Picture your favorite fantastical heroes–Sherlock Holmes, Harry Potter, Bilbo Baggins, Quentin Coldwater, Jon Snow, and Percy Jackson–embodied by a complacent ad man tasked with protecting the universe and you have Manfred Bugsbee, our reluctant hero, through whom we experience a world reminiscent of Earthsea, Narnia, Discworld, and The Dark Tower mythos. Michael Farfel has done his research in constructing a new epic tale aware of its fantasy and science-fiction predecessors; herein lies a story as inventive as it is cinematically inspired, a fully-imagined book sure to awaken the dormant heroes in all of us.

–Nathan Elias,
author of *Coil Quake Rift* and *The Reincarnations*

"Farfel crafts an epic tale with The Reluctant Journey of Manfred Bugsbee; equal parts fantasy and adventure, this story is entirely entertaining. It will hold your attention to the very end and leave you wanting more."

–Charis Emanon,
author of *51 Ways To End Your World*

"An engaging, intelligent, well-paced story. The author has created a realistic world with believable characters and where the magic is more subtle than the lightning-bolt-in-the-face magic of some fantasy books. I want to avoid spoilers, but I'll go so far as to say that the ´magic´ in this story delves much deeper into the spiritual realm than the wham blam cowboy style that is very prevalent and ultimately boring. Personally I found that very satisfying. The main characters: It's easier to empathise with a character when he/she has human flaws like self-doubt, both in him/herself and on a grander scale. It might be fantasy but it's these touches that make it feel almost like reading historical fiction, (from one of the more interesting, bloody and treacherous periods of history that is). It's also refreshing to read a book full of strong female characters that don't keep alluding to how strong and female they are - that's a given. They've got nothing to prove and they just get on with it, which gives them more credibility. Recommended to fans of the genre and to those who might like to give it a try."

–**Pete Peru,**
author of *The Reeking Hegs*

THE RELUCTANT JOURNEY OF MANFRED BUGSBEE

By
Michael Farfel

Montag Press ISBN: 978-1-957010-08-3
Design © 2022 Amit Dey

Montag Press Team:

Author photo: Joy Goh
Cover: cultarchives89
Editor: Charlie Franco
Managing Director: Charlie Franco

A Montag Press Book
www.montagpress.com
Montag Press
777 Morton Street, Unit B
San Francisco CA 94129 USA

Montag Press, the burning book with the hatchet cover, the skewed word mark and the portrayal of the long-suffering fireman mascot are trademarks of Montag Press.

Printed & Digitally Originated in the United States of America
10 9 8 7 6 5 4 3 2 1

DEDICATION

To my parents and the kid on the
hill with a sword.

TABLE OF CONTENTS

ACKNOWLEDGMENT

I'm forever grateful to Charlie and the whole Montag crew. It's a dream come true to work with such a patient and diligent editorial team.

I count my lucky stars to have such a wonderful and supportive family—Mom, Dad, Bridget and Dave. Thank you, a million times, over for giving my imagination space to grow. There's so much of each of you in this book.

Thanks to my beautiful wife and best friend, Honk. Your critical eye and infinite thoughtfulness have turned so many of my half-projects into wholes. Your belief keeps me moving. I love you.

Thanks so much to early readers of this work—The Ladybugs (Kyle, Colin, Nate and Jamison). Your insights helped me better understand my process.

Thanks to those who gave a final read—Christopher Kamrani, Mari Murdock, Nathan Elias, Pete Peru and Charis Emanon. Your willingness to help in the final stages of this project means the world.

Lastly, thanks to you, dear reader. There's nothing I want more than for you to have a little fun in the pages of this book. Thanks so much for spending some time with Manfred and me.

NO MAN AT ALL

Manfred Bugsbee sat at his desk and rubbed his temples as he tried to think of a clever ad for novelty throw pillows. His boss had given him the job a week ago, but he couldn't think of anything. It wouldn't be a large ad, just a 2x2 in the very back of a magazine. It was a test, a way to make sure he cared about the company, cared about the time he spent there—Manfred didn't care.

His body ached. He shifted from butt cheek to butt cheek and tried to find a position that didn't hurt his back. He blamed the chair. *It was an awful chair*, he thought, *rigid and unforgiving— no adjustments, no lumbar support.* It wasn't the chair though. Manfred was unhealthy. After she left, he slept too much and slept too little. No rhythm. He stopped exercising and developed quite the gut; beer and pizza almost every night. So, as he sat at his desk and stressed over throw pillows his sad body couldn't help but cry out.

"Fred, you look terrible," said his coworker, Jake.

Manfred tried to ignore him, but Jake was a professional hoverer. A human fly and his only real friend at the office.

"You been reading about the sun?" Jake asked.

Manfred looked at him.

"Crazy right?" Jake continued. "I love reading about that stuff."

Manfred nodded. "Yeah, the sun. Crazy."

"What're you doing tonight, Freddy? Let's get some pizza and a beer. Downtown. Be good for you man. Get out, have a little drink, have a little fun, you know?" Jake always nodded his head as he spoke, looked around nervously, and rarely made eye contact.

Manfred shook his head. "I gotta get these pillows done."

"You're still working on that? They're pillows, Freddy. Pillows. I'm working on the new erectile dysfunction pill. Full-page ad, my man."

Manfred straightened up in his chair. "full-page?"

Jake nodded. He always nodded. "Come out with me. Just for an hour or two. It'll be good for you. I'll buy."

"Fine," said Manfred. He knew it was the only way to get rid of Jake. Besides, you can't beat free beer.

"Alright, buddy. Good luck with those pillows."

Manfred felt sick. *How could they give Jake the erectile dysfunction ad?* E.D. was easy money. All you needed was a picture of an older man next to a younger woman. Simple as that. Hide the side effects at the bottom and you were golden. But throw pillows, that was complex. You had to know your audience, you had to convince people they needed them. You didn't have to convince anybody they needed sex.

Five o'clock came and with it, Jake and Manfred made their way to a bar downtown. Their usual spot, a sort of dingy, sort of colorful place with just enough ambiance to bring in the occasional female grad student. They sat by the entrance. Jake liked to be able to ogle women as soon as they entered the place, stake his claim, in his words. He ordered them a pitcher and a large pizza with everything on it.

"So, how you doing, bud?" asked Jake.

Manfred looked at him blankly.

"Come on, bro, it's been nearly a year. You've gotta get over her. Gone, bud. Like a cool breeze."

Manfred nodded. "I guess you're right. It's just…"

"No man. I get it. I get it. Did I tell you about the ad I'm working on?"

Manfred nodded. "You mentioned it."

"I'm thinking about the jet ski route. Maybe a sailboat. Just picture it, real curvy lady up front, tits out, seductive like, hair all blown back, and behind her, rolling up on a jet ski, some old fart, splashing water all over the place."

Manfred smiled as the knot grew in his stomach. He wanted that ad so bad. Easy money.

The food and beer arrived and the two men sat quietly as they ate and drank. Not much was said except for the occasional grunt of approval. It wasn't until their second pitcher of beer arrived that Jake motioned toward the front door. "Get a load of this." Manfred looked up expecting to see a group of young ladies getting ID'd, but instead, he saw a little, old man standing between two uninterested doormen. The old man was wiry and lithe. Couldn't have been much taller than five feet, totally eclipsed by the doormen. His face was covered by a white beard that blended into a mess of hair on his head. There were a few stringy, red hairs here and there from the man's younger years, but it was a mostly stark white mop of curls. He wore a tattered gray shawl and held a tree branch above his head and pointed with it from left to right. The doormen weren't entertained. He seemed to be looking for someone.

"Everyone is looking for someone, old man," said the meaner looking of the doormen. "Now get lost."

The old man pointed toward where Manfred and Jake were sitting. Jake watched the whole thing unfold and when the old man pointed toward them Jake touched his chest and laughed. "Me?"

The two doormen looked over. "Bum's with you, Jake?"

Jake poked Manfred who had already lost interest. "Yeah," Jake said with a chuckle. "He's with us."

The doormen looked at each other and shrugged. Before they let the old man in the larger of the two grabbed him by the shoulders. "You can go ahead but I'll be taking that." He reached down to take the old man's walking stick but as he tried to grab it the old man moved it ever so slightly and the doorman stumbled forward. The doorman would have fallen on his face had the old man not rebalanced him with a subtle push in the other direction. He then let the still unbalanced doorman take the stick and walked over toward Jake and Manfred's table.

The old man had to hop up to sit on an open barstool. He looked back and forth between them a few times and let out a heavy sigh. He grabbed Jake's beer and downed it in one gulp.

"So, which one of you is it?" he asked. "The fat one," he motioned toward Manfred, "or is it you?" he said and reached out toward Jake's face.

Jake swatted the old man's hand away. "Which one of us is what now?" Jake asked, looking at his now empty glass.

"Mindiidus," The old man said.

"Mindy-what-now?" Jake asked.

Manfred watched the scene unfold without much thought. He hadn't been paying attention when Jake called the old man over and had no idea why he was now sitting with them.

"Min-Dee-Eye-Dus," said the old man, sounding the word out. "Mindiidus. One is too fat and one hasn't the spirit." He poured himself another beer from the pitcher.

"Are you gonna pay for that?" Jake asked as he flicked the old man's shawl off the table.

"Gimme your hand," the old man said.

"I don't think so, buddy. You're not as fun as I thought you'd be and you kinda stink. How about you get lost?" Jake turned toward Manfred and the old man grabbed his hand. Jake moved to pull it away but couldn't. The old man had locked Jake's whole body up—Jake couldn't even speak. His eyes went wide with horror.

This got Manfred's attention and he leaned in toward the two of them. The old man turned Jake's hand over and traced lines across the palm and over his fingertips. He then brought it very close to his eyes, nearly touching it to his nose. He then released it and let out a grunt.

"It can't be the fat one, though," the old man mumbled to himself. "The Ulis should have come. I've no sight for this. Forcing me through the realms. Forcing me off the front lines."

Manfred finally realized that he was the fat one. "I'm not fat," he said.

"Pudgy then," the old man replied looking nowhere in particular. His face scrunched in thought. "It can't be the pudgy one."

After the old man released Jake's hand, Jake quietly slunk away from the table. Manfred, who was slightly buzzed, moved into the closer seat to get a better look at the old man. For how scarred his skin was, his face was quite cheerful—a lively glow to his cheeks and a healthy complexion. His eyes radiated a certain beauty from behind the mess of hair.

"What's your name, sir?" asked Manfred.

"Ain't no sir," the old man replied. He finally looked Manfred right in the eyes and a serene look washed over his face. "It just can't be," he said.

"What can't be?" Manfred asked.

The old man shook his head and slammed both hands on the table. "That ole hawk, the Ulis, doesn't know his ear from his ass. There's no time for this. The realm's 'll be undone at this rate."

"Realms?" Manfred asked.

"You're not the man I'm looking for. You're no man at all." The old man hopped out of his seat and turned right into an approaching doorman. Jake had asked them to intervene after being embarrassed by the vagrant.

"Alright little man. It's time to go," the doorman said.

"Yes. Yes. I am just on my way to see your ma," said the old man.

The doorman picked him up by the shoulders and brought him a full foot off the ground. They were now nose to nose.

"What's that?" the doorman asked.

"Your ma. She's waiting."

The doorman had enough and turned to throw the old man out of the bar, but the old man slipped out of his hands and left only the shawl to be thrown. The shawl went one way and the old man went the other. He stood shirtless in the doorway, a pair of loosely knit pants tied around his waist. He looked at Manfred one more time before disappearing into the night. People around the bar pointed and laughed at the poor doormen who had given up chase before they even reached the door. Strong men for certain, but they weren't paid enough to chase vagrants down the street.

Jake sat back down and laughed and rubbed his wrist. "What in the hell was that?"

Manfred was laughing too. "I've never seen anything like it. I wonder what he was on, crazy little bastard." Manfred motioned for a waitress to bring more beer but she shook her head.

"What the hell?" said Jake.

The manager approached their table. A suit with spiky black hair and two gold earrings. "It's time for you boys to leave."

"Huh?" both men looked at one another.

"You told security that that old guy was with you and it's too early for that type of trouble. Now, close up your tab and get lost."

"But he wasn't with us," Jake said in disbelief.

"Come on Jake. I don't have time for this. Close up and move on. It won't be me who asks again." The manager pointed toward the doormen who both smiled and waved.

"Couldn't even catch the old man," Manfred said under his breath.

"Excuse me," said the manager.

Manfred shook his head. "Nothing. We're leaving."

The manager picked up the shawl and threw it in Manfred's face. "And take this shit outta here while you let yourself out."

Manfred lifted his hands in surrender and put the shawl over his shoulder. He had to drag Jake out. Jake was the kind of person who wouldn't actually fight but tried his best to sound like he would. He yelled and hollered, flipped people off, and stomped his feet on his way. They made it out the door and were a few steps down the sidewalk when the old man's stick hit Manfred in the back.

"And take your old man's goddamn garbage," yelled the doorman who had thrown it at them.

Manfred picked up the stick. It was heavy and cold and smelled like a place he had once been as a child—somehow imbued with fresh mountain air. There was something else, a warmth in its center, a coursing of electricity. For a moment he was swept over with a memory that didn't seem to be his own. A forest fire jumping roads, a red-black sky. He swung the stick through the air and laughed.

"Hurry up," yelled Jake. "And stop playing with that damn thing."

THE SAINT

Manfred was in his apartment before ten o'clock. He threw the shawl behind a chair and put the stick in a corner. He made his way into the kitchen and boiled a pot of water. A tradition of nightly chamomile tea had been passed down to him from his parents who had both passed away when he was much younger. It was nice to wind down each night with their memory. His father always took it plain and his mother with honey. Manfred preferred the latter, two spoonfuls each night. He lay on the floor as the water started to roll.

His apartment was a stale remnant of his not-so-recent heartbreak. Photos of his ex lay face down on shelves and side tables. There was a bag of her clothes behind the couch. She would never come for it and he hadn't the heart to give them away. His friends had given up on telling him to move on. All in good time, he'd say. A superficial mantra that did little to coax him on.

The kettle whistled and he made the tea. The steam warmed his face and smoothed the lines of stress under his eyes. As it cooled, he stretched himself on his couch and rested the cup on his chest. He was still buzzed from the beers with Jake and there was no more comfortable place in his house to sober up than his couch. The cushions knew him well and absorbed his every woe. There he teetered for some time on the precipice of sleep and had a strange dream about the old man's walking stick. In his dream the stick was a blue, steel sword, the hilt bejeweled in jade and sapphire. He watched himself in an open field, wielding the weapon against hordes of scaly, gray-colored beasts. The sun above him flickered like a dying candle. A few times in the night he awoke to a buzzing sound that seemed to emanate from the stick, but he would only turn over and fall back asleep.

The morning came quick. Manfred's alarm clock screeched and tugged him off the couch. His eyes were still mostly closed as he rolled to his feet and stretched his arms in a mighty yawn. Somehow during the night, he had stripped down to his underwear. Across the room, a full-length mirror framed him perfectly. He chuckled to himself as he touched his belly and jiggled the ever-growing, happy paunch.

In Manfred's morning daze he didn't realize that the old man from last night was sitting at his breakfast counter, stirring a cup of tea with a calloused and crooked finger. His hands were a mess of broken and reset bones. Scars and bruised twists on every knuckle. The old man sat with his legs crossed, relaxed over his mug. Neither of them paid any attention to one another.

It wasn't until the old man spoke that Manfred realized he wasn't alone.

"Not the pudgy one," he said.

Manfred screeched and faced the man. His hands in a crude shape of defense, one arm guarding his face, the other held over his crotch. "How did you get in here?" he cried out.

"I'm here for my things," the old man said, still stirring his drink. He only acknowledged Manfred with a slight bend in his neck.

"You need to leave or… I'll… I'll call the police." Manfred inched toward the stick.

The old man stopped stirring and took a drink. "The signs were clear," he said. "No denying the sight of the Ulis, the prophecies of Kaseen."

"Please. Please leave," Manfred stuttered as he assumed a batter's stance and held the stick in both hands. "I don't want to hurt you."

The old man finally turned to face Manfred. His eyes were almost totally engulfed in shadow except for a slight yellow glow that escaped the darkness. His lips and chin were hidden under his thick beard. When he saw the awkward stance that Manfred had taken, he smiled.

"What is your name, son?" The old man asked, still holding the teacup.

"You're trespassing. I don't want to… but I will strike you, sir."

"Strike?" The old man's smile widened, revealing pearly white teeth, some capped with ruby red gems.

Manfred started a slow countdown. "Three." He tensed his shoulders and pointed his elbows out. "Two." He tried his best to keep both eyes open and focused on the old man's head. His jaw clenched tight. "One," he yelled and swung the stick, aiming timidly for the intruder's cheek.

The old man lazily ducked, almost as if by accident. The stick missed the top of his head by a cat's hair. Manfred spun from the force of his swing and ended up in much the same position he had started. The old intruder picked his teeth with the nail of a ragged pinkie. Manfred refocused and tried to come down on the old man's skull, who had somehow moved into a standing position. In a long fluid step, the old man was at Manfred's side and Manfred smashed his countertop. Manfred tried to turn into the old man and use the hilt of the stick to stab at him, but the old man moved in so close that Manfred couldn't move. He was stuck looking over his shoulder at the old man's beard. The old man took a step back and guided Manfred in a small circle before slamming the top of his head into Manfred's ear. That was all it took. The stick went flying and Manfred collapsed on the floor. The old man stood over him still holding his tea and laughed.

"Your name, boy?" he asked.

"Just take what you want," Manfred whimpered and covered his face.

"I want your name."

"I'm Man… Manfred," he stammered.

"Ah," the old man said and ran a free hand through his beard. "Maybe it's Fred I'm looking for. Where is this Fred?"

"Fred?"

"Your husband?"

Manfred sat up. "Husband?"

"You said you are the man of Fred. Where is he? This master of the house, this Fred."

The confusion of the situation didn't help alleviate the numbness of his ear and the fear of having a very fast, very old intruder in his apartment. "I'm Manfred. My name is Manfred Bugsbee. I'm not married. I don't know a Fred. Now, why are you in my house?"

"On a quest, I suppose. Figured you were the one I was a quest'n for. But I'm afraid there's been a mistake, Wilfred."

"Manfred."

"Whatever. Now, I must be on my way."

"Please," Manfred nodded toward the door.

The old man looked around Manfred's apartment. He tossed pillows and blankets on the floor and rummaged through the fridge. No stone unturned. Manfred followed behind him and asked what he was looking for and why he was there. But the old man just grunted, and occasionally sizing Manfred up, shook his head. He found his shawl and threw it over his shoulders and held his hand in front of Manfred, commanding him to stop.

"I am Saint Erneel if you must know. Protector of the Old Guard. Disciple to the Grand Ulis. Now, if you'll hand over the stick." Erneel stretched out his hand. Manfred leaned on the stick for support.

"You mean this stick," Manfred asked.

"Yes. My key home, boy. I must be on my way."

"Key?"

Erneel smiled and pointed at Manfred's front door. A light beamed out from under it and a tapping came from the other side. It was a dull light and Manfred couldn't remember if it had been there before, a switch had been flicked, or his mind had been so focused on the old man that all other sensations had been blocked out. He made his way toward the door and opened it. A large black bird flew in.

Manfred waved his arms above his head and stumbled around the room. The bird picked up the stick in his beak and gently laid it in Erneel's open palm. Then with a lightning-fast flick of his wrist, Erneel swatted Manfred behind the ear. A precise touch that took the air out of Manfred's legs and crumpled him to the ground. The bird along with Erneel let out a croak of laughter. They headed out the door and left Manfred drooling on his rug.

Manfred woke to the sound of his phone. It had been ringing off and on for the last hour. He tried to stand a few times but felt nauseous when he moved. He decided it best to lay there for a while with his eyes closed. The whole morning felt like a bump on the head. Make that two. There was dried blood on his ear, where Erneel struck first, and a goose egg on the back of his head. From where he lay, he could see that his front door was still open. This time there was no bright light shining from behind it—no birds, no old men. The phone beeped with notifications, banging at the drum of his injuries. He made it to his knees and then to his feet.

He tried to remember how drunk he had gotten the night before, but nothing extravagant came to mind. *Had Jake made him do shots?* he wondered as he rubbed his head. He thought of the old man and considered calling the police; report that his apartment had been broken into, that he had been assaulted.

He picked up his phone, slid the notifications out of the way, and dialed the first of the emergency numbers. But before he pressed send he laughed. He imagined what he'd say to the police; that a small homeless man had broken into his house, that he had stolen a cup of tea and stolen back a tree branch, that the old man had knocked him unconscious with the aid of a bird. He fell into his armchair and laughed until his stomach hurt. He remembered Jake's face when the old man had grabbed him at the bar. It was so bizarre, so absurd, that as he pieced the night together it only got funnier.

When he recovered from his bout of giggles he went through the notifications on his phone. Jake had called a few times, no doubt wanting to talk about the night before, or maybe he had lost his wallet again. Both of his sisters had called, too—they had probably talked to one another and realized that they hadn't heard from him in a while. His boss had also called and that made Manfred nervous. Had he committed to working today? He *was* behind. *Those damn throw pillows*, he thought.

He took a few deep breaths and tried to clear his head. He had to call his boss right away, but what would he say? He couldn't say he'd forgotten, he was already on thin ice. For the life of him he couldn't remember committing to work, but why else would his boss have called on a Saturday morning?

After pacing his apartment he mustered the courage to call. *Bite the bullet*, he thought, just say he was running a little late, had missed the train is all. The phone rang and went to voicemail. Unusual for his boss not to take an opportunity like this. There is no human more vulnerable than a man calling in late to work.

"Shit," he said aloud. He didn't want to go to work, but he began to get dressed. He'd call one more time, but the more he thought about it the more he thought maybe he *had* committed to an extra day.

His phone was ringing. It was Jake.

"Jake," Manfred answered.

"... Manfre... where the hell... the..." Jake's voice came in through heavy static. "... world..."

"I can't understand you, man. What's going on?"

"... sun... fire..." Jake was frantic.

"Jake, what the hell is going on?" Manfred repeated.

It clicked off. Manfred tried to call back, but nothing was going through, the phone wouldn't even ring. He tried to get online, but there was no connection. Manfred's stomach began to tense. Something strange was happening. He ran to his window and threw open the heavy black curtains. It was so dark outside. *How long was I out?* he wondered. His phone said it was one o'clock in the afternoon, but it looked closer to midnight.

Cars lined the street below his apartment, bumper to bumper traffic. People were weaving in and out on foot. Some cars had been abandoned on the sidewalk. Manfred opened his window to see if he could hear anything from the street below. He was met with faint sirens and the honk of horns, but underneath it all there was a growl, a persistent rumble.

He ran out of his front door into the long, shared hallway. Some of the neighbors had left their doors open in their haste to get out. He ducked his head into the open doors and called out but no one answered. When he got to the end of the hall he tried the elevator but it didn't come. He sprinted down the stairs, nearly tripping, forgetting momentarily that he was, in fact, pudgy.

By the time he made it to the street, he was winded and almost threw up. It didn't help matters that there was an intense smell of sulfur and something metallic in the air. The rumbling sound was even more apparent on the street level—the low bass of a broken sound system, steady and unforgiving. A woman bumped past him and he grabbed her arm.

"What the hell is going on?" he asked as he tried to catch his breath.

She was both confused and horrified by the question. She swatted at his hand and tried to walk away.

"Please," he cried out. "Just tell me what's happening."

She pointed to the sky above him.

Manfred followed her finger up and over his shoulder. She was pointing at the sun. Its intensity was masked by a green-black glow and Manfred was able to look right at it. Red clouds vibrated around it creating swirls of unearthly light. As he looked up the noise grew and grew until suddenly it broke and three bright flashes crossed the sky, each starting at the sun and disappearing into the distance. Manfred fell to his knees and covered his head.

A moment of true chaos erupted around him and the world. Cars crashed and buildings wailed with the echo from above. People screamed out for their children to hide, to cover themselves. Some ran out into the open, some ducked into doorways, and some tried to bury themselves under the asphalt—every one of them washed over in fear. Manfred didn't dare move. Then he heard the holler of an unfamiliar name.

"Mindiidus! Mindiidus!"

It was Erneel dashing out from an alley, full of loud commotion. He ran down the street and headed straight toward Manfred. His tattered shawl flapped against his sides and it waved about as he lunged over parked cars. His body twisted and turned between the panicked masses. Manfred tried to hide from him, tried to press his body into the street until he disappeared.

"There you are," Erneel said, as he stopped a few yards in front of him. "You'll have to do, old boy."

"Do what?" Manfred whimpered, guarding his head and trembling against the asphalt. "What's happening?"

Erneel dragged Manfred to his feet. "No time, son. No time." Erneel checked over his shoulders anxiously, as if expecting some evil to creep up on the two of them.

Manfred watched as Erneel stood there amongst the chaos around him. He was such a strange little man. Then he lifted his stick above his head and yelled something toward the sky. Had it been any other day Manfred may have felt bad for the man. Another delusional vagrant waving his possessions around. Manfred began to stand, but another crack of lightning put him back on the ground. This time though, the light came from Erneels stick and it glowed above his head. Erneel's voice rose above the terror around them. Manfred desperately wanted to be back in his bed—to wake up from this nightmare.

The glow faded and Erneel's shouts turned to whispers. He turned his back on Manfred and brought the stick down in a slicing motion. A yellow streak of light followed the movement and remained in the air in front of him. Manfred's head ached as he tried to make sense of what he was seeing. In front of Erneel, there appeared to be a tear in the fabric of reality. The old man had cut a hole in the universe and on the other side, Manfred swore he could see trees—many, many trees.

"Hurry up, Willifred," yelled Erneel who ducked through the tear, his body slowly disappearing beyond it. "Willifred," he yelled back. Manfred was frozen with fear.

"We must be going. We really must," Erneel hollered as he poked his head back out but Manfred would not move. Finally, Erneel pointed his stick through the hole and yelled, "Dogs, Willifred, dogs."

In the distance, a pack of dogs came running. Some large and some small. They barreled toward Manfred, a black chihuahua leading the pack. Manfred turned to see the ruckus as their barks and yips grew louder. He cried out as a German shepherd with a poodle at its heels overtook the lead, its brown teeth fully unfurled from its snout. Manfred turned toward Erneel and ran as fast as he could. He crashed into the old man and sent them both through the tear, leaving the hounds behind.

WHERE IS MY PHONE?

Manfred and Erneel landed in a heap. Erneel laughed hysterically and called Manfred all sorts of names. Manfred was in shock. His body was full of fear and tremors—the dogs, the sky quaking, the sun. He laid there for a moment until he realized he wasn't where he thought he was.

That is to say, moments earlier Manfred was under a black sky in the heart of a city, where mountains could be seen in the distance if you stood in the right place on the right day. Now he was somewhere quite different. He was lying in a thicket of tall green and brown grass. Wildflowers and butterflies fluttered on a cool breeze. Erneel was completely camouflaged by it. His presence only the trembling of weeds and wheezed laughter.

Manfred stood up and paced. He reached around the air for a fold or some hinge in the light—a door back to his city. No such luck. In the air there was only air. In every direction trees cut up and loomed over him, their tops unseeable beyond the canopy of leaves, the sky only breaking through in bits and pieces, so clean and clear. Manfred had forgotten what a clean sky looked like. He had forgotten the smell of free grass, cut only by the teeth of young animals. He picked up some rocks and a handful of dirt and checked carefully to see if they were real. He pulled out long weeds and pressed them against his face and took bites of them. Their bitter taste only confirmed that he was indeed awake and that he was miles and miles from where he had been.

"How did we get here?" Manfred asked.

"I'm not sure, but I think I'm getting the hang of it," Erneel replied.

"We're at least a hundred miles away from where we are... where we were," Manfred's voice was weak.

"No no, dear boy. We are where we are. Exactly where we were."

"What?" Manfred cried.

Erneel stood. He leaned on his stick and picked his teeth with the stock of a weed. "You see, Mr. Fred..."

"Manfred. It's Manfred Bugsbee."

Erneel looked at him vacantly. "What kind of ridiculous name is Manfred?"

"Please. Where are we? What's happening?"

Erneel smiled and moved in closer to him. "You see, Manfred, this is my realm. Connected to your realm by some waves and twists." Erneel seemed to be explaining it to himself as much as Manfred. "I was sent to your world to get you, or someone like you," he said.

"Like me?"

"Mindiidus, the new light-bearer. Troubled times ahead, my dear boy. Troubled times."

Manfred shook his head. "Nope, no. Absolutely not," he said and walked away, shaking his head all the while.

"Where are you going?" asked Erneel.

"Leave me alone. I'm going home."

Erneel nodded.

Manfred had heard enough. The old man was crazy and that was all there was to it. He had to get back home. He started by marching downhill. As he walked, he reached for his phone but his pockets were empty.

"Where is my phone?" he bellowed toward the sky and turned back to face Erneel.

"We must travel light through the layers. There's no space for tedious things," Erneel yelled back. "Now, your home is not that way. Your home is no way from here, fat man. Do you understand?"

"I'm not fat," Manfred cried out.

"You're not a lot of things. That much is clear. But we'll have to confirm with the Keeper before I can send you back."

"The what?"

"Just let me get my bearings and we can sort this all out," Erneel replied.

"I'm not going anywhere with you," Manfred said.

Erneel smiled and nodded then pointed his walking stick at Manfred, stopping it just short of his nose. "I'll drag you through this forest, all the way over the Blue Rocks of Reed. The Ulis wants you alive, but *how* alive is up to you. I'm growing weary, quite weary of your delaying. Now, move." Erneel looked around for a moment, picked up some grass, then decided on the right direction. He tilted his head in the direction and Manfred obliged. The little old man could be quite intimidating when he wanted to be.

They followed a rolling tree line that hugged a wispy little stream that was illuminated by exhausted rays of light. Manfred's knees screwed and buckled as he tried to keep his balance while they hiked on. His ankles popped and his flat feet ached. His usual walks were just to get coffee or catch a bus. Not as many roots and rocks in the city. There was the occasional homeless bundle or stack of garbage, but those were easily avoided.

Above the birds talked amongst themselves, out of sight, uninterested in Manfred and his stroke of bad luck. The leaves and branches of the ancient trees trembled and sent out their honeyed hum. It all sounded so ordered in Manfred's head, like they were taking turns, never trying to speak over one another.

Even though Manfred was scared and sick with anxiety, something about the place invigorated him. The smell of the trees and dirt, the taste of it on the air—it all washed over him. Even the steady flow of perspiration growing on his back felt different than it did in the city. Like it was growing from a better place, some human reserve he seldom tapped, and from that reserve, courage sprung forth. He began to plot his escape.

They had gone about a mile when Manfred dared to look over his shoulder. Erneel was lagging at some distance, muttering to himself and swatting his stick from side to side. Manfred took a deep breath and decided it was now or never. With one more look over his shoulder, he bolted. He took a hard right. There his face was immediately struck by a low-hanging branch, then another, and a few more. They broke the skin, but he wouldn't stop. With blood and sweatsting in his eyes, he ran harder than he had ever run. He waved his hands in front of him to clear the mess of the forest from his way. His mind was blank, the world in front of him nothing but a narrow slit of escape.

His heart banged against his ribs and it reminded him that he did not usually run. Fear and excitement had their hooks in and the forest flew past in a blur. He ran and ran. *This was his life now*, he thought. Escape, find a home, or die at the hand, or stick, of the old mysterious little man. The trees thinned and he took a moment to catch his breath at the bottom of a porous, black rock hill. He climbed onto a whitewashed clearing, the sun beaming down in all its cruel intensity. He didn't dare look back but somehow knew he had lost Erneel.

His whole body shook and the cuts on his face burned. His belly heaved under his shirt as he inhaled through painful cramps. Dizziness started to settle in, but he willed it away. He had to keep moving. His only plan, still, was to get as much distance between himself and Erneel as he could—then he'd worry about how to get home.

In a far corner of the clearing a lone, billowy, white tree extended from the barren earth. Strangely symmetrical, it waved its branches about. Manfred decided he'd rest under it once he'd made it across the opening, free from the weight of the sun. The rocks in the clearing made matters a thousand times worse. He tripped and hobbled like a lame horse toward death. Still, no sign of Erneel.

As he got closer to the tall ash-white tree he thought his mind was playing tricks on him. The movements of the tree weren't the sway of a young sapling, there was something deliberate, something animal—mirages of the heat and blood in his eyes. The sun was so bright that his brain knocked about in his head. *When did I last have water?* he thought. Manfred heard a commotion behind him and looked over his shoulder only to see Erneel running toward him, then bumping past.

Erneel stood between Manfred and the tree. His walking stick held out in front, firmly grasped in both hands.

"Fool," Erneel said.

Manfred finally realized his mind wasn't playing tricks on him. Whatever loomed in front of them was no tree, but some nightmare beast. Its body was the awkward shape of a human, nearly fifteen feet tall. Thick and grizzled white bark made up its arms and legs and rigid dead-looking leaves sprouted from its fingertips. Its head was only a thicker branch on top with a mess of roots that grew out of it. There was no face, only a round gap in the bark that glowed and pulsated.

"Outsider?" a booming voice came from somewhere inside the beast.

"Stay behind me," Erneel said to Manfred.

"Little saint," the beast continued and the two circled one another. Manfred held his hands against Erneel's back and followed him.

"What the hell is that?" Manfred whispered.

"Quiet," Erneel whispered and bumped his back into Manfred's hands, sending Manfred tumbling off of his feet. "Stay down." Erneel focused on the beast. "So, the Cloud is letting their Abominations run free now? Far from home aren't we?"

"Home is all," the beast responded and pounded its chest.

"We're farther away from the den than I thought," Erneel said to himself. "Leave us be, Kin."

Without warning the beast attacked. Its movements were gross and unrefined which made it easy for Erneel to keep his distance. He rolled and ducked under its mighty swings and hit at its legs and torso with his stick. The force of the beast's blows was extraordinary. Each time its mighty hands hit the ground, rocks shattered and the whole earth shook. Manfred tried to run, but the shaking of the earth was too much and left him crawling on his hands and knees. There was nothing for him to do but lay down and cover his face in horror.

Erneel raised his stick in the air and cried out, "Birds." Within moments, a flock of black birds descended upon the beast and pecked and bit at its face. The beast became unhinged as it swung its arms toward the sky. Erneel turned to check on Manfred who quivered on the ground. He reached down but Manfred rolled away from his touch.

"Get up," Erneel said calmly. "These birds will make quick work of him, boy. Best be on our way." Erneel reached down to grab Manfred one more time and as he did, a chance swing of the beast's arm reached him and he was tossed into a pile of rocks. The birds around the beast's head cawed in unison and moved to Erneel's side, tugging at his clothes. The beast walked toward his body and looked down at Manfred. The hole in its face shined so intensely that Manfred felt it even though he dared not look at it. The beast swatted the birds away and lifted Erneel with both hands. Its wooden fingers constricted around Erneel's small body.

"Little saint," it said. "Enemy."

The beast reached a long arm above its head and was about to bring it down with the full intention to crush Erneel's skull.

At the last minute, and as if from certain death, Erneel grabbed hold of its trunk head and dug an arm deep into the beast's face. The intense light of its face turned to putrid, ashen blood and sprayed out.

"My stick, boy," Erneel yelled down as he dug his arm deeper into the beast's head.

In a flash of courage, Manfred uncovered his face and jumped to his feet. He picked up Erneel's stick and ran into the fray. It was heavier than before and felt like steel. Erneel and the beast were latched against one another. Manfred took a long swing at the beast's torso, but misjudged the distance and fell right into a swinging knee of the beast. The blow landed just hard enough to disarm and put Manfred back on the ground. It didn't matter though, Erneel had got his arm deep into its face. The beast was on its way out. It tried a few more times in vain to pull Erneel off then crumpled into death as Erneel rolled to safety. His arms and face were covered in the blood of the thing.

"What the hell was that?" Manfred's words knocked into one another as a cloak of terror overcame him.

"A corruption of the Cloud. A very bad sign, indeed," Erneel spoke cautiously. "The patterns have shifted. Now it's time to get up."

Manfred crawled to his hands and feet.

"We must tread lightly. Get to the Keeper," said Erneel.

Manfred's eyes were wide with terror and his chest heaved as he tried to make sense of the world.

"What is that thing?" Manfred pointed toward the stick, his body still hunched over, trying not to vomit.

"My stick," Erneel replied dismissively.

"No," Manfred cried. "That is no stick."

"Yes, yes it is," Erneel said, his mind somewhere else.

Manfred put his face in his hands and whimpered. "What's happening?"

Erneel reached over and lightly touched Manfred's shoulder. "We must be moving, Mr. Fred."

"I don't understand." Manfred said as he pointed to the stick again, his body shaking. "I felt something when I held it."

Erneel nodded. "Good news, then. You may then be the man we were looking for after all."

Manfred heaved.

"First, catch your breath," Erneel said as he lifted his stick in the air and yelled out an unfamiliar word.

After a moment of quiet, two horses emerged from the forest. Erneel greeted them both as old friends. He kissed their noses and scratched their ears as they nuzzled against him.

"These two have offered to take us the rest of the way," Erneel said.

"Have offered?" Manfred asked, still queasy.

"Be nice to rest, wouldn't you agree?"

Manfred nodded and approached the smaller of the two horses. A beautiful golden-brown animal pressed its head against him as he approached. He had never seen a horse in the wild and was in awe as he ran his hand through its mane.

"She's an old friend," Erneel said as he slapped Manfred's back. "Now, up you go." Erneel helped Manfred onto the horse and then hopped onto the other.

They made their way out of the forest as the sun set in the distance. The landscapes changed in the moonlight. Purpling, dusk clouds formed in their path and rumbled from underfoot and overhead. Monoliths on the black horizon moved and cast shadows upon the smoke of the world.

Manfred had never ridden a horse before, but he made do. Sprawled out on the gentle creature, he waved in and out of sleep.

In his dreams he was late for work, frantically pressing at the lighted switches of his office elevator, wanting badly to be at his desk before the morning headcount. The elevator toyed with him, its doors opening and closing like a rusted carnival ride. In the dream, Erneel was behind him at each turn. Egging him on, never allowing him a clear enough mind to remember that great pitch idea he had for the throw pillows. He felt like he was on the cusp of the perfect advertisement. Erneel glowed and shuttered like a fluorescent light bulb—always just behind, always there just as Manfred's thoughts began to form.

In the real world, which still wasn't quite real to Manfred, Erneel led the way. They moved over jagged rocks, and slippery, dew-covered grass. All the while they closed in on a steep red mountain covered in a million years of blood from a thousand wars. At its base, a grove of willow trees waved their many arms. Had Manfred been more awake or had he any of the nautical awareness of his forefathers, he would have noticed that the two of them followed a spectacular pattern of stars.

Directly above the mountain, a brilliant, blue star sat unblinking. More massive than any of the distant stars that Manfred was used to in his world. Not quite as big as his sun, but so incandescent that it stained the path ahead of them in its intensity. The stars that led to it, the ones above the two men, were laid out in a perfect wave. An opalescent ghost of a universe was tucked in between their folds. Shimmering sapphire lines connected them in a complex aurora. On Manfred's earth, these stars would have been invisible behind the thick fog of night, but here in the land of Saint Erneels and tall beastly trees, brightness was a virtue not yet defeated by the din of man.

Not visible to either party, the red mountain was the beginning of a fjord against a violent sea far below. The ocean waves had been cutting into this side of the earth since near the beginning of time, and unbeknownst to Manfred, this had been the place of countless of those ancient battles, fought both from land and water, fortified by the crashing tide above it and the great sprawl below. As once the mountain was captured it was easily defended.

They closed in on the mountain, flat marble stones of red and white having been hammered into the path that led to its face. Manicured willows with golden, undulating leaves waved above them and tall rows of wildflowers narrowed the path at each side. It all led to an ominous square opening on the side of the mountain. From it, the sounds of life and music poured out.

Manfred was in awe.

"Welcome to Palis Mountain, the Keeper's den," Erneel said with a hint of fondness.

Once they reached the opening, they both dismounted their horses and Erneel waved for their mounts to leave. He scratched their necks and touched his head to theirs before they charged off into the distance and disappeared into the sprawl of the clear night.

BIRTHRIGHT

A giant stood guard at the entrance to the mountain cave. He stood nearly seven feet tall and was hunched over with the weight of his shoulders. His face was a wide block with a heavy nose and dark red lips. He wore ratted purple fabric around his waist that rested and swayed under his massive gut. He leaned against a well-used warhammer the size of Erneel. Behind him, the opening only went back a few feet. A cave not even big enough for a small animal, yet an intense warmth and the smell of food emanated from it. Manfred stared at his own feet, terrified by the man.

"The Little Saint returns," the man laughed and lightly touched Erneel with his free and gargantuan hand. "It's been a while, Ernie."

"Little Saint?" Manfred laughed, his fear lifting for a moment. "Ernie?"

Erneel gave them both a cold look and the laughter stopped abruptly. The man straightened, even taller now, at attention and

Ernie said, "Baxio. She's got you guarding the door now, does she? I'm surprised."

"Troubled times Ernie, uh, Erneel," his strong voice quivering slightly. "Sightings of the Cloud abound. Is this our man?" Baxio motioned toward Manfred with a look of curious disatisfaction.

"In all likelihood…" Erneel paused for a moment and looked back at Manfred. "No. But as you know, Bax, she is the Keeper and I, the errand boy," Erneel smiled. "She says jump and," Erneel tapped his stick at Manfred's feet making him hop slightly.

Baxio chuckled and nodded his head.

"May we?" Erneel asked.

Baxio shook his head. "She requires a sign, Erneel. Even from you. There is word that the Cloud already knows of his arrival."

"Explains the Abomination." Erneel looked over at Manfred for a moment. "You're a lot of trouble, Fred."

"Ma…"

Erneel cut him off with a grunt and lifted his right hand. A light glowed from his outstretched fingers. Manfred watched closely and squinted his eyes to catch as much as he could. The light pulsated as Erneel made the shape of a square and a barely visible yellow glow followed the path of his fingertips. Once the square was complete, he pushed his hand through and the lines turned a solid red, spun, and disappeared. Baxio nodded and moved to the side. Erneel had to pull Manfred forward, who stood transfixed and tried to see where the little shape had gone.

The cave behind Baxio twirled and shifted in a flash of light. Manfred covered his eyes in shock and when he looked again, he let out a nervous yelp. The cave behind Baxio had opened up a thousandfold and Erneel pushed him through the opening. Manfred's knees nearly gave way as they moved into a large open cavern filled with people. He looked back over his shoulder as the entryway faded away and left only a stone wall.

"Follow me, Fred," Erneel said as he quickly moved into what looked like a tavern.

The space was laid out like a dance hall, similar to the ones Jake frequented back home. Instead of steel beams and modern light displays, there were tall stone pillars and fire pits at each corner. In the center, a group of people danced to the music of an unseen band. Beautiful strings and percussion moved through them in waves. Men and women of all shapes and sizes twirled in loose-fitting gowns. They moved and shook in the way that only music and some kind of stimulate could facilitate, be it alcohol or fairy potions. At the edges of the dance floor tables were filled with food and drink. Dangerous-looking people sat around and laughed and nodded in the direction of Manfred and Erneel. Some lifted their hands in hello—Erneel ignored them all and continued to drag Manfred through the mess of dancers.

The smell of sweat and flowers reached out toward them. A woman with the glaze of drunk in her eyes grabbed Manfred's hand and twirled against him. Her gown was made of an airy fabric, embroidered with the shapes of weeds and blossoms. She pulled on his shirt and playfully grabbed at his belt loops. She laughed at his strange garments. Manfred held his hands up and tried to keep moving but the young lady stayed close and pressed against him. He could feel her warmth, her sharp body, and the humidity of people moving ever closer and couldn't help but feel excited. She whispered in a language he had never heard and kissed his cheek, then held his shoulders and leaned back. She went to kiss him again and Manfred closed his eyes in anticipation.

"Fireflies," he heard Erneel yell. Their lips had nearly touched when he opened his eyes to see a swarm of buzzy little flies between their faces. She inhaled one and coughed. The flies knocked around her head and banged against her eyelids. She stuck her tongue out at Erneel and cursed them both.

"What is this place?" Manfred said as he swatted the flies around his ears.

Erneel grabbed Manfred and pulled him close. "I won't kiss you, boy. We are short on time. No questions. No dancing."

They made it through the room without any more delays. The dancers and excitement stopped at the bottom of a set of stairs. Manfred thought for a moment that it seemed an odd place for a staircase, but laughed when he realized it was all odd. Manfred and Erneel were the only two people in the whole place to stand under them.

The stairs didn't appear to lead anywhere, just toward a stone wall with an engraving carved into it. Manfred groaned on each step. He was exhausted and starving and couldn't help but look over his shoulder at the people below them. They were all so carefree, so oblivious to the strangeness of the place. He thought about a chair he had in his apartment. How its soft cushions had begun to form to his body—he could almost feel it. He let out another groan, this time as long and sad as he could muster.

"This is it," Erneel said and sat on the floor in front of the engraving.

Manfred had to arch his neck to see the whole of it and even then, no light reached the top. What was visible was beautiful but did nothing to alleviate his confusion. The lower half was made up of vibrant red and black marble carved into the shape of flames and humans in the arc of battle. Grotesque beasts were cut into the translucent stones, ten feet high, bearlike things whose teeth and claws jutted out in stalactite forms. There was a violence to it that made Manfred feel dizzy, like the carnage of a wrecked car. The intricacy of it left him in awe, absorbed to the very core. The top half was eaten up by the darkness above. What he could see were crystalline, earthy stones that bled down into the battle below—drops of rain with curls of black that gave off the illusion of movement. Both scenes intermingled into a rock canvas of chaotic energy—flames and raindrops, beasts and their enemies.

"Marvelous, isn't it?" Erneel said, still sitting down, his stick laid out over his crossed legs.

Manfred nodded his head.

"It's been here since before the Corruption. Nearly as old as the realm itself."

"The Corruption?"

Erneel nodded. "Yes, the reason you're here. Now sit down," he motioned next to himself with his head.

"Why?" Manfred asked as he stared at the engraving.

"It's the only way to get in."

"In?"

Erneel nodded again and Manfred sat down.

"Close your eyes and relax," Erneel said.

As Manfred closed his eyes the room below them became quieter and quieter. He thought of the chair in his apartment, its deep seat perfect for Sunday naps. Many a book had been started there, but he always fell asleep before he had a chance to save his place. Here his butt grew numb from the hard floor. He wished he had one of those pillows he was supposed to be advertising. Their soft corduroy cases and thick down filling would be perfect for him right now. His back hurt. He opened his eyes for a moment and was hit with the shock of change. The engraving was still the same, but the tavern below and stairs behind them had disappeared, replaced with a solid whiteness. Above Erneel's head was another sign like the one he had drawn at the mountain's entrance. This one was much larger though and spiraled out from his head. Manfred reached to tap on his shoulder, to warn him that something strange was happening, but Erneel shook his head and whispered, "Eyes closed."

Manfred didn't argue, he closed his eyes again and laid down on the floor. The commotion and tumult that Erneel had dragged him through was begining to lift. He was so exhausted that laying down on the hard stone felt better than anything he could have imagined. A low humming sound came from somewhere in front of them and bathed his brain in an inviting warmth. The space was so quiet that Manfred was certain he could hear the blood flow through his veins and feel the murmur of his heart down through his feet.

"You look tired, my sweet Ernie," said a woman's voice.

"I'm afraid traveling the realms is not for an old man like me," Erneel replied.

"Is this our man?" continued the woman.

"Could be."

When Manfred opened his eyes, he found himself in a dark room—pitch black, except for a few beams of light that came down from above. Framed in that light he saw Erneel standing next to a beautiful woman. She looked to be in her early sixties with long, silver hair that went down past her waist. She wore a green cloak with a cloudy-white collar, her face sharp and refined. The two of them held hands as they spoke. Manfred remained seated, his breath shallow, praying not to intrude.

"He was where the Ulis said he'd be. However, my gut tells me there has been a mistake. He is an oddity, certainly, but no Mindiidus."

She looked down at Manfred and forced eye contact. Her eyes were as gold as the early morning. She smiled and looked at Erneel. "If he was where he was meant to be, we'll look into him. See what there is to read." She walked over to Manfred and put her hand under his chin and guided him to his feet. She moved around him, poked and prodded, smelled his hair, then stood back and held hands with Erneel again.

"Mr. Bugsbee, I am the Keeper of Signs. A disciple of the Hall of Signs and sworn protector of the realms. Do you know why you're here?"

Manfred shook his head and shied away from her eyes.

"Mr. Bugsbee, we have reason to believe you are a carrier of a great lineage. A lineage older than the Guard, from the time before the Corruption. I understand you've traveled through the Realms to be here?"

Manfred looked at Erneel who nodded his head. "I think so," Manfred replied.

"Your world is quite different from ours. Not much in enchantments or traditions. A very strange earth, yours."

"Then why am I here?" Manfred blurted out.

"Mr. Bugsbee, there are some who believe you to be Mindiidus. The great slayer of those who would harvest the sun. The fanatics of the Cloud."

"I'm no… Minda… Mindee… Moopy Guppy. I'm Manfred. Manfred Bugsbee." He surprised himself as he shouted

"We shall see. Now, take off your clothes."

"What?"

"For the test. Nothing can be hidden, Mr. Bugsbee. Now please." She mimicked the motions of disrobing.

"First, I want to go home," Manfred said and looked at Erneel. "I'm not doing this anymore."

Erneel let go of the Keeper's hand and moved to Manfred's side. He put his arm around him and spoke quietly, deliberately. "Boy, if this test reveals what is most likely, that you aren't who they think you are, then you can go home. But," he moved in close, "until they know, I can't take you back. You'll be fine. I don't believe it to be you either." Erneel returned to the Keeper's side and pointing at Manfred said, "Take 'em off."

Manfred realized he had no other option and slowly stripped down. All the while Erneel and the Keeper talked between themselves and ignored him. Finally he stood bare naked in the frigid room where he covered his privates as is the custom back on his earth.

"Now what?" Manfred yelled to get their attention.

"Stand still, Mr. Bugsbee," she replied.

Erneel sat down in front of her. She raised her hands to her eyes, pressed them lightly against the lids, chanted a guttural spell then moved them to her ears. Her eyes beamed at Manfred. A great building of words and sounds churned in her stomach and echoed through the room. She moved her hands to cover her mouth and the sounds reduced to a steady hum. She then pursed her lips, as if to kiss the air, and three small orbs of light escaped her mouth.

The orbs floated toward Manfred and buzzed around him like bees. They were the same honeyed color as her eyes. Manfred followed them the best he could. He circled as they did and ducked when they moved more aggressively toward his head. They darted around him and touched his skin, leaving cool burns that sent shivers through his body. Eventually, the orbs found their place and stopped moving—one above his head and the other two outside each knee. Once the one above him had settled, Manfred felt an intense shock shoot through him. It started as a sort of static ticking but built into an agonizing rod of solid electricity—down through the crown of his head and straight into the ground. His body was forced into a rigid straight line. The two orbs outside his knees helped him keep his balance. They all connected through pulses inside his body just below his belly button.

The Keeper then yelled out a powerful incantation that reverberated in his head and he was jerked off the ground. The orbs absorbed themselves into his body and brought with them an extraordinary coldness. He tried to scream but nothing came out. The orbs stirred inside him and scratched at his organs. They spiraled into his stomach then worked their way up through his chest, his throat, his jaw. The pain was unbelievable. He blacked out just as the orbs rested beneath the space between his eyes.

Manfred woke up with a terrible headache and his ears and throat burned with fever. He sat at the end of a long wooden table and on the other side, his parents drank tea. They were so young. His father with his dark black beard, manicured and touched with oil. Thick-rimmed glasses rested on his nose as he read the paper. His mother was so beautiful. Thick, curly hair rested and billowed above her ears, already with hints of gray. She tuned a radio.

"Would you like some more hot water, little Manny?" his mother asked.

He looked down at his hands. He held a teacup that he hadn't seen since he was a child. It was a porcelain mug with cartoon dogs painted on it that his father brought home from a business trip. The water inside was muddy and swirled with loose bits of tea. His hands felt cold.

He tried to respond, but nothing came. His mother tilted her head at him and gave him one of her marvelous smiles. Her teeth were immaculate, he'd always remember that. She joked that it was because she brushed them three times a day for fifteen minutes. He could hear his sisters arguing in the next room. It was like this every night. Some fight or another, some boy, and all the while he'd sit with his parents.

"This isn't right," he said.

His father looked over. "What's not right, ole Fred?"

"You shouldn't be here." Manfred felt the iciness build in his stomach. It was as if his organs were freezing and seizing up one by one.

"What's wrong?" his father asked. "Did you hear about the suns, the way they're all burning out?"

Manfred tried to stand but his body wouldn't listen. His mother made her way across the room and touched his forehead.

"Honey, he's got a fever. He's burning up," she sounded worried and kissed his cheek.

The coldness crept up his spine and outward to his skin. His body felt like it was melting into the chair. He looked into his mother's eyes and they were a bright flashing yellow.

"Green?" he said. "Your eyes are green."

His mother laughed. "Just like they've always been."

Soon the golden hue of her eyes was all he could see. He began to cry and his whole body shook in despair. There was nothing left but the coldness that had started in his stomach. It seeped out of his eyes in droplets, covered his face and soon his whole body. His entire world submerged. His parents disappeared and his cries were of agony and longing. He heard a crack of thunder and for a split-second saw Erneel and the Keeper staring down at him.

"Will he be all right?" Erneel asked.

"These tests are beyond human emotion, my Ernie. He'll be far from all right. Changed. Reborn." She pressed her hand over Manfred's eyes and the coldness was replaced with warmth.

He could not feel his body. The voices of Erneel and the Keeper were now only clicks and hums from a million miles away—echoes of a dying star. He could smell the tea and his mother's hair and then the darkness lifted.

Manfred tried to scream, but couldn't. He was somewhere as if in a dream, surrounded by mist, he could see the shapes and sprawl of a desert in the distance. Its vastness appearing in the gaps of storm clouds. As his body moved down, he felt the clouds' electricity traverse his veins and wind push up from the earth, cold and damp. He had no control over where he landed—pulled toward a plateau that stretched above the expanse. A lone man sat at its edge. As Manfred approached, he was struck with a sense of familiarity. He recognized something about the stranger.

The desert below was desiccated and infinite. Ashen trees with no leaves or fruit stood unmoving, their branches angular and wretched. Red rocks jutted up from the sand, windswept creations of another time, some arched and some broken. The sand was burdened within a brightness that reflected back on him, its intensity blinding. The sky was empty. There was no sun, no stars or moons to create light.

In the distance was a fire, its blue flames commingling with Manfred's breath. The way they flickered and weaved against the sky synched with the rising and falling of his chest. Human forms gathered around the great fire, shadowed, dancing bodies. They stepped to the flames like moths, some ritual, some howling.

Manfred settled on the plateau. At first, the man below him only seemed familiar, a body in a crowd, but the closer he got the more he became certain of something. He was moving toward a version of himself. The man sat with his legs crossed and didn't notice Manfred. His body was stronger than Manfred's. Sharp sinewy muscles pushed against his skin, red and black dirt covered his body.

Manfred moved to touch him. In that instant, he felt their bodies combine and he found himself sitting in his other's place looking back at nothing. He immediately felt the strength of the new body. The bones were solid and the mind was clear and focused. Memories of another life flooded Manfred as he looked in toward the fire.

He remembered fighting demons on dark nights, watching his brothers and sisters die—their bodies hurled into hellfire. He remembered kissing the feet of a woman whose hair curled and shimmered with bits of the universe, her mind the birthplace of all creation. He remembered dying. The way it felt, every atom pulled apart, every thought, every dream, crushed dismantled.

He gasped and hugged himself in pain as the memories coursed through him.

Soon he was no longer on the plateau, but down on the desert floor. He walked toward the flame. The shadowed humans in front of him were yelling out, their voices wicked with terror—screams like those of the songbirds of hell. In the fire he was a body that trembled with incandescence, it had no beginning and no end, surrounded and penetrated by smoke.

Above the body, a pattern of lines stretched into the sky—a kind of twisting turning map emerged from its head. The lines moved into the darkness, creating pathways to the great beyond. Manfred followed them with his eyes as they grew. They formed squares stacked on circles and bent into great spirals that vibrated stronger the longer he looked. The image took up the whole sky and wrapped up the earth below it. Soon it was all he could see. Its intensity pounded in his brain and flowed hot through his nerves.

Then he felt himself transfer to a new body again. He was looking out from the flames. He floated in the fire and could feel its heat course through him and the memories of yet another life struck him. He heard the voice of a woman.

"Scratch down the old world. Tear down their monument. Their wicked artifice. Those who ruin, make them bleed. Make them pay."

He could see her through the flames, dressed in elegant flowing garments, her eyes gone, replaced with small suns, her voice anxious strings.

"Take their rotted earth and cloud. Take their warm breath and life. Cull their roots."

Below him, the flames built up from a shifting, shimmering, silver pool. He looked into it and could see the cycles of life. The birth and death of a star, a man and woman in the throes of passion, a child's first step, his parents looking out and mouthing words of encouragement. Behind all of it, beyond the very depths of all sight, he knew he was looking at the history of his earth. Its body orbited the sun as fish and mammals tumbled out from the sea. The whole of its existence pushed against him.

The woman's voice cried out from beyond the flames, "To their death Mindiidus, to their death," and all that was left in the puddle was the sun. It waved in and out of permanence, smaller and larger, nothing, then everything.

Manfred was a total observer now, a step back from the world, bodiless. No more than a balloon tied to the universe that unfolded. The puddle disappeared along with the high flames as the world shook. A violent light enveloped each object held in his sight. The sanguine of the plain, the blue of the sky, the pale cracked skin of the man who had been burning, all brighter and brighter until with a cracking thunder everything vanished. Manfred returned to his own body, his eyes clenched against a growing headache.

Manfred could hear Erneel and the Keeper talking close by.

"I can't do this much longer, my love," said Erneel. "You know this, I should be on the front lines with Fenk. Our soldiers need me."

"Oh Ernie, my dear sweet Ernie. You must have faith. The Ulis found this man throughout all of existence. Your purpose is so much greater now. Please, if for no one else but me. Be patient."

"Patient? The Cloud are gathering their forces. Every day they become stronger. I'm a warrior, not an errand boy."

"How long has this war been waged? Since before I was born. And our daughter's children's children may have to fight it. If you could end it, wouldn't you?"

"It's all I've ever known."

Manfred opened his eyes. Ernie and the Keeper embraced and kissed. Manfred faked a cough to get their attention.

"Welcome back, Mr. Bugsbee," the Keeper smiled.

"Where am I?" Manfred asked, exhausted, unfamiliar with his new surroundings.

"We moved you to a room in my keep. Your body did not take kindly to the Viewing. We're on the right path now, I have no doubts." The Keeper said.

Erneel let out a grunt of disapproval and said, "Only a small piece. A very small piece."

Manfred sat up. Both Erneel and the Keeper offered hands to slow his movement. He looked around the room. It was a half-circle, his bed tucked against the straight wall. On the curve, massive arched windows stood open and let in a light breeze. Round pillars bisected each window—bright, ancient marble. Tucked under the windows were stone shelves lined with leather-bound books.

"When you're ready, Mr. Bugsbee, please, tell us what you saw," the Keeper urged.

"We know what he saw," said Erneel under his breath. The Keeper gave Erneel a stern glance as she offered Manfred a warm cup of tea.

Manfred grabbed the cup and took a few small sips and let the steam relax his face. "I saw myself, I suppose."

Erneel grunted again. "He supposes."

"Quiet, Ernie. Let him talk," Erneel and the Keeper locked eyes. Erneel's skin slightly blushed and he nodded and began to pace the room, his hands behind his back and his eyes on his feet.

"I don't know. It was a dream, I guess. I saw my family. I saw myself, or a version of me, I guess. Somewhere I have never been."

"Doing?" She asked.

"Watching. I saw a man burning at the stake, surrounded by a thousand human shadows."

"Sun Harvestors," she nodded. "What else?"

Erneel rubbed his face as he paced.

Manfred looked at her, confused.

"What else did you see or hear?" Erneel asked, his words abrupt.

"I heard a woman, but she didn't make any sense. She didn't say anything." Manfred took another drink from the cup.

"Nua'eeb was one of the first to turn toward the Cloud, an original Keeper, an evil woman," the Keeper said excitedly and rubbed Manfred's head with maternal kindness.

"She said *Mindiidus*, I remember that," Manfred said, following the excitement of the Keeper.

Erneel nodded his head and the Keeper couldn't help but smile. "Now listen," Erneel said to her. "We can't jump to conclusions. The Viewing is not foolproof. It is not perfect."

"Perfect? No such thing," the Keeper said, her smile more radiant than ever.

"You know what I mean. It checks for a connection. That's all. I could be just as connected to Mindiidus as he is. You know that. You project your hopes, my love. You see the world you want."

The Keeper nodded. "I certainly project. It is my duty as the Keeper of this realm to *project* my feelings. We would never have gone to find Mr. Bugsbee had it not been for my feelings and at the directions of the Ulis."

Erneel nodded and continued to pace again. "I know, I know."

"What you saw, Mr. Bugsbee, was a ritual of the Cloud. The man you saw, this *version of yourself*, we believe, is an ancestor of sorts. And those people you saw, the shadows, they were some of the first to move away from the order of our realm, driven to do harm by power. Harvestors, fanatics of The People of the Cloud."

"People of the Cloud?" Manfred asked.

"Corrupted," she responded, the word filled with surprising venom. "They fell away from our purpose, our divine ordinance of balance. Corrupted by strength, corrupted by weakness."

"And what's your purpose, exactly?" Manfred asked.

"Difficult to distill, Mr. Bugsbee. We are the guardians of order, we protect all the realms. Chosen by the Original Beings." She smiled as she spoke and Manfred could only reply with a feeble, "Oh."

Erneel put his hand on Manfred's. "Next, we see the Old Guard, Manfred. Their approval, the blessing of the Ulis," Erneel playfully pushed him, "and then it's off to battle."

"Battle?" Manfred's voice cracked.

"Rest. Your journey has been long and I'm afraid there is no turning back," said the Keeper. "We'll leave you now. Feel free to explore the keep. You'll find food just down the hall and a bath a little farther. I laid out some clothes for you." She pointed to an end table with three dark green robes stacked on top. "I know it's hard and you may be scared, but you have a birthright, Mr. Bugsbee."

"We'll see," nodded Erneel.

They left the room without giving Manfred a chance to question them further. His body was heavy with exhaustion and he felt sick. With nothing else for him to do he laid back down. It was the softest bed he had ever been in and right now, Manfred cherished comfort more than anything. He liked good food and he loved good coffee. He appreciated cinema and books, but give him a feather bed with cotton sheets and the rest didn't matter.

That made his predicament all the worse. He had none of his clothes, the comforts of his couch, or the smells of his room. Erneel had been dragging him through swamp and bug; things that, although necessary to the human spirit, Manfred had long ago traded in for high thread counts and pizza delivery. He tried to think about the insanity of the events that had led him here. The terrifying tree-demon, the sun outside his apartment, it all felt like a terrible dream. He couldn't focus and found himself thinking about his favorite cafe. The high-backed plush chairs that he could sink into, the way they smelled like perfume and espresso.

He slept most of the next days, venturing only from the room to the kitchen where there always seemed to be a bit of food just prepared, mostly rice and beans. Huge colorful blocks of vegetables he'd never seen or tasted before were laid out on the counter. A bright, orange, leafy cabbage became his favorite. It was sweet and creamy and he had taken to using a spoon to dig into bowls of warm brown rice with it.

His shirts and pants from before had been disregarded and he grew fond of the heavy green robes he had been offered. The insides were lined with soft airy cotton that kept their warmth but also allowed plenty of airflow. The outside was a thick cross-stitch of dry-treated grass. He was also given long underwear that tied loosely around his waist. As far as comfort, even under the circumstances, you couldn't beat the clothing.

He didn't understand where he was exactly. All that was clear was that he was somewhere else. A world like his own, similar shapes and rudiments, but filled with rituals and mysteries unlike anything he'd ever seen. He did understand enough of the landscape to know that he wouldn't survive long on his own, anyhow. His only hope was that it was maybe all a bad dream or at least a misunderstanding. Thinking it through, there wasn't much for him back in his realm: a job he hated, a lackluster love life, a family that had drifted apart more and more every year, and friends he rarely had the energy for. But it had all been his, and it was his home. There were moments of familiarity here, the sound of birds chirping, the taste of seawater on the wind, but he knew he didn't belong and probably never would.

Erneel visited him in his room. It felt nice to interact, but Erneel was elusive, and never gave Manfred much to go on. He only seemed to stop by as a curiosity, to see if Manfred had started to show signs of something bigger. A clear reference point for Erneel, who was still unconvinced.

"What's next then?" Manfred had asked. He had become anxious to leave the Keeper's home.

"Next, Manfred, we travel through the Drilding desert. A most unfortunate place, that."

"Unfortunate?"

"Miles of scorched earth. The quickest passage to the Old Guard. They'll decide your fate."

"The Viewing though. I felt something. I saw something. Isn't that enough?"

"Bah," Erneel was irritated. "Projections, Manfred. Projections of a good heart can be dangerous."

"You don't trust her?"

"She would die for me and I for her. But this is beyond what any of us have seen in our lives. Trust is not enough, boy. We are either certain or we are doomed. Maybe we are doomed either way." Erneel ran his hands through his beard. "We'll leave tomorrow. A long road ahead."

With that Erneel left the room and Manfred was left to ponder on the word, *doomed*.

YOU'LL FIND YOUR WAY

They had been traveling for quite some time before first light. They followed the coastline in the dark of early morning. Large, blue-beaked birds circled beyond them and dove into the violent ocean, pulling up red and white fish that shined in the moonlight. As the sun rose, they cut away from the sea toward steel-colored rocks and before long the beach was a distant memory.

They rode two pale horses. Each one was nearly six feet tall on all fours and magnificent. The one Erneel rode had dark amber eyes and scars all across its face. Manfred's was smaller with splashes of color throughout its mane. Friendly, somehow, the horse would tilt its ears back towards him and he'd scratch its neck. Manfred's saddle was cushioned and adorned with fur. He leaned back against rolled blankets and other pieces of bedding. As comfortable as a man like him could be so far from home.

Two pack mules carried supplies behind them and happily trotted along like dogs. Manfred could only guess what they had on their backs. A tent, some water, and food, he hoped.

"Beautiful animals," Manfred said as he rubbed the strong, slender neck of his horse. They had long since entered a red desert. Parched, little green plants made out a sparse pattern below them.

"Yes yes," Erneel muttered, half asleep.

"What are their names?"

"Names?" Erneel sat up on his horse and stretched his arms above his head.

"What do we call them?"

"We don't."

"Really? They're our friends, Erneel. Aren't they?"

"Friends? They are free. I give no name to free men or free animals, for that matter."

"Free? They're not free."

"How do you mean, not free?" Erneel looked over his shoulder and studied Manfred.

Manfred gestured to the bags on the mules and tapped the saddle of his horse.

"They answered the call. Here on their own volition, boy."

"What call?"

"You have seen me call on animals, no doubt?"

"Like at the Keep," Manfred replied, remembering the flies and his near kiss.

"Yes," Erneel laughed. "They are Cardinal Spirits of this land. Some wish to aid in the cause, some seek adventure. These four were called on this morning as you slept. Isn't that all you do? Sleep."

That was all Manfred wanted—sleep. "You mean they don't stay at the Keep?"

"When they wish to stay, they stay."

"And when they don't?"

"They don't."

"Why didn't you ask me if I wanted to join?"

"Because I don't care."

"But you care how the horses feel?"

"Ask yourself, Mr. Fred, if I let you go now, where would you go? Do you even know which direction we came from?"

Manfred pointed behind himself and realized even the gray mountains from the morning had disappeared. Wherever they were expanded red in all directions. He let out a nervous sigh.

Erneel smiled. "You're stuck with me, ole boy."

Manfred had to accept that Erneel could call animals out of thin air, that he had been a part of the killing of the giant spindly demon, and in that way it was all somehow connected. The uncertainty that scared him the most was that he too may somehow be important to this all.

Back on his earth, Manfred was just a low-paid ad man. The type of person lost in a large machine that no one quite knew the function of. Someone, somewhere, was being paid a lot of money for his work, but not him. Old men were taking month-long vacations with girls half their age. Politicians could be seen on the top floors of his building, taking donations. Important documents were being passed. No one person seemed to know what the goal was and no one cared. Clock in, clock out. *All for those damn throw pillows*, he thought.

Manfred had been good at his job. He was never so ambitious that he made the people above him nervous. He chose early on not to compete with them. To him, they always looked so tired, so agitated. Besides, he had decent benefits, he could afford his rent and he could go out for pizza and beer occasionally. What more could a man need? He laughed to himself.

"Something funny?" Erneel asked.

"Oh. Not really. Back home I was working on an ad for throw pillows and now I'm riding a horse. I'd never ridden a horse before I met you."

"It shows," replied Erneel.

"I guess it's not that bad, though," Manfred said and leaned back.

"It will be."

"It will be what?"

"That bad. You left a dying world for a broken one. This desert was once known as the Emarich Forest."

"This? A forest?" Manfred looked around, everything dead, emaciated, and covered in generations of sand.

"Lakes and rivers. Animals. Birdsong. The Cloud brings in energies that they can't control. It eats at the fabric of this place. Saps its beauty."

Manfred tried to picture a different landscape, but there was nothing there even for the imagination. A few smooth stones in the distance, some mirages, and tricks of light.

"You see those things," Erneel pointed toward the horizon. "Death Spires." They were tall cacti that hunched over against their own weight, the largest plants to be seen for miles. Leathery, orange speckled flesh with spines that twisted out like bedsprings. "They didn't exist before the Cloud came through here. Bad magic brings consequences."

"What do you mean?" Manfred asked.

"The Cloud steals light and power from other realms. When they cannot direct it, it only destroys. Tears through and leaves death upon death. The Spires are born from those dark spaces. And Manfred…"

"Yes?"

"Never touch a Spire."

Manfred nodded even though he didn't need to be told that. They were evil-looking things that moved unnaturally. Manfred thought they were following him, even though they didn't seem to have any eyes to speak of. Although at this point in his journey he wouldn't have been surprised if they did.

Folds of rolling clouds swallowed the horizon as evening rounded in above them, the sky still bright and hot. A welcome breeze drove down from above and cooled the sweat on Manfred's face, dust devils dancing in the glowing distance. Erneel pointed to a rockface in the monotony of the desert and said they would set up camp underneath.

Under the bluff, Erneel tasked Manfred with setting up their tent as he made a fire.

"Isn't there some magic spell? Some way you could just clap and say," Manfred clapped, "shelter?"

Erneel didn't look away from the fire. "Doesn't work like that." He gestured toward the ever-darkening sky. "Best hurry, Mr. Fred. Rain."

Manfred grunted and put his mind to work. He was determined to put the thing together on his own. The two mules walked around him as he laid out the pieces. The mules pressed their heads against him or against one another and nipped at his robe. The two horses had wandered off and swayed side to side in the breeze. Their shadowed bodies looked like some beasts and made Manfred uneasy.

The tent was simple enough—two large pieces of canvas, some rope, and a few support poles. The patchwork of newer-looking canvas stretched out where the stress of the supports was too much. Manfred only struggled for a minute when one of the mules pulled away with one of the ropes that made the spine of the thing. He had set it down behind him to adjust a pole and turned to see the mule twenty yards away with the rope dragging behind it. A few scratches behind the ear and the rope was returned.

"I got it, Ernie," Manfred said as he stood back in awe of his creation.

Erneel came over, leaving the roots and beans he was cooking over the fire, and kicked the corner of the tent where it all came together. The tent shook but did not fall.

"Maybe you are Mindiidus after all," he said.

Manfred's shoulders drooped.

"Lighten up, Manny. We may not live through the night. We must keep our spirits up."

"It's Manfred." Manfred replied.

"Let's eat then … Manfred."

They sat in silence and picked at the large root that Erneel had cooked. It looked like a carrot but came apart like the layers of an onion and the closer you got to the center the sweeter it became. The storm cloud never did what it had threatened. By the time it should have been over them it had disappeared and left in its wake a star-rich, clear, sky.

It was the most beautiful thing that Manfred had ever seen. You could see stars from the deepest reaches of the universe, small beads of light curling around each other. The more Manfred looked, the more depths he could see with each space opening up into another world of humming, breathing light. He ate his food in a daze as the countless galaxies unfolded above him.

"None like the desert sky here," Erneel said.

Manfred nodded.

"No matter how bad it gets, to see this sky, the orbit of Verus and Asai, clears the mind."

The night was quiet. Only the chewing sounds and the hush of the desert. Wind rustled the Spires, their strange needles dancing in the starlight. The horses and mules huddled together.

"What's in the beans, Ernie?"

"Excuse me?"

"They're just very good. I've never really liked beans."

"Ah, mushroom, the root of the Bray... Simple, really."

"What's the meat?" Manfred held up a fibrous red chunk.

"Meat?"

"It's fantastic," Manfred said with his mouthful.

"No, no. That's the Bray root. I don't partake in such cruelty."

"Hm?"

"Eating meat," Erneel snapped.

"Oh?"

"Vile thing to do, you ask me. To be honest. Imagine riding one of those horses with a belly full of their near cousins."

Manfred looked over at the huddled mass. They burred shoulder to shoulder and nipped at bothersome flies. "Sure, but what about chicken?"

"Is there a more regal class of animal than the bird?"

"Sorry," Manfred said, still chewing.

"Don't apologize to me, apologize to them," Erneel said as he tilted his head toward the horses and mules.

The horse he had been riding tilted its head at him and flared its nostrils. "Yeah, but they're smart, Ernie. I mean, not all animals are the same."

"A strange standard. Sameness. I'm afraid I'm too tired for this conversation. As a friendly piece of advice, though—don't kill the brothers of those you depend on."

Manfred rubbed his head and tried to make sense of what Erneel had said, but the old man just smiled and made his way to the tent.

Manfred sat a while and looked from the fire to the stars above. He tried to remember the last time he had gone camping. He and an ex-girlfriend would go out once or twice a year, but they'd always end up just camping out of her car or finding a motel. Plus, wherever they ended up, it always devolved into a fight. He had been out much more when he was younger with his family, but even then, they were never roughing it. His family had a small trailer that they'd take to lakes here and there. His sisters would sleep outside in a tent and he'd be left to fend for himself on the small couch inside.

He stretched his legs out in front of the fire and took it all in. Good food, warmth, the weight of an infinite sky, all for him.

"An adventure," he said aloud. The animals snorted at him. "I've never been on an adventure."

With that Manfred made his way to his part of the tent and he was asleep before his head hit the ground.

"Up, up, up," Manfred was startled awake by Erneel kicking him. "We're being tracked."

"Tracked?" Manfred said half-asleep.

"Up!"

Manfred followed Erneel out of the tent. It was still dark so it was easy to see that a fire had been built in the distance.

"Impossible to move, it is. Traitors in every corner. The Harvestors must have seen your entrance to the realm." Erneel talked quickly as he struck down the tent. "If we can move quickly, if we don't stop, we can make it to the edge of the desert. There we can find cover and reassess."

Manfred leaned against his horse while Erneel packed. He tried a few times to help but was worthless, still barely awake. They couldn't have slept more than a few hours and after such a long day of travel, his body was stiff with exhaustion. The mules mulled around near Erneel, his anxiety showing in them. Their flat, curious eyes followed his every move. Manfred fell asleep a few times where he stood, each time he was nudged awake by the strong fore-shoulder of his horse.

They made their way into the darkness, Erneel on high alert. The breeze and slopes of the night could be hiding any manner of enemy.

The fire behind them was smothered almost immediately, confirming Erneel's fear that whoever had lit it was on their trail. They pushed on as fast as the horses could carry. Manfred held on for dear life. His chest pressed against the pommel, his teeth and eyes clenched shut. Erneel urged the animals to press harder through the night and the breakneck pace took its toll. By the time the sun started to rise again, the horses started to slow, no longer able to keep the hurried pace.

Manfred was functioning almost entirely on auto-pilot. He was numb from fatigue and the jostling of his horse. Every so often a tremor of fear would work its way through his system, but it couldn't settle. It all felt more like a vivid dream than anything else.

Erneel threw some of the supplies off his horse, pots and pans and whatnot, and ordered Manfred to do the same. It helped them keep their slowing pace, but he could feel that the others were closing in.

Soon they could see the riders in the distance, specks on the horizon behind them.

"We'll have to fight," Erneel yelled.

The dream lifted and Manfred was alert to the unfolding horrors. He buried his face in his horse's mane and quietly begged to wake up.

Next, they could hear the commotion of their pursuers. The holler and whoop of the riders, the hooves in the desert—their leather and metal bangings.

"I'm sorry, boy. To have dragged you into this."

And in no time, they were overcome.

"Fight, Ole Fred. Fight."

There were five in total. Three men and two women. All dressed in red tunics. Their faces were covered in worn scarves that flagged in the wind. Each strapped with sun-yellowed leather armor across their chests and torso. Plated steel covered their biceps and forearms. Their horses were dressed for battle, chainmail, and gold lashings draped against their strong and scarred bodies. Each carried half-moon-shaped swords and used the hilts to hurry their horses on.

There was nowhere to run. Manfred and Erneel were surrounded.

"Why in such a hurry, Little Saint?" asked a woman as she dismounted. Her pale, agitated eyes moved from Erneel to Manfred.

"What errands we run across this desert are no concern of yours, Liadra."

"Did you think I would not track you down? Would not find you?" She asked.

Erneel smiled and nodded his head. "You're wasting your time."

"You killed my father!" She yelled.

Erneel let out a long sigh. "That I did. Your father, dear, was a bad man. A dumb man. An enemy to the very fabric of existence."

"Only to yours. Only to the power of the Guard," she was silent for a moment and looked over Erneel and his horse. "Where is your sword, Saint? Far from home without the famed Rocinallia?"

"Ah, my sweet sword, Rocinallia. I'm afraid for now, she rests," Erneel said, almost as if to himself.

"I had hoped to let you die with some honor," she looked toward Manfred. "And who is this?"

"He's nobody. No one of your concern."

"Does he speak?" she asked.

Erneel looked toward Manfred and shook his head.

"He looks awfully scared, Saint. Not like you to keep company with cowards."

"He's no one."

"One of many that will die for your sins, old man. Your whore wife, your whore daughter. Only a matter of time." She looked toward Manfred and demanded, "Who are you?"

Manfred tried to speak but when he opened his mouth all that came out was a barely audible whimpering noise.

"Leave him out of this," Erneel said.

Liadra stood for a moment in thought. "He couldn't be your—no, not the Relic Holder." She laughed. "It can't be, little Saint. This man has a belly."

This brought Manfred slightly back to himself. He had been a cloud of fear just before and she reminded him that he had a body, and with that reminder, he trembled from head to toe. Liadra walked toward him and as she did, Erneel hopped down from his horse and pulled his stick from its rigging. The rest of Liadra's compatriots dismounted as well. Manfred couldn't look away from her eyes. Unwavering, they held him—deep, like water going over his head. They pulled him in and sapped him of any strength he had.

"So, you're their man. Figured you'd be taller."

A few of her band laughed. Erneel shifted his feet quietly in the sand and she looked at him. "You're looking awfully tired, Saint. Do they have you skipping realms now? Already following the bastard Ulis' path?"

"Yours is a dead cause, Liadra," Erneel said. "A dangerous path."

Liadra laughed and motioned with her head toward Erneel. The other woman and one of the men approached him, weapons drawn. Liadra looked up at Manfred and winked. A momentary kindness flashed across her face. Her eyes were suddenly tranquil, almost inviting. He smiled and nodded at her. He felt seen, that in her gaze she saw him for who he was—a harmless interloper. Then, in one fluid motion, she pulled out her sword and cut off the head of his horse. The animal made a harsh clicking sound with its teeth—no time to shriek in pain. Its front legs spasmed then buckled and it fell to its side. Manfred tumbled forward and rolled into the horse's mixture of blood and sand. The other two men stood over him, unflinching, and Liadra pointed the serrated edge of her curved sword at his face, allowing the blood of his horse to drip on him. He raised his arms to assure her that he wouldn't move but couldn't stop himself from half hyperventilating, half crying as he was soaked in the animal's carnage. The horse lay next to him in two pieces, the eyes in its severed head still blinking.

"Stay put," Liadra said.

The two who charged Erneel swung at him. Their blades flashed in the rising sun. He sidestepped both of them, tripping the woman, who in turn, tripped the man. Erneel turned and brought a sharp knot of his stick across the man's ear and there was a terrible cracking sound. Blood poured from his eyes and nose. The woman stood, regained her footing, and swung at Erneel's stomach. He swatted the attack out of the way and brought his stick down between her eyes. She tried to attack again but was concussed and leaned over to hold her face. Erneel brought the stick down against the back of her head. She sprawled out in a plume of sand and released a wet croak from her lungs.

"Your numbers are thinning, child," he said and leaned on his stick. "Walk away."

The two standing over Manfred motioned toward Erneel, but Liadra raised her weapon in protest.

"Do they no longer let you carry a real weapon, little Saint?" Liadra said.

"After I killed your father, my dear, I had hoped to retire. But you and your cursed friends just won't let me." He held the stick out toward her.

All Manfred could do was hold his knees to his chest and quiver. His whole body was covered in the battle's blood. Uncontrollable noises built in his chest and soon a scream, that no matter how hard he tried to conceal, escaped. The two that stood above him looked down in disbelief.

Liadra and Erneel had locked in battle but Manfred could only hear the shuffle of their feet. He didn't look up until he felt something land just in front of him. Ernie had kicked Liadra hard in the stomach and she doubled over and nearly landed on Manfred.

"I'm surprised. For such an old man. You are still so fast," she said as she wiped sand from her face.

Erneel had a large cut at his temple that went across his forehead and just missed his right eye. He pushed a flap of skin to his face and looked at the blood in his hand.

"I'm sorry, Manny. I can't let you die out here. Not just yet," he said and raised his stick above his head.

A loud noise erupted and the animals scattered at the sound. One of the men above Manfred was knocked over by his stead and before he could stand, his head was crushed under its hooves. The other, caught up in the rigging of his horse, was dragged off into the distance. Manfred watched through his fingers as the horse and the man collided with one of the large evil-looking cacti. The needles of the thing twisted their way into them both, and with a violent bellow, arched its long slender top around them. The plant twisted itself around the man and his horse like a great snake absorbing its prey, the man's screams echoing against the open sky as he and the horse were disemboweled, their entrails commingled and splashed to the earth.

Erneel had cut through the sky as he had done on Manfred's earth, a gray glow emanating from beyond the fold.

Liadra charged at Erneel and brought down her sword. He blocked it just before it hit his head, but his stick shattered and the blade made it through to his shoulder. The old man had been able to slow down the downward momentum of her sword enough that it didn't quite make it to the bone. His robe quickly soaked through with blood. Liadra tried to pull away, but Erneel wrapped his arms around her waist and yelled to Manfred, "You'll find your way." Erneel threw himself and Liadra through the tear.

Flashing light erupted from the fold and pieces of Liadra's weapon shot out like shrapnel. And then it closed. Erneel and Liadra were gone. A pool of Ernie's blood was all that was left. It was then that Manfred passed out.

NEWFRIEND

When he opened his eyes, the sun had moved halfway across the sky—the world below, blue and empty and hot. Flies buzzed around his face and landed on his nose and forehead. He tried to lift his hand to swipe them away, but his arms were heavy, worthless. Something near him smelled awful, but he didn't seem to mind. He was comfortable in the sand. His butt and shoulders had sunken deep into it. *Like a fancy foam mattress*, he thought. There he relaxed, totally unmoving. He stared up at the sky and blew at the flies as they hopped from eyelash to cheek to brow. The horse lying next to him didn't do much either. Occasionally he thought it was saying something to him, a sort of gurgling, muttering. Manfred moved closer to hear what the animal was saying and was met first with a numbness and then an incredible jolt of energy. The sand around the horse's head had turned completely black with blood. The flies were innumerable and buzzed in unison, such that they echoed off the sky like a horn of war. He tried to stand, but his legs gave way. He was alone, covered in the mess of death.

He curled into the fetal position and was overcome with such awful terror that he almost cried out for his mother. Before now, this world had been terrible and scary. It had loomed over and jeered at him, but it had been manageable. Even the beast from the forest only seemed like some cartoonish nightmare. He could wake up from a nightmare. But this, the blood of that animal and the bodies of the two that Erneel had killed—he couldn't wake up from that, no matter how hard he shook himself.

When he finally managed to stumble back to his feet, he reached around in the space that Erneel and Liadra had been. There was blood and shattered bits of her sword in the sand where they had been. The rest was nothing—just a heavy desert sky and the unforgiving heat of the sun. His ears crisped and his throat dried. Sand picked up by the wind slashed across his face and everything in every direction was the same—an unrelenting horizon of dunes.

The two who had charged at Ernie laid shapeless in the sand, their blood coagulated in their wounds. He tried not to look at the one that had been trampled. It was no longer recognizable as human. Just a mess of rigid bones poking through flesh and hair.

He searched their bodies for supplies, all the while covering his nose and mouth. He could taste their death, and the smell, he could feel it in his lungs and stomach. An almost sweet rancor, like melons rotting, filled in the hot summer air. Between the two, he found one full canteen of water and some dried leaves that he hoped were food. The rest of the supplies must have been with the mules. He cried and cursed and walked in circles until he thought he saw one of the mules between flurries of sand. It may have only been a mix of shadows, but he had no other options. He tried to convince himself that it was courage that guided him away from the carnage and into the red swirls of desert and not complete desperation.

As he moved, the sand of the desert picked up. At times he could barely see beyond his nose. He tucked his face into his robe and moaned and sobbed with each step. His feet and back were tired and he drank too quickly from the canteen.

"Ernie, Erneel, Little Saint," he yelled into the spaces in front of him. He had no idea if he was traveling in a circle or a straight line. The strange-looking cactus were his only companions and they did nothing but frighten him. Their coiled appendages looked like angry snakes and snarled at him from all directions. Every so often he could see the mule moving around at the edges of his sight—a mirage, a guiding light.

"What have I done?" he cried. "Why have I been left here to die? I'm sorry. So sorry." He yelled as the sky turned purple, the first sign of moons and stars being born.

"I'll just go home now," he begged. "I have a great idea for those pillows anyway. Those damn pillows. I'll just… I'll just draw up a picture of a couch," he started laughing. "And I'll have myself on the couch. Naked!" He yelled so loud that his voice echoed back. *Naked — naked — naked.* He kept laughing. "Yeah, the pillows, I'll cover my balls with those stupid pillows. See how Frank upstairs feels about that. Frank, that bastard." He yelled again. *Bastard — bastard — bastard.* With this, he tripped and fell face-first into the sand and screamed into it and pounded his fists. "Frank," he yelled into the sand. "Frank, I quit. I can't do this anymore. Erneel. Erneel, you stupid ass, why'd you have to leave me here to die? Why would you drag me into this hell? I hardly know you."

He punched and struggled against the sand and continued to yell incoherently. He was having a full-throated tantrum. As he rolled along the ground, granules of the ancient earth filled his robe, his pockets, the creases of his body, but he didn't care. He could feel his death. Beautiful though she was, she hovered over him, pointing and laughing, ready to take him at any moment. He rolled onto his back and looked up at the sky. There was a bright crescent moon. Outside of its light, golden stars peeked through the purpling dusk. Crimson ones too, that shimmered and shook, moved toward each other as if in conversation, then disappeared. *They seemed so close*, Manfred thought. He reached up and tried to grab them. His arms were heavy. His movements felt trapped in molasses.

The sky turned black and his body melted into the night—sucked into desperate sleep. So deep that his mind could not wander, instead, it fixated on a memory. The piercing cold eyes of the Keeper stared down at him while he lay in her soft bed.

He could feel Erneel trying to wake him for their journey. *That small man, that devil.* He could see him pacing the room in circles. His harsh beard, its few red hairs mashed into the white. He could hear him: *clomp, clomp, clomp.* Erneel was speaking, but Manfred couldn't understand. He just wanted to sleep. But Erneel wouldn't stop: *clomp, clomp, clomp.* Erneel's robe brushed across Manfred's face as the old man tried to tug him awake. He wasn't talking anymore, just breathing heavily through his nose, so close to Manfred's face. *What awful breath—stupid holier-than-thou doesn't eat meat*, thought Manfred. His breath smelled like garbage and farts. He hated him, desperately. Why couldn't he just let him sleep? He didn't want to go on any adventure anymore.

But Erneel was persistent and grabbed Manfred by the sleeve. Tugging on him, nibbling, biting. Manfred's eyes shot open and he cried out. Something was eating him alive. He swatted at where the beast had begun its feast and rolled to his feet. The animal reared away and huffed through its chapped nose.

It was one of the mules.

Manfred yelled out to it. The mule, having no name, he tried every greeting he could think of. 'Hello. Hi. How are you?' It stood calmly and matted its teeth. Manfred hugged the animal and kissed its rough furred head and cried into its matted brown curls.

"Thank god you found me," Manfred said between scratches of the mule's ears. "You've come to save me. To save me," He cried and laughed all at once.

The mule turned its head from side to side and stared blankly at him. Manfred assumed it understood him as it had understood Erneel and kept talking with it.

"What happened back there? Who were those people?" Manfred asked.

The mule flared its nostrils.

"I'm sorry he's dead," Manfred whimpered. "It's all my fault."

The mule continued to mash its teeth and blink its brown eyes.

"Dead. He's dead. But you've saved me," Manfred reached out to pet the mule some more, but it avoided his touch. "Yes, yes. We need to get going. Where are we going? He told you, right? The way he does. The way he tells animals things." Manfred nodded his head as he spoke and looked over his shoulders, half expecting the rest of the animal pack to show up.

The mule brayed, adjusted its back haunches, and started to walk away.

"I should follow you then? Right, okay."

Manfred forgot how tired he was and brushed the sand off the best he could.

"Should I just, uh, get on you then? That makes the most sense right?"

The mule moved just fast enough that Manfred had to jog to keep up.

"Okay, if you'll just slow down, I'll hop on."

The mule didn't slow.

"Okay. That's fine."

Manfred tried to run and hop on, but the mule shrugged him off. Manfred tumbled in the sand and the mule kept walking.

"Fine," he said as he got back up. "Fine, I'll just follow you then."

The mule slowed down and let Manfred catch up. He tried to jump on again one more time, but the animal turned and nipped at him. Manfred raised his hands in defeat. "Okay, okay, I'll just follow." He rested his hand on its rear haunch and they walked together through the desert.

Once the cold of the night had taken over, the mule finally let Manfred ride it, and before he knew it, Manfred was asleep again, balancing gentle on the warm back of his animal companion.

Manfred woke up as he tumbled into the sand. The mule had changed its pace as the desert cooled and moisture filled the air. Manfred scrambled to his feet to see where the mule had gone. It had run toward a sparse grouping of green and yellow ferns that staggered out from the desert's edge. There a valley opened up beyond the desert and led toward the beginnings of what appeared to be a mountain pass. Had he not been so thirsty he may have stood in awe. Red rocks lined the valley walls and spiraled toward some center, and at that center was a basin of water, and that was all he could see. The whole of the sky reflected from it and pulled him toward it. Just past the basin, three willowy trees of gilded bark stretched out, their leaves a humid nightgreen. He made his way down a rocky path, fixated on the basin of bright clear water. His legs twisted and turned against him, filled with exhaustion, his robe catching on every stick and twig.

Hidden from Manfred's view, around the basin and below the trees, were eight people of varying shapes and sizes, all balanced on their heads. Their legs were folded and their arms, from elbow to palm, formed triangles of support on the dirt below. A low tremolo escaped from their noses and reverberated off the stones of the valley. All wore ratted, canvas pants, tied tightly at the stomach. Some had ornate tattoos on their faces, crisscrossing triangles around their eyes with intricate spirals and dots connecting them.

The men had long, wiry beards that curled out from their faces, groomed with wax and oil. Everyone was bare-chested. The woman's breasts heaved in each breath toward their necks. The men had designs drawn across their chests with the earth-colored clays in the shapes of trees and roots. They were all situated in what was the exact and complete end of the desert, where sand continued into the valley, but stopped abruptly at their strange ritual and was replaced with a lush garden of flowers and high, flowing grass. Long fat blades whipped softly against the statued figures. The humid air formed a pleasant mist around them.

Seven of them had their eyes closed, their faces as calm as night. Only the occasional twitch of their lips gave away their living condition. From a distance, they looked like works of ritual art—nothing more than expertly balanced rocks. Vibrant, bespeckled bugs moved freely on them and hopped from limb to limb. The bugs crawled unpatterned across their exposed bodies, never causing a fidget or tremor on their hosts.

One of them, the young man, had his eyes wide open. They were pale-yellow and full of the moon's light. His bald head rested in the sand, he had no beard, only scruff. His face was red with the strain of blood. Where the rest looked as if they were born inverted, set to stay on their heads for all eternity, he swayed slightly from side to side.

When Manfred realized what he had stumbled into, fell to the ground and moaned in anguish. "Water. Please give me water." None of the seven creatures budged at his request except the young man who rolled to his feet and moved toward Manfred.

"Water…" Manfred pleaded. "… Ernie."

The young man pointed at the shallow basin and Manfred fell face-first into the bowl, lapping at it like a dog. He removed his robe and tried to scrub the blood and sand from his hair as he drank. The seven remained unmoving.

"Easy, newfriend," said the young man. "You'll get sick. Get very sick."

Manfred lifted himself from the bowl to catch his breath, the water dark with the blood and dirt that had caked into his face. "Erneel… Ernie…" Manfred stammered and put his face back in the bowl, drinking and splashing it against his bare chest.

"You're not the Saint?"

Manfred spoke between gulps of water, "No… gone… Old Guard."

The young man sat next to Manfred and looked him up and down. "You've lost your way. We're not of the Guard. Lost."

Manfred looked at the group around him. "Who?"

The young man stood up and pointed in a circle at his others. "We are the Sacred Kin."

Manfred shook his head.

The young man looked confused but seemed eager to tell Manfred about his group. "Builders of trees? Rebuilders. The Kin."

Manfred continued to drink. "No… other world."

"Another world? To meet with the Old Guard?" The young man sat with his head cocked and examined Manfred. "What do they call you in this other world?"

"Manfred." He laid down next to the bowl of water and looked up through leaves toward the dark sky. "You are the Sacred Kids?"

"Kin. The Sacred Kin. I'm Os'halla, defender of the ways."

"Ways?" Manfred's body relaxed into the grass beneath him.

"Disciples of the Essential Ways. Rebuilders. Dedicated to harmony." He gestured to the other seven. "We create roots, we connect. We create." Os'halla showed Manfred the top of his head, where small roots had begun to grow out from his clean-shaven scalp. "Do you see?"

Manfred's vision was blurred and he was dizzy, but he could see something growing out of the man's head—small brown nobs of wood. "Roots?" he asked.

He nodded. "With practice, we Turn."

"Turn?" Manfred felt like he was hallucinating. He was so exhausted and drained that this man seemed like nothing more than a dream.

"Turn toward nature, create new green, become trees. Become."

A shock ran through Manfred and he jumped to his feet. "No," he cried out. "We killed it... it tried to kill us. A tree-beast."

Os'halla rolled away from Manfred. "Oh, no. That is not us, newfriend. Stolen by the Cloud. Altar Breakers. Abominations of our practice. It is not us." Os'halla raised his hands to try and calm Manfred down. "Please sit. Those are wicked things. Wicked. You are safe here. Safe."

Manfred's mind raced, but he was so weak. "That tree tried to kill me. It was one of your... brothers?"

"Was. Broken spirits come to our hollow to learn. You see. No patience. They grow roots, but don't quiet. Too loud. Their minds. The Cloud calls for them. Holds them in their corruption."

Manfred took a few deep breaths.

"The Saint, you said, the Saint?" asked Os'halla, trying to calm Manfred.

"Killed... by Liadra."

"Liadra? The Bone King's daughter killed the Saint?" Os'halla scratched his head. "Worrisome. So worrisome."

Manfred began to cry.

Os'halla pulled Manfred to his feet. "Don't cry, newfriend. Two-day trip to the Old Guard. I'll take you. As my duty. Duty of the Kin."

Manfred looked at him through tear-filled eyes. "You will?"

"The Kin follow the path. When the wind blows, we feel it on our skin. When it rains, we drink. When the path sends the lost, we find them. You are lost. I am bound to guide you and to guide."

Os'halla walked Manfred to a hereto unseen small lean-to that rested against a valley wall. Manfred's heart and legs were exhausted. The floor of the lean-to was covered with layers of dried moss and a few heavy blankets.

"Rest here. There are clean robes in the corner. Find comfort, newfriend." Os'halla pointed to the bed and Manfred couldn't resist the temptation of a soft place to lie down. He crawled in and covered himself with a heavy wool-like blanket, not caring anymore who this stranger was. The fatigue was so immense that he fell asleep immediately. Before Os'halla returned to his others, he waved his hands over a small pit outside the lean-to and a fire started within, its warmth reflecting onto Manfred.

Manfred was home in his apartment. Its objects buzzed in a blue haze. The paint on the walls cracked and vibrated and he could hear a loud moaning at his door—a great dying cackle. He swung the door open just as the elevator down the hall closed. He ran to the stairs and made it down to the lobby as a shadowy figure exited through the main doors. He pushed out onto the street. Above, the sky pulsated black, the sun a swirl of metallic blue and white. It blinked with Manfred's movements. Ahead, he could see Erneel slumped over at the edge of the road with Liadra's sword sunk into his head.

Manfred tried to reach him, but with each step he took, Erneel moved farther away, shrinking as he did.

Beyond the cityscape, a rolling thunder clapped against the sky and the sound built toward him. It convulsed through the city streets until it revealed itself as those of the hooves of many horses.

Liadra and her band burst out from an alleyway near Erneel. She rode the horse she had decapitated in the desert, its head hanging by a thread, its guts billowing out from its throat. She lifted Erneel by the sword stuck in his head and tossed him into the sky, his body drifting up into the air toward the sun.

Manfred cried out and brought the attention of the horde. They galloped toward him and the whole universe shook. He wanted to run, jump under a car, or crawl back up into his apartment building. But he stood fast. Suddenly, he held a spear and in that there was confidence. He felt a surge. The spear was eight feet long, seven in wood, and the last foot, a slender arched bone carved to a point. The bone shone brightly under the dying sun.

Liadra and hers rounded upon him and he pointed the great weapon at her and the headless horse. Each of the hordes froze, and in a great shudder they too began to drift up into the sky as Erneel had done, caught by the sun's gravity. The buildings and the streets followed suit. And then Manfred felt his own body being stretched out at each atom.

He opened his eyes and he was still in the bed of moss. He breathed in the air of the place. The small fire popped and hissed out the smell of sage, the stars cutting through the leaves above him. With one more breath he fell back asleep.

THE SACRED KIN

When Manfred awoke he was drenched in sweat and wrapped tightly in the heavy blanket. His elbows pressed against his ribs and both legs were tangled and stuck. It was cooler here than in the middle of the desert, but it did not matter. His throat was dry so that it hurt and his head was pounding. He tried to maneuver out of the blanket, but with each twist, the fabric constricted tighter around him. He needed water and he needed out of the bed. The dark wool fibers of the blanket scratched at his sun-peeling ears and neck. He rolled out of the lean-to in a painful and breathless frenzy. He finally freed himself from the blanket with what felt like Herculean effort.

He grabbed a robe from a stack near the lean-to. It was stark white cotton. The strange cleanliness of the thing gave him energy and he had a moment of comfort.

Before him, Os'halla had laid out a plate of dried fruits and vegetables and a large jug of water. Before he put the new robe on he used the jug to douse his body. He rubbed the dirt and sweat away and let it fall to the ground. He then guzzled as much water as he could. Nothing had ever felt so rewarding. He felt it in his stomach and his lungs, all the way down to his feet. Between gulps, he stuffed his face with fruit, and couldn't remember the last time he had tasted food so good. Happily he leaned against the red rocks and gorged himself. Eventually he threw up next to a small tree.

The lean-to was built into the rockface behind him. He hadn't realized it the night before, but where the desert abruptly ended at this valley, he was at the bottom of it. The lean-to sat above where Os'halla and the others had been last night and if Manfred had walked forward a few feet, he'd have noticed that most of them were now gone. Only Os'halla and two others remained.

While Manfred was peeing on a red rock, a woman came up behind him. He had just enough time to finish and cover himself as he turned to face her. She was one of the women from the night before, no longer standing on her head, but still bare-chested. Her hair was matted with red dirt and flowers. Two long green roots grew out from the crown of her head, diverging and intersecting into a single point. Manfred put his hands in front of his face, trying not to look at her boobs, and looked down at her feet.

"Don't be scared," she said. "We are glad that you've eaten all that we've left for you."

Manfred lowered his hands and nodded, still looking down.

"I'm Axealo," she said as she bowed her head.

Manfred looked at her for a moment and quickly looked back down. "I'm Manfred," he stuttered.

"We are glad you found us, Manfred. The desert is no place, no place at all. Please come sit with us while the Warrior Green trains."

Manfred followed her down to where he had found them the night before.

Os'halla stood in front of the basin that had first quenched Manfred's thirst. His hands were held in prayer and a long gold chain stretched out of the water. The chain stood at nearly six feet tall and swayed back and forth like a cobra. Somehow it moved on its own accord and made Manfred uneasy. He looked back and forth from Axealo's exposed back to the chain. She motioned for him to sit next to a man who watched Os'halla.

"Manfred, this is Gehgard the Green."

The man nodded without taking his eyes off of Os'halla. "Welcome to this day, Manfred."

Gehgard sat with his legs crossed, his whole body tattooed with dotted shapes, his gut hanging down over his knees. He was bald like Os'halla but the roots on his head were much thicker. It looked like a single frizzy dreadlock, but on closer inspection, it was a cord of smaller roots winding together.

Os'halla smiled at Manfred and quickly looked back at the chain. As he did, the chain coiled back and darted at his face. Os'halla slipped the attack and took a long, circular step around the basin. The chain attacked again, swinging at his head, then cutting at his legs, but Os'halla avoided each charge with ease. He jumped and ducked in fluid motions. It was like a dance. Os'halla moved in a small circle around the basin as he rolled and spun to avoid the chain's whip.

Gehgard followed Os'halla with his eyes and winced and clapped his hands each time Os'halla dodged an attack. "Good movement, good flow. Stay present, follow along, feel its will," he said.

Doing so, Os'halla stayed just out of reach of the chain. He toyed with it as it began to speed up, its attacks harder and more precise. When Os'halla could no longer avoid it altogether, he pressed his forearms against it and seemed to absorb its movements. The chain wrapped itself around his neck and he turned and replaced his neck with an arm, then softly push it away. Manfred couldn't make out what was happening. The chain was so rigid and heavy and Os'halla's reactions to it were so elegant and soft.

Manfred took his eyes off of Os'halla and the chain for a split second to look at Axealo's breasts, a reflex more than anything, and at that exact moment, Gehgard looked at him.

Manfred blushed and looked back toward Os'halla.

"Stranger?" Gehgard said. "We understand you're to meet with the Guard. Settle this business?"

Manfred looked at him. Gehgard's beard was completely gray, yet he didn't look over thirty years of age.

"Man of little words, I see." Gehgard looked back toward Os'halla and yelled, "Relax."

Os'halla and the chain were going full speed and Os'halla had started to take damage, his whole upper body red from the chain's strikes and tugs. The chain had wrapped itself around his legs and while he struggled to free himself, it poked at his head like a mischievous younger brother.

Axealo patted Manfred's leg to get his attention and without thinking he looked at her chest again before making eye contact.

"Sorry," he said.

She looked at him quizzically. "The Warrior Green says you're from another world?"

Manfred nodded, staring at her forehead with all of his strength.

"And you look to meet with the Old Guard?"

He continued nodding.

"And you've never heard of the Kin?"

He shook his head and she laughed.

"And the Saint is dead?"

Manfred looked her in the eyes and felt his tears welling up within him.

"It's about time. The Little Saint has been tempting fate for a hundred years," said Gehgard. "I always did tell him he'd die long before me."

Manfred looked at Gehgard in disbelief. "Who are you people?"

"Haven't you been told? We are the builders of forests, descendants of the Green God. The question is, who are you?" Gehgard said. He still winced and cringed along with Os'halla's movements.

"I've told you, I'm Manfred."

"Manfred. From another world," Gehgard nodded. "What name is that? What other world?"

Manfred looked from Gehgard to Axealo for help. "I don't know, from the regular earth," he said.

"Man of Regular Earth, you say. A man who tumbles into our world and speaks our language?" Gehgard was looking at Manfred now out of the corner of his eye.

"Speaks your language?" Manfred asked.

"Not many have the *Many-Tongues*," Gehgard said. "Why again were you in the care of Erneel?"

"The '*Many-tongues*?'"

"A man who speaks the language of worlds he's never been is a man beyond the worlds, wouldn't you say?" Gehgard looked at Axealo, who nodded her head. "Os'halla, we must take him to the village, protect him, sort this out. Do you not think?"

Axealo kept nodding and said, "Our work can wait."

"Work?" Manfred asked.

Axealo pointed toward the desert above them. "The Earth-Breakers broke the forest, where was once green and lush. They brought down a sun, brought down a forest. We work to rebuild."

Manfred squinted at her, confused.

"The Cloud worked in energies that they could not control, Man of Regular Earth," said Gehgard. "It scorched the earth above us, all the way to the sea. So it is for us to put our breath to work and rebuild." He pointed to the trees above them. "Just this has taken us so long and now we hear the Cloud rises again."

Manfred shook his head and let out an aggravated sigh. "None of this makes sense," he said and stood up. He pointed at Axealo and shouted, "For starters, why are you all naked?"

Axealo and Gehgard looked at one another then back at Manfred.

"And what is he doing with that chain?" Manfred said as he pointed at Os'halla.

Hearing that, the chain fell to the ground and Os'halla turned to respond. "Pract…" But before he could finish the chain had sprung up and slapped him across the face. Os'halla fell to the ground and the chain slipped back and disappeared deep into the basin.

"He's practicing," said Axealo.

"He's the guardian of the Kin, the Warrior Green," said Gehgard.

Os'halla stood up. "The Warrior," he said as he brushed himself off.

"You'll stay the day with us," said Axealo, "and tomorrow Os'halla will take you to the Guard."

Manfred sighed. He knew he had no choice.

That night, they sat around a fire while Gehgard told the Kin's story of creation.

"Before time was time," he said, his face glowing in the dark flames. "Before time was time, Manfred, there were only the three. The Green God, the Wax Child, and the Red Star." He leaned in so close to the fire that Manfred was nervous his beard would catch on fire. "The universe was a great nothing that stretched in all directions forever, a blackness of such vastness that it still hangs over us to this day. And at the center of that blackness, spinning freely of her own design, rested the Red Star. Her body was so compact, so dense, that it could not be seen by the naked eye."

"There were no eyes to see her," Axealo added.

"Even now, with the eyes of a thousand men and the resolve of a million explorers, the Red Star remains unseen." He leaned back and rubbed his stomach and continued, "The Red Star laid out and her red hair and her red body created the first light and from that light was born the Green God. At first, he was a mere reflection of her brightness, only existing on the farthest reaches of the nothing, only existing as the sparkle of her eye. And he was nothing and nothing more. An orb caught in the empty folds, appearing, growing, moving through the void."

"Somehow, somehow," repeated Axealo.

Gehgard nodded as he spoke, "The two remained outside of time. Always searching for one another but only catching glimpses of themselves, other reflections, ghosts, and little else. Before she had created light, and by chance created the Green God, the Red Sun knew nothing of loneliness because there was nothing to long for. She had spent the beginnings of eternity relaxed and happy in the warmth of her redness, of her nothingness. But once the Green God appeared, a flicker in the distance, the Red Sun's heart grew cold, and it grew a loneliness and a sadness. When they finally did meet, their love was so strong that just on sight of one another the Wax Child was born. The Wax Child being the first true substance of all existence. The Red Sun, she is light, the Green God, he is spirit, and the Wax Child, they are earth. And for a long while, the three of them lived in harmony. The Red Sun at the center and Wax and Green beyond. But Wax grew, taking up space and the nothingness became cramped. They, the Wax Child, were a formless shape, floating and growing."

"No, no, no," said Axealo. "They were a thousand shapes. They were all spread out."

"Do you want to tell the story, Axe?" Gehgard asked as he looked at her and Os'halla laughed.

She nodded and took over. "You see, Manfred, they all loved each other. It was awful. It was congested. There was nowhere to hide. The Red Sun created new light, new centers, so the nothingness could expand and give the Wax Child room to grow. But no matter the size of the nothingness, it was never enough for Wax. In this space Green would get lost, the new lights too much for him. So Green grew angry with the Red Sun for she had not considered him as she created light. And Red Sun was angry with Wax for being ungrateful, and Wax … they just kept growing."

"You're rushing it," interrupted Gehgard. "This happens over countless generations."

"This happened before time," said Axealo, "there were no generations. Only them."

Gehgard chuckled. "I suppose."

Axealo cleared her throat. "Then the wars began. Red and Green fighting, each dodging Wax, until the nothingness, that was so fragile, so perfectly placed on an altar, shattered." Axealo threw a handful of something in the fire and it cracked and popped like fireworks. "Red remained outside of time, but Green and Wax and the new light she had created spread out, pieces and pieces in the shattered nothingness."

Gehgard piped in, "And Green, in his sorrow for losing the Red Sun, searches the pieces of the Wax Child for a clue, a way back to the center. And each time Green sits down with Wax and they get to talking, new life is formed. These trees, the water, all gifts of their word, the spirits mixed with the earth, and thus we are born."

"Does he ever find her?" Manfred asked, feeling himself fall asleep.

Axealo put her head on Gehgard's shoulder. "Whenever there is love, she is found. Whenever there is sorrow, she is found."

The two of them glowed in the fire light. It danced around them and for a moment highlighted the color in their eyes. Gehgard's a cool green and Axealo's a bright flashing red.

They both laughed.

"It is said," Gehgard continued, "that once the Wax Child descends on man, cuts through the many realms, speaks the many tongues, there will be a final battle and all will be reset and harmony shall be complete."

"We are their followers. In us, as is in you, are the spirit and first light. Descendants of the Green God." said Gehgard. "Now you better get some sleep, Manfred. It is a two-day trip to the Guard."

Manfred was already asleep, too exhausted to see the allusions to his journey and the excitement in Gehgard and Axealo's faces as they looked at him.

A GOOD SIGN

The next morning, Manfred expected to see Gehgard and Axealo by the basin while Os'halla and he ate breakfast, but they were gone.

"Where'd they go?" he asked.

"Preparations," said Os'halla.

Manfred tilted his head.

"To fix a broken forest takes time, it takes work. Takes time," Os'halla said. "But now they prepare for the end."

"So," Manfred asked between bites of chewy bread, "what were you doing yesterday, with that chain thingy?"

"Practicing."

"Practicing for what?"

"Yielding."

"Yielding?"

"We seek peace, but there is always war. Always."

Manfred took a long drink of water and nodded his head dubiously. "By yielding?"

"Cultivate the bend and there is no break."

Manfred shrugged.

"Hit me," said Os'halla.

"What?"

"I will show you."

Os'halla stood up and Manfred smiled. He outweighed Os'halla by a good sixty pounds and had a few inches on him. Now that Manfred was looking at him, Os'halla actually looked malnourished.

Os'halla returned the smile and nodded his head again. "Hit me." He put his hands behind his back and stuck out his chin. "Hit. Me."

"I need to get to the Old Guard."

"First, hit me and then I will take you."

"I don't wanna hurt you, man," Manfred said as he slowly got to his feet. "You're kinda frail."

Os'halla stuck his chin out further.

"Fine, but I warned you." Manfred chuckled to himself and Os'halla looked at him blankly.

Os'halla slapped his chin lightly and nodded his head.

Manfred let out a heavy sigh and took a half-hearted swing at Os'halla's face. It landed and Manfred raised his hands. "Okay, now can we go."

Os'halla shook his head then pointed at his face. "Hit. Me."

"Fine," Manfred sighed again, then stretched his right arm back, opened his chest, and stood on his tippy toes. "Ready, then?"

Os'halla smiled.

Manfred swung with all his might. His disposition. The sun. Erneel's death. The confusion. All weighed in and his whole body formed itself behind the blow.

When the punch landed, Manfred felt a sensation he had never felt before. He felt the strike land, but not as it should. Os'halla's body was empty. There was nothing to stop the force, there was nowhere for it to go, so it just returned to its origin and put Manfred on the ground.

Manfred looked up at Os'halla and said, "I should've known."

Os'halla helped him up. "Known?"

Manfred wiped the dirt off of himself and looked at Os'halla impatiently. "Everything can kill me out here."

Os'halla smiled.

"Now will you take me?" Manfred asked, embarrassed.

"What is the rush?"

"The rush is, I want to go home."

"Home is the Old Guard?"

"No. Home. Earth… uh… the regular one."

"Man of Regular Earth, regular man," Os'halla said.

"Old Guard is Erneel, Erneel brought me here," Manfred said frustrated.

"And he is dead."

Manfred put his face in his hands in exasperation.

Os'halla patted him hard on the shoulder. "It's a day's hike through the canyon. Then a day over the pass. Let us go now."

Manfred peaked from his hands. "Thank you."

"It is my duty, newfriend."

Os'halla led the way and did not wait. He only brought one thing with him, a bo staff. It was made of what looked like still-living wood. A vibrant, younggreen color, as if Os'halla had just plucked it up from the ground—a sapling just being born. The only disruption to its color were a few black knicks of battle. The pathway into the mountain range was narrow and without footholds. Os'halla disappeared at each bend and hopped over downed boulders as if they weren't even there. Manfred knew he couldn't keep up and could only hope that Os'halla would be there in the end. There was no time for the claustrophobia that moved through him either. The walls were so tight in some places that he had to suck in his gut and walk sideways. Each time the walls closed in and he felt their awful pressure, he'd will himself on. The terror of the desert behind him was enough to push him forward.

As the sun broke through the small slits above them, the canyon opened up and Manfred could breathe. He called out to Os'halla, "Can we slow down?"

Os'halla let Manfred catch up. "Newfriend, you're right. There is no need to rush. No need."

Manfred nodded. "Thank you, and it's just Manfred."

"Manfred, newfriend."

"I don't do this so much back home," Manfred said as he caught his breath.

"And what did you do?"

Manfred thought for a minute. "To stay in shape?"

Os'halla examined Manfred. "Shape?"

"I…" Manfred tried to think of a lie, but nothing came.

"You what?"

"I don't. So, how long have you been with the Kin?" Manfred asked.

"I was young," Os'halla said, "very young. My mother had died in Freea and I, too, was close. A cold season, as I remember,

remember. In her life and her strength, she had traveled with many—old believers and new. She told me of the Kin, of their commitment to life and their reverence of death. Of death. Before she died, I knew my path would lead to them. Would lead. So, I wandered, in my sickness, as you did, out of the desert into our refuge of grass. Gehgard took me in. And there I remained, committed, empowered, by the path. Remained a protector and a lookout."

"Lookout for what?"

Os'halla shrugged.

"For me?" Manfred asked.

Os'halla smiled. "For you and all things like you."

Two hawks flew across the sky, one right at the heel of the other. Their wings and tail feathers cut across the blue sky. Os'halla pointed them out just as the larger of the two turned over and grabbed the other in its talons. The two birds shrieked and twisted above the two men, flying and grappling until they disappeared above the canyon walls.

"A good sign," Os'halla said.

"What do you mean?"

Os'halla looked at him confused. "A struggle above the canyon wall, a struggle below. All things move forward. All things are harmonious."

The next few miles took the men up slippery moss and corroded sandstone. Manfred had to concentrate on each step. He spent most of his time on all fours to keep from falling backward. Every so often Os'halla would let Manfred catch up to give him a small bite of food or some water or point out some bird or other critter.

It occurred to Manfred that he had no idea where they were going. For all he knew, Os'halla could be a member of the Cloud, pulling him deep into a quiet cavern to sacrifice him to some strange god. If Os'halla was planning on killing him, at least for the time being, he was being fed and afforded some kindness. Manfred knew he wouldn't find relief or comfort again until he could sprawl out on his small couch and listen to the hum of his humidifier. He longed to pull at the fabric of his favorite cotton shirt.

"We'll break for the night up here," Os'halla yelled down a few switchbacks ahead.

Manfred wanted to jump for joy, but his legs were so tired all he could do was raise his hand and give a slight wave. Each day on this new earth Manfred was faced with an exhaustion worse than the last. When he was in the desert, he couldn't imagine being more tired, and now as he looked back, it seemed almost pleasant to be holding on to the pack mule.

The switchbacks opened into a large clearing of soft white sand. Small, wispy, purple trees sprouted out from the corners. By the time Manfred reached it, Os'halla had already reached the center of the clearing and was sitting down.

"We'll rest here," Os'halla said as Manfred made his way toward him.

Manfred caught up and immediately fell to his side. "It's all I've ever wanted."

Os'halla waved his hands over a dead tree and it burst into flames. Shadows scampered about as Os'halla pulled a few of the smaller trees out of the ground and directed Manfred to eat the bulbous earth-colored roots.

The roots were bitter but their moisture filled Manfred with a warmth he had not felt in some time. The more he ate the happier he became and, surprisingly, the more he hiccuped. Together they sat around the fire and told stories.

"… and I wake up and this old man, this devil, is sitting at my counter, eating my food—hic—and I, I don't know what came over me—hic—but I charged him, and I ended up right on my ass—hic—hic—"

"You charged the Saint? The little Saint." Os'halla looked at Manfred wide-eyed.

"—hic—he was trespassing," Manfred laughed. "The old man was trespassing and it's—hic—my house. You know. A man has to protect his own home. His house. And then there's you—hic—. Tell me, are you trying to kill me, man?"

Os'halla tilted his head at Manfred but didn't respond.

"Are you trying to kill me? Everything out here—hic—is trying to kill me. I saw a cat," Manfred paused for a moment," I mean a cactus, I saw a cactus eat a man and his horse. Are you trying—hic—to eat me?" He stood up and wobbled back and forth. "Are you getting me drunk? So you can kill me?"

Os'halla laughed. "Sit down, newfriend. I am not trying to kill."

"But, you, earlier," Manfred did some karate moves in the air, "you—hic—told me to hit you and I fell over."

Os'halla nodded.

"And that was violent—hic—and rude."

"Would you like to learn?" Os'halla said and stood up.

"You're not gonna try and—hic—kill me?"

Os'halla shook his head. "Just stand up straight and relax." Manfred stood as straight as he could, but his head would not hold still. Os'halla put both hands on Manfred's chest and lightly pushed down and as he did Manfred felt steadier. It felt like Os'halla was pushing straight down on his shoulders, somehow pressing him into the earth. Os'halla tapped the insides of Manfred's knees with his right foot. "Bend your legs here. Feel the weight. Fill your lungs. Your lungs must be full. Let the breath burn through you, let it seep into the sand." Manfred breathed out and Os'halla's hands became even heavier. Os'halla gently adjusted Manfred's knees again and removed his hand from his chest. "Keep breathing like that. Emptiness starts with fullness. Breathe and release and breathe."

"Close your eyes and keep breathing," Os'halla said and positioned himself in a loose fighting stance. Manfred took two deep breaths before Os'halla threw a hard right punch to his chest. Manfred felt a jolt of pain, but it quickly subsided. The force of the blow went down through his body and sprung back out through Os'halla's hand.

Manfred opened his eyes and rubbed his chest.

"Not bad," Os'halla smiled.

Manfred continued to rub his chest, feeling drunk again. "It felt like it went right through me. How did you do that? —hic—"

"You did, newfriend. Practice and you'll be an empty vessel in no time. No time." Os'halla chuckled at the confused look on Manfred's face.

Manfred looked at Os'halla for a moment, then without saying a word he laid down in the warm sand and was snoring within seconds.

He woke up the next morning covered in dew. He had slept so well that he didn't notice the small droplets of water that had formed on his body. But when he did notice, they made him feel feverish—a sticky humid restless feeling. The sand around him was damp and the canyon chilled. He moaned as he got to his feet and staggered toward the nearest wall. He peed with one hand and wiped the dew from his hair with the other. On top of everything else, he was hungover. Whatever was in those roots from the other night had packed quite the punch.

Os'halla had been awake for a while and had made a small fire against the opposite wall and its heat reflected against him. Manfred wanted to ask him where breakfast was, but before he could speak, Os'halla raised his hand and pointed to a spot next to him. Manfred took the hint and tried to emulate Os'halla's posture. He relaxed his shoulders, the point of his head held high and his chin tucked in. Manfred's breath was loud and labored, his mouth agape. Os'halla, on the other hand, seemed not to be breathing at all, somehow taking air in through his head, or his pores, or those strange little roots. They stood there until the fire flickered to its death.

Os'halla then turned toward Manfred who seemed surprised to see him just standing there.

"Just through there," he said and gestured ahead of them. "By nightfall, we'll be in Arkis'el, the village of the Old Guard."

Manfred nodded and they made their way out of the clearing.

The opening narrowed quickly into another slot canyon and forced the two men to squeeze and contort to find each new foothold. There were times when the ground would disappear below them and they had to climb in a spread-eagle sort of way. Manfred marveled at the newfound abilities of his own body. He was sore and tired and scared, but somehow able. He breathed in the orange dust of the walls and felt almost excited to see what was next to come.

After a last steep crawl, they emerged. Manfred, who had been so focused on the climb, was overcome with momentary vertigo when he saw where they were. He knew they had been going up, he had felt it in his legs and in his shortness of breath. But he couldn't have imagined how high they were and how quickly the world had dropped away in front of them.

The two men stood atop a mountain that overlooked a lush valley. Fields of some crop, wheat-like, waved in voluminous patterns. Small huts and their fires dotted the terrain. Os'halla pointed across the valley and Manfred followed his arm with an intense wave of vertigo.

"Arkis'el."

On the far side of the valley, a great jewel of a city was embedded in the mountain range and folded into the clouds above.

"Hopefully they are expecting you," Os'halla said as he stretched out against a spindly tree.

"Why do you say that, expecting me?" Manfred said as he caught his breath.

"Not the most peaceful times, not the most peaceful people."

"I thought the Old Guard were the good guys."

"Steadiers. Steady is not not good, not not violence. Steady is steady. They do what they must to achieve it. What they must do."

"What do you mean?"

"When your ship is tumbling to its doom in the Mawayla Sea, when your sails are torn and the mast has splintered, you must bring it back on course with all your might." Os'halla smiled as he spoke. "Keep it moving. Though treacherous ahead." With that, he started down the crude path carved out against the mountainside.

Mountain goats grazed along the path and called out to each other, their bleats making Manfred nervous. He could feel the echo of the cries in his bones. During moments when he began to daydream, remember the cool of his apartment and the young ladies that frequented the cafes on the street below, the goats' voices brought him back. Their bleats forced him to focus on the cliffs around him and the wall that grew behind him as he and his guide made their way down. The canyons were so much safer—a slip-up down there and he'd only fall a few feet—out here, it would mean certain death.

The sun followed them for the trip down. It started high above and arched over the great meadow as they moved through switchbacks and thin ridges of loose rock. Os'halla pointed out the sky-colored birds that tiptoed through the sage of the stone and the razor-backed lizards that were as long as Manfred's arms. The lizards licked the cool of the rocks and their oval eyes rolled around in search of flies. Manfred did his best to avoid them and they returned the favor.

They made it off the mountain before the sun had totally disappeared. It was still a few hours' walk across the verdant fields before they would be at the gates of the village.

They moved in a peaceful silence. Lines of huts could be seen off in both directions and shadows of human forms moved silently around them. Manfred imagined small families sitting down for dinner after a long day of toiling in the fields. It felt good to think of people doing normal things. Instead of going on quests or flying across splits in reality. He tried to imagine them eating burgers and fries, or mashed potatoes, something real, no more watered-down cabbage or alcoholic roots. He thought of the viewing and the Keeper's eyes. They had seared themselves in his memory. She had so much faith in him. But what could he do? He cowered when faced with the abomination in the forest. He watched, dumbfounded, as Erneel was killed. Erneel knew it was a fool's errand. Why couldn't he have just left Manfred alone?

As Manfred was lost in thought, the fields moved beneath their feet and they closed in on the great village.

THE SAINT IS DEAD

The pillars and large gate of the village stared down at them as they closed in. Beyond the gate, the village was embedded in the rockface of a mountain which towered into blackening clouds. What he saw was so vast that it made Manfred dizzy. Large swaths of new masonry stood out against the ancient passage where the gate and walls had been patched over generations. Corridors of light revealed themselves through small slits—flames flickering out and casting shadows on the ever-darkening path in front of them.

Manfred watched as a small beam of light flashed across the sky. He smiled. It looked like something the Keeper would've produced. A beautiful redness that traveled fast and folded and fluttered in the wind.

Os'halla had to tackle him to the ground as the flaming arrow landed behind them.

"Tell them who you are," Os'halla yelled out.

Another arrow landed just below them.

"Wait, wait!" Os'halla called toward the wall. He was back on his feet, his hands above his head.

Manfred crawled to his feet and Os'halla nudged him forward.

"I'm here to speak with the…" Manfred's chest heaved with fear, "the Old Guard."

There was a long moment of silence. All that could be heard was the burning of the arrows and the chirp of locusts.

"Speak up or the next arrow goes up your ass," a voice from the darkness.

Os'halla pushed Manfred forward a few more steps.

"I am here to speak with the Old Guard," Manfred yelled, his voice cracking.

"And who are you to speak with the Guard?" The voice yelled back.

"I… I am Manfred Bugsbee."

"The Guard expects no *bee bugs*. This is your last warning. The Guard is accepting no visitors."

Manfred looked back at Os'halla and shook his head.

"Tell them who sent you, Manfred," Os'halla urged.

"The Keeper," Manfred cried out. "… Saint Erneel."

Another silence from the tower, this time longer than the last. The locust's cry was deafening. Finally, a new voice called out. A woman this time. "Where is the Saint?"

"Ambushed," Manfred tried to yell but he couldn't. "Ernie is gone."

"Speak up," shouted the woman. "Where is Erneel?"

Manfred fell to his knees and began to weep.

Os'halla put his hand on Manfred's shoulder and yelled back, "The Saint is dead."

Another silence. This time, not even the locusts dared call out. Without warning, a hail of fiery arrows screeched across the sky. Os'halla pushed Manfred to the ground and used his bo to deflect and parry the onslaught. Had Manfred not been huddling in the dirt he'd have seen an expert warrior at play. The arrows were clearly directed beyond the two men, but Os'halla took it as a moment of practice. He swiped and snapped through whatever arrows got too close. He twirled his bo and used it to kick up clods of dirt that met the arrows mid-flight—almost gleefully, Os'halla danced with the wall of fire that fell. As the pace of arrows slowed Os'halla leaned down and comforted Manfred.

"Do not move," the woman's voice called out.

From the darkness, four horsemen appeared. Two with large bows at the ready, all donned in armor. The bowman wore chainmail hoods over their faces. The hoods covered their shoulders and hung down over their chests. Their torsos were covered with plated steel. The other horsemen wore heavy flat-black armor. Neither wore a helmet, gold and black neck guards sat atop their dented chest plates. None of them spoke except one man who seemed to be in charge. He was a tired looking man, blue-black bags under his eyes and wrinkles that confused the age of his face. He leaned down toward Manfred and Os'halla and demanded, "you have news of the Little Saint?"

Manfred couldn't speak.

"He came from the Drilding Desert…" said Os'halla.

The man cut Os'halla off and drew his sword. "And who are you?"

"Os'halla, Green of the Sacred Kin. I'm bound to get this man to the Guard. To the Guard."

The man rubbed his chin in contemplation then gestured with his sword for Os'halla to continue.

"Your Saint brought him here from another realm. Now your Saint is gone," Os'halla continued.

The man let out a heavy sigh and replied. "Do you carry a sign?"

Manfred shook his head and whimpered. He did not dare to lift his eyes from the ground.

The man sighed again and motioned for the bowmen to let down their weapons. "Tie their hands."

One of the bowmen hopped down from his horse and tied both of their hands and threw the other end of the rope up to the man giving orders.

Slowly the gate opened with the whirl and buzz of some unseen mechanism. Men and women clad in armor called out from towers on either side of the opening. Their words as mechanical as the gate, the commands and replies of trained militants. Manfred and Os'halla were pulled into a large, dark corridor and the doors closed behind them. An archway at the end revealed the village.

Unsurprisingly, Manfred had found himself in another very strange place. Ancient, steely cobblestones led up the middle of the village. Tall graying buildings stacked on top of one another leaned and teetered into the night sky. Bridgeways with tapestries and laundry thrown over them passed above their heads as they moved up the path. Smaller roads splintered off the main way and led down narrow pathways, lighted by flames and dark, silent commerce. Figures looked out from the sideroads at the prisoners, held back by guards at each turn.

Manfred had his shoulders up and was slouched over in a position of total defeat. The bits of wind that made it through his robe went straight to his bones. He wanted to lie down in the middle of the street, but his body had entered into a sort of autopilot—he could hear the village and the trot of hooves, he could even feel himself moving, but he was retreating into himself with every new step. The cold and the terror of his journey so far assured him that there would be no answers here.

The bowmen broke off after a while through the village. They said nothing and disappeared down one of the sideroads. The other two men talked amongst themselves. There was something in their voices that Manfred couldn't place—anxiety and uncertainty, to be sure, hints of sorrow—but behind it was a sense of excitement and anticipation. Manfred figured they knew what Erneel's mission had been, to find Mindiidus and bring him here. It added to his despair to think he was about to let them down. He still had no idea where he fitted into this realm, and with each passing moment, he wanted to fit in less and less.

"Do you know what Erneel was tasked with?" asked one of the riders to the other.

"I know some."

"Then what?"

"It is all mired. Ancient secrets—ancient hopes. You know that."

"Who is he, then?" the rider motioned toward Manfred, who still walked with his head down.

"No one of importance."

"You allow *no one of importance* to see the Old Guard, unannounced. After the death of the Bone King being so recent. Come on, Tansrit. Do you take me for a fool?"

"I take you for a soldier, Rucks. I know what you know. Which is what they tell me. And they tell me very little. There have been members of the Cloud captured in our valley and Fenk's army is losing on more fronts than anyone wants to admit. Even the Holst have come out of hiding. I'm sure this man is nothing more than another in a long line of false premonitions from Kaseen. If this man can help, he'll help. If not, he'll die."

Rucks leaned closer to Tansrit and whispered, "I've heard he's here to deal with the Harvestors. There are stories that they've come back. That they're disrupting other worlds again. That their power builds"

Tansrit pushed him away and laughed. "You've been spending too much time with the farmers. Delusions of a different time."

"Well who's the other guy?" Rucks asked, slightly crestfallen.

"Sacred Kin. Neutrals. Nature worshippers. Always the ones to bring in stragglers. No better than the Order of the Gray Marsh. You know Yarley, the stranger the stranger, the warmer the welcome."

The two men laughed.

They continued through the village. It truly was an ancient town carved deep into the face of a mountain. Each road started from its middle and circled outward to the walls. In every direction, gigantic stones stretched into the sky that connected and blended into the mountains in the distance.

Soon the group had made it to the centerpiece of the village and up a steep set of stairs to their final destination—a Citadel that rested at the edge of the village, nestled into the cliff walls behind. Manfred's whole body ached with exhaustion and each step filled him with despair. He was sure his legs would soon give out.

They were greeted at the top of the stairs by a young woman who stood in the entryway and smiled. She was slight and pale. She wore a simple black shawl and a fragrant perfume. Manfred only looked at her feet, but the perfume made him ache for home even more.

"I will take them from here, Tansrit," she said. "They have convened in the White Room."

Tansrit bowed to the woman and gave Manfred and Os'halla a final stern glare.

Together they stood in a vast foyer, lit all around by candles and oil lamps. Diverging staircases and hallways led into infinite shadows. The halls were lined with paintings and banners that billowed slightly on the wind of the place. It was cold and the coldness reflected off the stone walls.

"They say you are with the Sacred Kin?" she said to Os'halla, her quiet voice carrying throughout the large room as if meant for others to hear. "It has been years since your people have blessed us with a visit." Without giving him time to respond she turned her attention to Manfred. "And you, my friend, there appears to have been quite a bit of fuss about you."

Manfred nodded to her.

"You two must be hungry. Coming over the mountain as you did. There is plenty of food here with the Guard. Now, Mr.

Bugsbee, I must warn you, they will have a lot of questions. Some of them won't be as nice as the good Saint Ernie, er, Erneel." She laughed and turned her attention to Os'halla. "… and I'm afraid, Mr?"

"Os'halla. Os is fine."

"Mr. Os'halla. While everyone here appreciates your service you will be asked to wait in another room. This is all very sensitive. You do understand?"

Os'halla looked at Manfred and asked with a nod of his head if he would be alright alone. Manfred returned the gesture. Although he was quite terrified of what was behind the door, Manfred figured there wasn't much arguing with the nice lady. Os'halla made an elegant bow at the woman in compliance.

"Ah, very well. My name is Colri, by the way."

Colri led the two down a long arched hallway. Paintings of royal-looking men and women adorned the walls. She directed Os'halla into an open door. Inside, a chubby man with a tired face greeted him. Colri introduced him as the night cook and after a few pleasantries, she took Manfred by the hand and guided him farther down the hall. After a few flights of stairs and long dark hallways, they reached a dead end.

"Are you ready, Mr. Bugsbee?" Colri asked and put her hand on his shoulder.

Manfred nodded a response without looking at her.

Colri stepped toward the wall in front of them and made a circular shape with both hands, a trail of blue light followed her fingertips, then built into a large square. She pushed the shape forward and the wall faded away. She faced Manfred and curtsied, then motioned for him to go through.

Manfred found himself in a white marble room. At the peak of the ceiling was a triangle window and even though it was night outside, a bright, warm light shined through it. In the center of the room, four men and one woman sat at a round, wooden table. They spoke amongst themselves and didn't acknowledge Manfred. Manfred turned back to ask Colri what he should do, but she had disappeared along with the door. *Abandoned again*, he thought.

Finally, a round-bodied man approached him. He was near Manfred's height but twice the width.

"Many questions, friend," the man said and bowed in introduction. "I am Saylu and we are the Guard." He motioned toward the others behind him who all rose and approached.

The woman was next. "This is Kaseen, our Divine Warden." She made praying hands at him and smiled. Her hair was so white that it looked blue and her eyes burned with the same radiance as the Keeper's.

Next was a large bald man. "And Delute, the Saint's Second," Salyu nodded toward the man. Tattoos of birds and fish covered his hands and the crown of his head.

"Fenk and Yarley," Saylu motioned to the last two. Fenk was small like Erneel but much younger. He had a long black ponytail and was the only one carrying a weapon. A curved scabbard hung from his waist. He looked at Manfred with near, complete disgust.

"Fenk is our Commandant of Arms. He leads the greatest army in the history of all our realms."

Yarley was the oldest of the crew and walked hunched over with the aid of two canes. He nodded his head toward Manfred.

If Yarley had been able to stand up he would have been eight feet tall, but his body was so crooked and bent, he had to look up to make eye contact with Manfred. Manfred expected a final introduction, rather everyone in the room looked at Yarley with a sort of awe, as if waiting to hear how he'd introduced himself. He didn't.

After the introductions, Saylu motioned for Manfred to sit in the only open chair left in the circle. He assumed it must have belonged to Erneel's and a knot tightened in his stomach.

"We understand you were separated from Erneel in the desert?" said Saylu, with a forced calm.

Manfred nodded his head.

"What happened?"

"Liadra," Manfred said and tried to read the faces of the room.

"She was alone?"

"No. Five, maybe six. Erneel killed a few, the others," Manfred took a deep breath, "died in the commotion."

"Commotion?"

"Erneel… he did a thing," Manfred tried to imitate the *thing*, raising his arms and doing his best at miming interdimensional travel. "They went somewhere else. It was loud. It scared the horses." Manfred paused again and looked at his feet. "… who trampled the others."

Saylu nodded his head. "And Erneel was bringing you here?"

"Yes."

"Did he say why?"

"The Keeper, she thinks I might be someone I'm not."

"Someone you're not?"

"Mindiidus."

Yarley stood up from his seat and moved slowly toward Manfred, his canes and shuffle echoing in the domed room. Once he reached him, he put his hand on Manfred's shoulder for balance and spoke, "So sure of who you are?"

Manfred squinted his eyes in confusion. The old man's face was nothing but wrinkles, all of his features sunken into the folds of his skin. His eyes were bright though, two small slits of brilliance.

Yarley continued, "And in such a great and vast universe to be so sure in." He then turned to face the rest of the Guard and pointed toward each one as he spoke. "In getting him here, through the treacherousness that lies between, Little Saint and the Keeper appear to have put their faith in this man. I trust you'll get to the bottom of this." With that, he tapped a stick on the ground and disappeared in a puff of redolent smoke, a smell like burnt sage.

Kaseen smiled. "Always with the riddles, old man."

Saylu continued his questions as if nothing out of the ordinary had happened. "You had a Viewing?"

Manfred nodded.

Saylu gestured for Manfred to fill in the story.

Manfred shook his head. "It was all so strange. There was a fire. At first, it was in front of me. Then I was in it. And a woman's voice, she called me Mindiidus. Harvestors. The Keeper seemed impressed. Erneel, not so much."

"Stubborn one, the Saint," Kaseen chimed in.

Manfred smiled at her.

Saylu continued. "Do you remember the woman's name?"

Manfred thought for a moment then said, "Naba Noodles?"

Delute and Kaseen both laughed.

Saylu nodded. "Nuaba Ooli. One of the first to fall. Did they tell you anything about her? About what you saw?"

"A little."

Fenk slammed his fists on the table and abruptly stood up. "Now is no time to give this outsider a history lesson? The realms are in decay. I would be much better served recruiting real warriors, preparing for the battles to come. The Clouds numbers are growing. Pencaut and his men took the village of Selup and Gray Tower is under siege. He is emboldened while we chase ghosts like this here. Soon they'll come for the Village and Tansrit's soldiers won't be able to stop them. I left my men to meet with the Guard, with the Saint. This man is a waste of our time. Worse yet, he occupies the time of our best warriors."

Kaseen replied, "The Ulis and the Keeper brought this man in, Fenk. Your war is of the physical and this man may be the key to restoring all the realms, restoring our strength."

"Physical?" Fenk said in disbelief. "Yes, it is my troops that are being hacked apart by the Cloud, it is me that has to tell grieving mothers that their daughters won't be returning for the Ulchy harvest. Thousands have died, woman. Thousands more will when the Gray Tower falls. The Ulis and his old prophecies haven't saved a life in a hundred years, you fools."

"Old prophecies?" Kaseen said her nostrils flaring. "It's our history, our reality. The Ulis pinpointed this man out of the web of the whole of existence. It is no mere prophecy."

Manfred tried to focus on what they were saying, he tried to keep track of each new name and place, but his mind kept wandering, reminding him how tired he was, and how the chair he was sitting in, although very uncomfortable, would be the perfect place for a nap. Other times all he could think was how weird everyone was dressed. Their utilitarian robes cinched together with little ropes or small knotted buttons. Everyone in the room was suddenly bickering and Manfred was totally zoned out—he even worried for a moment that he had left the milk out in his apartment.

"The Ulis is a decrepit old bird," Fenk said and puffed up his shoulders.

Kaseen let out a strange angry noise and Manfred started paying attention again.

Saylu raised his voice. "Quiet. Fenk, we have never questioned your commitment. Yarley has put his full faith in your ability to ready our armies. But Mr. Bugsbee is here now and he will receive our full patience and attention."

Kaseen and Fenk sat back down and made sure the whole room knew they weren't looking at one another.

Saylu touched Manfred's knee and then leaned back in his chair. "My apologies, Mr. Bugsbee, where was I?" Saylu shot Kaseen and Fenk a dirty look before continuing. "What you saw in your viewing and what you heard are of great importance to this realm, to all the realms. Nuaba was a powerful Keeper, and one of the first to fall away from our purpose, to seek power and devastation. That pyre was one of the first incarnations of the true and complete destructiveness of the Cloud. You traveled through the Drilding Desert, yes?"

Manfred nodded his head.

"Before the corruption, that was a lush forest. Rivers, valleys and fields of beauty unmatched in all the realms. But Nuaba and her kind, the Harvestors, in their quest for power brought death to our home. They brought fire to our realm, unmatched and unbridled. Until you came along."

"Me?" Manfred asked, focusing with all of his might.

"An ancestor of sorts. Connected beyond time."

"Mindiidus," Kaseen blurted out. "And the Relics. Did they mention the Relics?"

Manfred shook his head.

Saylu raised his hand to quiet Kaseen. "The Relics are all that are left of the original Mindiidus. His bones remain. And the bones are a conduit of your power."

Manfred remembered the power he had felt when he held Erneel's staff in the grove. "Is the stick Erneel carries a Relic?"

Kaseen opened her mouth to speak but Saylu spoke first. "Not exactly. Erneel's staff is embedded with certain energies, but nothing like the Relics. You felt an energy from it, though?"

Manfred shrugged his shoulders and half nodded.

"That is good, very good."

Manfred took a deep breath. "Can you please just tell me why I'm here?"

"It's yet to be seen. But when your original died, when he gave up his life in the fires of the Cloud, his body was separated through all of space and time. Gifted into realms we've yet to explore. Multiplied through the gates and bridges of all eternity. His bones, the only lasting physical piece of him, the Relics, are imbued with a power we've yet to completely comprehend. We believe," he looked at Kaseen, "that you are an incarnation of that great warrior, a chance in the cosmic battle that builds."

Manfred rubbed his hands through his hair. He was losing focus again. He was so tired and scared and frustrated and these people made zero sense. "I am no warrior."

From the space that Manfred had entered the room came a loud commotion. A banging, a grinding, then a great deal of sparks. From the sparks, a woman appeared. Manfred quickly stood up in fear, sure that another beast was coming to kill him.

"Welcome, young lady," Kaseen said across the room.

The woman moved toward Manfred. Had Manfred not been terrified as she approached him, he may have found her attractive, in the way a fly may find the spider glorious before its brains are sucked out. She grabbed him by the chest and pulled him close. The heat of her breath pushed up his nose and into his eyes.

"Where is he?" she demanded.

"Who?" Manfred replied, forgetting most of his life for an instant. He turned away to see if any of the Guard had planned on helping him.

Saylu stood up and tried to console the woman. "We're getting to that, Looma. Please, calm down."

Looma didn't take her hands or eyes off of Manfred. "Now. We are getting to it now. Where is he?"

"Ernie?" Manfred asked, regaining his wits slightly.

"Of course, who else?" She pushed Manfred into his chair and turned away from him. "Where is Erneel? The man who dragged you across the desert. Where is he?"

Manfred drooped into the chair and wanted to disappear altogether. "I'm so sorry. He's dead," He was, again, on the verge of tears. "Liadra stabbed him."

Looma's face twisted for a moment in what looked like anguish, but instead, she burst into a hearty laugh that scared Manfred almost more than when she had grabbed him. "My father has been on the front lines of every battle this realm has seen in the last hundred years. He has killed all manner of abomination. Broke the necks of thousands of would-be Sun Harvestors. You're telling me the Bone King's whore-daughter *killed* him?" She looked at Manfred again and he held eye contact with her for fear that if he looked away she'd kill him. He no longer felt like crying, instead, he felt that if he was suddenly blinked out of existence, that would be for the best.

"I'm sorry," he repeated. His voice trembled. "I watched her blade cut into him."

"Delute?" Looma turned her attention to the large bald man. "How many times have you seen my father stabbed?"

He began to count his fingers and quickly cycled through both hands then started over. He scratched his head, held out both hands with each finger stretched out, and replied, "A lot".

"A lot," Looma repeated. She now addressed the whole of the room. "I have said this, my father has said this—we need warriors for this battle, not—" she pointed at Manfred, "uncarved blocks of fat. And now, one of your greatest warriors is lost in some outer realm because of a fool's errand. An uncertainty."

"Here, here," said Fenk, delighted. "The girl is right."

"Girl?" responded Looma.

"I'm with you, Looms," said Fenk. "That's why you should be home with your mother preparing the Three."

Looma seemed to blush for a moment, but before she could speak Kaseen interjected, "The Three will be ready if needed, Fenk. Leave them to the professionals."

"Professional liars," barked Fenk.

"All of you be quiet. Looma, if you wish to stay in here, then you had better calm down. If Tansrit knew you had burst in here like this he'd have you out running watch on the Outer Crest."

Kaseen laughed. "If you don't think Tansrit saw this coming, Saylu, then you've lost your edge."

Saylu glared at Kaseen.

Manfred stood back up. "I agree with them. You need warriors. I don't belong here."

"*That* is yet to be determined, Mr. Bugsbee. Yarley, the Ulis and…" Saylu looked at Looma. "Your parents, the Keeper and the Saint, believe this man is Mindiidus. I will not discount the intuitions of the greatest minds and defenders of this realm. Now, hush."

"Fine," said Fenk. "But enough talk. Test him."

Saylu nodded at Fenk. "You're right." He then looked at Manfred. "We have a Relic. If the power in you can get you to the Harvestors, you should be able to manifest a weapon. The only force that can break through their barriers."

"Manifest a weapon?" Manfred said as he sounded the words out to try and make sense of them.

Saylu shook his head. "Did Erneel explain nothing? Mindiidus, your lineage, was a sword-bearer. A now extinct and ancient tribe of warriors that could call upon weapons given the right conduit. As far as we know, it's the only power in the universe that can end the work of the Harvestors. The power you felt when you held Erneel's staff is to us another indicator of your abilities. Although it does point to you being a descendant from sword-bearers, that isn't enough. You have to be tested up against a Relic. Bring it here, Delute."

Delute pulled a large red staff from behind where he was sitting. It was the full span of his arms and not quite the thickness of his index finger. In the middle, a charred, crooked bone made a crude cross guard. Delute extended it toward Manfred.

Manfred held the stick in his hand and looked around the room. Everyone stared on in anticipation.

He let out a full-bodied sigh. "I don't know what this is. I don't know what you want me to do."

"Call upon a sword. A weapon," directed Saylu.

Manfred mouthed the words, *call upon a sword,* and then replied, "those words don't mean anything in that order."

"How about if you don't figure it out, I'll cut off your balls," Looma said.

Delute and Fenk both chuckled.

"It is inside you, Mr. Bugsbee. Just allow a weapon to manifest," said Saylu unconvincingly as he gave Kaseen a worried look.

Manfred closed his eyes and tried to make sense of what they were saying. He remembered the feeling that coursed through him when he ran at the beast in the forest, or when he first picked up Ernie's staff outside the bar. A lightness, an electricity—now he just felt hungry. Then he thought of the impending castration from Looma and was overcome with despair.

"Manifest a weapon," he said to himself. Instead of a weapon though his muddled mind started thinking of advertising pitches for the throw pillows he was supposed to be working on. Were they feather or synthetic? He tried to remember.

Suddenly, he could feel the Keeper's eyes, their full intensity staring down at him as she called out, "Baxio."

"What's a Baxio?" Manfred said aloud.

"Baxio?" Delute laughed. "Baxio served with him during the Western Plight. That ole' crow."

Manfred looked at Delute and it came back to him, the guard at the Keeper's Den, his large hammer. He could see it as clear as day. The head of it, a stone black with flat surfaces on both sides, perfect for crushing compact cars or large skulls. The handle was as big around as Manfred's thigh—an earth-brown wood with a long blood-spattered rope tied around the end of it and secured to the man's wrist.

Manfred could feel the branch change in his hand—growing. Slowly, it doubled in size and he had to hold onto it with both hands. It kept growing. He hugged it to his body and allowed the bottom to rest on the floor and the top to rest against his chest. For a moment he thought he had control of the situation—he could feel a pulse of energy, an intensity, a magic. But the thing kept growing—heavier and heavier. Soon it began to teeter against him. He caught it and it teetered the other way. He caught it again, its full weight pressed against him. It was too much and he had to dive out of the way. The large hammer, fully formed, crashed against the ground and in the blink of an eye withered back to its original form.

Saylu hurried to Manfred and helped him up. The rest of the Guard looked on in disbelief. Kaseen smiled from ear to ear and shook her head with excitement.

"It's a start," Saylu said as he helped Manfred to his feet. "Time for you to rest. There is much for us to think about, Mr. Bugsbee, much to think about."

The Guard talked amongst themselves as Saylu showed Manfred back through the entryway where Colri intercepted him. She talked at him like a leaking faucet. Assured him that Os'halla was taken care of in a room overlooking the village. She told him about her childhood, the way the boys used to make fun of her, how her father fought alongside Erneel and Tansrit in a place called Spiral Oaks, how she had briefly dated Delute, but his only love was the sea. It all just bubbled out of her. Finally they made it to the room he'd be sleeping in.

"Is there anything else I can do?" she asked.

Manfred shook his head.

Once Colri had gone, Manfred sat on his bed for some time. He was exhausted, but his mind was a hornet's nest of anxiety. He tried to make sense of all of the people he had just met and all the things they had talked about. It was clear that some battle was moving toward its epoch and he could turn sticks into hammers. Noone seemed to trust him, though— hell, he didn't trust himself. The longer he thought about his time in the White Room the more it felt like a bad dream, like the terrible meetings he was forced to sit in on back home. The ones when the Corporate talking heads would come along and explain one problem or another and Manfred would just nod his head, watching the hands on the clock overhead, counting down the minutes until he could go home to his couch and savor a cold beer.

Manfred could really use a beer.

REVELATIONS

Manfred woke up in the early afternoon. The bed wasn't quite as soft as the one at the Keeper's den but he didn't complain. Compared to where he had been sleeping the last few days, it was heaven. When he finally made it out of bed he put on a fresh robe. His room looked over a courtyard in the interior of the Citadel. He looked out and could see Os'halla meditating under a dark purple tree. Children had gathered around to try and emulate him. Their legs waved back and forth as they tried to center their hips above their heads, a moment of stillness, then they'd tumble over, laughing all along. Every so often Os'halla would open an eye and smile and the children would run away and hide behind the rocks and trees.

In Manfred's room, there was a large bathtub with water constantly flowing through it. It took him no convincing to get into the clear water. Nothing had felt so good in his life. The warm flow of the water pulled all the sand and dirt from his skin and turned the water black. He shook grass and clods of dirt from his hair and scrubbed himself clean. Before long, after plenty of scrubbing, the water was clear. Manfred leaned back and put his feet up.

"So help me god, I'll stay here all day," he said aloud as he smiled.

There was a knock at the door.

"Go away," he yelled and splashed water against his face. "I'm busy."

The door burst open. It was Looma.

Manfred let out a screech and sunk into the tub.

Looma was no longer dressed for battle. She wore a sheer sky-blue dress underneath a black shawl. Manfred took a moment and noted that she was, to his surprise, quite beautiful. Her hair braided and twisted around her neck and her eyes were like her mother's—an unearthly brightness went wherever they did. She had a deep scar across her right cheek that went down her chin, jumped and reemerged on her collarbone before it disappeared behind her shawl. Manfred hoped to one day ask her how she had gotten it.

"Get out. I'm to take you to the Ulis," she said as if Manfred wasn't hiding in the bathtub.

"Uh… right now?" Manfred asked sheepishly, trying to cover his body the best he could.

"Yes, now, right now," she replied.

"I'm sorry," Manfred said. "I just haven't been able to take a bath in days."

"Don't care."

Manfred let out an involuntary groan.

"What's the problem?" she asked, staring at him.

"I just, could you, uh, turn around?" Manfred responded.

She turned around.

Manfred made his way out of the tub, never taking his eyes off her, ready at any moment to dive back in. He dried off and got dressed.

They took a side door out of the Citadel and a spiral staircase down into the noise of the village. The roads were packed with carts and people wearing bright, silk clothing. The clatter of the city echoed off the tall brick buildings that loomed above them. People pointed at him and ducked behind one another with their heads together. They recognized him as an outsider, but there was something else to it. A sense of curiosity and awe swept over their faces when they looked from him to Looma. She kept a short leash, grabbing his collar whenever he strayed too far. The crowds opened up for them.

An old woman broke from the crowd and grabbed Manfred's sleeve. Her face was covered by a bright, white headdress, her black eyes peered out.

"Dear traveler," she said. "You are lost, but we recognize you. A gray man cometh to us from the sky."

Manfred leaned in. "You recognize me?"

"You are the light," she said.

"The what?"

Looma grabbed Manfred from the crowd and tugged him toward her.

"Old woman, go back to your nest," Looma said as she stood between the two.

The woman pointed toward the sky. "We know your task, of the Three, you are. Here to protect us from the broken skyline. But you are no Saint. No Keeper."

Looma grabbed the woman. "I don't care whose protection you're under, hag. Back to your nest."

The old woman laughed and pulled Manfred's hands to her face and kissed them. "The young wolf is misguided, Mindiidus." She turned and disappeared back into the crowd.

Manfred looked at Looma. "You hear that? Mindiidus." He smiled.

"False prophecy spreads quickly around these parts. Now, we're late."

Looma pulled him under an archway into a grove of spindly, black trees. Other women, like the one who had confronted him, walked around silently, all wearing white headscarves, their hands pressed together at their waists.

"Who are these people?" Manfred asked.

"Fools," Looma said. "This way."

They walked a dirt-worn path toward a round structure in the middle. It was an unceremonious building that looked like it was there by accident. Like a moon had crashed into the earth and been left to gather vines. Small shapes were carved into it and billows of smoke came out of them—squares, circles, and spirals, like the things Erneel had thrown above his head. A round wooden door was the only entrance.

"What is this place?" Manfred asked.

Looma grunted. "The Hall of Signs." She opened the door and pushed him inside.

A deep, beautiful hum emanated through the room. Manfred recognized the inside of the building as a place of worship, as if it was some kind of church. Wooden benches made up most of the floor and were split down the middle, leading to a pulpit in front. Multi-colored candles were grouped on all sides. Pools of wax had accumulated all around and covered the floor in large, reflective swaths. The candles must have been burning for generations.

Kaseen met them as they entered.

"Welcome, Looma." They hugged and Kaseen bowed her head toward Manfred. "Welcome to the Hall of Signs, Mindiidus."

He bowed awkwardly at the recognition.

Kaseen was in full regalia. A long white dress with symbols that matched the cutouts on the building. Her long hair hung behind her in a single braid, adorned with flowers and frayed fabrics.

"The Ulis," Looma said impatiently.

"Always in a rush, Looms."

"My father is missing," Looma snapped.

"No one knows the importance of the Saint more than I. But that is no reason to be rude to our guest." Kaseen raised her hand at Looma's attempt to argue. Looma sat down on one of the benches.

"What is this place?" Manfred asked again.

"A place of contemplation. A place to remember the bigger picture."

"Ah," Manfred said and nodded his head.

"The place where we discovered you."

Manfred squinted his eyes then looked at Looma who rolled hers.

"You must have seen the Saint make Signs?"

"Sure."

"The Signs are an ancient protection passed down through generations. Nothing more sacred throughout the land."

"Oh," Manfred continued nodding and smiling.

"You, Manfred Bugsbee, were born with a sign above your head. The last time it was seen was at the birth of your first—our Mindiidus. Marked, of course, by the Ulis."

"What's an Ulis?"

Someone was finally answering his questions and he couldn't help but ask them all.

"The Ulis holds the map of the Realms. Controlled in his mind. He found you within the pages of that map."

"Please, Kaseen, we are running out of time." Looma stood up.

"Do treat the Ulis with more respect, dear."

Kaseen led them behind the pulpit to a marble statue. A strange little thing. It looked human except for its extra arms and legs. Depending on where you stood, it either looked like a gnarled hand or a Hindu goddess. Kaseen did a sign above it, much more complex than anything Manfred had seen before. She used both hands and moved them to some unseen rhythm. She bobbed her head as she worked and Manfred swore he could hear music in the distance. She looked much like a conductor but instead of strings and brass being produced, it was streaks of light. When she finished, a grand design of intricate light floated above the statue. Squares inside circles and spirals that twisted outward. The design hovered for a heartbeat then fell to the statue. Like with all their tricks, the statue melted and revealed a staircase into darkness.

They followed Kaseen down a maze of hallways, through doorways adorned with silver and gold, down another spiral staircase that seemed to go on forever, until finally, they entered a small room filled with dust, books, and a frail old man wearing large spectacles.

"Ulis," said Kaseen. "This is Mr. Bugsbee, our Mindiidus."

Slowly the Ulis made his way across the room, dragging his right foot as he did. Even in his slow movements, there was a spryness to him—a look of agility beneath the furrows of time. He wore an elaborate gown with lines of black silk and gilded spirals. He reached his hand out to Looma who took it in a kind hello. He then took both hands and put them on Manfred's chest and stretched his crooked spine up to look at his face. The Ulis squinted his eyes so much that they seemed to close.

"Haven't seen you for quite some time." The Ulis' voice was as dusty as the room, cracked and raw.

"I don't think we've ever met," Manfred replied

"Maybe so. Maybe not." He laughed and gestured toward some seats in the middle of the room. "Shall we get to it then?"

Before they all sat, Kaseen bowed reverently to everyone. Looma and Manfred bowed back. Manfred was still feeling and looking awkward as he hunched over, more of a tense nod than anything. Kaseen took the hands of the Ulis and kissed them, after which he touched his hands to his forehead. Kaseen told them she'd be waiting upstairs and left.

Manfred and Looma nodded and the three of them sat down. The Ulis crossed his legs and nodded his head in deep contemplation. Manfred and Looma both sat on the edge of their seats. No one made a sound until the Ulis began to snore.

Manfred and Looma looked at each other in confusion.

"Ulis," Looma said and lightly kicked his chair.

The Ulis sat up, startled, he looked around the room. "Who's there?"

"Looma and Bugsbee. You were about to tell us something."

"Oh… Yes, yes. Looma, my dear. I have some good news and some terrible news."

Looma nodded impatiently.

"We have found your father."

"He's alive?" Manfred gasped.

"Yes, yes. That is the good news."

"And the bad?" Looma asked.

"Take a look for yourselves." Ulis took his glasses off and gestured above the three of them.

Above them was a mass of tightly wound cobwebs. Millions of complex designs ran over and weaved into each other—up and up and into darkness. It both terrified and mystified Manfred.

"We don't have your vision, Ulis," said Looma, unphased by the clutter above.

"Oh, yes, yes, silly me." The Ulis replied and shaped a blue sphere of light in his hands and the whole room went dark. Manfred gripped the sides of his chair in anticipation of another ride like in the Keeper's den. When The Ulis pushed the sphere up toward the cobwebs, it splashed against them and burst in every direction, the blue light illuminating each twist and turn of the webbing. The Ulis made another sphere, red this time, and no bigger than a pea. He tossed it up and it crashed against the blue and spread out in small pinpoints across the three-dimensional canvas.

"It's beautiful," Manfred whispered, completely enthralled.

"It's everything," said the Ulis

Looma sighed impatiently. "The bad news, Ulis. What is the bad news?"

"The bad news? Ah, yes, bad news," the Ulis pointed toward a red dot that started to blink rapidly. "That's your father."

"And where is that?" Looma asked.

The Ulis' eyes widened. "The Bleak, muh'dear."

"The Bleak?" Looma asked.

Manfred was surprised to hear a hint of nervousness in her voice.

"Afraid so," replied the Ulis.

"Why?" asked Looma. "Why would my father travel to such a hideous place?"

"Hideous?" Manfred said, mostly to himself.

"I'm afraid, among other things, dear girl, we sent your father before he was ready, having been a warrior of light for so long. But the path of the Ulis is no easy task. It is rigid. We gave him the tools of travel, but took away his dear sword, Rocinallia."

"You're saying he couldn't handle Liadra without his sword?" Looma asked in disbelief.

The Ulis shrugged his shoulders. "I suppose he didn't want to find out. He probably figured that Mindiidus would be safer alone in the desert than in the hands of the Cloud."

Looma was becoming very frustrated. "Is there anything else?"

"Yarley sets up a portal to the Bleak. You two and Delute are tasked with bringing back our dear friend."

Looma stood up and threw her chair to the ground and Manfred ducked down. "A portal. You're sending us through a portal. You expect this man to survive a portal? Has the Old

Guard gone mad? Why on earth would Yarley want to send someone untrained into the Bleak?"

"Delute chose you alone. But Yarley insists the sword-bearer accompany." The Ulis bowed his head then added sternly, "His word is final."

"It is too dangerous for him," Looma replied.

"Too dangerous?" Manfred groaned.

Looma let out an angry grunt and left the room and made as much commotion as she could.

"Very," said the Ulis. "Nothing left but black towers'n'bugs."

"They're only sending three of us?"

"If Erneel is still alive when you get there, that'll make four," the Ulis smiled.

Manfred sighed.

"Sadness?" the Ulis asked.

"I need to know why I am here, Ulis. I can't help any of you. I'm no warrior."

The Ulis motioned for Manfred to come closer and Manfred scooched his chair forward. The Ulis placed his hand on his shoulder and asked, "Your world was ending?"

Manfred shrugged.

The Ulis nodded. "Your world *is* ending. Worlds end. Warriors begin. You'll know what you are when you are. Now. I've research to do. I heard voices I've not heard for some time."

Manfred nodded.

The Ulis turned back to the map above him. It flashed and twirled and the Ulis moved his hands inside of it, pulling on strands as the universe unfolded. He was able to zoom in on different spaces, some shook with a violent light, others were steady and blinked in and out. With each gesture of the Ulis, the map would change and Manfred began to notice something. Beneath the ever-changing pattern was a green shape. Something beyond all the commotion. Manfred reached his hand in to point at it.

"What is that?"

The Ulis didn't turn to face him. "The Cloud brings powers it cannot control. Oary…"

"What?"

The Ulis turned to face Manfred and looked surprised to see him, "What're you still doing here?"

"Huh?"

"It is unfolding, boy. You best be on your way."

"Oh," Manfred said.

The Ulis nodded his head and in an unceremonious gesture flicked his hand at Manfred. Manfred stood for a moment confused at what he should do. Eventually, the Ulis started snoring again, his body bouncing slightly in his chair. With that, Manfred left the room and returned to meet with Looma.

"Did the old man have anything else to say?" she asked.

"Do any of you ever have anything to say, really?" he paused, "aside from, 'Manfred, old boy, you're surely going to die soon'?" he laughed.

She smiled and said, "Delute chose me."

"What?"

"He trusts me. Why they would send you, I have no idea."

"Haven't I already been through a portal?"

She looked at him confused. "What? No. What my father does is different. A portal is a thing outside of time and space. It doesn't involve the magic of the Saint."

"Oh," Manfred said sarcastically.

"My father cuts through the fabric of the realms. Very dangerous, especially for two or more people. Portals can only be accessed by the Ulis."

"I thought Yarley was sending us through."

She squinted her eyes at him. "They are all Ulis."

"What?"

She grunted impatiently. "We need to get some rest, Bugsbee. Tomorrow will be a great deal of dread."

"Oh?" Manfred said and hoped Looma would follow with a joke, instead, she turned and walked back toward the stairs.

Kaseen was waiting for them. Manfred exited last and the statue reformed behind him. Looma hugged Kaseen and told her she needed to prepare. They kissed each other on the cheeks.

"I'm going to keep Manfred for a bit, Looma. I'll send him when we're through," Kaseen said.

"You won't get lost now, will you Bugsbee? Most roads lead to the Citadel anyway and Tansrit's men will keep their eye on you." Looma said impatiently and left without another word.

"Sit down, Manfred," Kaseen said and motioned to a place next to her. "Tell me, how are you feeling?"

"How am I?" he asked. "I hate it here. I hate everything about this place. I'm terrified all the time. No one lets me sleep. I haven't walked this much in my whole life. You people send me through spaces and times and viewings and portals. I'm in hell. That's how I feel."

She laughed.

"And you all think it's so damn funny," he continued.

"I'm sorry, Manfred, but this is your birthright."

"My birthright is marketing. I make ads."

She looked at him absently. "The Ulis showed you his map, did he not?"

Manfred nodded.

"On that map, we have watched you your whole life. Prepared at any moment to bring you in, to find out if you truly held the power of Mindiidus."

"Well, I'm not and the Old Guard knows it."

Kaseen rose and walked toward the pulpit and gestured for Manfred to stay seated. She returned with a massive book bound in time-worn, red bark.

"From the beginning," she smiled as she caressed the face of the book then turned the pages delicately. "Before you and before me, before your world, there was this realm. Born from the breath of creation. An establishment of rule, we were. Aids to the Oarygus. The great architects of reality." She touched her forehead in ritual. "A single tribe. The true Old Guard."

Again, Manfred was desperately trying to keep up. "*True* Old Guard?"

"What you see today is only a remnant. A stay of ritual. The Oarygus designed this realm to help them watch over the other worlds. They created a Ulis to watch, a map always in his protection. His disciple was made to defend, to fix everything broken in the other worlds."

"Ernie?"

Kaseen nodded her head. "The most important relationship in our history. Consistent. Since the very beginning. The Saint guards and protects the realms that the Ulis oversees. Then the Saint takes over and so on and so on. For countless years, you understand. Even in secrecy after the Corruption. When the tribes split and the People of the Cloud originated. You see, we were all made as equals. Stewards of the great cause. The cause of balance. Only interfering when realms were truly pulling against that balance, and even then, only slightly. Never bringing war, working strategically, a light breeze. If an issue couldn't be resolved, we were called off, and the Oarygus would take care of it with earthquakes, asteroids, floods. Whatever they could pull from nature. They would destroy and rewrite. The People of the Cloud reveled in that destruction. They lusted after that power. The split was small at first, philosophical. They demanded the Saint become a warrior—a killer. Bringing armies into the other realms, dismantling them before the Original Beings, the Oarygus, even had a chance to intervene. It went on like this for a generation. Councils were set up to determine when intervention was necessary. It was civil, democratic, even. A few miscalculations led to the decimation of some peaceful realms, destroying most of their life, turning them to ruin, and it forced the hand of the Oarygus. They revoked our purpose, turning us into just another realm. No longer the guardians of balance. Only the Ulis and the Saint were allowed to remain, their import too high to throw away. The Oarygus handled the Cloud without mercy, spreading their ashes on the four winds, they drew a line that none would dare cross. The lower ranks became subservient, terrified to meet the fate of their others. Some were allowed to return to the fold of the Guard, who had become mere politicians, owners of land, only symbols of what was. Some began to explore our earth. To set up villages and create worlds for themselves. An era of peace. Purposeless, but peace nonetheless." She paused and looked through the book for a moment. "Then came the Harvestors." She had found a page in the book with an illustration. A stock of a man, painted in harsh white, heavy-handed splatter, empty black eyes. Naked except for ornamental jewelry made from charred, black bones, and gold flowers. She tapped her finger on the face of the Harvestor as if to pound the image into Manfred's brain.

"I saw them during the viewing."

She continued tapping, not missing a beat. "The Keeper, the evil witch, a hero in her time, Nuaba, she stole the secrets of the Saint. She discovered that the realms touched every so often, and sometimes when they touched certain areas became weak. She and her followers developed their practice. Bastardized the glory and magic of the Signs. Instead of opening doors, they started creating pathways to other realms, making ways to siphon the power of other suns. At first, the power only dispersed into our realm. They had nowhere to put it and it turned much of our earth into deserts—uninhabitable sands. The Guard was naive then, complacent in their power. The Cloud became stronger, smarter. Soon, they could burn through entire villages. Destroy whole worlds if left to their devices. They tore through villages, burning down fields with the turn of their hand. With it they brought ruin on top of ruin. Never before had our realm seen such carnage, such destruction. The Guard was so oblivious, so unprepared, that in no time the Cloud had taken over, reigning supreme. For a thousand years the Oarygus were nowhere to be seen."

"A thousand years?"

She made a slow circle with her right index finger. "Time was different then, it flowed in strange shapes, as if the Harvestors were burning through the whole of the continuum, breaking the barriers of reality. We mustn't let them regain that power, Mindiidus. We must stop them." She smiled and flipped through the book some more. "*You* must stop them, dear boy." She pointed to another picture of a man holding a skull, his body draped in blood. "After countless years, it is believed that the Oarygus conjured a great power and put it in you."

"Not me," Manfred shook his head

She looked up from the book confused, her thoughts still absorbed in its pages.

"I am me now. There's no other me. None of this makes any goddamn sense."

"Of course it's you. Time doesn't matter—thousands— millions—you're bigger than that, Mindiidus."

"Manfred," he said, agitated. He had been engrossed in her story. But the connections she tried to make with his reality were too much. "How can you be sure that any of this is true? And here you people plan to send me against some all-powerful demons, some fire thingies." He stood up and was pacing. "Why do you have so much faith in all of this? Why bring me into this mess?"

"The signs, Mindiidus. The signs."

He grimaced. "Signs."

"During the rise of the Cloud, the great fall of our realm, the Holders of the Sign stayed well hidden. Away from combat, away from the prying eye of the Cloud's mercenaries. We continued the tradition of Ulis and Saint. We kept the lineage intact—the secrets, the maps of the realms all kept safe by the Keepers. Many of us were tortured, burned and torn apart. The Cloud could only do so much without the map, the mind of a Ulis. With the map, they'd have access to every realm in existence. Without it, they had to count on luck, hoping that our world would rub against another. But they closed in. We could only hide for so long. And then the firstborn, the great Mindiidus showed up on the Ulis' map. It was like nothing he'd ever seen before—a bright beacon, a sign complex and simple in one, like an ever-twirling spiral. That sign has only ever been seen twice. Once then and then once again over you. It was calling out from your earth, in our time of need." She was talking fast and hardly breathed. A near sermon.

"He was the same way as you are now—unsure—a peasant with no allegiance. But we tracked him down, certain of his importance. Nothing could be more important. We knew the Oarygus were calling out to us, telling us he was the weapon, our savior. He had visions of the time before time, views only the Oarygus could have seen in the blanks before reality. And that is the truth of it, the whole of it. After that, the tables turned. We were able to defeat the Cloud. The Original Beings returned. They restored balance and took away the abilities of the Cloud, forcing them under our rule. That was the last time anyone has seen the Oarygus. After that, they left. They left the realms to themselves, tired of fixing our problems, on to bigger things, I suppose. But they will return. No doubt that is why they have sent for you. You are the first sign of their awakening."

"No one sent me. You took me from my home. You gave me no choice."

"I understand, Mindiidus, you are scared. You didn't ask for this burden. We are all given strength and weakness, my friend. We are given room to grow within the power of the Signs. We are rushing you and I apologize for that. I know it's in you. I know you will bring order." She touched his shoulder and he felt sick.

"Now go back to the Citadel. Get your rest. Second to the Saint, there are no safer hands to be in than Delute's. And Looma, ever passionate, ever powerful. A warrior's warrior. She means well and she is good to those she trusts."

Kaseen walked Manfred out and made sure he could find his way back. She bowed to him and kissed his hand. When he was far enough out of her sight he tried to wipe the feeling of the kiss off of himself, as if it stained him. He felt unworthy and annoyed by all of the ritual and legend that she had bestowed upon him.

Two women in headscarves followed Manfred back to the Citadel. They kept a good distance, but every time he looked over his shoulder, he could see them as they bumped through the crowd. People avoided him now like he was a leper. They pulled their children to the opposite side of the street and pointed at him and the ladies behind him.

He also noticed more and more military men as he made his way. On ledges and bridges above the village, they stood guard. Archers watched the spaces around him and pointed as he made his way through the winding streets. Some walked through the crowds and pretended not to notice him, but it was obvious that all eyes were on him. He considered running, just for the sport of it, to try and lift the depression that was building in him. But he couldn't, he was sapped of all his energy, sick and tired.

He made his way to the steps of the Citadel where Os'halla was sitting.

"Newfriend," Os'halla yelled out with a smile.

Manfred waved halfheartedly.

"How are you, Os'halla?" Manfred asked sitting beside him.

"Haven't spent time here since I was a child. Not bad. Not bad."

"And they're treating you alright?"

Os'halla nodded. "All kind. All nervous. All worried."

"All jack asses," Manfred said. "What've you been up to?"

"Connecting."

"Oh yeah? With the locals?"

Os'halla shook his head. "With the earth. A powerful energy courses below us, into the root of the world—this world. It's the way of the Kin. You never know what the days will bring. You never know what ground will need my energy. And when I may need the ground's."

Manfred nodded. "Do you think I'm going to die, Os?"

"Of course," Os'halla responded.

Manfred put his face in his hands and sighed.

"Do you mean in the portal?"

Manfred looked up. "How'd you know about the portal?"

"I guess we're going on an adventure tomorrow. An adventure."

Manfred wanted to cry. "You mean—you're coming with us?"

Os'halla nodded. "The old man, a Ulis once, I believe, he said I should. I agreed. There are many plants in the Bleak I wish to bring home."

Manfred stood up and hugged Os'halla. "I'm so glad you're coming too. I hate this place, Os'halla. I really do."

Os'halla patted Manfred on the back. "Get some rest, Man of Regular. Tomorrow we see a new world, bright and new."

Manfred spent the rest of the day in his room. He was afraid that if he left, he'd be dragged to another strange place. His only visitor came as the day was winding down. A young man brought him food and a cup of tea. Manfred hadn't noticed, but he was too nervous all day to think about food, but as soon as he smelled it, he was struck with hunger. He thanked the young man, who nodded his head but wouldn't leave.

"Was there something else you needed?"

"Um... Looma said I had to stay until you finished your tea," the young man said timidly.

"Why?" Manfred asked.

"She says you won't sleep without it. She says you'll be even more useless without sleep. It's trunkweed, you'll be asleep before you know it."

"Fine," Manfred said. He drank the whole of it in one gulp and presented the bottom of the cup aggressively to the young man. "Go tell that cranky bitch I drank it."

The young man made a strange choking noise and his eyes almost jumped out of his head and he left the room without another word.

Manfred ate the food and before long felt a wave of exhaustion pour over him. He barely made it to the bed and was asleep before the sun set. The trunkweed did the trick, without it, his mind would have been a cloud of anxiety—no place to prepare for more of the unknown.

MANFRED BUGSBEE AND
THE BLEAK FOUR

Looma and two armored guards woke Manfred the next day while it was still dark, a heavy parcel landing on his bed.

"You'll be needing that. It is from Kaseen." Looma said and pointed at the parcel. "It should keep you in one piece once the stabbing starts."

Manfred unfolded the package to reveal tightly reinforced fabric armor. Lightweight for the size and feel of it with flexible plates sewn throughout. It had been used before—quite a bit. It was covered in restitches and blood stains.

"It was her brother's, a great warrior. A dead warrior. You should be honored to wear it."

Manfred nodded and ran his hands over the armor.

"Should I put it on, then?" he asked shyly, still covered by the large blanket of his bed.

Looma nodded and she and the two guards left the room.

Manfred dressed in front of a mirror near the tub. He stood in front of it and almost laughed out loud. The man he saw was barely recognizable, like he had aged ten years since entering the realm. There were small cuts all over his face that mixed with his scruffy facial hair. His hair was curly like it had been when he was young. He ran his hands through it and smiled. The armor he wore was too big at the shoulders and hips. He felt like a cartoon version of himself, something he would've drawn as a child, disproportionate and mismatched. When he exited, Looma looked him over and stifled a laugh.

"You're not quite as big as Aulrich was, but that'll have to do. Let's go."

Delute and Yarley were talking by the table in the White Room. Os'halla stood alone and carried a large pack on his back and his bo staff.

The portal was on the far side of the room. Even though Manfred had never seen anything like it, there was no mistaking it. A transparent blue half-circle came out of the floor and rippled with every movement in the room. Even their breath affected the shape of the thing. Beyond it was the static of a television, fluttering between the wall of the room and a wavering, shimmering light. More a distorted window to the other side of the room than an entryway to some other dimension. It made the room hot and Manfred nauseous.

"He is arrived," Yarley said to Manfred putting an abrupt end to his and Delute's conversation.

Manfred nodded his head, one eye on the portal.

"And the kin will accompany," Yarley pointed to Os'halla.

Manfred made himself smile.

"I don't like this, Yarley," said Looma.

"It is not *your* like that matters, dear. In and out. Bring back our Saint."

Looma began to speak again, but Yarley shook his head. He handed Manfred a stick like the one Erneel carried. "The Saint carries a relic. He'd be better with this and you with that." Yarley let out a hollow laugh. "On with it then, the balance crumbles." He pointed toward the portal.

"But, what am I supposed to do? I'll only get in the way." Manfred protested. "I just don't understand the point of sending me."

"He doesn't understand," Delute joked. "The man doesn't understand, Yarley."

"*Understand. Like.* No time for all of this. Just *do*." Yarley looked from Manfred to Looma as he spoke.

Manfred looked at the portal then Delute and Looma, and even they seemed cautious of it. It was flat yet somehow miles deep, it had the forbidden gravitas of a well in a horror movie. Manfred walked toward it and felt dizzy and unbalanced. The shape of the portal pulled in on him and weighed him down. Manfred was the first to walk through to the other side of the room.

Soon, after everyone had passed, they stood side by side. From their new vantage, the portal looked less threatening. It was colder on this side, but the fluttering of it had stopped and they could see Yarley as clear as day, his crooked body moved back and forth. The blue of the portal seemed to start from his middle. Small lines of light formed around their bodies, some took on familiar shapes, squares and triangles, while others flashed from one to another. Os'halla tried to grab them but they eluded his every movement. The shapes were solid and incorporeal all at once. Shifting from liquid forms to leaden objects, blinking in and out of existence. Looma stood silently and followed the shapes with her eyes. As the blue of the circle in front of them became brighter and brighter they could no longer see Yarley. Slowly the shapes connected around them and worked into the spaces between the four. The puzzle of reality was becoming and unbecoming. And then complete darkness.

Manfred was stuck in a memory.

He was whale watching off the California coast. He remembered everything. How it took his legs so long to get used to the ocean. How it was nonrefundable. And how the captain said they may not even see any sea life, let alone whales. It was a fat-headed woman that first saw the great white things. Her straight red hair was wet from the splash of waves when she called out, "A wee'ul, a wee'ul off thuh starberd." Sure enough, a whale had arched its body above the ocean and its massive being unleashed furls of foamy water against the sides of the boat as it plunged back into the verdant crests. The sky was so clear. He walked back and forth on the long open deck as a pod of the beasts swam abreast, the salty air and mist of the sea filling his lungs.

The memory was so bright.

He was taken in by the swirls of blue and green water as they broke against the steel of the ship. The high-piercing siren of the whales echoed in his body and shook in his toes and through his shin bones, banging against his thighs, through his hollow stomach, and rattling inside his ribcage, until the sound burst out through his eyes. He blinked and the whales floated out of the water. They wagged their massive caudal fins like puppies' tails. He laughed at their awkward bodies.

The red-headed woman was calling out, "Wee'uls, as far as the eye can see, ma. Wee'uls. Papa, wee'uls. Larry, Larry, yuh ever seen such a thin'?"

He caught the eye of one of the large beasts, it was bloodshot and vibrated in its socket. He leaned over the bow of the ship to get a closer look. Its skin changed as he examined it, transformed into the jagged rocks of a mountain's face. Green trees sprouted from its sides and small black animals climbed from peak to peak. It was so close to Manfred now that he couldn't breathe, there was no space between them—he could feel the whale swimming in his lungs. But, no matter how hard he reached out he couldn't touch it. It was there and not, in all directions.

The woman whispered, "So strange, Larry. They're like somethin' straight from the bible. Gray as Ole Abraham's beard."

The great mammal dissolved into a black swirling mass and Manfred felt his body stretch out toward infinite horizons. He was no longer a human form, but a crude representation of one that flagged in the wind. He could hear Delute laughing hysterically, the laugh of white-hot horror. Looma called out lists of names and Os'halla was somewhere close breathing very heavily. Manfred's body had been stretched to the ends of the universe and there was too much to look at. So he closed his eyes.

"Wee'uls. Wee'uls. Wee'uls, papa. Wee'uls."

Darkness again.

He heard the crash of waves. The light wind of early morning and his insides felt the tingle of sleep. He opened his eyes and could see the portal moving away. He focused on it until it disappeared beyond an alien landscape. He found himself in a charcoal-dusted field. Once again, he was in a new world not his own. His three companions laid out on the ground next to him, each one rolling in fits of horror.

"What's wrong?" Manfred called out in a panic. He held Os'halla's face, then Looma's. He reached out for Delute's hand and gripped it firmly. "Delute, it's alright. We made it through. It's okay."

Os'halla cried out, "I died." He rocked back and forth. "I'm dead. Dead!"

Delute held his chest and yelled out, "What hell?" He rubbed his temples and tried to stand. His legs gave way and the large man crumbled to the ground.

Looma shook violently.

"We made it, we're okay." Manfred kept saying. "We made it."

Looma caught her breath and spoke, "I've never felt such pain. Never." She was crying. "Bitter hell."

Manfred sat next to her and patted her back. She looked at him and the cold of her eyes softened for a moment before she shrugged his hand away.

Manfred began to panic. Although he felt just fine, his new friends all seemed to be on the brink of death. He gave them each water and tried his best to calm them down. After what felt like an eternity, they all started feeling better, even embarrassed by how they had been acting. Manfred asked, but they couldn't explain the awfulness they had felt in the portal.

Delute, Looma and Os'halla spent much of the rest of the day gathering their wits. The portal had taken a toll on them. Manfred felt energized and seeing that they were weakened by it gave him a boost of confidence. Looma looked at him with a curiosity that, although unnerving, felt nice.

"Can I look around?" Manfred asked Delute.

Delute nodded. "Not too far."

Nothing was left of the sun except a yellow haze that glistened in the distance, its light casting shadows that made Manfred walk on his tip-toes, ready at any second to run back to camp. Tall grizzled, battered vines pulsed and glowed against the earth and dug in and out of the dirt in long, arching waves. A chemical buzz emerged from the plants and hummed in the air. The earth itself pulsed, blowing out gasses from its core, great gusts of fetid, sulphuric steam, the ground covered in soot. Each step he took raised wafts of it and underneath red microcosms of veiny plants spread out like spiderwebs. They darkened under the weight of his footsteps and regained their luminance as he lifted his feet.

A way from where they entered this strange place, twisted metal beams unfolded out from the earth's surface, withered from the harshness of time. He moved closer to them and ran his hand over the stone frames that raised and lowered in the ground like the bones of some primordial beast. As he moved farther away from the group he was filled with an eerie calm, that of an explorer, a man being born into the unknown. He imagined himself as an astronaut stumbling onto a barren world and sensed some familiars of his architecture buried beneath its ruin.

Nothing stirred except for the sway of tall black metal pillars. They creaked and reached into the darkest pits of Manfred's imagination. With every step a part of him wanted to turn back, to return to the comfort of his compatriots, but he could not. He could picture city streets dividing the structures from one another—brimming with the rituals of life, the children, and the commerce of his home. Yet it all remained foreign. He was looking into the past and future all at once. Even the metal wasn't square like the I-beams of his earth. They were rounded and stretched out like taffy that wrapped around itself for support, shimmering in the low light.

Before long he found himself separated from the party. He could hear them and see the smoke from a fire they built, yet the separation felt infinite. He reached the first of the steel pillars, it bowed and cried in the wind. He touched it against his bare skin and was surprised by the cool of it. He traced its intricacies. It was the only one still free-standing, stretched out from the ground at least thirty feet in the air. The rest were bent or broken—rusted mammoth tusks disappearing into the dust of the place.

The beam he leaned against was made up of two distinct pieces that wrapped around each other. No rivets or nails held them together, rather a corroded weld tacked out in a thousand different places. The more he looked at it and felt the curve of the thing, the more it reminded him of home. He thought of the condos going up all around his city and the constant restorations that took place on the streets below his apartment and was swept with dread. He imagined his small corner of the world being slowly sucked dry until all that was left were its iron bones like those here. He sat down next to the pillar and cried. Under the strange sky, supported by the even stranger landscape, he felt his first moment of release since his arrival. The tears were of sorrow and a strange seed of hope, in the death of this planet he saw purpose in what the Guard had been asking him to do. To help his world avoid the fate of this one would be worth fighting for. He allowed himself to stay where he was until the voices of his others called out to him.

When Manfred made it back to camp the three of them were next to a fire Os'halla had built. Delute acknowledged him with a grunt as he paced back and forth, singing a song and shadow boxing. Looma was sitting down and sharpening her weapon. Manfred sat next to her and watched as she worked the thing over. The blade was a dark silver that glistened in the heat of the fire. It was no longer than her forearm and curved slightly at the end with a few serrated sections—meant for tearing out guts, Manfred imagined. The handle of it was nearly twice as long, made from what looked like ivory and redwood. A two-handed weapon. Good for getting in close, disrupting enemies that tried to work from a distance. On the end of the handle was a balanced pommel, a square, cloudy-white stone.

"That's beautiful," Manfred said.

Looma didn't look up from her task but replied. "She's seen a lot. The farmers east of my village use it to harvest crops, call it a Sejon. My father taught me how to use it to defend those farmers."

"Fascinating," Manfred replied, surprised that Looma revealed so much.

She smiled. "What is it you do back home, swordbearer?"

"I work in advertisements. I'm working on one for pillows. What I really want is the erectile dysfunction one. It's super easy money."

"What?"

"My job."

"Sounds awful."

Manfred nodded again. "The benefits are pretty good, though."

Looma squinted her eyes at him. "Benefits? Right."

Manfred smiled. "So, how long have you lived with the Old Guard?"

"Long time."

"Oh? Nice place."

Looma nodded.

"Your mother is the Keeper? Her place on the ocean, that's a beautiful place."

"I lived there for a while when I was young," she softened a bit.

"Oh?"

"My father was leading an army. Fighting in a great war." She slashed the air a few times with her weapon. "Wanted me safe. Had hoped I'd give up. Hoped I'd too become a Keeper and not a warrior like him."

Manfred continued smiling. "Looks like that didn't work out."

Looma pointed her weapon at Manfred. "How did you make it through the portal so easily?"

He shrugged his shoulders. "I don't know. At first, I thought I was going to panic, but then—I don't know."

"You don't know much, do you?"

Manfred shook his head.

Night came quickly and coldly. The sky was a darkness that Manfred had never known. If not for the glowing plants on the ground the world would have been pitch black. There was no moon and no stars to be seen. They ducked into the bedding that the Guard had supplied and tried their best to sleep before the morning's trek toward the unknown.

"What was this place?" Manfred asked Os'halla as he tried to fall asleep.

"What do you mean?" Os'halla responded.

"So barren. Where is the life?"

Os'halla chuckled softly. "Life is different here. Once like yours and ours. Life on top. Now it's within. Within."

"Underground?"

"Some. But it is all around. All around. Those plants absorb the dim light of the sun. Like veins, pumping throughout the surface, then feeding into the core. The light is turned to gas and the gas flows out and creates a protective dust. The dust keeps the plants from getting eaten. Getting eaten."

"Eaten by what? I haven't seen any animals."

"The portal scared them off, but they're around. Not many visitors come through here." Os'halla chuckled again.

"How do you know all that about the plants?"

"I'm Kin, Manny. We know plants."

"What was it like before?"

"Advanced, ancient, I'd say. But you'd have to ask your Ulis, yours. He'd know better."

"Do you think Erneel's alive?"

Os'halla was quiet for some time. "He is the Saint. Strongest of the realm. If anyone can survive the harshness of this place, it's him. Try and get some sleep. There is another long day tomorrow, newfriend."

Manfred was surprised at how calm his mind was when he finally closed his eyes. Sleep came in seconds. Something about the dark of the place.

In the morning Delute mapped out their destination. Erneel had last appeared less than a mile away, near a hill of volcanic rocks. The Ulis' measurements were never exact, time and space were different throughout the realms, but the Saint carried a strong sign and there was little doubt that he had been up there or would be very soon. Delute plotted out their approach—simple, he and Looma would take the lead and Manfred and Os'halla would follow and observe. If worse came to worse they'd have to help carry Erneel back down. If Erneel was unconscious, they'd have to nurse him back to health before returning home, since he was the only one among them that could create a connection between the two realms. If he was dead, they'd have to wait until Yarley sent help, which could be days, weeks, or even months.

They wasted no time getting to the rocks. The dark sky encircled the peak and commingled in smoke and red steam.

The four moved slowly, careful of their footing. They were able to approach the top from a mostly lazy slope that only occasionally became treacherous, but even at its worst Manfred could crawl from rock to rock with ease. The thick mist reflected the sun and hilltops broke through in the distance giving the illusion that they were quite high.

Suddenly, a loud screech erupted above them. It was the unmistakable wail and shake of some terrible beast. They all tucked into the hillside and made themselves as small as they could. Delute looked back at Looma. His eyes flashed a moment of confusion that turned to worry as he looked farther down toward Manfred and Os'halla.

Manfred's whole body shook with fear. He didn't dare make eye contact. He pressed his face against the cold ground. The screech came again and a gruesome shadow-thing took flight above them. Its massive head darkened against the dawn-black sky, followed by a serpentine body that writhed and slithered in flight. It was there and gone in a flash as it disappeared into the mist.

Manfred looked toward Os, his eyes wide with terror.

"Mother-beast," Os'halla whispered.

Delute looked at Looma. "Of course *your* father would awaken the Kai'Va."

Delute and Looma continued up the slope.

Manfred tried not to move. He pressed his body as flat as humanly possible against the hillside. Os'halla stayed with him.

"It's just as much below you as it is above you, Manny. Safer near Delute and Looma. Much safer."

Manfred looked down and felt sick. "It could be anywhere," he whispered then burst up the hill in fear.

Delute tackled Manfred to the ground as he came running over the top and pressed his hand over Manfred's mouth. "Behave yourself," he whispered.

The four of them stood on a plateau of reflective, volcanic rock, smoothed by an eternity of wind. From here they could better see the alien world they inhabited through breaks in the mist. The veins of the surface plants illuminated the ground and pulsated in unison. Plumes of thick smoke billowed out from the earth's surface. Whatever beast they had seen move above them was long gone. It had disappeared either into the gray-brown clouds forming above them or the hiss of fog and steam below. The horizon exploded with color as the dying sun twisted itself into the day. Their destination was on the far side of the plateau—the opening of a dormant volcano. Intuitively they knew two things—Erneel was somewhere inside the hill and that is where the beast had come from.

"If the Kai'Va has awakened, then her whole body will be aware of us soon," said Delute, mostly to Looma. "We'll have to be quick. We don't want to shed any of our blood for her." He looked back at Manfred and Os'halla. "Stay behind us. Keep an eye out for her and stay low. If she comes back, try and stay out of her belly."

Manfred's stomach crept into his throat. He could only acknowledge Delute by blinking his eyes—dopey, terrified Manfred.

Delute continued, "You'll be fine. Kai'Va won't concern herself with us if we're quiet. And Ernie," Delute smiled. "Ernie is as quiet as a lamb."

As they made their way across the plateau a sound from within became more distinct. It was the sound of struggle.

Something, or more likely some things, was moving toward the surface. Animal cries and yelps boiled up from the depths. With the side of her weapon, Looma slapped Erneel's stick tied to Manfred's back and nodded a demand for preparation. He fumbled with it and dropped it, then picked it up and held it in both hands before turning and running as fast as he could.

The other three stood their ground as the first of the noisemakers erupted from the cavern. Looma swung at it without hesitation, but the small creature ducked under her blow and cried out, "Looma, little wolf. RUN."

It was Erneel, covered in blood and soot. His robe was torn and tied crossways over his shoulder. He looked at his daughter and smiled, but didn't slow down. The shrieking of whatever had been following him intensified. Before the other three could follow suit, two beasts sprang out. They were smaller versions of the thing they had seen fly off. Four or five feet long, made of snapping, twisting tendons. Their snake-like bodies were covered in black waving fur with mouths like bear traps that revealed crisscrossed incisors and long red tongues. One flew over Looma's head and as it did, she sliced its underbelly from head to tail, and its yellow putrid organs spewed out. The other one made it to Os'halla, who slammed the butt of his bo staff into its open mouth, its head stopped as its body flipped over him. Delute dove on top of it and snapped its neck with a great twist of his upper body.

Looma yelled out a war cry, proud of her kill.

One more human form emerged from the cavern—Liadra. She was pale-white and sickly, as she stumbled forth. Her face and body were bruised and matted with blood. Looma grabbed her and threw her to the ground and Delute moved to kill her, but Erneel yelled for them to stop, yelled for them all to run.

Manfred and Erneel made it halfway to the edge. They stopped and turned back just as a swarm of beasts shot out of the hole and swelled into the sky. They rose like a school of fish, blending into a terrifying battle flag. Delute, Looma, Liadra, and Os'halla ran toward Manfred and Erneel as Erneel crawled down the slope. The beasts rose high in the air before drifting down, their fur fluttering like leaves as they did—a giant mass of near beauty. The great body landed between the separated party and splashed outward and spread out in all directions. The dark agents moved out to the far reaches of the plateau and encircled the whole of the rescuers. This forced Erneel to return to Manfred's side. A handful of the beasts remained where they had landed and howled in chorus. None of the animals attacked, undulating on the peripheries of war.

Looma couldn't take her eyes off of Liadra.

"Why is she alive?" Looma yelled to her father.

"Not now. It is not important. We must focus," he replied then turned to Manfred. "Meant to give you this earlier, ole boy." He handed Manfred a charred piece of bone and took the stick Manfred was holding. "Better than nothing, I suppose."

Manfred held the bone in his hand and a coolness swept over him and for a moment he wasn't scared.

Then the beasts attacked. They swirled and swung their massive tails as they dove over one another and chomped at the wind.

Os'halla moved in circles and figure-eights around the beasts. He swung his bo in full arcs and used the end to stab at them. He dug it into their ribs and down their throats. The animals couldn't reach him, their attacks too wild, too aggressive. He could counter their every movement.

Looma shouted and met the beasts head-on. She slashed at the animals and switched from one hand to two. Her weapon was never in the same place and neither was she. She swung the heel of her feet at their noses and slammed the toe of her boots into their jaws. Every movement she made was violent and precise.

Delute wrestled and tried to tear out their tongues, to jab his fingers into their bellies and find the very things that made them tick. Short stone knives fixed to his palms made grabbing and ripping a glorious and grotesque act. Soon his hands were covered in the fur and flesh of the demons.

Liadra fought the best she could but was mostly worthless, delirious. Her weapon had been lost when Erneel pulled her through the tear so she grabbed and kicked at any animals that got close enough. Even in the heat of battle Looma and Delute kept an eye on her, occasionally giving up good positions to keep her in sight.

Erneel held Manfred with one hand and moved with the beasts as their mirror image. The animals could not reach nor corner him. Their large heads bounced into one another with dull cracks when they tried. From a distance, the stick would whip across their eyes and he'd float to their side with one hand always pulling Manfred. He twisted the beasts up like origami, then struck across their snouts.

The relic did not change in Manfred's hand as it had in the White Room, but a soft blue light emanated from it. The gnawed bone was still visible within the transparent hue. He stayed close to Erneel and did little but get in the way. Occasionally he was able to pull from some depth outside of his experience and parry an attack or swat away a sneaking enemy that had bypassed Erneel. With each blow he landed, the bone became heavier in his hand, a weight that pushed down into his feet and sturdied him.

The creatures took a great deal of damage at first. They rushed in and pushed over one another, only getting in each other's way. A few quick deaths and gruesome injuries forced the creatures to reassess their strategy. They no longer focused on Manfred and his others separately, instead, they attacked as one, right then left, from out to in and forced the rescue party to the center of the plateau. The six of them were no longer able to spread the beasts into weaker pieces. The creatures communicated with howls and murmurs that spilled out of their nightmare jaws.

Delute was the first to suffer from their building steadiness. While he wrestled with one and attempted to use it as a weapon against its brethren, another latched onto his leg and tossed him into a defensive scramble. The animals piled on him and if not for Liadra he'd have been killed. Liadra dove on top of the pile, knees first, and used her elbows and her teeth to pry back the beasts. Once Delute had enough wiggle room he erupted from the pack and sent them all flying back, including Liadra. He pulled her up by the scruff of her armor and threw her back into battle. Delute's leg was losing blood and he had to shy away from the battle to care for it.

Looma took a hard blow across the head from a wild tail and was knocked off balance while she watched Liadra help Delute. She was quickly overcome by three of the beasts. From the ground, she kicked and stabbed at the animals, able to keep them back momentarily. One passed her guard and dove for her neck but Os'halla knocked it away, the ends of his bo staff glowing with fire.

"Make room," Erneel yelled out. "Make room."

Erneel had to open a connection back into their realm. The creatures sensed his urgency and began to focus on him. They launched their serpent bodies at him, sacrificing fur and flesh to make sure he couldn't finish the ritual.

Delute pushed Liadra and Os'halla forward and yelled, "Hold fast. Defend our Saint."

Liadra and Os'halla were the outer circle. Os'halla used the reach of his staff to keep the creatures back as far as he could, the lighted ends worked to injure and intimidate. Liadra stood just behind him and swung and kicked with as much ferocity as she could muster. Looma, being the second line of defense, sliced and stabbed at whatever made it past the two. Lastly, Delute used his body as a final shield, putting himself in front of Erneel and Manfred. He used his elbows and knees to bounce the tiring creatures back. Manfred's weapon glowed intensely and he helped where he could. Every so often the light of the relic would touch an animal and it would yelp and jump back with such intensity that Manfred would nearly drop the thing.

Delute's injury slowed him dramatically. He persisted though and would defend Erneel's life even if it meant his demise. Their history was a flood of moments like this. The beasts slowed as the warriors, backed up against one another, began fighting with more and more purpose. A rush of adrenaline had overcome them, and they all knew it was now or never.

Erneel was able to open a connection but it visibly drained him.

"Is that home, Ernie? Are you sure?" yelled Delute.

"As sure as I can be, old friend," Ernie replied from one knee.

With surprising force and speed, Liadra pulled Os'halla's bo from his hands and hurled it at Looma. Looma was able to parry it but wasn't fast enough to reset as Liadra ran past her. Delute moved to grab her, but Liadra pushed a hard kick into his wound and he buckled in agony. Manfred tripped over himself as he tried to stop her from diving through the tear. She made it through. There was a flash of light and Erneel collapsed. The tear was gone.

The commotion of Ernie's work scared the beast and pushed them back enough for Manfred and the rest to regain their wits.

"Escaped," cried out Looma as she lifted her father to his feet. "How could you let *her* escape?"

Erneel had to lean on his stick and catch his breath. "We are trapped, little wolf. I'm sorry."

Delute was still down. He sat with one hand pressed against his leg. "We'll be fine, Ernie. We've been here before. Just like Spiral Oaks," he laughed and winced and laughed again.

Soon the beasts regained some of their courage and moved in again. They continued circling and yelping and snapping their jaws and rearing up like cobras. But their lunges turned into feints and mere ghosts, attempts to show heart. The warriors were the same. Manfred had been pushed to the front with Os'halla and had to engage. No matter how scared he was there was nowhere to run. The Relic had formed into a glowing, blue club and repelled the beasts when he struck them. Each time he landed a blow he felt lighter, more confident.

The battle became a game of fatigue, where whoever exhausted first would be totally dismantled. Just as the warriors seemed to have gained the upper hand, the beasts afraid of Os'halla's fire, the blue glow of Manfred's weapon, and the undying tenacity of Looma, the stalemate broke. A roar careened from the sky, thunder, and the sounds of hell. Manfred looked up and felt all energy and confidence immediately sap from his body. He wanted to cry, but instead, he laughed and pointed. The mother of the beasts had returned. She circled the plateau and her children all looked up and greeted her. A soft noise came out of them—an almost pleasant purring, the world shaking with her presence. The leviathan beast landed and a plume of blood-addled dust rose to meet her. Many of her children retreated to their cavern, dragging their wounded and dead. The few that stayed behind tucked into the ragged fur of their mother. She encircled the party with her long body and rested her head on her tail, the eyes of her children peering out from the folds of her body.

Her luminescent silver fur reflected the skylight, filled with burs and bits of earth. Her face, the parts not covered with hair, was pallid, umber, calloused from years of strife. Red scars and deep gashes covered her jowls and crooked muzzle. Vibrant, sad eyes looked down at each member of the party, one by one, her hinged jaw opening slightly and pulsating with breath, rank gusts of air pouring out onto the party. Her eyes finally rested on Manfred.

"You," the beast whispered. Manfred jumped back and looked toward his friends. They had become unmoving, frozen by some dark magic. "Meddlers," the beast continued.

"What have you done?" croaked Manfred as he looked at his friends.

"Done? Is ours. Is our body." The beast licked at the earth with her cracked and fetid tongue.

"We were only protecting our friend. Trying to bring him home." Manfred pleaded.

"Home? Meddlers." She swung her head side to side.

"We're not trying to meddle. We just want to go home. They wouldn't let us leave." Manfred pointed at the smaller creatures.

"Kill you, light-eater. Kill you, earth-ruiner. Dare return?"

"No, that's not us. We're on your side."

"Sides? Only one. Fu'Kai'Va."

"Please, just let us leave."

The great beast bowed her head in a moment of contemplation. "Why?" the word echoing in all corners of the universe.

"We're going to kill the ones who… who ate your light."

The beast blew a plume of black ash from her nose. "Cannot kill. Only one."

"Me," Manfred said, holding out the relic.

The great animal crossed her eyes on the weapon. "Of the Sword?"

Manfred nodded. "I am Mindiidus. I have returned," he said.

The beast lifted its body then slammed back down. The vibration pushed Manfred back. "Kai of the Sword. Leave." She opened her mouth as wide as it would allow and breathed out a thick, rancid mist. Manfred lifted his hands in fear and disgust as it overtook him and the party.

He felt dizzy and disembodied. Then he was somewhere else yet again.

HARD TIMES

The five of them emerged from a thick fog a few miles outside of the Village of the Old Guard. Looma took a swing at where the beast's head would have been and nearly fell over.

"Where are we?" she stammered. "The Village? Delute?" she yelled.

Delute, who had lost a lot of blood, laid out in the field unmoving. He remained stone-faced but his skin was starting to lose its color. Looma ran to a nearby farmhouse and banged on the door.

"The relic suits you, boy," said Erneel as he leaned hard on his stick, his legs weak.

"Are you alright?" Manfred asked.

"It takes a lot out of a man," he replied as he slowly sat down. "Check on the rest, won't you?"

A woman and two small children had come to the door. On seeing Delute's condition in her field, the woman ran to his attention.

"If we leave him here, he's sure to die," the woman yelled. "Get him into my house." She pointed at Os'halla. "Get his shoulders." Then to Looma. "Grab his legs, child." Lastly, she looked at Manfred who was still standing next to Erneel. "Don't just stand there. Do something, or he'll die."

They pulled Delute into the house. Even with Os'halla and Manfred lifting at the shoulders and Looma and the woman at the feet it took all of their strength to drag him in. The house was a single room with a loft above. In the center, a large wood-burning stove flickered out its warmth, connected to the ceiling by a clay pipe. After the woman threw off the bedding, they laid Delute down on one of two bare bed frames. His moans of pain almost sounded like laughter.

"Suzett, the *black-oak honey*," the woman called out to her small daughter. "And *earth-brine*. Hurry, my girl. The honey."

Suzett brought her mother two jars. One was filled with black granulated honey and the other looked like mud.

"His pants," she called out.

Os'halla and Looma helped pull his armored pants down, exposing his strong legs. There was more blood than wound, the beast had hit him in just the right spot and Delute was being drained.

The woman washed her hands in a basin by the fire and went to work. She filled the wound with the mud to stop the bleeding and Delute only shrieked once. Then to help disinfect the wound, she worked the honey in circles and folded it into the mud. Delute held Looma's arm in one hand and bit a leather strap wrapped around his other, his face scrunched into a painful knot. The woman focused less on Delute than Looma. She made small talk and occasionally pushed down on Delute's leg as he squirmed. "I'll tie you down if I have to," she promised. The mixture on his leg had begun to solidify and the blood no longer oozed out.

All the while Os'halla juggled dolls for the two young girls, Suzett and Breena. Every time they'd try to get a clear view of the field surgery, he'd catch a doll on his foot or in his mouth. The two girls laughed and goaded him on.

Manfred was worthless. He sat in a chair that faced the fire and every time he heard Delute struggle against the help he felt like he would throw up. To see Delute reduced to a squirming mess was almost as scary as standing in the shadow of Fu'Kai'Va. The power of the Relic no longer calmed him. In this small hut, he felt nothing but despair.

When Erneel joined them, he was tired and spoke in small bits and pieces. "Called on a horse," he gestured to the door. "Ride to the Guard, Looma."

Os'halla took the two girls outside to see the horse while Looma assured Delute that he was in good hands and they'd all be home soon. She hugged her father on the way out. Manfred witnessed it all through his fingertips. Erneel was noticeably frail in his movements. Manfred offered his chair, but Erneel refused and moved to Delute's side. The old saint nodded toward the woman then his friend's leg.

"It'll be fine," she said knowingly. "Bring me some *grayfern* will you?"

Erneel grabbed a jar and raised it toward her.

"Grayfern, you oaf. That's *thistle'ar*. Do you want him to shit himself?"

Manfred sat up and almost laughed.

"Yes yes, *grayfern*, here it is." Erneel found the right jar and brought it over.

"Under your tongue, dear," she said and slipped a piece into Delute's mouth. "You'll sleep like a baby and it'll bend out the poisons."

She moved back to the basin and washed her hands. "Out fighting for the good of the world?"

Erneel bowed his head solemnly and replied, "Hard times."

"Perpetual," she said as she grabbed Erneel's hand and put it on Delute's leg. "Pressure. Some food?"

"Thank you," Erneel responded.

Looma had gone on to get help from the Guard and Delute was fast asleep. The two girls were outside playing in the field while Os'halla, Manfred, and Erneel sat with the woman at a small wooden table. She had prepared beans and some old-looking bits of bread. It was mostly quiet with the occasional sigh of appreciation as they chewed their food. The woman watched them closely.

"When I was six years old, I worked these same fields with my father. I can't remember his face, but I'll always remember the way he smelled." She looked at each man and they smiled and nodded. "When the crops were high, he'd hold me above them and point to Arkis'el, the home of the Old Guard. He promised to take me there one day. Said if we had a good season we could holiday there. It never happened. I knew it never would. I knew how fathers were. They lie to their daughters. They make hope from nothing. Those were good years. Long warm summers. I'm sure you remember." She forced eye contact with Erneel.

"Then came your enemies. They burned down our house and our crops. My younger brother died in the fields. Burned alive. I remember that smell too." She held Erneel's gaze. "Since that day I've hated the Cloud. My father swore revenge, joined your army. Left my mother and me in charge of the farm. We rebuilt our house, tilled the fields. We did well. I was proud. A little man like you," she reached out for Erneel, "brought us a letter one day. With a great seal and a thousand signatures, my father had died. Killed thousands of miles away. 'On the front lines,' the little man said. 'A brave warrior. Helped run the Cloud out of a farming village like ours.' I was proud. My father's death brought me hope. Another lie," she laughed and poured them all drinks. "I have lived on this farm my whole life. Was married here. Buried my mother here. When the fighting had started again, my oldest son joined your army." She tried to conceal a guttural sob. "He was young. His father would've joined too, had he not gone lame working the land. My boy, though, was strong. Kind. Believed the Cloud was a great evil, believed they had to be stopped. A great evil." She laughed again and took a long drink. "The first time he came home from battle he had new scars. Nearly lost an eye. He told my daughters about oceans and mountains, beasts hundreds of feet tall. They didn't want dresses anymore, they wanted swords and shields." She was quiet for a while, the only noise came from her hands as she rubbed them together, dry and cracked. "The second letter I received from your guard had fewer signatures." She smiled. "A great evil is watching you. You snakes." She pointed at Erneel with both hands.

"What was your son's name?" Erneel asked.

She covered her face and sighed, "you'll never know his name. Never," she shouted. "And you," she pointed at Manfred, whispering now, "when you die fighting another man's war what will they send your mother?" She sat back in her chair and stared into nothingness. They sat quietly until the daughters came in and excitedly announced the arrival of more horses.

Three members of the Guard had returned with Looma. Two men on horses along with Looma and a woman with a horse-drawn cart. They carried Delute out.

Erneel held the woman's hands and they both cried as they said goodbye. The woman pulled her children close and they watched as Manfred and the rest piled onto the cart and rode off toward the village.

Manfred counted the huts as they passed, trying to take his mind away from Delute. The huts lined up against the tall dark purple crops that whistled in the breeze. Mothers held their children back from running toward the convoy, but they couldn't contain their excitement. The children yelled and waved their small hands. Work-worn men held them on their shoulders and pointed out the swords and armor and whispered what an honor it was to see the Saint and his men. Manfred fell asleep against Os'halla and when he woke they were at the gates of the village with Tansrit greeting them.

"Welcome home, Erneel." He said as two of his men loaded Delute onto a gurney. "A new one for you, facing Kai'Va."

"Yes, yes. Do they know we're here?"

Tansrit nodded. "Fenk and Saylu are in the White Room."

"Fine." He turned to Looma and Os'halla. "You two go with Delute, he'll need friends when he wakes. And Mr. Bugsbee, you come with me."

Tansrit looked at Manfred. "Didn't think he'd survive."

"Better than most," replied Erneel.

Salyu and Fenk greeted them in the White Room.

"Harvestors move to the Auswhary islands," Salyu said before anyone could sit down. "And Liadra was seen near Ghulil Pass."

Erneel shook his head and thought for a moment. "She's faster than her old man. Faster than a lot of the Cloud. She's getting stronger."

"What happened in the Bleak, Ernie?" asked Saylu.

"Yes, old man, what happened? Why is Liadra back in our realm and not dead?" Fenk urged.

Erneel sighed. "If not for her I'd have died. Simple as that. She knew I was her only ticket home. When we landed in that cursed land of dust I was cut deep." He opened his robe to reveal a line of crude stitchwork. "She stitched me up with a bone of that place and fiber from her armor."

"You grow foolish," said Fenk, "you should have killed her then and there."

Erneel nodded his head back and forth. "I suppose."

"It was a mistake not to kill her. If she's already through Ghulil she'll be on a ship to the Aushwary coast long before your men are ready," said Fenk.

Erneel looked at Saylu. "He's right. We have little time to get to her and close down their siphon. The Harvestors are getting quite strong and I fear they look to summon."

"Summon?" Manfred asked.

"Another unfounded prophecy of Kaseen," Fenk barked.

Erneel looked back at Fenk. "She no longer talks of defeating the Guard. She talks of tearing apart the fabric of existence. Manfred's earth is only the beginning. With that power, the Oarygus may return. May sleep in our realm."

"You've spent too much time under a dead sun I think," Fenk said.

Saylu spoke up, "there is no doubt if the Harvestors fortify their connection with Manfred's earth his home will soon be lost." Saylu looked at Manfred.

"Lost?" Manfred asked.

"Who cares?" asked Fenk. "If there is a summoning, if the Oarygus do return, it won't matter if the armies of the Cloud have already burnt through our world. Gray Tower has fallen, time is running out. They'll be at the villages soon enough."

Saylu lifted his hand to quiet Fenk and spoke to Manfred, "every day your earth grows colder. Soon there will be no turning back. Both for your realm and ours. Total chaos. Without the sun your planet dies, no more than a floating rock." Saylu looked at Fenk. "You know that the Harvestors need to be dealt with, Fenk. This is a war fought on more than one front. It always has been."

Manfred thought of the dead structures he had seen in the Bleak.

Fenk stood up irritated. "Erneel," he walked toward Ernie. "You should have killed her, old man?"

Erneel nodded. "A risk, I'll admit."

"Risk?" Fenk yelled.

Erneel continued to nod.

"That's no risk. It's careless."

Erneel stood up. "You forget much of this realm is under the protection of Kaseen and the Ulis."

"You count on your old protections and superstitions as the world crumbles. All in the hopes that this man," Fenk pointed toward Manfred without taking his eyes off of Erneel, "will be able to save us. This uncertainty."

"He *is* Mindiidus."

"Bah," grunted Fenk. The two men stood toe to toe.

"This is not the time," Saylu urged.

Fenk looked at Saylu. "While Erneel and his men worry about old magic and ancient birthrights, Pencaut Elo and the Cloud grow stronger. Tangibly. How many villages have fallen now, Saylu?"

Saylu shook his head.

Fenk continued, "in the time since this man came to our realm, five more have fallen. We are not invincible. We lose the trust and respect of our people as you chase ghosts. There will be nothing left to save, Erneel. You and Delute are needed on the front. And the *Keeper's Three*, free them up, Erneel. Let them do what they do best. Protect us. We need them. We need you on the front lines."

Erneel ran his hands through his beard. "He spoke with Kai'Va, Fenk. I saw it with my own eyes. He's the key, he has to be."

"You know what your problem is, Erneel? You think you can stop all war, all bloodshed. You can't. Since before you were born, before Yarley, there has been war and it will always be. We cannot stop all war, Erneel, but we can put an end to this one. Give the realm time for peace. To rebuild. But I need our forces concentrated. All this prophecy does is divide our men. It weakens them to think there is an absolute end. Why even fight if this man can put an end to it with the wave of his hand?"

Erneel opened his mouth to speak but said nothing. In a flash of light, Yarley appeared in the room. "Right, right," said Yarley, a blue fog pouring off of him. Erneel looked at him absently.

"Divided, Fenk. We cannot win this on the body alone. If the Oarygus return, it matters not the blood we shed."

"The Oarygus haven't been seen for thousands of years, Yarley," said Fenk.

"The Ulis sees," Yarley nodded his head, "an ancient shape."

"He's a sign," Erneel gestured at Manfred. "A sign of their return. It's clear, Fenk. The Cloud looks to summon the Oarygus."

"The Oarygus are a myth," replied Fenk, his voice unsure. "The Ulis has been wrong before. Been wrong a hundred times."

"Yes, yes," said Yarley. "That is why you fight a war and the Saint prepares for the end."

Fenk let out a heavy sigh and sat down.

"Has the boy proven himself?" Yarley asked Erneel.

Erneel looked at Manfred and shrugged his shoulders.

"Talked with the Mother, eh boy?" Yarley leaned toward Manfred.

"I guess," Manfred replied.

"You guess and guess, child. What do you know?"

Manfred looked toward Erneel for help, but Ernie would not look at him.

"I don't know what you mean."

"You felt?"

"I felt sick."

"You felt her voice. Few can feel across the realms. Few like you. And the relic?"

Manfred pulled the bone off his back and held it out.

"You felt its pulse?"

Manfred nodded.

"What's next?" Erneel interrupted. "If the Ulis is right, we're running out of time."

"You and the Bleak Four must go to the Aushwary. To stop the Harvestors and bring Liadra back. If they seek to awaken death, killing them only makes them stronger."

Erneel pointed at Fenk. "Fenk is right. No more hopping realms, the war is here now. Tomorrow I will retrieve Rocinallia and we put an end to the Harvestors."

"Who is Rocinallia," Manfred asked.

"My sword," said Ernie.

Fenk clapped his hands together. "Finally some sense, old man."

"Fenk will continue fortifying our troops and once Delute is ready you'll take his ship," Saylu said, who had been quiet ever since Yarley mentioned the Oarygus.

Yarley disappeared before Saylu finished speaking and the other three sat quietly.

DEAD EYES FINALLY DYING

They were on the ocean for quite some time aboard Delute's ship, the *Stone Sail*. In the afternoons the crew took to sparring. For the first few nights, Manfred watched from the helm. Delute and Looma always started it. Like siblings cooped up in the back of a car they'd push each other until one snapped, usually Looma. Her temper was legendary and Manfred swore he saw fear in Delute's eyes when they'd first come to blows.

Delute's fight was control. He used his strength and size to wear you down. He'd laugh and absorb shots to the body and top of the head. Then he'd pull you in and squeeze out whatever energy you had left. He never moved backward. He fought like a building wave, and when the wave broke, so did his opponent.

Looma was like a boulder crashing down a mountain. Every strike was followed up harder and faster; working from the force of the last, taking any opening, any path. To Manfred it looked chaotic, elbows and knees, palms, fists, she even charged in with her shoulders and hips—always in a straight line. It worked to counter Delute. Whenever he'd catch her and try to pull her into a stronger hold, he'd be met with the sharp points of her elbows or even the crown of her head. Delute tended to walk away with the advantage but was always winded after his bouts with her. Whereas no matter the defeat, Looma was always ready for the next fight.

The fights between Os'halla and Looma were the most exciting. For every strike, a counter, for every advantage, a sacrifice. So much like a dance that Manfred heard music in his head as they fought. Os'halla with his circling could get behind Looma, but Looma was always making space for herself—kicks to the shin, palms to the bladder, and kidneys. During the whole journey, there was only one decisive victory between the two of them. Os'halla was knocked out cold when he mistimed a turn and with his back to Looma, she swept his legs. He spent the rest of the day quietly nursing a large goose egg on the back of his head.

Erneel always entered reluctantly, but by the end, he'd be laughing hysterically as whoever he faced tried to land a single blow. Erneel moved in the same circles as Os'halla and was always just out of reach. Os'halla's movements looked fluid, but there was an obvious structure to them. Erneel on the other hand moved entirely based on his opponent, always exactly where they didn't want him to be. With Delute, he was just far enough to stay out of his grasp, with Looma, he was so close that her attacks were smothered before they could gain momentum. Os'halla's circling was pointless, with each turn, Erneel would force him to spin back the other way. If Os'halla attacked left, Erneel would be right. If he attacked high, low—every movement was met with an empty space.

When Manfred finally joined in, they all made it painfully clear that his abilities were not innate. Without a relic he was clumsy. Delute allowed him the most free-range. He'd absorb Manfred's strikes with a loose cover, take a few hits then pull him into a clinch and toss him aside. Os'halla was less patient and mostly used Manfred as target practice. He never fully committed to his strikes but he made sure Manfred was aware of each one.

Looma was consistent in her harshness. The first time they touched hands Manfred made the mistake of *going easy* on her. Out of sportsmanship, she gave the lesser fighter one free shot at the beginning, and he weakly pushed at her head. After that, all bets were off. She jabbed her fingers into his ribs and knocked her knees into the fat of his thighs. Every strike he threw was blocked with the edge of an elbow or a tap to the throat or groin. After that, he'd sit down and count the new bruises, never quite sure where they had all come from.

Erneel rarely sparred with Manfred but every so often he would pull him aside and remind him to slow down.

"How can I slow down with your daughter trying to take my head off?"

Erneel laughed. "There's no need to rush, my boy, the fight isn't going anywhere. The Relics reach into you. You understand? This power comes from you, Manny. Slow down. Watch. Feel. Attack when there is something to attack. No need fighting a battle that isn't there."

Manfred only ever landed a few good blows and they always came from someone else rushing in. Whether it was Os'halla turning too quickly or Looma going in for the kill. For Manfred, it felt like luck, but he was learning.

One lucky hit came against Looma after she had put Manfred off balance and immediately tried to knock him to the ground. She moved quickly with both hands toward his head, but all Manfred had to do was lift his elbow as he fell back. The point of it dug right under her heart. She gasped, more in surprise than pain, and before Manfred could regain his balance she had already thrown him over her shoulder. Even as his back slammed into the wood planks of the ship it felt like a small victory.

"It won't happen again," Looma said as she helped him up. "Not too bad, though, Bugsbee."

On a clear night, Manfred was left to watch the helm. To calm his stomach he held onto the mast and searched for the horizon. He thought back to the dessert. He thought about how Liadra had sliced through the neck of that horse with nothing more than a flick of her wrist. The warm spray of the ocean that splashed against his neck reminded him of the blood of the poor animal and the waves sounded like her laughter. He then thought of how weak she looked in the Bleak. She had been a shell of his first introduction, yet she still escaped. She was resilient and quick-witted. Soon they'd be facing her again and he didn't feel ready, didn't feel anything other than nausea when thinking back to her. He had begun to love and trust the rest of the crew, but he could feel that they were still unsure of him—unsure and willing to sacrifice him if need be. All the while, the slap of the ocean against the hull seemed to call out. "Sa-cri-fice, sa-cri-fice."

As Manfred was lost in thought Delute emerged from the lower deck, stark nude, his body luminescent under the pale light of the moon. Earlier that night Erneel and he had taken to drinking a pungent sludge that Delute kept on board. Manfred tried a sip but nearly passed out from the fumes alone. The two warriors exchanged stories, laughed, cried, and even came to blows before falling into their hammocks. Delute now hung from the side of the ship and peed and laughed hysterically. He wobbled around the deck and climbed the main mast. At its peak, he howled at the moon. Manfred could hear him over the crash of the ocean and half expected him to come down a werewolf. It wasn't until he heard a high-pitched squeal that he looked back to see Delute hanging upside down in a mess of ropes. Manfred hurried to his friend's attention, but Delute fell head first onto the deck before he could get there, a weighty thud echoing across the ship.

"Delute," Manfred yelled out. "Are you okay?"

"Manny, ole boy," Delute said. "Where did that little man put m'drink?"

"Ernie?"

"M'drink, m'boy. Where's it?" Delute managed to move to a sitting position.

"You hit your head pretty hard, Delute. Are you okay?"

Delute grabbed Manfred by the shoulders and pulled his face close. His breath was rank. "The night sea, m'boy. Isn't she the most beautiful thing you—hic—ever seen?"

Manfred struggled to keep from inhaling Delute's breath.

"You fairing aright, m'boy?"

Manfred nodded and Delute let go of his shoulders.

"I was smaller than you when I first set sail," he poked Manfred in the chest and laughed. "Smaller than that wee ole man, with his beady eyes and m'drink. That old shrump. Wee—hic—Erneel," he kept laughing. "Where is he, m'boy?"

"He's asleep, Delute. Down below." Manfred tried to maintain eye contact with him but Delute's eyes had the faraway fuzz of a near blackout drunk.

"I was sold to sea merchants, you know? Folks owed a debt, the saltwater price, the brine." He rubbed his head as he spoke. "My father's life or mine. Sold to the ocean and I grew to love her. The taste—hic—of her. The blue of her eyes." He pointed out into the darkness. "For ten years they kept me. Taught me everything I know about a ship. About a life out here. My home."

"Ten years?"

"Aye, and it was your boy, Erneel, who saved me," he laughed again.

"Oh?"

"Sure as a squall is a lady. The merchant, fat, angry man, beard as yellow as piss—hic—a rotten one. Called—hic—himself, Blood Island. Ole Blood dealt in the fringe—weapons and slaves, treachery of all stripe. If you had money, his ship was yours. It was all I knew; all manner of wickedness bound to the bottom, stored in the hull. I can still hear the cries, Manny." There was a hard focus in Delutes eyes for a moment, but they quickly wavered. "Charred my very soul. But it was my life. Ole Blood had shown me the earth—hic—the whole of it. That ship was nothing but bare-bones, the Twig, he called it; woulda sunk had any other miserable shrump been at the helm. A heart as thin as paper, a mind for the sea. Like your Ulis, a map of the currents in Ole Blood's blood—hic—hic—You see here and here." Delute pointed to a scar on his chest and a tattoo of a severed head on his stomach. "Faced the Daylight Warriors with Ole Blood. My first kill. Weren't old enough even to lay with the wenches of the Hoallary Coast. Weren't old enough to kill. I killed and killed," he looked into the distance. "Was the Saint who stole me from Blood. From Blood and his ways."

"Stole?"

"Ah, the wee welp, Erneel. Blood had got in deep. As deep as you can. The most vicious recesses. Were hauling a prisoner for—hic—called the Checkered Men. A roaming band of mercenaries. May have had Yarley's brother, er, son, held captive. Hard to keep track, you know. We had held up at a port in Iiree Bay, one last stop with the goods on hand, when the first sign of Erneel came crashing down on us. Ugly-beaked sea birds with tail feathers as long as y'are tall fell out of the sky and attacked the crew. We'd dealt with angry foul out on the waves. A wild hair 'n they'd reign down. Was different now— patterned, unified. Knocking some of the newer crew straight off the deck. I sut there laughing. But the merchant turned pale as the main sheet. I remember him looking down at me, shined in sweat. He saw death a'coming. Like a breath a smoke, Erneel— hic—and his boys run aboard. Our crew were some Checkered and some other. All aching to die—be that for money, be that for fun." Delute took a deep breath. "I'd seen death on every coast in every port. But this was carnage complete." He paused again and looked over Manfred's shoulder. "Where'd you say that drink was, ole Manny?"

Manfred shrugged. "I don't know. You and Ernie probably finished it off."

"That nasty, ole' bird. Probably cuddled up to it right now. Where was I?"

"Carnage."

"Ah, it were a sight. Erneel and his famed sword, Rocinallia. The greatest weapon to ever grace the Realm. Greater even than the ole Keeper's Three. Before he had started skipping realms, he and that sword cut through men like weeds. Ole Blood knew his time was up. Did not run. Did not beg. Charged straight at wee—hic—Ernie, howling like a crow, foaming at the mouth, teeth buckled in a scream," Delute rubbed his eyes for a moment. "Would have done just as good diving head first from the nest. Erneel didn't even turn to face him. Stuck out his sword and Blood Island ran himself through. I had hated Ole Blood, but he had raised me, had been a figure of sorts, a father." He rubbed his eyes again. "Wee Ernie saw me coming the whole way. Blood still—hic—standing with Rocinallia stuck through his neck. Dead eyes finally dying. I weren't much to deal with. The ole shrump played with me for a wink, dodging me like a flame to the wind. Put me down with a swift kick to the tailbone." Delute laughed. "Been in a lot of fights, never been knocked down like that." He swayed his head back and forth. "The drink, boy, where is it?"

"I still don't know."

"Ah," his head still swaying. "That was that. The old man put me down like a stone. Coulda killed me. Instead he took me in. Always had good intuition. Knows people. Knows the world." He pointed a long, tattooed finger at Manfred. "That's why I trust in you, ole Manny."

Manfred smiled, a sense of pride welling in his stomach.

"If that ole rickety bag a bones is willing to fight by your side, by the light, so is this ole—hic—drunk." Delute pulled Manfred's face to his, eye to eye, stinking breath nearly suffocating him, and said, "I'd die for you, boy, die dead." And kissed Manfred on both cheeks before pushing him away.

Manfred suddenly felt like crying. The welling of pride built in his throat and to stop from bawling he asked, "What happened next? After Ernie saved you."

"History, boy. Some moments stick, some don't. Best not dwell on the ones we've lost." Delute stood up with the help of Manfred and pointed his head toward the entrance to the lower deck. "You go to bed. I'll take the helm, dear friend. You see that?" He pointed to a wisp of red clouds in the distance.

"Storm's a'coming."

A violent bending of the boat's slats against the squall of waves woke Manfred. The *Stone Sail* tossed and leaped through the ocean. He made his way to the upper deck, holding on to each railing and rope, his knuckles white. The rest of the crew were already up and tending to the great storm. Delute was at the helm, long thick ropes tied around each limb secured him in place as walls of black water splashed across the deck. Looma had fastened herself in the crow's nest and yelled down what she saw. Most of her voice was lost to the breath of the sea. Os'halla and Erneel took to the rigging of the ship and helped Delute the best they could.

"Red water, red sky," Delute yelled out to no one in particular. He then motioned for Manfred to join him. "Take the helm, won't ya?"

Manfred hesitated but a large wave crashed against the bow of the boat and launched him into Delute's arms.

Delute unraveled himself from the ropes and set them on Manfred. "I'll be right back. Just keep her on track with Looma's arm." He pointed up to Looma who was barely visible in the mist, periodically disappearing behind the flap of sails, her arm outstretched.

Manfred held the helm so tightly that he could feel the whole of the sea in his hands. Delute disappeared and reemerged with a large cask of the drink that he and Erneel had been into the night before. He used it to push Manfred out of the way. "Take a seat, Manny, and hold on." With one hand he steered the ship and with the other, he took long drinks.

The rain whipped across the deck like a herd of crazed animals and tossed anything that wasn't tied down into the ocean's open mouth. Manfred sprawled himself against the deck and held on for dear life. Delute sang, his voice an ugly mess of grunts and vibrato.

> *Oh, they promised a drink*
> *So tall, that I think*
> *I'd swim in her all year.*
> *Oh, they promised a swell*
> *From straight out of hell*
> *I suppose I'll be dying out here.*
> *Oh, there's a red in the skies*
> *Like my fair lady's eyes*
> *Who ended her life on a pier.*

As he sang an ominous solid bump came from the starboard side of the boat, different than the shock of waves. It came again.

"Not now," cried Delute, breaking from his song for a drink. He pointed for Manfred to look over the side. As he did there was another bump and a terrible mass emerged from the water, a large blue-black beast. A cephalopod of sorts, an eighth the size of the ship. It glowed like a Chinese lantern. On seeing it Manfred let out a shriek that competed with the yell of the ocean and tried to bury his whole body back into the ship.

Delute chuckled. "Don't worry. Like your boy Ernie, only seaweeds for them."

Two more emerged from the water. Each glowed a different color. They shot above the highest sail before diving back into the tumult.

"With you?" Delute yelled down to Erneel who shook his head. "Can you tell them to leave?" Erneel shook his head again and Delute continued to sing—louder now.

> *Oh, they take us for fools,*
> *Our loves back at home,*
> *They think that sea water*
> *Be more than a tomb.*
> *They write us love letters,*
> *and lay with our brothers,*
> *Oh, they take us for fools back home.*

The animals wailed and yelped as they jumped in and out of the water. Even as the weather calmed and the red of the sky turned blue, there was no break for the ship. The animals created wells of their own as they careened above the mast. A few times Looma was nearly knocked down by the spouts of water the creatures pulled behind them. She howled in pure jubilance and reached out with both hands to touch them. Manfred could only peer through his fingers.

The animals had more tentacles than an octopus, some with more than twenty. Their long arms were covered in dark spots that radiated in contrast to the sky. Their sequined, shimmering, bulbous heads bloomed like flowers and shook and pulsed. Their screams vibrated through the whole ship, all the way into the bones of the crew. They wrapped their tentacles around one another and flew off in the opposite direction, playing a game and the poor ship was just their playtoy.

When the animals departed, they left the ship in a condition not much worse than before. Some rope needed untangling and there was a small tear in the mainsheet which Delute took to fixing. Manfred took the helm and tried to catch his breath.

"What were those?" He asked Os.

"Phalila Fish. A very good sign. Very smart animals, very smart," Os'halla said gleefully.

"A good sign? What do you mean? They almost killed us."

"Oh. They were only playing. We were never in any real trouble. Did you know that Phalila Fish can live for three days above water? They breed on land. They mate for life. I love Phalila Fish. I love them."

Manfred nodded along.

"Females can have up to forty tentacles, Manny. Did you know that? Forty! Can have."

Manfred began to shake his head.

"And the males, when they fight, they fight on land. It's a test of endurance, of who can hold their breath longer. Weren't they truly majestic, newfriend? Majestic."

The next day they saw birds and the day after that they saw land. Os'halla drank tea and told Manfred what he knew of the realms as they moved in on the Aushwary Peninsula.

"Most people of this realm don't care about your world. They don't even know it exists. If the Cloud chooses to tear through another realm, they don't see your villages burn, only their own. The Cloud gets more powerful, more powerful. They enforce their morality; they kill those that stand in their way. This stretch of land, the islands around it have no real strategic value, value. The Guard and the Cloud often forget about them, often forget. Ignore them. Nothing changes. Forever outliers have used them as hiding places. As long as they don't align, the greater powers leave them alone."

"Sounds like home."

"Most of the realms fall into the same issues."

Manfred nodded.

"They exist side by side. Same building blocks, different outcomes. The Bleak is unrecognizable now, but at its birth and in its youth, it may have looked just like yours, like mine. Like home."

"How many have been destroyed like the Bleak?"

"We'll never know. The Cloud at the height of their power tore through many. Many have found new ways of life. Many."

Manfred looked out over the ocean. They both steadied themselves on the railing as waves churned against the ship.

"Ecta Noon is an interesting one. It's said to be a mistake in the process, but we in the Kin don't believe in mistakes. Don't believe. Nature, even unknown nature, follows the path. It is all rumors, not even the Saint or the Ulis have seen Ecta. I've heard it's square, I've heard it's a living planet. Alive." Os'halla laughed. "I've heard it all."

"So how do you know any of this?"

Os'halla smiled. "The Kin are scholars. Gehgard knows much. Has taught me of ours and others. We are students of the path from all corners of the world. We don't just sit around and hum. We teach each other. We teach. Examine the world and the world beyond."

"So how many are there?"

"Realms? They may be infinite. It could have been repeated for all eternity."

Manfred shook his head as he tried to picture the magnitude of it all. Space had always fascinated him. Its expanse was unknowable, now there were more and more degrees being stacked on top of it. What was once merely unknowable had become laced with the unfathomable. He leaned in close to Os'halla and asked. "What are the Oarygus?"

Os'halla nodded his head. "Some believe this whole thing is accidental. They believe the sky was born from the sky and the ocean from the ocean. From the ocean. The separate realms are just chance. However, there have been occasions of tinkering. Moments in our history where great changes have occurred. Changes that can't be explained by the natural world."

"Miracles?"

"The Young Gods—Oarygus, they're believed to be, like Mindiidus, beyond the realms. Occupying the realms and not."

"Why would Ernie be worried about them?"

"In their lives, the Oarygus become architects of earths. They build anew, they destroy. Had they not existed there would be no existence at all. This realm, in its history, is beholden to them. Beholden. Long history of protection. The Young Gods are volatile. Need energy. They've been known to nest. To find an earth with energy and burrow inside of it, deplete it."

"Why would the Cloud want that? Want to bring them here?"

Os'halla shrugged his shoulders. "They are fanatics. They have been under the thumb of the Guard for generations. Some, like Liadra, wish for destruction. The power they pull from your sun resides in our earth. Calls out to the Young Gods."

"Aren't they afraid they'll destroy everything?" asked Manfred.

"Destruction is only a part of life. Only one of the steps. Only one."

"To kill a whole planet, though?"

Os'halla shrugged again.

"What do you believe?"

"I've never seen the Oarygus."

Manfred tilted his head inquisitively.

Os'halla continued. "The Kin deals with what is tangible. What is felt. Things that are beyond the senses are just that. Until I see or feel an Oarygus, a Young God, they are and they aren't."

Manfred looked down at his feet. "Looma said ..."

"Looma doesn't understand the Kin. Looma is born and bred a warrior. Held by the Guard her whole life. She thinks because we sit in fields and worship trees that we are soothsayers and purely mystics."

"Don't your friends turn into trees?"

Os'halla laughed. "I have seen it, it is."

"What about… haven't I seen you make fire out of thin air?"

"Warm the belly. Warm the hands. Warm the earth. It is not that hard."

"This place doesn't make sense to me, Os."

Os'halla nodded and poured the rest of his tea overboard. "The realms are full of mystery. Full."

Manfred said nothing for a minute, then asked nervously. "What happens if when we reach the Harvestors and I can't get to them? What if the guard is wrong about the power of the relic?"

Os'halla laughed and patted Manfred on the back. "Then we die."

AUSHWARY PENINSULA

There was no welcome committee as they neared the beach, the stars shimmering in the barren sand. Driftwood acted like black holes and absorbed the night sky. Jagged cliffs loomed out from the sand and bisected the sky. Lights of village life could be seen beyond the cliffs. A welcome sight to the seasick travelers.

They all tumbled from the ship in a daze. Delute was the only one sad to see dry land, even Erneel knelt and rubbed his hands in the dirt. From where they landed there was only one way up to the village. They'd have to climb. It was nearly one hundred feet straight up. Ropes and chains had been attached over the years to be used as guides with footholds and ledges that appeared and disappeared into the crumbling rock face. Manfred's stomach lurched as he tried to make sense of the path forward. Erneel patted him on the back. "It's not as bad as it looks. Took Looma up this very wall before she could even talk."

"Is there no other way?" Manfred groaned.

"The front gates," Erneel laughed. "But there's no time for that."

"Shouldn't we rest awhile?"

Erneel grabbed Manfred by the arm and pulled him close. "Manny, you need to be strong. This wall, what lies beyond this wall, is no match for Mindiidus. You are a warrior; I can promise you that." Erneel winked at him. "I promise once we bring Liadra back to the village you'll get a nice long break. Maybe go back to the Den and find that young lady that wanted to dance with you," he chuckled.

Delute and Looma made it to the first notch of the climb. Like children on a summer outing, they laughed and crawled over one another. It made Manfred dizzy just watching them. Looking at the steepness of the wall made his knees shake and his stomach knot.

"Os and I will follow you up. Catch what falls." Erneel joked, urging Manfred up.

Manfred responded with a timid grunt and a nod of his head. He grabbed the first of the ropes and made his way up. Most of the footholds were sturdy enough and he was surprised at how strong he felt. At home Manfred couldn't even do a single pull-up, now he moved around with ease, his whole body working in harmony.

"Take it slow," Os'halla yelled up. "Only a little ways to go."

When he became scared, he reminded himself that there was no turning back. It was up or nowhere. He even found solace in the thought that what was at the top of the cliff could be a million times worse than the climb—or the fall, for that matter. There could be a dragon or an army of unknown beasts waiting to smash his brains to bits. The villagers could be cannibals, picking their teeth with the bones of small children.

Strange where a man finds comfort.

Looma and Delute had long since cleared the top by the time Manfred dragged himself over. The cliff sloped down into the village of the Auswhary. Manfred was taken aback at its expanse; it was truly magnificent. As with the Guard, the buildings had been carved out of hills and rock faces, reinforced with grass and dried mud. Enormous stone spires with lit windows arched into the night sky. The village was so quiet that Manfred could hear the village's allegiance flags whipping in the wind.

He didn't feel the dart hit his neck but he did feel the poison. He took a few steps and turned back to see Erneel and Os'halla surrounded by cloaked figures. Manfred's vision blurred as he fell to his knees but he could track a struggle. The blurry blob that was Ernie bounced from enemy to enemy, tossing them over his shoulder, rolling to their sides and between their legs. Manfred couldn't make the foes out at all—in fact they looked more like billowing, black sheets than any human form. Os'halla was slightly closer to Manfred and Manfred could make out some of the details of the fight. It started intensely with Os'halla bludgeoning every assailant that came in reach, his bo staff whistling and whipping through the air, until he created enough space to run toward Manfred. But as Os'halla moved closer his movements slowed, like his body was being overcome by some invisible quicksand. Manfred tried to stand. One last jolt of energy as the poison made its way to his heart. He saw the cloaks, like dark stuttering storm clouds, close in on Erneel's prostrate body. Os'halla reached out his hand and Manfred grabbed it as they were both knocked to the ground. Completely overcome in the shadow of their foes. Manfred tried to yell, but the poison had pulled his tongue to the back of his throat.

He felt himself being dragged. Creatures in dark hooded robes walked on all sides and talked in a language he could not understand. Whatever they had hit him with seeped through his veins and coursed from organ to organ, the world coming in and out of view in shakes. At long last he could make out a hallway, barely lit and carved out of stone and dirt.

His body didn't feel like it belonged to him. He looked from the hooded creatures to his legs but felt no connection. He tried to struggle, to twist himself free of their grasp, but it was no use—he could feel the genesis of his movements, but it was as if they never made it to their destination. The figures threw him into an open room and locked the door behind them.

Os'halla spoke from the darkness.

"They have the rest of us somewhere else. They are only concerned with known members of the Guard. Known members. We appear to have fallen into a trap. Some poison, likely Illthorn of Oak."

Manfred only understood half of what Os'halla was saying. The harder he tried to focus the more tired he became. Soon he was falling in and out of sleep, still aware of Os'halla and the darkness of the room.

When he woke up, he waved his hands around and searched for Os'halla. "Os? Os, where are we?"

Os'halla rolled to a sitting position and touched Manfred's hand. "I'm right here, newfriend. All I know is that they have the Saint."

"The Cloud?"

"We'd already be dead."

"What do we do then? How do we get out of here?" Manfred asked frantically.

"We wait and wait."

Manfred stood up and felt around the walls until he found the door. He banged on it and yelled as loud as he could.

"You're not very good at waiting, are you?"

"They could be torturing our friends, Os'halla. They could be dead. How can I just wait?"

"It's all you can do."

"I don't have to do anything," Manfred replied.

"We are prisoners, Manny. We wait. Prisoners."

"There has to be a way out, we have to help them."

Manfred punched the door and lurched back in pain.

"Sit with me, Manfred. They'll come eventually and we'll get to the bottom of this. We're not dead. That is a good sign."

Manfred sat down. "A good sign? Everything is a good sign with you. How can you not be worried? Terrified? It's so dark."

"I am always worried. But I know, as you do, that we cannot worry down these four walls. We cannot worry through the door."

Manfred stood up and paced the small room. "Accept defeat then?"

"Accept, yes. Defeat, no. Our friends are strong, resilient. You need to sit down. There is still poison in you. Poison."

"I'm fine. You're fine," Manfred replied impatiently. "We need a plan."

"Then sit."

Manfred sat down again. "Fine, what's the plan?"

"Wait."

"Dammit," Manfred yelled.

"You need to release the poison."

"What?"

"Yield. It has left my body already because it has nothing to hold on to."

Manfred shook his head, annoyed, woeful.

"Release, Manny. Release."

Manfred felt the dark mass of poison tumble through his stomach and pull down on his lungs. His fear was all that kept him from passing out again. Os'halla rolled back onto his head and closed his eyes. "Breathe for a while, Manfred. We'll need you at your best in the times yet to come."

Manfred closed his eyes and took slow deep breaths. The poison did its best to keep his attention on his stomach. His heart rapped in his chest as he tried to imagine something useful—a way to escape the room and find his friends. He tried to imagine what the rest of the structure they were in looked like. At first, he could see long dark hallways, each one turning toward another, leading to dead ends and stone doors. He tried to follow them, to feel the cool walls and see the dim lights. But the walls turned to ash and the floors folded into nothingness. The darkness was so profound that it made the room they were in seem both infinitely large and small. He tried to think of the hallways again and where they led, but they narrowed and constricted on him like a snake. He had to stand up.

"Os, I can't. I can't sit here and wait," he said and paced the room.

"Don't think of it as waiting then."

"Then what?"

"Preparing. Think of it as preparing. We are all preparing. The Saint, wherever he is, whether in distress or pleasure, is fortified. Is actively prepared. Breathe. Prepare and breathe."

"Every time I try to concentrate on my breath it just gets worse. The darkness, Os. The darkness is driving me crazy. How am I supposed to prepare and for what?"

"For death."

"What?" Manfred stopped pacing.

"In death, there can be no fear. In death."

Manfred sat back down. "That doesn't make any sense, Os." He put his head in his hands in frustration.

"Try," Os'halla said as he rolled to Manfred's side. "Try not to focus on your breath, but on the spaces that your breath occupies. First in your mouth, then your throat, your lungs. Release it into your skin, your belly. Preparing for death is only looking at life. Only looking. When fear takes over, find death."

Manfred closed his eyes again and tried to feel his breath. His mind was still wandering down the dark hallways, but each time they began to shake or turn into evil things, he'd find his breath again—in his chest and his feet, in his ears and tongue. It tethered him to the ground and guided him toward moments of release.

As he sat, the silence around him grew, and he could hear things that just moments before had hid themselves behind the beat of his heart and the buzz of his anxieties. Soon the room flexed and settled and he heard a strange sound coming from Os'halla's head, something like the sound of worms digging their way into the dirt. Manfred realized it must be the strange roots.

With all the traveling they had been doing Os'halla had not had many chances to nurture his connection. Manfred didn't understand what the goal was, but he respected the commitment and the sense of ritual. Back home, Manfred had very little ritual in his life. Besides his nightly cups of tea, his weekly bouts of internal yelling, his bi-monthly existential meltdowns, he had nothing as powerful and profound as Os'halla's meditation. It was a real part of him, more important to him than sleeping or eating.

Manfred imagined himself laying on the floor of his apartment. Stretched out under his favorite blanket. A warm summer breeze blew through an open window. He could feel his head sinking into a soft corduroy pillow, its grooves making lines against his tired face. He ran his hands over the lines and smiled. He pictured a beautiful well-rested woman with pillow lines on her face. You wouldn't even have to show the pillow. "Brilliant," he said aloud.

"What's brilliant?" asked Os'halla.

Manfred sat up. "I figured out my ad."

"Your what?"

"Oh, I just, I'm feeling much better."

The poison had lost its hold on him and as it faded, he felt the strength of his friends, Looma and Delute who were forged from the strongest metals. It would take a whole army to even dent their resolve. Wherever they were now, they couldn't be hurt, he just knew it. And the ole' Saint, Manfred laughed out loud and pictured him surrounded by some terrible hounds, playing tricks on them, pretending to throw a tennis ball while hiding it behind his back. Os'halla was right. They could wait. He meditated on the great and terrifying things he had seen while in this realm. The large tentacled beasts that almost killed them in the ocean. The battle with the Fu'Kai'Va, resolved in the end by dialogue rather than more death. He could still feel the relic, the way it built something inside of him, the way it pulled great powers from his very depths.

The Mother, Fu'Kai'Va, had spoken of its others as a collective as if each of the beasts was a limb instead of a different entity. Manfred remembered reading about how bees used their collective mind to protect themselves. The Fu'Kai'Va may have evolved in the same way—short on resources, they banded together like schools of fish. He felt sad the more he thought about the Kai'Va. They were only trying to protect themselves. He and his friends were trespassing on the Fu's already broken world. They were only protecting their home and Manfred and his friends slaughtered them—piled the odd-bodied creatures toward a dead sun.

"Os, are we murderers?" he asked suddenly.

Os'halla opened one eye, still balanced on his head. "What?"

"The Fu'Kai'Va. We went into their world and killed them. Are we the bad guys?"

"Violence begets violence. We were there for the Saint. It could have gone much further had she not reached out to you. To you."

Manfred nodded.

"There will always be war. It is woven into the whole of the universe. It is people like you that know when to rise above it. To rise above."

"And the Cloud? They are evil? They deserve death."

Os'halla rolled into a sitting position. "They are manipulators, I suppose. If left unchecked every realm would be sorted into chaos. The years that they have been in control have been mired with atrocity and genocide. The Guard isn't perfect, but they are decent."

"Decent?"

"There is no good and bad in the world. Only possible futures each with its troubles. The Cloud wants a future of dust. Of dust. The Guard hopes to avoid that."

"Where do you fit in then, Os?"

"This path, then another."

"I dragged you into all of this. I'm so sorry."

Os'halla chuckled. "There is nothing avoidable in this life. Now we must rest. They'll be coming for us soon."

Manfred and Os'halla were both asleep when the door opened. Five hooded creatures, two with spears with bludgeons at each tip and the other three had two swords on their left side, one long and one short. Creatures isn't quite right, but behind the hoods, in the darkness, these people seemed monstrous. Shadows caught their scarred faces and revealed their blank, military stares. The two with spears poked at Manfred and Os'halla until they awoke and were on their feet. With head gestures and pointing with their weapons all of them entered the hall. Manfred and Os'halla led the pack, prodded on by those weapons.

"Where are you taking us?" Manfred asked. "Please."

No one answered.

Os'halla walked lazily, his arms and legs drooped like a child's. A few times Os'halla's escort had to nudge him hard in the back to get him moving.

"What's wrong with you?" Manfred whispered.

"Tired is all, newfriend. Maybe it is the poison. The poison."

They continued down the many dark halls, occasionally lit by portholes to the sky and flames from small corridors on the sides. Manfred tried to look back at their guides but was only able to catch glimpses before being prodded onward. Their robes were uniform black and they all walked with a similar slide. Some seemed nervous, some agitated.

Os'halla began to slouch more and more. Moving slower and slower, the creature behind him had little compassion and pushed hard with his spear. Manfred had never seen Os'halla like this and began to worry even more. What if all of Os'halla's talk didn't mean anything? What if the poison was still in both of their bodies, just waiting to kill them?

"Os, are you sure you're okay?" Manfred whispered.

"Just tired. Feeling oh so tired."

Os'halla was now completely hunched over, his hands on his thighs, walking with nothing more than a slow shuffle and belabored breath. Manfred reached to comfort him, but his hand was smacked away by one of the spears. Os'halla had almost completely stopped moving and the creature guiding him had had enough. Frustrated, he pulled his spear back to give Os'halla a full-bodied strike to the ribs. Just as the weapon touched him Os'halla slipped away from it and the creature stumbled forward. Os'halla spun and grabbed the spear of the creature that guided Manfred. Quickly, Os'halla threw that creature against the wall.

Manfred was so surprised that he hopped forward with a yelp and nearly fell over.

The hallway was good for directing traffic, but it took away the creature's advantage in numbers. The three creatures that took up the back of the party had to dodge their comrade as he bounced off the wall and tumbled behind them. When Manfred regained his footing, he pounced on the creature that had fallen forward and delivered a knee to the side of his head. The creature slumped to the ground, unconscious. Manfred and Os'halla stood shoulder to shoulder, now both armed with spears.

Two of the remaining three had unsheathed the longer of their swords and began to move in more deliberate shuffles, foot to foot, raising dust as they did, the points of their weapons extended. The third remained unaffected by the commotion around him. His only change came in slower steps, his hands both resting lightly on the smaller of his two swords.

Manfred and Os'halla walked backward in crossed steps. The spear was heavy in Manfred's hands, so different from the lightness of the relic. He knew he had to play the part though. He moved the weapon back and forth, eye level with his enemies. He and Os'halla took turns looking over their shoulders, never daring more than a glance. The two that had been disarmed were now at the back, but the calmer one, their clear leader, motioned for them to leave. One helped the other to his feet and they disappeared back down the hallway.

The five that were left made their way down the narrow hall. The dirt of the cavern floor had been kicked up from the skirmish, lending the space a brown glow. A stillness hung over them, the hesitation before all-out war. The one in charge no longer even touched his weapons, instead, he crossed his fingers comfortably across his chest.

The end of the hall was approaching, a closed stone door. Manfred and Os'halla knew they were running out of time—it was now or never.

Manfred acted first with the impatience of an untrained warrior. He lurched his spear at the creature right of center. But what was in his mind was in his action and he was tentative. He wasn't sure what they wanted or where they were headed. Up and to this point the creatures hadn't been overly aggressive. They didn't charge Os'halla and Manfred when their comrades were disarmed. Manfred was scared and uncertain about his attack.

Os'halla's attacks held much more intention, non-lethal, but to the point. He attacked the front inside shin of the creature to his left. Using the flat side of the bludgeon he forced the creature into an awkward open step. Os'halla then brought the weapon straight up into his enemy's groin. The one who held up the rear still had his hands clasped across his chest, walking slower and slower.

Manfred's tentative stabs nearly got his head chopped off. His opponent allowed Manfred a few more lazy jabs to pull him in. Once Manfred tried for a more promising blow the creature parried hard and forced Manfred to stretch. The creature hesitated and gave Os'halla just enough time to bring his weapon across and protect Manfred's neck.

After that, Manfred all but hid behind Os'halla, who continued walking backward with his weapon cutting the hallway diagonally in half. The leader motioned for the last two to leave. He then reached up and removed his hood, revealing a deeply scarred human face. Paper white skin stretched over red and black scar tissue, the victim of horrendous burns. His eyes were a bloodshot mess that shifted lazily from Os'halla to Manfred. He smiled and revealed crooked, chipped teeth.

"I am Bealzut. And this could all have been much easier." With that, he threw his long sword hilt first at Manfred's head.

Os'halla blocked it easily as it flew toward them. But as he blocked it, Bealzut lunged and cut Manfred's spear in half with his shorter sword. Manfred took two hard swings at Bealzut's head with the remainder of his weapon. Both times the bones of his arms were met with the hilt of Bealzut's sword. Os'halla turned quickly to face Bealzut, and as he did Bealzut guided the tip of Os'halla's spear toward the ceiling. The momentum of Os'halla's turn stuck the tip of the spear into the hard-packed dirt above.

Bealzut chuckled and kicked his long sword up to his free hand. He now stood in the shape of a square. The dagger in his forehand pointed up and the long sword over his head made a right angle in front of him. Manfred and Os'halla now had their back to the long hallway.

Manfred rubbed his arms while Os'halla freed up his spear. Bealzut took slow crossing steps backward, rarely letting either foot completely leave the ground. He clicked the tips of his weapons together in a nagging rhythm and smiled behind the blades. Os'halla was cautious, knowing if he committed fully to one blade or another, he'd leave himself open. The spear was too long and cumbersome in the narrow hallway. Manfred's was shorter since it had been cut, but he lacked the depth of practice to realize its advantage.

The blades that Bealzut carried were both slightly curved and only sharp on one side. In the mostly dark of the hallway, they caught each shimmer of light, winding Manfred's nerves tighter and tighter. As the clicking of the weapons and the occasional glare of light worked their magic on him, Manfred made a move and dashed forward, using a long step that Erneel had shown him on the ship and leading with his hips to give the illusion of space. As quickly as he came in, he was disarmed. Bealzut used the sides of both blades, making a point to only cause blunt trauma. Although painful, the strikes were not critical.

"He won't hurt us," Os'halla said to Manfred who was now sitting on the floor rubbing the side of his head.

"I'm very hurt," Manfred cried out, still holding his head.

"So sure?" Bealzut asked.

"You could have killed us both already. Already," said Os'halla.

"Flies and spiders," Bealzut said.

"Where are you taking us?" Os'halla demanded.

Bealzut looked behind himself and shrugged. "Who leads the way?"

"Where are our friends?" Manfred asked through labored breaths.

Bealzut put both of his weapons back in the scabbards and rolled up the sleeves of his robe, revealing even more of his smoke scarred skin. "It matters not."

"Where are they?" Os'halla shrieked. His yell surprised Manfred. Os'halla had lost patience and Bealzut was set on a fight.

Os'halla threw down his spear and charged Bealzut. They locked together like two elk, arms like antlers—hooves and teeth. Huffing and puffing, they struggled for position. They threw knees and uppercuts, the knock of their knuckles and bones rebounding down the hallway. Manfred tried one last time to intervene, but Bealzut pushed a front kick into his bladder and put him back on the floor with an awful grunt. Os'halla was more of a handful than Bealzut had anticipated, but he seemed to relish the chance to go head to head with him and laughed and smiled all the while

Os'halla squirmed out of most of Bealzut's holds, but never for long and never without consequence. Manfred watched from a fetal position on the floor, through covered eyes. The doorway was getting closer. Light shone from under it as they moved away from Manfred. Finally, in a great heave, Os'halla lost his footing and became so top-heavy that with a simple pull Bealzut sent him flying into the door. Os'halla crashed through and tumbled into the next room.

Manfred was still on the ground, watching as Bealzut charged through the open door. The noises from the other side were chaotic. Things breaking and crashing off walls followed by the rising voices of more unseen foes. Manfred struggled to his feet and limped down the hall. He dragged one foot and groaned with each step—certain that Os'halla and his death were on the other side.

He entered a large room with vaulted ceilings, supported at each corner by ancient timbers. There were small fireplaces all around that acted as lanterns. Like the hallway, most of the structure of the place was made from packed dirt, from the walls to the high ceilings. On one side of the room, a long table was covered in food and drink. On the other, small, sunless flowers sprouted from the shadows. Their stems looked like fine crystalware and the bulbs were a transparent white pink.

As he scanned the room, he was greeted by the happy faces of Looma, Erneel, and Delute. They all stood on the far side of the room and laughed hysterically. Two of Bealzut's others were laughing too.

"What is this?" Manfred shrieked, holding his side.

Erneel made the first response. "Old friends," he said and gestured to the men next to him.

"They were trying to kill us," Manfred yelled.

"Kill?" Bealzut said with a shrug of his shoulders.

"Os'halla?" Manfred asked, looking for confirmation.

Os'halla shook his head. "Was only toying with us. Toying."

"Is this a joke?" Manfred demanded.

"No joke," replied Delute. "We didn't know their intentions. They didn't know ours."

"Friends?" Manfred asked.

Erneel nodded his head. "Greylit and I have had run-ins before." He patted one of the others on the back, a very tall man in the same garb as Bealzut. His hood was pulled back and revealed an auburn, pockmarked face. "Fought side by side at the Battle of the Tren."

"Aye," said Greylit as he pushed Erneel lightly on the arm.

"Had us locked up," Manfred was sick.

"Sorry. We were clearing some things up, old boy. Truly sorry."

"On high alert in these parts," Greylit chimed in.

Manfred shook his head with disgust and Erneel made his way over to him. "We were ambushed and separated, Manfred. These things take time."

Manfred was angry, but he was also weak and smelled food. "I can't ever catch up," he said and sat down and dug into the hard breads and vegetables that were laid out on the table.

"You're the Little Saint then?" asked Bealzut.

Erneel smiled and nodded.

"And that's Rocinallia?" Bealzut asked, enamored by Erneel's sword. "It's said you were a great warrior in your time."

"Was I?" Ernie smiled.

"Maybe it's my time," said Bealzut with surprising seriousness. "Care to spar, Saint?"

Ernie looked at Greylit. "Does this one ever shut up?"

Greylit smiled. "He did the same to me when first we met. Wouldn't shut up until I put him down. Not as easy as you'd think."

Erneel laughed and in one fluid, singular movement pulled the sword from his back, sliced through the stem of one of the strange flowers, caught the head, and handed it to Bealzut.

It was Manfred's first time seeing the famed Rocinallia unsheathed. It looked more like a long, heavily damaged chef's knife than some legendary weapon of mass destruction. It had an ostentatious, square pommel that melded into a half, hand guard. The cross-section looked like an afterthought, a piece of well-worn steel that looked to be tied on with scrap bits of halyard. Manfred was unimpressed and huffed as he thought to himself, *who names a sword?*

Bealzut held the flower in his hand and looked at the cut, dumbfounded. He didn't say another word.

"Another day, maybe," Erneel said and turned back to his conversation with Greylit.

They caught Manfred and Os'halla up the best they could. Greylit and his men had been hired by the inhabitants of the island. The Cloud had been seen scouting the area for quite some time and had recruited some of the young Aushwary to their cause. Manfred asked as many questions as they'd allow.

"Why not just side with the Guard?"

"It's not that simple. The Aushwary are sovereign, always have been." Greylit responded. "Once you raise arms against the Cloud there's no turning back. It brings only death."

"Won't the Guard protect them?"

"Where is this man from?" asked Greylit. "Nothing is ever that easy. The Guard aren't what they used to be, I'm sorry Erneel but it's true. Their influence diminishes with each new night."

"So, what do you do then?"

"We have certain abilities, no reason to waste them."

"Mercenaries?"

"We've been called worse."

"Where are the Aushwary? We didn't see anyone when we landed."

"In hiding since the Cloud settled in. Three Aushwary have died and they called on us for protection."

"How did you get here so fast?"

"We are Holst. We are everywhere."

Manfred looked at Erneel. "How did they get the drop on us? On you?"

Erneel shrugged. "A slight miscalculation. A minor setback."

Delute laughed. "That's what the Holst do, Manny. They *get-the-drop* on folks."

"What's next then?"

"We stay here. Do what we've been paid to do. You go on and do whatever you had planned on doing," responded Greylit

"After you almost killed us. Don't you owe some help?"

"Retribution?"

"Yes."

"Believe me, boy. The Guard owes the Holst more than you'll ever know."

Greylit gave Manfred and the rest of the crew extra supplies and all of their weapons back. "Trusted you with a relic, did they?" he said as he handed Manfred back the bone. "Must be worse than I thought."

Manfred nodded nervously.

"Be careful you don't get the whole world destroyed," Greylit said. Manfred anticipated a joke or a *good luck* to follow but Greylit just gave him a stern and pensive look.

With that Greylit led them to an open room with a few beds built into the wall. He told them they could stay for the night but in the morning, they'd have to leave. Liadra and her crew had already started their work on the far side of the peninsula. One night was all they could spare.

FLOWERS AND WOLVES

They made their way into the Aushwary jungle the next day and Manfred knew that this was it—that they'd emerge on the other side, weapons and bodies at the ready, faced with some final task. He watched as Looma and Delute carved through thick leaves and branches in front of him. They were so calm and ever-playful, outdoing one another with each downed plant. Delute tore some up from their roots and Looma sliced through stocks as thick as her leg. All the while Os'halla moved behind them and picked up each plant and examined it. He'd taste each one and bring them to his nose, taking full breaths to see what rewards they hid. Erneel was mostly quiet. Occasionally small birds would drift down toward him and rest on his shoulders. He'd pet and whisper to them, hold them in his hand for a moment, then release them back into the dense jungle.

It was humid and Manfred could feel his hair curl. When he was a kid, his family spent summers on the coast. His mother and sisters like to play in the water, tackling waves and drifting under the warm sun. He'd lay next to his father and listen to him read aloud, always some manual on the local marine life. When it cooled they'd fish, rarely ever catching anything. His sisters and he always shared one of the poles and bickered and fought and laughed. The rare tug on the line was enough to put them into a frenzy. They'd dance around in the sand and call out for their dad. Manfred's hair was curly then, his skin sore from the sun. He couldn't help but smile.

"We're being followed," said Erneel.

Manfred's eyes widened and the weapon on his back began to glow. Looma and Delute slowed their pursuit of the hanging plants. Os'halla stayed back but turned to face the direction they had come.

"Not an enemy," Erneel said.

"Greylit?" Asked Delute.

"One of his men. I don't know how they ambushed us before. So loud in these trees." continued Ernie. "We'll let him catch up."

They continued, slower now, their movements hushed. Looma stopped butchering everything that came in her way and opted to push what she could to the side. They kept moving. The terrain changed below them as if it were alive, sharp ascents and descents, curves against rolling bits of decaying foliage, trees bent down, burdened by large oozing pods. Os'halla continued to poke and prod at every piece of life he could find.

They cut into a mud-slick clearing, an unlucky area that had been uncovered by the jungle's canopy. Thick muck made it necessary to walk with high knees. Erneel, unlike the rest of the crew, was able to walk without sinking. Manfred had the worst time of it, nearly losing his shoes several times. When they made it to the far side of the clearing the member of Greylit's party made himself known. It was Bealzut.

"Received permission," he called out.

"Permission for what?" Looma replied.

"To be your disciple," he said as he slowly made his way across the clearing.

Looma laughed. "I think he's talking to you, old man."

Erneel put his head down and said under his breath, "No time for this."

Bealzut made his way across the mud. He moved awkwardly and had to hold his robe up. He looked like a caricature of a rich woman in an expensive dress. A far different image from the warrior Manfred and Os'halla had just faced. When he finally caught up with them, he presented Erneel with the flower he had cut the night before.

"Saint, the cut is perfect. I have traveled the world. Challenged countless experts—Herscha the Great, the Brun King—even the Clearwater blacksmiths were no match for me. But I have never seen anything like this."

Manfred leaned in to see what was so special about the cut. It was merely ordinary, unexceptional, to say the least. He had had girlfriends, he had even bought them flowers, he knew to cut them at an angle and place them in water—add that plant food and there you have it.

"What am I missing?" asked Manfred.

Bealzut looked at him for a moment before returning his focus to Erneel. "You must take me as your student."

Erneel shook his head.

"Saint, I cannot take no for an answer."

Erneel grunted and kept walking.

"What is so special about the flower?" Manfred asked again.

"How can this man be the *Grunghek*, the relic holder. No brains at all. No sight for battle," said Bealzut without looking at Manfred.

Manfred with the relic tied to his back felt much more confident. He was still upset about the way he and Os'halla had been treated below the town. He puffed out his chest and moved toward Bealzut. Bealzut put one hand on his shoulder and showed him the flower with the other.

"Let me explain, *Grung*. Only an expert, a singular master, could cut with such grace, such delicacy. Look closely at the angle of it, the arch of separation. Do you even notice that the flower has not wilted in the slightest? It doesn't even know it has been severed from its root. Grand and perfect expertise."

As Manfred leaned in to examine it, Bealzut loosened the knot that held the relic to his back.

"Can you see it yet?" Bealzut asked and lobbed the flower to him. Manfred backed up to catch it and as he did the relic fell from his back and he tripped over it, almost knocking over Os'halla, who had caught the flower behind him.

Manfred grabbed the relic and jumped to his feet. It was glowing and taking on the shape of a framing hammer. He could feel the white-hot power of it flow through him. Bealzut cocked his head at the weapon, a look of vague interest flashed across his face, then he crossed his hands at his side and rested them on the handles of his two swords.

Looma and Delute circled back, interested to see the relic in action, especially against someone who had given Os'halla a run for his money. Os'halla wasn't interested in the fight, he had sat down and was taking great pains to examine the cut flower.

Manfred and Bealzut circled for a moment, stepping over weeds and downed tree trunks. Erneel briefly allowed it to go on before stepping between the two of them. Bealzut immediately relaxed his guard and put his arms behind his back, happy to finally have Erneel's full attention. Manfred kept pacing, red-faced.

"Greylit knows I don't take disciples. You need to return to the village. The survivors of Liadra's pack will come back once we're done. They'll have something to prove and be quite desperate. That village needs you much more than we do."

"At least allow me to fight by your side. The Holst can handle a few stragglers."

"We could use him," Delute called back. "We're walking into a whole lot of trouble."

Manfred was still upset, but Os'halla had pulled him back and was trying to show him something of the flower.

"You have no patience," Ernie said to Bealzut. "This mission requires lightness, steadiness."

"I can be patient. I will wait here until you accept me."

"I will never accept you. You may come with us but only because I know Greylit would never send me an inept and Delute is right, we need the help. But if a scratch befalls any of my men while fighting at your side, no mercenary group on this earth will accept you."

"You'll have failed the Little Saint," said Delute with a chuckle. "No man can come back from that."

Bealzut bowed his head. "I'd sooner die than allow harm in your midst, great teacher."

Erneel grunted and shook his head.

The group continued through the broken terrain. Os'halla took his own path and examined the many different exotic plants. Every so often he rejoined the group with something for them to taste or smell. One time he handed Manfred a small fruit with long slender arms that knotted around itself. Manfred hungrily took it from him but just as he brought it to his mouth the fruit came alive. It unraveled with the grotesque movements of a spider. Manfred gasped in fear and dropped it. Os'halla laughed and laughed before explaining to Manfred that the plant he was about to eat wasn't alive. It was just reacting to the warmth of his hand. The plant had evolved to spread itself out and wrap around anything providing warmth like humans and other passing animals.

Os'halla picked the fruit back up and ripped pieces off for each person. It took Manfred a while to get the courage to eat the thing. It squirmed in his hand like a squid. When he finally did, he was rewarded with cool, instant, and complete hydration. The juice of the fruit pumped a cool breath through his whole body and for a moment the colors of the world were more vibrant.

Soon the forest fell away and sand mixed in with grasses and weeds appeared below them and they knew they were close. You could taste the salt of the ocean in the air. A crimson bird landed on Erneel's shoulder and chirped in his ear.

"Liadra has more men than we thought and a few members of the Kin," he looked toward Os'halla. "It is in the valley just beyond this crest." He pointed toward a rock ledge that emerged over the jungle that remained. "We'll have a good vantage up there. I'll call on the spirits of this place for help, but there are no guarantees. It's

a lot to ask. Our enemy has the ocean to their back," Erneel continued. "No place to retreat. These men are fierce. Some hardened by
battle, committed to their cause. Others are piss-poor, recruited
by the Cloud with the promise of money, land, and adventure. It
won't take time to know who's who. They'll all fight, though, tooth
and nail." Erneel pointed at Os'halla. "You and I will deal with
your brothers. You know them better than any of us. The birds will
help scatter the rest. Work them straight down the middle. Looma
and Delute, you'll thin the herd. Once the birds and what other
spirits I can bring on board set them to chaos, you two work the
flanks. Bealzut, I don't know what you're worth, but you and Manfred will take up the rear. Anything that tries to get away will be
left to you two. Once we clear a path, the Harvestors will be yours,
Manfred. Let the relic guide you."

"What about Liadra?" Asked Delute.

"She'll be about. Best to bring her back alive, but I won't
make the same mistake again. Kill her if you have the chance,"
Erneel said. "Now, give yourselves a moment. I'll see who's
friendly around these parts." With that, Erneel sat down, worked
his breath, and chanted quietly to the canopy above.

Delute and Bealzut found a patch of grass and sparred
playfully. Looma and Manfred lounged next to a small stream.
Os'halla found a patch of grass between some trees and began
his work of calling upon the powers with which he was familiar.

"Looma," Manfred said, "Do you think I'm ready?"

Looma had one hand in the stream. "Does it matter? When
we go over that crest, there is no turning back. Ready or not,"
she said.

Manfred felt a shiver go through his body. "How did you know you were ready?"

"For what?"

"Your first battle."

She sat upright. "I was lucky. My first battle came to me. I was ambushed on a supply run outside the Drilding Desert. No time to think. No time to worry. Just fight or be buried, Bugsbee."

"What if I run?"

"You won't."

"I'm not so sure, Looma. I'm scared."

Looma pointed to her father. "That man—the great Saint of the realms, the most feared warrior this world has ever seen—is afraid of spiders."

Manfred shook his head in disbelief.

"It's true, Manny. He doesn't even dare visit the Ulis. He cowers under that web. Like a child. I've never seen anything like it."

"There's no way, Looma."

"It is the truth. Screeches like a peasant girl, he does."

Manfred laughed.

Looma nodded her head and smiled and laid back down.

Manfred stayed seated and tried his best not to run away.

As night came three large wolves appeared from the jungle. Their ears were long and pointed and their mouths were full of crooked black teeth. Bealzut was the only member of the crew alarmed by this. Although Manfred felt a knot in his stomach brought on by the unfamiliarity, he knew immediately that they were friends of Erneel.

The three animals approached Erneel as he meditated and each nuzzled against him as he opened his eyes. He pressed his face into the fur between their ears and whispered to them. Looma sat petting them and tried to pick up the conversation from her father the best she could. A massive wolf with flaxen fur at each of its paws and a curled-red streak across its eyes came over to Manfred. On all fours, it was nearly as tall as him.

"Hi," said Manfred. It pressed its nose against him a few times and almost knocked him over. Manfred looked toward Erneel for help but he was busy with the other wolves. "I'm… uh… I'm Manfred," he stuttered.

The wolf licked Manfred's arm and lightly nipped at his hair.

"Are you sure you wanna do this?" Manfred asked. "We could all die."

The wolf pressed its nose against Manfred one more time and returned to Erneel and the other wolves.

"Good friends," Erneel said as he leaned against the one that had just been with Manfred. "One of their fold was killed by the Cloud a day ago and they wish to help. Said they felt your presence," Erneel said as he looked toward Manfred.

The party moved to the top of the crest. Still hidden from the Cloud, Erneel sent a few birds to fly above and report back the exact layout.

Farthest from them on a finger of land that reached into the ocean, three Sun Harvestors stood around a glowing pool. They had already begun their ritual. They screamed like demons and pounded their chests—arrhythmic, unsettling beats. They held hands in ceremony and moved around the ever-darkening space between them.

On guard and protecting the space just in front of the Harvestors, were two of Os'halla's corrupted brothers. Their limbs hung like torturous pendulums and their bright flashing eyes scanned the world around them.

The rest of the camp laid out between them and the Harvestors. Three ragged canvas tents with smoke pouring out sheltered some of the few dozen armored men and women of the Cloud. There was a tension about them, they were anxious for battle. Some of them marched in crude formations, while others sat and sharpened their weapons.

After the birds laid out the field to Erneel, he sat with the wolves. He communicated to them in a language of movement and touch. Erneel then drew out a plan in a patch of dirt, giving everyone a direction and a place. He assured them that it wouldn't be easy, that they all might die. Everyone smiled and touched arms, each ready to dive in.

As the Relic burned in Manfred's hand, it gave him strength and balance, but he was still quite scared—still out of his depth. Os'halla and Looma did well to calm him down, joking and reminding him he held the most powerful weapon in all the realms.

"We'll do all the work," said Looma. "These men are dangerous, but they're no match for Manfred Bugsbee and the Bleak Four."

"Yes. Yes," said Os'halla. "We'll clear a path for you, my brother. As simple as that." Os'halla twirled his bo above his head. "Simple."

Erneel pulled Manfred aside moments before he gave the first orders to attack.

"How do you feel, ole boy?"

Manfred shook his head. "Scared, Ernie, that's all."

"It is good to be scared." Ernie knocked his hand against the Relic. "This here is in good hands, my friend. Just stay back, out of the way, until there is an opening. The Holst will protect you."

"How will I know when it's time?"

"You will know."

As they spoke a war horn sounded from the enemy camp. There was no more waiting. Erneel patted Manfred on the back one more time and ordered the first wave of attacks.

IN BLOOD

The birds were the first wave. A chaotic display of heroics. The smaller ones acted as diversion and reconnaissance. They'd dive straight at the helmeted faces of Liadra's troops then veer away at the last second. This left many of the lesser warriors sprawled out on the ground and gave Erneel and the rest a view of the weaker sections of their force. The small birds continued their assault as the larger ones entered the fold. Their talons and beaks ripped at whatever was in reach. Some threw themselves into the fire pits and went out like momentary phoenixes, flying the best they could while aflame and stuck with arrows. They flew into the dry grass and lit it on fire. Quickly the scene turned to hell.

The clamor of it was like nothing Manfred had ever heard. Battle cries and the wails of fear mixed with the heckling and shrieks of the birds. The fire popped and hissed and bodies scattered back and forth, swinging their swords in all directions, creating deathly whistles in the humid air.

The wolves were next. Looma rode one of the larger ones, howling as if she were one of them. Her hair flowed in the gusts of war, dipping and waving in fluttering beauty. The hounds crashed through the center of the enemy horde. Larger than life, they took no time carving what they could to bits. Looma rolled toward a dizzy, weak flank and pushed them toward death, either into the flapping jaws of the wolves or the growing flames. Those she couldn't direct, she engaged, slicing and bashing, her face quickly becoming a mess of blood and dirt—caked in the carnage, a nightmare warrior manifest.

Delute advanced with her and the wolves. He careened on all fours, a mammalian wrecking ball, ripping and tearing into the other flank. He tanked off the limbs of what he could and threw them into the air and bellowed forth, the blades on his hands making ribbons of his foes. The enemy seemed to gravitate toward him. Even as they tried to run, the calamity of his movements sucked them in. Once in his orbit, there was no escaping their mutilation. Manfred forced himself to watch as the horrors of war unfolded.

The enemy forces that tried to run had nowhere to go. Manfred and Bealzut stood guard at the only escape route. These were the bottom rung of Liadra's fleet, supplied with used armor and rusted half-weapons. Men and women who had turned to the Cloud for easy work, a chance for adventure, and a sense of power, often driven out of their hometowns. Many were cold-blooded killers, murderous outcasts whose only skills were blind lust. Many were far too young to have their fates sealed, but here their lives were cut short. Soon becoming nothing but food for the vultures.

A man in tattered chainmail came up the hill toward Manfred, the first of many. Both his ears were bleeding from the bird attacks and he had lost his weapon. He was a round-faced adolescent. Manfred's stomach ached as he realized the boy was crying. All of the strength he had from the relic seeped out of him. Manfred was about to run when another of the Cloud hit the boy in the head with a hammer. The boy crumpled to the ground and another cried out, "Deserter," and stepped over the body toward Manfred.

There was no more time for remorse. The itch of the relic returned and Manfred could do nothing but attack. Bealzut stood in front and protected him the best he could, his weapons moving in stripes of blood.

Erneel and Os'halla held off. They watched from the crest. The Kin remained outside the battle, swatting away members of the Cloud that tried to escape toward the ocean, a final obstacle before the Harvestors. Erneel knew waking them too early would be a death blow. His men were doing fine, animals and all, but they had mostly only dealt with cannon fodder.

Os'halla rocked back and forth against his bo, eager to help his friends. He had never seen a corrupted Kin in the flesh. He had only ever heard stories of their terrible bodies. One moment they had been transcendent beings attuned to the greatest secrets of nature, then plucked out of the ground like rigid weeds, their placid minds were replaced with the war horns of the Cloud. The balance of the Kin worked for many, the center path, but for some, it forced a fragile equilibrium, so easily and dangerously put off.

A direct line opened and Erneel nodded to Os'halla. A moment longer and the line would have disappeared any sooner and they'd be sucked into the margins of war.

The Kin were more developed than the one Manfred had seen when he first entered the realm. Where that one was mostly a spindly creature, like an uprooted sapling, these two were heavy trunked demons. They had the thick skin of whitebark, solid, and in the shape of scales. One was shaped much like a human with two legs and arms, and a knotted head twenty feet above the field. The other was more like a god of the ancient east—six arms formed around its midsection. In the distance this tactical disfigurement was unseen. The abomination had held its arms close to its body. Immediately on entering the battle, it released them—the blossoming of a horrific flower.

Erneel directed Os'halla toward the lesser and made a low stance in front of the many-limbed beast.

The limbs made the beast unbalanced to the benefit and hindrance of both sides. It wiped out two of its party and one of the large wolves in a lumbering turn of its body. The wolf's spine broke like a toothpick as the creature bowled it through a mass of warriors.

After its clumsy entrance, the Kin made itself into a steadier shape. Its legs and three of its arms pushed down against the ground while the other arms raised in preparation to smash Erneel and whatever else he could get in its grasp.

Os'halla faced the smaller of the Kin and it recognized him as a brother.

"Far from home?" came a voice from somewhere in its belly.

Os'halla drummed his bo against the ground. "The Kin is always home."

Without warning the Kin attacked, its body an angular weapon. Os'halla stayed as far back as he could and used the tip of his bo to find breaks in the flesh of the beast. It was a dance that he could not lead. All he could do was allow the Kin to throw him away from the rest of the battle and try to open a path for Manfred.

Erneel moved in half circles in front of the other beast, its stone-shaped face following him crookedly as it pressed its body closer and closer to the ground. Erneel's movements were rhythmic. He knew the beast's first attack would be direct. Knowing that the Kin were mostly untrained, instinctive, he wanted to create unbalance. When the beast finally did lunge, it used the force of its limbs that had been pressed against the ground. As it charged, it threw every appendage straight at Erneel, and his earlier movements paid off. It directed its body at where Erneel should have been, but he feinted and was able to slice through one of its arms before jumping to its back. He held Rocinallia around the beast's thick neck and had control for a split second. The beast shook into a violent frenzy and tried everything to pull him off. It slapped its long arms at him and swung its whole body against the ground. Erneel struggled the best he could to counter the weight of the angry thing, their fight quickly turning into an awful, blood-slick mess.

As the lesser trained of Liadra's force began to thin and run for the hills, her more skilled warriors began to show their strength. None were as intensely trained as Erneel and the rest, or lucky, in Manfred's case, but they had numbers and it showed in the field. A spear had taken Looma's ear clean off and a wild kick had worked to close her right eye. She was able to slow the blood loss as Bealzut lent her cover, but had no time to catch her breath. Delute's sutured injury from the battle in the Bleak had begun to throb and some of the more experienced enemies took to aiming for it in hopes to reopen any advantage. All the while, both sides were forced to dodge the Kin as Os'halla and Erneel attempted to dismantle them.

Of the four only one wolf remained, the others having fought bravely and sent many of Liadra's forces running toward the sea, but when its brother was killed by the giant Kin the last wolf lost heart and dragged him back into the trees. Birds still occasionally crashed into the battle, with less frequency and far less strategy, even occasionally attacking the members they wished to help. The battlefield was quickly thick with blood and feathers, discarded limbs from Delute's frenzy, and ever-shifting flames that erupted and flagged from side-to-side.

The relic glowed orange in Manfred's hands and had taken on the shape of a longsword. It was perfect for creating distance between him and the enemy. None of them dared step to him directly, only taking sideswipes and attempts from behind. The relic created a great awareness in him and with that, he was able to turn and cross anything that meant to do him harm. The blade itself felt tied to him, penetrating his bones, guiding him with a warrior's mind of some time past. Meanwhile, a clear path to the Harvestors was being cemented. Erneel and Os'halla wrestled with the large beasts and sacrificed any tactical advantage they had to move the Kin out of Manfred's way.

As soon as an opening revealed itself Manfred charged the Harvestors. There was an electric hum in the air—the static before the cataclysm. The Harvestors were still a hundred paces in front of him when Liadra appeared, her face not yet dirtied from the carnage, a fresh scar across her brow.

"Not so quick, errand boy." She rushed Manfred with two blades of war above her. She knocked them together and sparks fell over her face. He knew the relic would not be enough. Every time he blocked an attack he felt the continuity of the relic skip, reverting his mind to the docile hiccup it had been back home. He tried to focus between strikes, but she knew that persistence was key and laid blow after blow. She separated his weight, disconnected his feet from his hands, his hands from the weapon, and his mind from the battle. She was constantly two and three steps ahead of him. Her steady eyes and wind-chapped face were all Manfred could see. He had built her up so much. From the first moment he saw her in the desert, he was terrified of her. And that even Ernie approached her with caution meant very few others, if any, could defeat her. Yet, she was only human, a fanatic, yes, but just a person. And her humanity, her small, almost fragile-looking face, scared him now more than anything. More than the Kai Va, more than Os'halla's fallen brothers.

She lured him into an opening painfully obvious, but he was so outwitted that when she presented her neck for the chopping, he swung with all his might. She dodged his attack and his weapon slammed into the ground and shook him to the soles of his feet. Before he could regain his footing, she kicked him hard in the hand. He heard and felt three fingers break and the relic fell and returned to its form of bone. She kicked him again, this time in the face. His teeth cracked down on his tongue and his mouth filled with blood.

Manfred laid on the ground, sprawled out as if in the comfort of a nap. He felt just fine except for the taste of iron at the back of his throat. He thought about how long it had been since he had tasted French fries. There was a small diner just below his apartment building that served discounted milkshakes every Thursday. It was his go-to for dates. There was a woman who started working at the coffee shop he went to on Friday mornings before work. Days before Erneel dragged him into this mess he had broken the ice with her. He had wanted to buy her a chocolate milkshake. He had wanted to kiss her and smell her hair.

"The Harvestors. The Harvestors." Manfred could hear Delute yelling. He sounded so far away. "The Harvestors."

Manfred turned his head and the daydream lifted. Delute was wrestling with Liadra. She was yelling as he headbutted her and called out to Manfred. "Go, Manny. Go."

Manfred rolled to his feet and grabbed the relic. His right hand was rendered useless by Liadra's kick so he used his left. The relic still glowed but didn't change from its original form. He spit out a few teeth and hacked up blood, but kept moving. His bottom lip was cut open from the inside. He ran. The electric buzz of the Harvestors grew and grew until he felt like he was in the middle of it. The relic remained unchanged as he came within steps of his goal. The Harvestors were chanting and breathing heavily from their stomachs. They yelled and pounded their weapons against the ground.

Manfred's destiny was in front of him. The Harvestors wicked magic that Kaseen had tried to explain, that he had seen a version of himself confront in the Keeper's Den, was little more than three naked men standing around a black, reflective tide pool. He could feel its energy. He felt their power pulse with every guttural chant and phantasmal movement. They were human bodies for certain, but affixed to their practice by way of some spectral evil. Their unshadowed bodies were hyper-focused on their task as if they were alone and their magic was the entire universe.

He looked back over his shoulder as Liadra's sword cut clean through Delute's leg. Severed from the knee, he fell forward. Manfred yelled and took a step back toward his friend when one of the Harvestors broke rank and engaged him.

"He returns," the Harvestor said through clenched teeth. He was taller than Manfred, skinny and malnourished in the face. His cheekbones jutted out and stretched his gnarled skin. Quivering veins crept under his eyes and nose. Naked except for ornamental jewelry around his neck and waist, a mess of small bones tied together with coarse hair. His body was covered in black blood and earth.

Manfred's eyes were on the Harvestor but his mind was behind him. He could hear Looma screaming. Different from her growling war cry, some all-powerful rage seeped out of her every pore. He wanted to look back, to run back, but the eyes of the Harvestor kept him—small round windows, glazed over with hard focus, unblinking.

"Too late," the Harvestor said. "Your earth. Your friends. Your life. Be gone." The Harvestor struck itself on the head with its free hand. A line of blood appeared and he laughed. The other hand held its weapon, the length of his arm, a pointed spear, from rock or bone. Sharp things were netted in and around it, some rusted barbed wire, teeth, and hollow bones. The Harvestor shook it in Manfred's face and out rattled an unearthly melody.

The relic remained the same in shape but began to change in weight. Manfred could feel it grow heavier and heavier as the center of the earth tugged on it. In two quick motions, Manfred had the Harvestor on the ground. He knocked the weapon from his hand then struck up under his jaw and laid him out. Manfred mounted his fallen enemy and in three heavy strikes collapsed his skull, sending particles of brain and blood into the air around them.

The relic grew even heavier as the next Harvestor approached, leaving the strange black pool to be manned by only one. The Harvestor attacked but its advance was cut short and with very little effort. Manfred grabbed its face and twisted—its neck broken, its brain unhinged from its heart.

The last Harvestor kept to its duties of chanting into the abyss. Once Manfred was upon him the relic became so heavy that he could no longer hold it. It fell from his hand and was pulled into the center of the dark pool. Manfred's body felt weak and defeated, but he grabbed the Harvestor and turned toward him in confrontation. The Harvestor seemed to look through him, his mouth hanging open as if surprised by Manfred's presence, oblivious to the battle that waged around him.

The two of them locked arms. The Harvestors' weapon was made useless by Manfred's proximity. They clawed and twisted in struggle, every free arm latched on to another, every opening met with a fingernail or tooth. Manfred's broken hand begged for him to stop. There was no stopping. The Harvestor was much stronger than Manfred, but Manfred did well to reduce leverage and movement. Every step back the Harvester took, Manfred followed and kept him in an embrace. He aimed his chin into the Harvestor's eyes and collarbone, trying to make every movement, every strike painful.

The dance lasted a short time. The Harvestor finally broke free, enough space to bring his weapon down across Manfred's back. The spines of the small spear tore into Manfred's flesh and sprawled him out. He tucked himself into the fetal position, blood spurting from his back. He groaned in small sputters as the Harvestor returned to his operation and flung the blood from his spear into the growing darkness of his magic. Manfred managed to roll to his back. Birds flew down to help but were repelled by some unseen energy, their feathers and beaks pushed back in frenetic sparks.

Even though he was no longer holding the relic, he could feel its presence. The intense weight of it still pulled down on him, melding through his bones. The deep cuts in his back and his broken fingers radiated with its energy. He could see light coming from it, a pulsing coal over flames. Manfred had no idea what was going on on the battlefield. He didn't know that Os'halla and Erneel had overpowered the Kin, tangled them up like melted wax, that most of Liadra's forces had hightailed back into the island's interior, others trying to swim out to sea. He didn't know that Looma and Bealzut had Liadra cornered, and it was taking everything in Looma's power not to kill her. He didn't know his friend Delute had taken one final breath of saltwater air—all he knew was he had to get to the relic.

In one great heave, tapping into a reserve of strength hidden even from himself, Manfred threw his body onto the relic and the pool above where the Harvestor stood. On touching it Manfred was overcome with its coldness as if he'd been submerged in a frozen lake. He could hear his parents calling out from the ocean, his sisters laughing at him as he was knocked over by waves. He screamed as his body began to burn, white-hot agony poured out from his organs, from each and every cell in his body, the blinding heat swirling inside of him until it spilled out into the world in vibrations. Everything turned white—pitched toward the sun. His screams turned into a dry howl as he felt his skin melt away.

Manfred looked into the small pool, worn into the edge of the ocean, and time collapsed. He could see his earth, human faces flashing on flexing circles. Pale eyes sunken in—all framed in desolation, full of fear and brimming with horrors. He screamed out a warning. "The world is dying." Flowers wilted and grass turned to ash on hilltops. Hysteria and war broke out at each corner of his cooling earth. Leaders and peasants pointed their dying fingers at their dying sun, their tears turning into oceans and their oceans filling with blood.

The pool turned and twisted in metallic ripples, its colors colliding and folding in on one another. Waves of it splashed against Manfred's face and as it did, other realms came into view. Dead worlds in states of decompose engulfed him—the smell of charred remains filling his mouth. The entrails of melting bodies burst out in all corners of Manfred's new reality. His body arched in pure agony. Wailing-dying children cried out for mercy, choking on viscera and soot. Their fingers filed down to nubs as they scraped at the ice and stone. Manfred's eyes and ears pressed in on his skull, his teeth begining to crack—his tongue lapping at gallons of blood and the bile conjured up from his stomach.

Pain. Ultimate. A thousand worlds and countless lives were deconstructed in each sinew of his body.

A high-pitched, unearthly sound emanated from where Manfred touched the relic. Folds of violent wind shot out and shook the earth around him, forcing him back to himself. The Harvestor was engulfed by the reaction—its atoms torn apart and its body disappearing into a coral mist. Nothing was left but drops of dew and floating flakes of charcoal. The pain from before that somehow had lasted infinitely now lasted barely half a breath. A new feeling replaced the anguish. Whatever poured out of the relic and the pool below him found the spaces in his body that needed work. The deep punctures covering his back, his hand, and jaw were filled with a force of healing. An amber warmth laid over him and soothed his every ache.

The ocean pool and the relic disappeared in a burst of light and Manfred was left shaking on the ground, surrounded by a cloak of energy. He stumbled out of the cloud of dust and electricity. All of his clothes had been burned off and his naked body was hunched over in exhaustion. His hair was powdered with ash and coagulated blood, his mind blank. A sense of relief was all that pulled him forward. He grabbed a bloody scrap of armor from the ground to cover himself where he could.

"Their magic, boy?" Erneel yelled from across the battlefield. He too was covered in blood and stood next to heaps of the enemy force. It looked like he was holding on to one of them but Manfred couldn't tell.

Manfred nodded his head and presented the only sign that came to mind, a thumbs up. It felt good and heroic.

Near the waterline the twisted shape of one of the lost Kin was sprawled out, its body still fidgeting, caked in the tar of its blood. Sap oozed from it in slow gobs. Once a leviathan of terror, now only a breathless monument to their battle. Manfred couldn't see the other but he knew it too was gone. To Manfred, it felt like hundreds of corpses stretched back from the beachhead into the jungle. He had never seen so much carnage in his life and it multiplied in his head, the adrenaline lifting from his body as the viscera of war revealed itself. He fell to his knees and vomited.

RITUALS OF LIFE

Through watery eyes, he saw Looma kneeling next to something. It was Delute—unmoving. A ship in the desert. Manfred made his way over and bent down next to the two. Looma put her hand on his back and leaned her head into his and began to cry. Even though he felt certain his body had been drained of all energy, and that tears would be a great miracle, he knelt sobbing over his dead friend.

Os'halla and Bealzut stood nearby, completely silent. They knew that their words could do nothing but harm. Os'halla knelt too and touched them both in a quiet embrace. The light of the sun rested on the sea as their hearts broke.

Erneel dragged Liadra toward them by the hair. She was a mess of silence and gore—shallow breaths barely escaped her gaping mouth.

Looma stood and looked her father in the eyes and said in a near whisper, "We kill her. We kill her right now."

Erneel shook his head.

"For his earth?" Looma cried out and pointed down at Manfred.

"For the realms, Looma," he replied, his voice unsure.

Looma spat at Liadra.

"We need to know what's left."

"She comes home under your protection, and Delute?" Looma whimpered. "And Delute doesn't come home at all? That is what the Guard wants?"

"I have fought beside him since before you were born. He protected your mother during the Black Peril. He's my oldest friend, Looma." Erneel's face scrunched into a sad, small shape for a moment and he turned away. "I'm sorry."

Erneel tied Liadra to a sturdy tree and left her with Manfred. Looma and Erneel gathered bark and thick grass from their surroundings to start the burial rites. Os'halla convinced Bealzut to help gather the bodies of their fallen enemies. Manfred sat between Delute and Liadra.

"Why?" Manfred asked, almost to himself. "Delute was kind. He was a good man." He wanted to cry, but couldn't. "It should have been you—I should have stopped you." He held Liadra's face in his hands. Her eyes were glazed over and swelling up in bruised, vibrant patterns. Manfred felt a moment of sadness pull through him and then rage. He punched her in the nose as hard as he could. It didn't feel how he expected, a slight resistance, and then her nose gave way to mush. She let out a labored, painful grunt.

"I'm sorry," he said and the tears finally began to flow. "I'm sorry." He forced himself to look at her. It was impossible to tell how old she was. In the desert Manfred had assumed she was his age, only having led a harsher life. Now, she looked so old. There was an innocence in her fragility, the way each breath slowly rolled out of her, like a newborn in the first struggles of life—a contradiction.

"Look at me. Open your eyes. Look at me," he was yelling now, unintelligible. It was as if she wasn't there. Nothing existed in that body—no pain, no sorrow—just enough breath to keep the soul trapped, and no matter how loud Manfred yelled, or how hard he pulled on her, there would be no reaction. He sat between the two bodies, one hand resting on the cheek of Delute and the other gripped in the bloodied hair of Liadra.

By the time Looma and Erneel had returned, Manfred had fallen asleep. Exhaustion he had never felt before washed over him and he was hollow to the world around him. When he opened his eyes, Looma and Erneel stood over him. They carried large bundles of bark and flowers.

"Delute was born under the sign of Marrest," Erneel said. "And so he will be set free by that sign. Will you help us, Manfred?"

Manfred nodded.

Looma and Erneel laid out what they had brought— orange flowers with large spade-shaped petals and small black flowers that looked like bunches of balloons. They also had loose pieces of bark, thick grass, and yellowing weeds, all to be joined together with a rich smelling sap from some of the trees around them.

Manfred watched silently as the other two undressed Delute. They washed him the best they could, using canteens they had pulled off of the dead men to carry the salt water. Looma let out a guttural cry when she saw the wound that had killed him. A hole flapped over with skin that went all the way through his chest, just below his heart.

Once they had scrubbed away the blood and dirt, they wrapped him in the things they had gathered and took great pains not to make eye contact with one another. Occasionally they'd reach a hand out toward one another in a gesture of understanding and hold each other's fingers, or caress a shoulder, each doing their best to hold back their tears. Slowly Manfred joined in.

First, they wrapped him tightly in bark and grass, covering everything except his face. Next, they took the pungent sap and handfuls of flowers and pressed them into the shroud. There was no pattern to it, Manfred just followed the movements of his two friends and they made the body beautiful.

Delute's face was left uncovered and Erneel used chalk from soft, powdery white stones and charcoal to draw symbols above Delute's eyelids and cheeks—small bird shapes on the large quiet face. Erneel kissed the dead man's eyes as he worked and etched out a story on his old friend. He whispered things into his ears and pressed his cheek against his forehead. Erneel's voice was inaudible, but the ocean seemed to break each time he leaned in and gently crash with every word.

After sealing the bark underneath Delute, Ernie made a small torch. The three of them then pulled Delute's body near to the ocean. It didn't need to be explained to Manfred that that was where he'd be laid to rest. Delute may well have been a fish or a bird at sea. The ocean was calm as it coaxed its friend in as if telling him and the rest that it would be okay, that Delute would be taken care of. Manfred parted ways and let Looma and Erneel continue without him. He returned to the shore and watched as the three of them continued into the ocean until the water was up to Erneel's neck. They kissed their friend one more time before Ernie touched the torch to Delute's feet and the tide pulled him out to sea.

Erneel, Looma, and Manfred stood on the shore holding hands and watched for as long as they could see the flame. In a sudden swell of fire, Delute's body erupted on the horizon. Looma cried out and Erneel fell to the ground. Their friend was free from the bonds of life and allowed to turn to smoke and ash and rest in the ocean's depths.

They sat at the water's edge and watched the smoke disappear. Manfred helped Erneel to his feet and they left Looma alone. She wanted to stay until there was nothing left, to keep her friend as close as possible for as long as possible. Delute was like her brother. He had taught her to fight before her father had. When she was young, Erneel wanted nothing more for her to be a farmer or to work with Saylu in politics. But Delute couldn't deny the fight in her, the purity of discipline and skill she had been born with. As she sat, she felt a cold she had never felt before. Erneel covered her with a blanket but it did little to find warmth for her.

Manfred, Erneel, and Bealzut took to setting up camp. They went through the tents of the Cloud to find what was useful. They started a fire and picked at scraps of food. Bealzut was mostly quiet but informed Erneel that the Holst could help them get back home, that they had ways. Erneel thanked him and told him that he did well in the fight, that the Guard could use men like him. Unmoved and stone-faced, Bealzut struggled to conceal his excitement.

All the while, Os'halla prepared for another burial rite next to the large pile of bodies that Bealzut had helped stack. They formed the pile on a patch of dry earth. It was a gruesome scene. The bodies of the Cloud were mucked over, coagulated in blood, their faces all stretched out in final gasps. Os'halla asked to be alone and meditated on his head in front of the bodies. Tears ran down his forehead as he took steady breaths and hummed from his stomach.

Manfred watched Os'halla's ritual in bits and pieces as he helped Erneel with the camp. Patches of grass popped up around the bodies. The blood of the deceased took on the form of a great nutrient in the barren area. The process moved slowly, but the nature in which Manfred watched made it even more astonishing. He would check in every so often as the sun moved across the sky. The grass grew in inches. Each time he looked, the bodies were more covered. The budding grass and fetid carnage struggled for space and the grass was winning. Butterflies and small bees appeared in waves. They sat down on the corpses and hopped from limb to blade of grass. Flowers sprouted from the eye sockets and wounds of the dead and in only a few hours the mound had changed. Although the limbs of the fallen were still visible and made for a grisly altar, there was a beauty to it, a restfulness to the flower-covered enemies' bodies.

Looma didn't leave the ocean's side until the moon had risen and there was no sign left of the sun. All but Os'halla sat around a large fire. They drank wine, all quiet, unblinking. They ate out of necessity—the dry bitter rations of their enemies, tasting all the more bitter. Occasionally they would all adjust as if on cue, to remind one another they still existed, that the fire hadn't become all that was left of reality.

Bealzut was the first to go to sleep. He stood up and apologized in a whisper that no one heard. Erneel was next. Hard to say if he went to sleep, rather, he stood and leaned on Rocinallia for a while then headed into the woods. Manfred moved to ask where he was going, but Looma shook her head.

"I'm sorry Looma," Manfred said, the burden of stillness still too heavy.

She let out a full-bodied sigh. "You don't believe in silence, do you?"

Manfred was embarrassed, but she was right. He never had enough willpower for silence. "Delute was kind to me from the start. He didn't treat me like an outsider."

"But you are," Looma said, never looking away from the fire.

Manfred stood up and paced. "I said I was sorry, Looma. He was my friend, too. I don't want to be here. I don't want any of this."

"Shut up. He wasn't your friend. He was my brother. Now he's dead. Dead for *your* earth."

"I was dragged into this, Looma. I didn't ask for any of it."

Looma only nodded her head.

"Please. I am so sorry I couldn't save him."

She stood up. "Shut up. I don't blame you, no one blames you. This isn't your fight. The Guard," she said through clenched teeth, "is worthless. They put out fires, they push back against the Cloud, but it doesn't matter. They all cross their fingers on the myth, the hope, of your birthright, Mindiidus." She smiled and spit into the fire. "I am sorry you were dragged into this. I'm sorry that *my* friend is dead. I'm sorry *you* talk so much." She grabbed him by the chest and pulled him close. "Now leave me alone." She stifled her anguish and disappeared into the night, taking with her what was left of the wine.

Morning came quickly and with little sleep. Looma was standing out by the ocean. Bealzut helped Erneel pack what they could salvage for the journey home. Os'halla was the only one sitting. He was exhausted and sat in front of what was left of the fire.

Manfred looked down to the place Os'halla had been working the night before. A beautiful hill of flowers and tall grass was all that was left of his ritual. Manfred walked down to examine it closer. Bees worked in a frenzy on the fresh plants. Flutters of wind moved the new shape like a single organism. It waved and turned itself in a dance. Not until he got within a few feet was he reminded of its origins. It reeked of rotting flesh. Although beautiful, the smell was so repugnant he couldn't get any closer.

"What is that?" Manfred asked.

"Life," Os'halla responded quietly.

"Life?"

Os'halla nodded his head.

"What becomes of the dead?" Manfred asked as he looked out toward the ocean.

"A return. Our friend Delute hasn't gone anywhere in particular, rather, he has returned to everything. Not bound, not stuck, he is released. Our friend. Released."

"His spirit?"

"Spirit is nature. Nothing solid. Nothing connected. All solid and all connected. He has only left one vessel for the next."

Manfred put his arm over Os'halla's shoulder and sat with him.

Os'halla pointed to the place where he stacked the bodies. "The work of the Kin. Not easy to help in the transition." He then pointed toward the ocean. "You and Ernie and Looms did well in sending him off. The ocean craved him and he, the ocean. Life is hard, newfriend. Hard." Os'halla closed his eyes and quickly fell into deep thought.

They took their time getting back to the Aushwary village. It was a somber journey. Os'halla and Bealzut stayed in the back. The other three took turns dragging Liadra. She was able to walk, but that was about it. She didn't speak and looked to be hardly breathing at times. Erneel had patched her up and given her a few stitches, the minimum requirements so she wouldn't bleed out.

Manfred looked at her often when he wasn't tasked with pulling her and felt the tinge of empathy. Wasn't she someone's daughter? Didn't she also have a life, a family? These feelings were made easy by her state. She wasn't constantly laughing or speaking in diabolical squeaks. She was just a pale, defeated thing, not even fully human. He tried to imagine a different version of her. Back in the desert, her eyes had held a momentary kindness—a blip of something. That was just before she slaughtered his horse. He couldn't help but wonder what could create such abject cruelty.

"What will we do with her, Ernie?" Manfred asked.

"The guard will have some questions for her. Then she dies."

Looma clapped her hands together in joy on hearing her father's judgment.

"Just like that?" asked Manfred.

"This is war, Manfred. She sealed her fate by bringing those Harvestors to this island. Bringing countless other dangers too."

"She sealed her fate killing Delute," Looma said and tugged on the rope that secured her.

"Didn't she save you in the Bleak?" Asked Manfred.

Looma shot him a cold look and Erneel replied, "She saved herself, Manfred. You can't still be that stupid."

Manfred put his head down and kept moving. He wanted to escape the realities of war. The death of good men, the death of justice. It was all too heavy. They made their way back to the Aushwary village where Greylit and a few of his men received them.

"I'm sorry that we didn't intervene, Erneel. You know our rules," said Greylit as they met.

Erneel nodded his head. "We'll need a place to lay our heads. We'll need food. In the morning we leave."

Greylit nodded to his men and they led the way into the village. It was still quiet, but some of the people had come out of hiding. They lined the streets and watched Erneel and his crew. Some ran out to touch and thank him, but he refused their gestures—turning them away with a grunt and a scornful gaze.

The small band of warriors, and their prisoner, were brought to a small ornate house in the center of the village. It was a different type of structure from the rest, tedious and human, clearly an aesthetic monument amongst the tall windswept buildings that surrounded it. A square, two-story building with white marbled columns under the pitch of a dark black roof. Standing in front of the only entrance was a plump woman.

She was middle-aged with dark, colorfully adorned hair that curled over her heavy cheeks and along her thick neck. She was elegant and her movements were graceful and spry as she bowed to each of the warriors.

"Erneel, the great Shepherd," she said and bowed to him lower than she had to anyone else. "It has been a long time since the Guard has come this way. Has it not?"

Erneel nodded his head. "Aye."

"It seems our world is falling apart," she said. "But I'm sure it's nothing new to you. Seems that the great wars never really end."

Erneel shook his head. "I'm afraid not, Shaleest. I am sorry that your people have been dragged in once again."

She touched his shoulder. "The price we pay for remaining on the sidelines, I'm afraid. Only some truly respect our neutrality. I'm sorry for the loss of your friend. I realize you had a mission, another reason for being here, but his death will be remembered by my people as a defense of all of us. No doubt a great warrior."

Erneel touched her hand on his shoulder. "A good man," he said.

"You'll be staying here tonight," she said as she turned and waved her hands at the building in front of them. With her back now facing them, she asked, "And your prisoner, will she cause any issues?"

"She's barely alive," Erneel assured.

As they made their way into the building, Manfred leaned into Looma and asked, "Great Shepherd?"

Looma looked at him lazily and yanked on Liadra's rope. "My father is many things. Long before I was born, he brought the Aushwary and the Guard together for a brief period. The union was short-lived, but people remember it."

Shaleest opened the doors in front of them and gestured for them to enter. The first room was a small banquet hall. Food had already been put out and a few members of the household greeted them and offered drinks and places to sit. Erneel tied Liadra to a post in the corner. The crew ate and drank while Shaleest and a few others waited on them.

"It hasn't been this bad in quite some time," said Shaleest as she poured Erneel more wine.

Ernie nodded.

"Who's the prisoner?" she asked.

Ernie held the cup in front of himself and thought for a while. "Daughter of the Bone King."

Looma let out a laugh.

"The Bone King? He led the Cloud for nearly a century," Shaleest said. "Through a time of peace, even."

"Peace?" Looma said.

"Relative," Shaleest responded. "Quiet. Nothing like this. They say their armies knock at your door. That it's inevitable."

"War," Looma said and looked at Liadra.

"Bigger than we've seen in my lifetime." Shaleest continued, "Does it end here, Erneel?"

"Afraid not," Erneel replied, contemplating his cup. "The Harvestors are only a piece of the puzzle. Fenk and our armies are spread into almost every known region."

"Do you know how the Bone King died?" Looma asked.

Shaleest nodded. "Killed in the Citadel, right? By the Saint himself."

Looma nodded. "But do you know how?" She stood up and walked toward Liadra.

"That's enough, Looma," Erneel said.

"No, no," Looma insisted. "The Bone King came to the village to negotiate a treaty. Came in good faith. Came with less than a dozen men. The Guard let him in, treated him as an equal. Remember?"

Erneel looked at Looma.

"Of course you remember. He nearly killed you. Nearly killed Yarley. Nearly gained access to the Ulis." Looma knelt in front of Liadra with a cup of wine. "That day my father killed yours. He struck out his eyes and knocked his liar's tongue right down his throat. The Bone King erased with a turn of the great blade, Rocinallia." Looma slowly poured her wine over Liadra's head. "And you'll die. Like your father. Like your men. All for nothing."

"Enough," shouted Erneel.

Looma drank what was left of her wine.

"You all must be so tired," Shaleest said, trying to relieve the tension.

Ernie nodded and made his way toward Shaleest. "Please come visit the village when this is all over. You know how beautiful it can be."

The two of them hugged and Shaleest gathered her people and left.

Looma sat in front of Liadra. "I'll take watch tonight," she said.

Ernie shook his head.

"I'm not going to kill her," she said. "You have my word."

Ernie didn't take his eyes off of her.

"You don't trust me?"

"With life itself, my dear. Take watch."

Os'halla and Bealzut had gone to bed sometime earlier and now Erneel and Manfred retired.

Looma paced the room.

Static electricity settled in Manfred's room and woke him when it fizzled at his ears. At first, he didn't move, afraid that if he did, a terrible shock would erupt from his stomach. He remembered feeling this way as a child. After his mother tucked him in and kissed his forehead, he would lay awake and stare at the ceiling while a buzz worked its way through his bones. He could never explain it, like some struggle against tiredness—a frenetic anxiety. He'd call out for help and his father would come in, tea in hand, and sing to back him to sleep. He thought of calling out for Looma.

When the feeling subsided, he crawled out of bed. The banquet hall was quiet and Liadra and Looma slept in a corner. Liadra was secure at the post with the chains and rope, her breath shallow. She didn't look like she'd make it through the night. Looma was out cold, one hand gripping her weapon and the other tangled in Liadra's hair.

He stood outside and watched a storm build over the jungle, splinters of light darting from cloud to cloud under illuminated sheets of rain. The static in his bones started up again and just as it did an oddity occurred. At first, he thought it was a trick of exhaustion, but it happened again and again. Where each lightning bolt should have faded into nothingness, they remained. It was as if the plate of the universe had been dropped and shattered. Schisms of dark and light spread out above him and a great exhale built up from the ground and crashed against the cracking sky. Perfect squares and circles manifested and hovered in the darkness far beyond his reach. Somehow, both solid and not, they vibrated and shrieked like glaciers falling into the sea. He tried to run back into the house, but the terrors unfolding had him transfixed.

The sky had gone from a beautiful storm of stars and clouds to an awful and complex puzzle. Bright colors connected all around him. He yelled to anyone that could hear, "What's happening to me?" No one answered. Whatever was coming created itself from the air in his lungs. It pulled from the heavens and from his chest the essence of its existence. Then in a flash, it all returned to normal. The sky bowed back to the near, complete dark of night, the moon just visible above the roiling, distant clouds.

As he caught his breath and tried to make sense of what had just happened, a being of intense luminescence descended upon him. It was not the shape of a human, instead, it drifted between two and three-dimensional forms. At moments it looked like a pair of mutilated conjoined hands—the fingers moving to scratch at the palm. The objects never stayed the same. A hand in one instance would bend in innumerable folds and reveal a new swirling mass of shapes. It seemed to be creating itself rather than moving—existing in one corporeal state and then another, untying and manifesting reality in sometimes fluid sometimes stuttered steps. It made its way over and through the structures of the village. Manfred couldn't move—the electricity in his bones fastening him to where he stood.

The shape moved ever closer, constantly shifting from a paper-thin intangible flat to extensions inconceivable to the human eye. He cowered in fear. The thing, whatever it was, filled his veins and the depths of his consciousness with ice and dread. It was miles and inches away from him all at once. He removed his hands from over his eyes to watch, resigned to its ubiquity.

The thing hovered over him and moved along with his breath. Shutters of light made up some form of a body that appeared to blink in and out of existence. Manfred sat up and tried to get a better look. From what he could tell, it seemed to partly exist in his mind. As he looked at it, it revealed itself to be both a pinprick at the edge of his universe and the whole of the world around him. He felt it get closer and closer to his face until it pressed against the small hairs of his nose. Then there was a flash of white light and the thing moved past him into the building.

Manfred pulled himself to his feet and chased after the being. The banquet hall was just as he left it. Liadra and Looma were still unmoving, laid out in an almost pleasant manner, their heads just barely touching. He opened his mouth to shout for help but no sound escaped. He heard movement behind him and turned so quickly that he lost his balance and fell, his head striking the corner of the grand table. After so many battles and heroic feats he was undone by a stationary object—knocked out cold.

Manfred awoke the next morning, wound tightly in the blankets of his bed, to the sound of his door opening. His head pounded and the night before was a vague memory, something like a shadow being filled with light.

"Do you do anything but sleep?" Erneel asked, frustrated.

Manfred sat up. "I had the strangest dream last night."

"It's all a strange dream, boy. Now get up," Erneel said and slammed the door.

They wasted no time getting to the ship. Greylit and his men took the party down through tunnels and switchbacks carved under the city. A less direct path than the one they used before, but it made the transport of their prisoner much safer.

A collective pain ran through all of them when they laid eyes upon the *Stone Sail*. It remained where it had been as if nothing had happened, each plank of wood a reminder of Delute's laughter.

Greylit stood with them on the beach. "You'll be alright then, old friend?"

Erneel nodded. "It's a good ship and I know her well. May we meet again on more peaceful fronts." The two embraced.

Greylit grabbed Bealzut's arm as he passed. "You're unmarked now, Brother Beal. If it weren't for the Saint, this release would never have been allowed. May we never meet on two sides of a blade."

Bealzut took a moment longer with Greylit before boarding. The Holst were warriors above mercenaries and all respected his choice to follow Erneel, another reminder of Erneel's importance throughout the realm. Seeing this young warrior leave behind his friends to voyage into the unknown all in the service of a man who treated him more as an annoyance than anything reaffirmed the mystic. It also gave Manfred a small sense of pride. Erneel had taken Manfred in, sought him out from all the realms. Very few could say that, even less with the passing of Delute.

They were all quiet as the ship left the beach and slipped out into the sea.

The ocean was subdued. Erneel took the helm and locked Liadra in the hold. Bealzut tried to keep himself busy and display his worth. Looma was quiet and took to drinking. She shied away from anyone's company. Os'halla and Manfred busied themselves with the food. They cooked all day with the supplies that the Holst and Aushwary had sent them off with.

Os'halla told Manfred about all the new plants he had discovered, the beauty of their simplicity, the way each one had carved out a small niche for itself, never deviating from their purpose. He marveled at the fundamental similarities he could see in all of them. Even though each looked so different, tasted so different, they all acted in accordance with base survival. Even the plants in the Bleak, so alien, could be reduced in the same way.

"At our root, we are all the same," Os'halla explained as they chopped up long lines of vegetables. He held up a green slice. "You're no different than this. Not different from me. We all die. We return to the body of the earth, the earth, and are born again. Our roots are constantly growing, beyond time, beyond space. You see, newfriend, you see?"

Manfred grabbed the vegetable and took a bite. "Sure. I'm a vegetable, I get it."

Os'halla laughed. "It's not like that, we all have a purpose and a function, but reduced we are dirt. We are the dust of all the realms. Of all."

Manfred found comfort in Os'halla's words. Os'halla never said it outright but hinted that Delute in some way was not dead, instead, he was only moving through the different phases of life. Manfred wished that he could impart those ideas to Looma, or to Erneel, but they all rarely spoke now, and when they did it was abrasive and short.

They arrived in a port town on a sunny afternoon. Manfred's stomach had become so used to the sway of the sea that his first few steps on land nearly saw him fall over. Os'halla had to catch him and remind him to slow down, pick a point, and focus. Erneel and Bealzut carried Liadra out onto the pier. She could barely move, barely even open her eyes.

Erneel had sent birds ahead of them to tell the Guard of their arrival and a caravan awaited them. Twenty or more warriors with weapons and armor at the ready, led by Tansrit, helped unload their supplies and by nightfall they were ready to head back to Arkis'el. Liadra was locked away in a windowless metal carriage.

Looma would not be traveling with them. Erneel had requisitioned a wagon and five horsemen from the caravan to escort her to the Keeper's den.

"Fenk and his men have made some ground in the last few days, but the Cloud is closing in on the Village. It's our last stronghold. Once it falls… It cannot fall. Your mother will have started the ritual of the *Three*. I should have left you home, my dear. Left you to prepare." Ernie said to Looma.

She hugged him. "I would have never stayed. Liadra had to be stopped. The Harvestors had to be stopped." She had tears in her eyes as she spoke. "I loved Delute. You loved him. I'm afraid I won't be ready."

"The *Three* are a part of you, just like your mother. Just like the Keepers before her. The Village needs you, my dear. That is all you need to know."

They embraced one more time before Looma left.

AN OLD FRIEND

Manfred and Erneel sat atop a wagon at the head of the caravan. Erneel tried his best to allow for a silent ride, but Manfred couldn't help but ask questions. His heart was heavy and he knew few other ways to fill the void.

"What about when you call on animals, doesn't that count as magic?"

Erneel looked at Manfred through squinted eyes having hoped that his questions were done. "What do you mean?"

"It's weird, Ernie. Even you have to admit that."

Erneel shook his head. "I learned it like all other things."

Manfred nodded. "Did the Ulis teach you? Yarley?"

Ernie let out a long sigh. "When I was young, very young, I was sent away. To the House of the Red Order. I was much younger than Looma then. Hadn't seen any of the world and knew nothing about myself. A terrible place for a child, the House. Most of the children there were nothing more than spoiled criminals. The worst of the worst. Small devils. I wasn't like them. I was bad because of boredom, not intention—nothing rooted. My family's business had nothing to hold me."

"Business?"

"Merchants. My father owned a small store on the trade route of Gheyst. His father's, so too his father's father's. A pattern I wished to avoid," he let out a subdued chuckle. "So I made friends with the homeless, the prostitutes, downtrodden folks who had seen the world, had taken risks. The ostracized had the lessons I wanted to learn. They knew the world, the whole of it. My parents weren't ever really there. They cared for me, I suppose, but they never did have time for me. Eventually, I became too much trouble, so they sent me off, boarded me off. The House was meant to civilize us, teach us manners and etiquette, how to talk to royalty, how to appreciate and submit to power." He paused and looked into the distance and a smile crept across his lips. "But dear boy, they also taught fencing," he laughed. "I remember the first time they handed me a wooden sword and put me in the ring against an older classmate. Gran Heele. I'll always remember his pimpled, oblong face. The kids called him Rocks. Was built like stone, that boy. I was terrified. Had been in fights before, but I was always pummeled, always left broken. I closed my eyes and charged him with all of my might. He hit me so hard on the top of my head, I lost a tooth." He laughed again. "Had to stay in the nurses' quarters for two days. I cried and cried. But I came back, stood in front of Rocks again. He tried to go easy on me, but I slashed at his shins as hard as I could. I wanted him to either kill me or teach me a lesson. So he smashed my head again and again. After the third time with the nurses, the Headmaster told me I couldn't fence anymore, said I was too weak—too reckless. While the other boys learned to fight, they put me on grounds duty. That's where I met her, ole Mayharooth, Haroo. Ill-tempered old crow. The first day I was assigned to her, she said, "Do good and I'll take you as a student." I laughed at her and she threw me a bucket. Didn't talk to me for weeks after that, pointed and grunted. Would swat me with long weeds when I got off task. Her only friends were the birds and the snakes."

"Oh, so she taught you how to talk with the animals?" said Manfred, feeling clever.

Erneel looked at him out of the corner of his eyes and shook his head. "Can't you see I'm reminiscing, boy? Be patient." He looked toward the sky and took a slow deep breath. "Now, where was I?"

"Uh… Hair'O?"

"Ha Roo, Haroo." He corrected. "Yes. A real mystery, that woman. Tall and angular, all limbs, gangly and feline. Could shake the top of a fruit tree. Pretty face, if not for the deep scars. Drank and stunk. Barely spoke and when she did, she would tell stories of wars in the farthest reaches of the country. Gargantuan mountain demons. Great evil red-feathered hawks. The stuff of dreams. Fantastic lies as far as I was concerned. She was a groundskeeper at a school for rich brats. I ignored her and did my work. The older kids made fun of her, tried to torment her. Nothing eviler than young men, you know. She took it all in stride—she could not be bothered. Did her job well, took pride in it. Up every morning with the sun. Slept maybe three hours a night. Early on it looked like lunacy, the commitment of a simple mind. Simple, yes. I didn't understand simple then, you see. The first thing she taught me was connection. Sneaky ole bag. The brooms. She would correct me when I cleaned, make sure the broom was always connected. Pressed against whatever object needed cleaning. She'd say, 'What you hold in your hand is your hand or it's nothing. All things connected.' It made it easier, made the hours helping her less exhausting. I could do it with my eyes closed. I could feel if an insect was in the way. Hours and hours working on a method and I never even knew it."

"A method?" Manfred didn't realize the old saint was talking to a memory at this point.

"It was months and months before they allowed me to start fencing again. Unlike the rest of the boys, I never grew. Stayed small. Hated it then. Grew into it." He smiled. "The first time I approached an opponent, without thinking, I attached the tip of my sword to theirs and they were stuck. They would try to push it away or back up, but I stayed with 'em. Never giving them a huff of space. Eventually, though, they'd always put me down. Connection only goes so far, you see."

"I don't understand, Ernie."

Erneel looked at him. His eyes squinted like he was examining a foreign object. "What?"

"She didn't teach you how to fight?"

"The great teachers never spend much time teaching. Once she saw I could follow my opponents and stick with them, she moved me on to new practices. New tasks. I began to beat out the rugs at the end of every week. She showed me how to swing from my waist, conserve my energy, protect my elbows and shoulders from coming undone. It took all day. Hundreds of heavy matted rugs, full of thick mud and twigs. I got strong. I got fast. I still didn't realize where it was coming from. I thought I was just changing as a man. But it was Haroo. I started being able to hold my own against the bigger boys. Following their movements the same way the broom attached to the angles and curves of the fine cabinetry in the teachers' quarters. Strike hard against the soft of their stomachs and drag down like I was clearing away dirt."

Manfred nodded as Erneel spoke. He pictured young Ernie fighting off his enemies with a broom, being yelled at by a gangly woman.

"Haroo was only there for my first two years and I have never seen her since she left. Maybe dead. Maybe not. A few months before she did disappear, we were cleaning the headmaster's room and I asked her about the animals, how they seemed attracted to her, almost friendly. She smiled, elusive at first, saying she had been one in a past life, a snake in the mouth of a bird. I remember those words; I remember picturing it as a boy as she spoke. After some time she explained it to me, calling them Cardinal Spirits—more than animals, she said. Connected, like your boy Os'halla, each one rooted in something bigger than itself. She told me I could speak to them, too, if I opened up to it." He chuckled. "The sages never make sense, dear boy. Talk in riddles. I tried opening up. Tried listening to them in the night, but nothing came of it. Truly, it wasn't until she left that they started coming around. Started listening. I suppose that was her final gift to me. Ole Mayharooth— haven't said that name in quite some time. Thank you, Manfred."

"Thank you?"

Erneel patted Manfred on the back and said he needed to rest for a while. With that, he hopped into the wagon below and Manfred was left trying to speak to animals around him.

The journey home was much slower going than the approach had been. The larger caravan took back roads to avoid being dragged into battle. Fires of war could be seen over almost every hill. Manfred spent much of his time sleeping in a cot, mostly because he truly was exhausted, but Erneel had also ordered him to rest. Every time they stopped to rest the horses, Manfred and Os'halla would explore their surroundings. Like two kids on a road trip, they'd hit the ground running. A few days out from the village they stopped near a lake to rest for the day. Os'halla and Manfred sat under a tree and threw rocks as far as they could into the water.

"It's time for me to leave," Os'halla said. "My time."

"What do you mean?" Manfred felt a knot in his stomach. "I can't do this on my own."

"Never alone. You have the great Saint to guide you," Os'halla smiled. "I have to return to help the Kin. To prepare for what comes next. Prepare."

"And what's next?"

"Hard to say, Manny. Hard to say. Liadra and hers brought great energy into this realm. The Kin must sort through it. See where it ended up. Seek to cleanse. To cleanse. To protect the Village of the Old Guard is not my battle, I'm afraid."

"It's not mine either, Os."

"You must know by now, Man of Regular."

"What do you mean?"

"It is all your battle. The realms called out to you. You and you."

"If it's not your battle, why come in the first place?" Manfred felt angry.

"Bound to help, Manny."

"You've said that," Manfred snapped

"It is an oath of the Kin. Help those who are lost and there were none more lost than you." He smiled. "No longer, brother. The realms have found their Mindiidus. Have found."

Manfred shook his head. "Mindiidus would've saved Delute."

Os'halla looked out over the lake.

"It's true. If I were this great warrior, this great savior, then why would he die?"

"It is the way of the world. Of life."

"No, Os. He is dead because I couldn't save him. Because I'm not Mindiidus."

"Do you remember when we first met?"

"Of course."

"People don't just stumble into the grove. Protected for thousands of years from prying eyes. Yet there you were, near dead, emerged from the desert. Emerged. Thirsty. Emerged. Lost. I'm sorry, Manfred, but for all your failings, which there are many, you are who they say you are. Mindiidus. As you slept, Axealo and I spoke. She had seen you in dreams. Foresaw your emergence. Thirsty. Lost. I'd not have killed for you on that island, in the Bleak, if it wasn't true. Wasn't true."

"Why tell me this now?"

"Why tell you at all? Faith in a man can be his death. Faith. I had to watch you. Had to be near you. You lack confidence and your uncertainty is a sickness. Stay close to the little Saint. And don't forget to breathe."

They stood above the shallows of the lake. Os'halla put his hands on Manfred's shoulders and looked him up and down before pulling him close and kissing his forehead. With that, Os'halla left. He took nothing with him except his staff and a handful of flowers.

DESTRUCTION,
RENEWAL AND REBIRTH

When they reached the village Liadra was unloaded by Tansrit's men and brought to the infirmary. She was still pale and sickly, but some of her color had returned. She smiled and laughed at Manfred as she was loaded from one cart to the next. Her laughter devolved into a coughing fit and she was soon spitting up blood.

The roads leading to the Citadel were quiet, intense. The only life was armored men and stray dogs. The villagers had been made to stay home under a strict curfew.

Manfred spent the next few days watching the guards from a balcony of the Citadel. He amused himself by searching for Bealzut amongst the ranks. He wasn't hard to find, walking, nearly dragging his feet next to the large disciplined guards. He had been given hand-me-down armor that fit his body awkwardly and his two swords were much different than the issued sabers the rest of the men carried.

Other than that, Manfred spent his days trying to meditate. He thought a lot about Os'halla and his ability to stay calm in battle. Manfred needed calm. There was something in the air. Erneel barely visited him and when he did, he was either drunk or almost completely silent. He'd just look at Manfred across the room before wandering off. The one time he spoke was to tell Manfred that they'd be meeting with Liadra soon. Erneel explained that Tansrit's men weren't able to get anything from her. That they had been too easy on her. He told Manfred that if Saylu couldn't get any information from her, Yarley would perform a Viewing. That he would be a lot less delicate than the Keeper had been, he said. Manfred didn't want to think about it. He had hoped he would never have to hear her voice again. Had hoped she'd just die in captivity.

He practiced the posture Os'halla had shown him. He tried his best to release all of his fears or at least control them. He was getting better and better, and some days he could stand for hours. There were even moments when his mind would go completely blank and the world would disappear.

Often in these moments, he'd be brought back by an image of Liadra's sword stabbing through Delute. Then Delute's blood would splash out and spread itself into each pore of Manfred's mind—violently knocking against his solitude. He could still hear Looma scream. It filled him with such intense sorrow that the first time it happened he began to cry, his whole body trembling. He could also hear Os'halla's voice coaching him to relax. Sometimes he could and sometimes he couldn't— Manfred was finding a balance.

Erneel and Manfred met with Liadra in the White Room after a few days' rest. Yarley sat in the far corner and Saylu sat between her and three armored guards. Liadra was shackled at the waist, leaving her arms free, her chair bolted to the floor. She fidgeted constantly and touched the chain and the stitches on her face and neck, the guards watching her every movement like hungry wolves.

Saylu was in the middle of questioning Liadra. "We're giving you a chance to choose the right path. To end the bloodshed."

She spat on the floor.

"The Harvestors can no longer hide, and when we find them," Saylu motioned toward Manfred, "Mr. Bugsbee can break through their fields. Put an end to your work."

Liadra smiled.

"You saw him in action, Liadra. There is no denying his power.'"

"Power?" she whispered. "You don't know power."

"Oh?" responded Saylu.

"My people have been carving up the universe since time began. Your prophesied may have closed one door, but our prophecy brings it all down. To ash." She laughed.

"And what is your prophecy?"

Liadra tried to force eye contact with Manfred, but he looked at the floor. "Mindiidus. Mindiidus. Could not save the sailor. Could not save your earth. What can you do?"

"You know what he can do," said Saylu.

"The poor boy can't even speak for himself," Liadra said, never taking her eyes off of Manfred. "You were busy when I stuck the sailor. I had heard stories of him. Heard he was a thousand feet tall. Unkillable," she laughed and looked toward Erneel. "Your protege. Not many under your wing these days."

Erneel sat with his legs crossed and rubbed his face. "Delute's his name, dear girl."

Liadra smiled. "Of course. The pirate. The two of you were legendary. The Battle at Gray Hill, Moss Island. Legendary. Tell your stories from the Gild Sea to the Ash Fields. Now they will tell stories of me." She stretched her arms above her head. "Undone the Saint's very best. Me. Where a million others have failed."

"You're wasting your time, Saylu. Let Yarley scrape through her already." Erneel said.

"Perhaps," Saylu replied quietly.

"Why not have the Keeper do it," Liadra said. "Please. Please, take me to her. I can meet the followers of that whore. They'll die, too. And your daughter," Liadra laughed. "Precious little thing. Is she the next to hold the mantle of Saint? Who, just like you—can't protect her friends." She laughed and coughed up blood. "I watched her face as the sailor died. Weak."

"Delute," Erneel said and adjusted in his seat.

"What's a name to a dead man, anyhow?" She wiped the blood from her mouth. "And little Looma, wasn't she his student? I'd have rather killed you in front of her, but I'm sure that hurt just as bad. Do you think they were lovers, old man? Maybe he stuck her through like I did him?"

In a fluid dash, Erneel moved across the room and backhanded Liadra and brought Rocinallia to her neck. The guards tried to stop him, but he was too fast. Saylu stood up and yelled, "No, don't kill her!"

Erneel cut Saylu off and slowly pressed Rocinallia into Liadra's skin. "Should've killed you in the desert. In the Bleak. Should've let Looma kill you on the beach." He looked over his shoulder at Saylu who was still pleading with him. "I won't kill her. Time will kill her." He turned back to Liadra. "My friend died at your hands, but he died to protect the realms. You'll die in a cage while I kill all of your brothers and sisters. Just like I killed your father."

"You have no idea what is coming," she managed to say—the pressure of the blade building at her throat.

"I'm afraid I've seen it all." Rocinallia broke the skin and a crimson spot of blood appeared. "I need a drink." He turned to Saylu. "We're wasting our time with her."

Erneel patted Manfred on the shoulder as he left the room.

"The Saint is slipping," Liadra said, wiping the blood from her neck.

Salyu let out a deep breath and sat down.

Liadra pointed toward Yarley. "Once a Ulis, now a feeble ancient nothingness. There's nothing you can dig from my mind that won't befall you all soon enough. So… unremarkable. So… frail." Her words trailed off.

"He knows what you have been up to. He and the Ulis are how we found you with the Aushwary and they'll find the rest of the Harvestors, too. You can make it easy though, Liadra. Call off your Harvestors. Bring peace," said Salyu.

"It doesn't matter. The armies of the earth will be at your door soon enough," she said.

"You know the spaces between the realms are fragile, Liadra. The Cloud goes too far pushing those boundaries. The whole of the structure could collapse. Bringing the end. The total end."

"A blessed day, watching it all crumble."

"This cycle can end here. The last time the Cloud played with these forces it resulted in decades of bloodshed. You can end it."

"The Old Guard doesn't exist without bloodshed" Liadra smiled. "We don't wish to control this earth. No more. We aim for the fabric. Existence itself. The army of the Cloud," she laughed, "they don't matter anymore. Me. My Harvestors. End it all."

Yarley approached her and the two guards followed closely and made sure to keep him out of her arms' length.

"A change is coming," she said and looked at Yarley with a sort of subdued reverence. "The Cloud fights you at all fronts. But the Harvestors, they bring down the whole of it. The fabric will not tear. It will burn."

"Forces beyond you, young lady," Yarley said, leaning from side to side on his canes.

She shook her head. "Bring back Erneel. Let him kill me. It doesn't matter."

"No?" asked Yarley.

"While you sit here, we call out," she pointed toward Manfred. "Destroy his earth. Destroy all earths. You know how this will end."

"In this story, all that is set in stone is your demise, I'm afraid," he said, contemplating Liadra's face.

"They return. We bring them home. They are tired of earths like your errand boy's. They will wash the whole thing clean."

"My earth?" Manfred asked.

"Ah, he speaks," she said. "Yes, you and the wicked children. Less than dirt. They have grown tired. They want us to finish you off, to kill the disease. One by one."

"What disease?" Manfred continued, the haze of fear that covered him lifting slightly.

"The disease of the realms. How many earths did they make? Each covered in living greens and reds. They wish to eradicate those who have wasted the gift. The Harvestors are their vehicle. We are the instrument. The Bleak was a cesspool filled with wretched beasts. We fixed it. Just as we will do with yours." She spat on the floor again.

"A level of piety your ancestors lacked," said Yarley.

"They had not known such power—led astray. The realm has never seen such power," she laughed. "We bring all-out destruction. Renewal. Rebirth."

"Who brings?" Yarley's old face squinted as if willing her to speak.

Liadra looked at him and smiled.

"Who?"

"Oarygus. Oarygus. They return."

Yarley shook his head. "What have you done? You're less than a speck of dust to them, my dear."

Liadra sat quietly for a moment and tapped her fingers absently. She fixed her eyes on Manfred. "You are special, then? Important? Could not save the fisherman. Could not keep your precious relic. There will always be more Harvestors. Men willing to die. Willing to commit themselves to the ritual. To the truth. Order and cleanliness require fire and ash."

Manfred leaned on the table. He wanted to slap her as Erneel had done, but he couldn't move. Transfixed by Liadra's repugnance, her relentless commitment to her curse.

"They came to us, after all these years, eons, they came back to us." She pounded her fist against her chest, paying no mind to her broken ribs. "They told us it was time to kill the Gray Earth, begin the destruction of all the wasted realms." She pointed at Manfred then pounded her chest again. "It will all be ours. No more pesky Guard. And once the power transfers, once the reckoning is bestowed, we will be all-powerful. Not even they could stop us." She was yelling now. "Rotten earth upon earth, begone. No longer left in the hands of dirty children." She pounded her chest one more time then reached out toward Yarley. Two guards stepped in front of him.

Saylu pulled Yarley back and told him to sit down. "You stupid girl, if the Oarygus were here the Ulis would have known."

"He knows. He must."

Saylu and Yarley exchanged concerned looks.

Manfred began to feel a strange static in the room. At first, to his horror, he thought it was the feeling of the Harvestors. But it was something different. He looked back at Yarley to see if he felt it, too. Yarley didn't meet his eyes, instead, he seemed to be speaking quietly to himself.

"Can you feel that?" Manfred asked aloud.

Liadra laughed hysterically and one of the guards yelled at her to shut up.

"You give us no other choice," Saylu said in an exhausted, tentative way.

The guard who had been yelling reached down to forcefully cover Liadra's mouth and when he touched her, he evaporated in a pulse of light, armor and all. The force of whatever happened threw everyone to the ground except Liadra and Yarley, who almost seemed unfazed as he got his footing. Liadra was terrified.

She screamed in gut-wrenching agony. The two remaining guards drew their weapons. The chains around Liadra's waist became red hot and burst. Shrapnel shot across the room and a piece of it lodged itself in the head of one of the guards. He fell dead to the floor as Liadra's body rose from the chair. She was still screaming. Her whole body went rigid then limp as blood poured from her eyes and mouth. The last guard charged the hanging body, but upon his weapon making contact, he, too, disappeared in a shock of light.

Whatever Liadra had been was now dead. Her body floated through the air toward Saylu who turned his back and yelled for Yarley to get Manfred out. Before he could finish, he suffered the same fate as the two guards. A mist of blood was all that was left. Manfred lunged at her, but Yarley tripped him and pushed him out of the way. Manfred could only watch as Liadra's lifeless body raised its arms and reached out for Yarley. He did nothing to avoid her touch, instead, he seemed to welcome it. When Liadra's hands finally touched him, he did not evaporate like the others, rather, a transmission occurred. Lights and whirlwinds of sound erupted from Liadra's face and entered Yarley's head through a stream of a thousand movements and a million colors. Liadra's body melted away and left a final, unceremonious stain of blood and bone.

Yarley cried out as his long awkward body straightened to its full height of nearly seven feet. His eyes brightened within his sunken face and they looked like two full and complete universes. A halo of darkness emanated from his body. Manfred tried to get up again but the energy that pulsated from Yarley kept him on the ground.

The room began to spin. Manfred could only see Yarley, but the rest of the space turned black. Yarley moved back and forth like a tuning fork, his whole body vibrating and spreading out. Yarley was whispering something under his breath. As the words formed, shapes like those Manfred had seen in the portal began to manifest. Squares and angular bits of unreality stacked against each other and moved toward and through him. Manfred tried to help, tried to scream, but his body was being pulled apart. A terrible screeching noise, like the seizing of an engine screaming through an untuned radio, burst through the room. Manfred tried to reach out toward Yarley for balance, but it was no use. The unsteadiness of the room made it impossible for him to move.

Suddenly the lights went out. He could still hear the screeching—shrill, broken vibrations.

Manfred was somewhere else. The room was pulsating. He took slow deep breaths into his stomach and tried to focus.

"Manfred. Manfred, what are you doing here? How did you get here?" He heard the words but the voice was twisted and echoed in on itself.

The room slowed down and Manfred fell to the ground. There was a cool breeze flowing through the room and the smell of the ocean.

"Manfred." The voice became clear. "How?"

It was Looma she ran to his side. "How did you get here?"

"I have no idea. Where are we?"

"My mother's. What is going on?"

"Yar... Yarley, something's wrong. Liadra's dead."

"Good. How? What's happening?"

"No, Looma, you don't understand. Something is wrong with Yarley. Saylu is dead."

"Saylu?" she said as the ache of more dead friends drove through her. "What are you talking about?"

"I don't know. Something is wrong, Looma. Where is your mother? We need to get Ernie out of there." He had a hard time speaking.

"Why? What happened?" she repeated herself out of fear.

"Your mother," he cried out. "Get your mother."

Looma ran out of the room. Although the room had stopped spinning his stomach was still trying to settle. He could still see Yarley's eyes, like small vacuums, breathing pulsating orbs, singed into his mind.

The Keeper arrived.

"Get him water." the Keeper ordered Looma, who left the room again.

"What's happening?" Manfred asked as the Keeper put her hands on him trying to calm his body.

"You tell me."

Manfred straightened up the best he could and told her what he had just seen unfold. She nodded along with him, the shadows of the room casting upon her face.

"The Ulis warned of something like this," she said more to herself than anything. "He wasn't sure. Couldn't be sure of their return."

"What about the Ulis?" Manfred was afraid to ask.

"He's not dead. I'd know. Neither is Erneel." She made her best face of comfort and wiped her eyes as she did. "They'd have gone to the Realm Unknown."

Manfred looked at her.

"It's a space between the realms. An accident of creation. Not even the Oarygus can access it. Erneel and the Ulis will remain there until it's safe to return."

"And Yarley?"

The Keeper shook her head. "An Oarygus nests in him. He'll be able to contain the embodiment for a while and Kaseen will have suspended the White Room."

"Suspended?"

"I'm sorry, Manfred. I forget you're new here sometimes. It's hard to explain exactly, but the room exists in waves of connection. The connection has been severed."

"Is it like the Unknown Realm?"

The Keeper shrugged. "Not exactly. Not really. It's safe, for now. But the embodiment will only get stronger."

"Will Tansrit evacuate the village then?"

She shook her head. "The Cloud's army closes in from all directions." She let out a heavy sigh and sat down next to Manfred. "It's trouble. It's so much trouble."

Looma returned with water.

"What's happening?" Looma demanded.

"Finality, dear. It is upon us."

Looma moved toward her but she raised her hand and pointed at Manfred. "Tend to Mindiidus. I must prepare." Looma didn't try to argue as the Keeper left the room.

"What is going on?" Looma said to Manfred.

Manfred could only shake his head. He was still weak.

Looma sat down next to him on the floor and put her head on his shoulder.

They sat for some time in silence.

THE REALM UNKNOWN

Days passed without any word from the Village. Then early one morning Manfred was summoned to the Keeper's room. Bealzut stood at the far side. Two of the Keeper's men held his arms. Manfred tried to move toward him but the Keeper held her hand up.

"He says Ernie sent him but brings no sign," she said.

Manfred nodded. "Yes, yes. This is Bealzut." He looked at him. "Bealzut, how are you? What's going on?"

Bealzut smiled and nodded his head. "Grunghek. I'm fine. I'm thirsty."

"Why did he send *you*?" asked the Keeper.

"I am his most trusted disciple," replied Bealzut.

The Keeper shook her head. "That you are not."

Bealzut smiled. "The message had to arrive and we Holst are slippery. No one but me could've been here so quickly."

The Keeper was still shaking her head.

"He and the Ulis are safe, I can assure you."

"I know that."

Bealzut cocked his head. "He wishes for me to escort the boy warrior to the Realm Unknown."

"Boy?" said Manfred. "I'm probably older than you are."

"Age? A child is a person lost. A person out of their depth," Bealzut said looking at the Keeper all along.

Manfred grunted.

"There is no way he wants to send Manfred to the Unknown," said the Keeper, almost to herself.

Bealzut pulled a small bone from his sleeve, no bigger than a toothpick.

"How'd you get that in here? What is that?" demanded the Keeper.

"A Relic," he said. "The Saint entrusted me with a Relic. None other."

The Keeper reached out for it, but Bealzut refused. "Do you trust me, woman?"

The Keeper made a spiral shape with one hand and pointed at Bealzut with the other. "No," she said.

He tried to put the Relic back in his sleeve but couldn't move. A tremor shot through his body and the bone popped out of his hand and into the Keeper's. She made the same spiral motion and Bealzut relaxed into his chair with a sigh.

"Teach me?" he asked.

"Is he always this chatty?" the Keeper asked Manfred who nodded his head. "Ernie doesn't like chatty."

She held the bone in front of her face and turned it over a few times. Her eyes brightened and Manfred held the arms of his chair. He remembered the small orbs of light she had used to see into his past and began to sweat.

Bealzut looked at him. "What's wrong, child?"

The bone began to float in the air between the Keeper's hands and a ray of light connected it to her forehead.

"Oh," said Bealzut, his eyes wide with interest.

The Keeper made three signs above and below the bone and the ray of light disappeared.

"A Relic," she said. She looked at Bealzut her eyes glowing gold. "To the Unknown?"

Bealzut nodded.

"I have never," she said. "An ancient magic. You both may die," she continued and looked from one to the other.

Manfred gulped and Bealzut smiled.

"At first light in the west garden," she said. "I must prepare. When you enter the garden do not say a word, understood?"

Both men nodded as she explained that the Realm Unknown was the most delicate of actualities. That it existed in all things but required an acceptance of its unreality before one could enter. She spoke, almost as if to herself, and laughed when she said she had never sent anyone there and that even the slightest mistake could lead to cataclysms beyond her imagination.

"You both have fragile minds," she said, "and in that fragility, there are infinite dangers and potentials."

Manfred was, for what felt like the millionth time, listening along as someone explained the very high likelihood that he'd soon be killed in the most inventive bizarre way. The Keeper finally dismissed the two men.

"I looked for the Kin, the tree head," Bealzut said as they walked down the hallway.

Manfred looked at him.

"Could not find the grove. Few things a Holst can't find. If the builders of forests are in hiding then they must know."

"Know what?"

Bealzut stopped walking. "If we fail there will be much for them to do." He laughed and patted Manfred on the back.

The next morning they met in a walled-in terrace garden overlooking the ocean. Summering flowers competed with dew-covered ferns against the garden walls. The ground was overrun with unkempt vines that dipped and twisted along dirt paths. The Keeper sat by a fish pond fed by two bright, diverging streams. Fish splashed about and jumped in and out of the water, their iridescent fins like bolts of lightning. There was no ceiling and high above them peach-colored, spade-leafed trees grew out from the walls. Manfred felt dizzy as he watched them sway about. Bits of their color fell to the garden floor. *Os would be in heaven in a room like this*, Manfred thought.

The Keeper ushered them over and the three of them sat between four massive rocks covered in a kaleidoscope of lichen. She wore a thick, tightly woven shawl—the drab gray simplicity of it stood out against the brilliance of the garden. Two other women entered behind Bealzut and Manfred and wore the same fabric—one red, one white. It was clear there would be no introductions, as the ritual required a complete silence. The women handed Manfred and Bealzut each clay cups then took their place behind the Keeper.

She motioned for them to drink. Manfred took a small sip and smiled, surprised that it tasted mostly like water with a little metallic aftertaste. The Keeper motioned for him to drink again and mimed shaking an empty cup. Manfred downed the thing and Bealzut did the same. The two women touched hands behind the Keeper.

The drink bubbled in Manfred's stomach. It was warm and made him tired. Out of the corner of his eye, Manfred saw movement. At first, he thought it was the billowing of a tree, but came into focus as a tall sickly-looking man. Manfred couldn't help but gasp—it was clear that whatever liquid he had drunk was playing tricks on him. The Keeper pressed her finger to her lips and her eyes glowed as bright as he had ever seen. All the colors of the garden became more vibrant and even though he dared not look up at the canopy of leaves, he could feel them moving in his skin—he could feel their reflection in his bones.

The sickly man held a live bird in each hand. They squawked as he made his way toward the group. The man wore a tattered robe worn through in some places and held together with unpatterned patchwork. He reached out to Manfred with one of the birds as it struggled against his fingers, its small beak opening and closing in desperation. The Keeper nodded for Manfred to take it, and the same for Bealzut. Manfred looked down at the small bird and felt sick. Its sad, round eyes darted left and right and it chirped so loudly Manfred thought his eardrums might burst. The Keeper snapped her fingers to get their attention and made a crushing motion with her hands.

Manfred shook his head in disbelief and mouthed the word 'no.' The Keeper did the motion again this time more forcefully. Manfred looked down at the bird and felt tears well up in his eyes. The Keeper snapped her fingers again and forced eye contact with him. The power of her gaze ran through him and he knew he couldn't refuse. He turned his head away from the bird and began to squeeze. At first, it felt like it should crush easily—soft feathers reinforced by delicate bones—but the longer he squeezed the harder it became. He had to look down a few times to make sure it was still a bird. It was. The bird didn't seem to care about what was happening. Still chirping, still looking from side to side, then suddenly it gave way. The bird vanished in a white plume of smoke. The smoke poured into Manfred's nose and mouth and he felt such a violent knock in his brain that he nearly passed out.

The smoke swirled in his lungs and stomach like a snake. It wrapped itself around each organ until it sat somewhere deep inside and formed a rock in his stomach, so heavy that he couldn't stand. He looked up and tried to catch his breath and saw the two birds above the Keeper's head. They flapped their wings like hummingbirds and each figure eight pulsed in his brain. He looked higher and the leaves had turned into one large swath of paint with flecks of sky scattered throughout. Bealzut laid on his side and held his legs in the fetal position and fidgeted in agony. The Keeper smiled at Manfred.

"The ritual is nearly complete. Drunk water from the primordial well and letting go of your reality," she looked at the two birds above her. "Beyond here is the beyond. The Realm Unknown forms within and without you. Please, won't you tell my dearest Ernie, I'm tired of war." With that, she closed her eyes in meditation and the other two women took over.

They first helped Bealzut to his feet. He was drenched in sweat and begged them for water. They shook their heads, no. The stone in Manfred's stomach lifted as the two women offered him their hands. He felt a momentary lightness. The two women walked in front of the men and beckoned them to follow. Manfred and Bealzut moved slowly and leaned against one another for support.

"I'm not sure I can go on," said Bealzut as they exited the garden, through a door that Manfred didn't remember seeing before.

They now moved through a long-arched hallway.

"We must," said Manfred.

The two women were so far in front of the men that they could barely see them, just small blurs of red and white in the distance. The hallway sloped downward and they had to shuffle their feet so as not to fall. The path was slippery with dust and their bodies ached.

"I am Holst," said Bealzut. "And this is nowhere."

"What do you mean?" asked Manfred as they made their way toward the two women.

"Holst is always aware. We are everywhere. Not now. Not here."

Manfred patted Bealzut's back. "The Saint needs us. He's close, I can feel it."

The two women stopped and waited in front of a small doorway. Manfred reached for the door but the woman in the red shawl stopped him.

"Mindiidus and the Holst must be wary of the great Unknown. Created and uncreated as a trap. Real and unreal as a place of refuge. Beyond this door there is nothing. There is only space unfolding." She pulled a small bone from her sleeve and handed it to Manfred—another Relic.

The woman disrobed. Her freckled body was beautiful in the dark hall and Manfred felt the urge to sit down. She wrapped her shawl around Bealzut and disappeared in a cloud of smoke. The other woman did the same. She was just as beautiful and all the pain in Manfred's body lifted for a moment as she looked him in the eyes, completely naked.

"When I am gone, cover your head," she said.

"Why?" asked Manfred.

"Skies are known to fall as new realities emerge," she answered.

She wrapped the shawl around him and disappeared.

Bealzut and Manfred looked at each other for a moment, caught their breath then ducked through the door.

They were back in the garden. A few steps and the door behind them was gone. It was nighttime and the moon was barely a sliver in the purpling sky. Manfred felt calm and let Bealzut lead the way. They walked in the wavering grass and took care not to trip over the vines.

"Back in the garden?" asked Manfred.

Bealzut shrugged. "Not exactly, not quite."

Manfred looked down at the grass. "It's growing," he said. "Same with the trees," he pointed toward some in the distance.

Bealzut stopped walking and bent his knees. He motioned for Manfred to lower too. They both took a defensive position. The grass kept getting longer, first to their knees, then their hips, each piece popping out of the ground. Not growing, but being pulled up. Soon, the grass floated past their heads. Bits of dirt rose with their little bulbous ends. The trees in the distance did the same and a sound like grinding gears built as the roots yanked up from the ground. Large knots of earth swayed in the sky as each piece of nature floated up.

The two men stayed crouched and looked from one another to the plants above them, which moved up as if buoyed by rising water. Up and up—until everything stopped and hovered in the sky.

"What now?" asked Bealzut, still crouched, looking from side to side.

Manfred shook his head.

"Keep moving?"

Manfred nodded and the two men continued. They kept their heads down and moved slowly over the new holes in the ground. With each step they took Manfred could feel something churning inside of him. He took it for anxiety. Fear that they were headed nowhere or to just another one of the Keeper's games. But as the feeling grew, he realized it was a weight outside his body. He looked up at the floating trees, their large roots like nightmare animals, some as big as a car.

Manfred was overcome by a terrifying premonition. He grabbed Bealzut and yelled, "Get down." The weight he felt was coming from the plants—they were about to fall back to earth. His yell turned into a scream, then the squeak of a tired throat. The two men huddled on the ground and covered their heads as all of earth fell in on them.

Manfred grabbed Bealzut's hand so as to not die alone. Soon they were crushed. He felt his body pancake, each organ and bone that held him up, flattened. He dissolved as Bealzut screamed in utter agony.

Manfred opened his eyes to complete darkness. Bealzut was no longer screaming. He could sense that the Keeper and Looma were close. He called out and reached for them but felt only a profound coldness.

"I'm not ready," said Looma.

"There is no ready, dear." responded the Keeper.

Manfred could feel them moving.

"With your father and the Ulis stuck beyond and myself overseeing these two men, you must. You must try and slow the Cloud."

"I haven't trained since I was a child. Not since Delute put a sword in my hand."

"The power is in you, Looma. It is yours."

"Where are they?" Looma asked.

"Here."

Manfred could make out rudimentary shapes in the darkness. The Keeper extended a bag to Looma.

"So small."

"Only to conceal their power, dear Looma. You've yet to see them on the battlefield."

"And there are three?"

Looma poured the contents of the bag onto a table. Three unremarkable rocks.

"What is that?" asked Manfred.

They couldn't hear him.

"You'll have a few days to practice. We should've kept you here, Looma. Trained you."

"No," said Looma. "I've fought by the best men in the realms. If I'd have stayed here, what would I be fighting for?"

Manfred felt the two women embrace. "The three will drain you, Looma. Kaseen will help you. She will fortify you. You are so strong, like your father."

"Is he safe?"

"I don't know. In the Unknown, all things are alive and dead. I can sense his presence but it is warped. Stretched and divided. And Mindiidus. I don't know if that unfortunate man can survive all of this realm hopping. The Ulis and your father have prepared for it. Have taken vows. Have said their thousand oaths. And the Holst…" the Keeper sighed, "We have sent them into a dangerous place."

"They can handle it. I know they can. I've seen Mindiidus in battle. Against the Harvestors. Against Kai'Va. And Bealzut is a true warrior."

"I hope you're right, Looma."

Manfred felt the two women fade away.

The two men opened their eyes and moved to their feet, their bodies heavy and stiff with pain. They grabbed each other and quietly examined one another. Bealzut's eyes were completely bloodshot, his pupils pulsating violently. Blood dripped from his ears and nose and he wiped it away as he stepped back from Manfred.

Manfred was in no better shape. His head pounded and his whole body shook. He tried to remain calm and breathe, but it was no use. He had to let the tremors move through him. They started in his feet and worked their way through his stomach and chest before they released out of his head in a yell. He felt better but still shivered as he and Bealzut surveyed their surroundings.

They were standing on a marble floor almost indistinguishable from the Keeper's den. So familiar that if not for the rest of their world, Manfred would've thought they were in a secret room of the Den. They stood outside under a cloudless sky that stretched in all directions. The moon moved in a slow wide circle—a scavenger watching its prey.

"Did you hear them?" asked Manfred.

"Who?" Bealzut said.

"Looma and the Keeper."

Bealzut shook his head. "When?"

"Just now."

"I heard nothing. Only felt the flames of my youth."

"Said something about the Keeper's Three."

Bealzut looked Manfred over. "A machine of war. If they call on them, they must have little hope for us."

Manfred nodded. "What are the Three?"

Bealzut scratched his face. "I've never seen them in action. An ancient weapon of the Order of the Sign, the Keepers. From when war was all this realm knew. Mountains that rise from nothing and can barrel through an enemy fleet. Guided by one, but controlled by many. It means the Guard is scared. It means a return to darker times."

The landscape changed around them as they walked, at first in subtle ways. The marble they had started on became fine white sand. Manfred leaned down to touch it and remembered the desert with Ernie. In a flash, he watched as Liadra cut him in half. He let the sand run through his fingers as blood splashed in his mind. When he stood back up the sky had changed—blue and white clouds in a reddening sky.

Angular stone mountains rose on the horizon and Manfred was sure they hadn't been there before. A white dot against the mountains flicked in and out of view. He pointed and Bealzut nodded. They moved toward the object.

Manfred knelt to touch the sand again. It was soft between his fingers. He rubbed his palms together to feel its warmth and touched his face so he could smell it. He let grains fall and as he did, he heard Bealzut yelling.

"No, Erneel. It's us. It's your sword-bearer."

Manfred looked up to find himself in yet another place, something like the White Room, but different—scattered. He could hear the grains of sand as they fell, like springs bursting from a clock. The walls were yellowed and above him hung the Ulis. The old body swayed from its feet, his hands outstretched toward Manfred. Manfred reached up and heard Bealzut yell again.

"I will not fight you, Saint. Not like this."

Manfred turned around to see Erneel approach Bealzut. Both men had weapons raised. Crude, unrefined things. The Saint held a rusty ax and Bealzut, a charred wooden club.

"Step aside, Holst."

Erneel's beard went all the way down to his waist, twice as long as Manfred had remembered it.

"What are you doing, Saint?" Bealzut cried out.

Erneel swung the ax in two quick arcs and Bealzut jumped back.

"No more man of regular earth, ole boy. The Relic. Where is she?" Erneel swung again, this time just missing Bealzut's foot. Sparks flew up and Manfred was looking down at the sand again.

Then the room was gone along with Erneel and the Ulis. Bealzut looked back and motioned for him to hurry. Manfred caught up but it was slow going and the world was changing fast. The mountains pushed back the sky and heatwaves murmured off every object.

"Stay calm. This place is a wicked shadow."

"But where is Ernie?"

"What do you mean?"

"We were just with him, he was trying to kill you."

Bealzut looked at Manfred confused. "The Saint is ahead of us. In the distance. He must be."

"How do you know?"

Bealzut touched his head. "Many tools of the Holst. One is a sense. A sense of man. A sense of direction."

"What are Holst?" Manfred thought asking questions might try and soothe the fragmentation he felt rising in him.

"Greatest warriors in the realm. Oldest order outside of the Guard. The Guard's claim is to protect the realms—we protect the people. Wherever there is fear and giants, we are. Wherever there are demon hordes, we are."

"When did you join?" Even though Manfred was talking, he felt as if he was watching the conversation from somewhere else. As if, stuck in a dream.

"Join?" Bealzut rubbed his hands. "The Holst takes what is theirs."

The two men kept walking toward their destination.

"When we protect a village, we take a fee. That fee is a child. That child is Holst."

"You take children?" Manfred pressed.

"We take Holst. They are everywhere. Born with the sense. Born with the strength."

"Wait, wait, wait." Manfred was feeling faint. "You take kids? Kidnapping?"

Bealzut shook his head. "Where we met, the Aushwary, they had two young women who were Holst. The Aushwary needed protections, so we made a trade. Jailuh now trains with the Holst. She'll become a great warrior. Her sense will be fostered."

"You said there were two."

"The Holst takes one."

"I need to sit down."

Bealzut watched as Manfred sat down and they were in the room again.

Manfred couldn't reach the Ulis but felt that he was cold. His skin was pale and drenched with sweat as he swayed overhead.

"What have you done to the Ulis?" cried Bealzut as he dodged another ax blow.

"I don't want to kill you, Holst. But I will protect the realms. That's all I'm good for, that's all that's left."

Manfred was still reaching for the Ulis, his body stretching all the way.

"The Relic, Manfred. Where is it?"

Bealzut dropped his weapon and raised his hands. "Saint. We are here to bring you back. Please. Release the Ulis. Let us return to the Keep."

Ernie threw the ax at Manfred and Bealzut dove to catch it. While he was extended, Erneel lunged across the room and kicked Bealzut in the ribs. Bealzut let out a hollow sound and fell to the ground. Erneel reached out toward Manfred. "The relic, boy. I know you have it."

The yellow of the walls made Manfred dizzy and he wanted to lie down. "The relic," he said. "It's right here." Before he could hand it over, Bealzut jumped on Erneel's back and used the handle of the ax to choke him.

"Bealzut. No," Manfred yelled as the yellow of the room overtook him and he laid down beneath the Ulis.

Manfred felt the sand cool beneath his body again and the red of the sky was near complete with only dots of sickly yellowed stars showing through the veil.

"We're almost there, child." Bealzut pointed, "Just there."

In front of them was a small stone building. He could see two objects moving along within a pulsing light. Bealzut pulled Manfred to his feet. "This place is changing. If we don't hurry, I'm afraid we'll be stuck forever. The Saint will be lost. On your feet."

Manfred stood, the sky filling with storm clouds, and he could feel the rain building up. The mountains stretched out like aspen trees and shook and waved in the red sky.

"I'm thirsty, Bealzut. Can't we rest?"

"We'll drink soon. Just keep moving."

Manfred's legs were heavy and with each step his thirst grew. Their destination faded in and out of sight. At once there, a certain stopping point, then gone in a rolling mist. He looked down at his feet and yelped. The sand was up to his knees. "Bealzut, wait," he yelled. But Bealzut was up to his waist, too. He turned his head and Manfred saw fear in the warrior's eyes. Manfred reached down to free his legs but they wouldn't budge. He looked up again.

Erneel stood over Bealzut with a stone held above his head. Bealzut was barely moving, except for shallow breaths.

"Please. Ernie. What are you doing?" Manfred asked, extending the Relic to him.

Ernie tossed the rock to the side. "Manny, my dear. You've done just fine. It's all just fine." He picked up the Relic and moved toward Manfred, slowly. "The Ulis is dying, boy. I am his disciple. A failure." He rolled the relic back and forth in his hands. "I cannot fail the realms. The Holst would try to stop me." He pointed at Bealzut.

"No, Ernie. We're here to bring you back. Back to save the realms. To stop the Oarygus." Manfred said.

"You are here to become Mindiidus. To give over to death. No more simple Man of Regular Earth. The stakes are too high."

"I don't understand."

Ernie laughed and looked up at the Ulis. "I told you he wouldn't understand."

"What are you doing to the Ulis?" Manfred cried out.

"Doing? He's asleep. Conserving his energy. Do you know how long we've been here?"

Manfred began to speak, but Ernie moved closer to him and asked the Ulis, "Where did you say?"

The Ulis didn't respond.

"Was it the right side or the left side, old man?" He clapped his hands together then waved the Relic at the Ulis. "Wake up, wake up."

Ernie grabbed Manfred by the arm and looked him in the eyes. "The left side, I guess. I'm sorry, Manfred. It will only hurt for a minute and it may only kill you." He raised the relic and brought it down toward Manfred's neck.

Manfred closed his eyes and was in the sand again. It was past his chest and he could no longer see Bealzut, just small plumes of dust from where he had gone under. The moon spiraled above.

He considered praying and realized he hadn't thought about any god in quite some time.

The sand was above his head now and forced its way into his mouth and down into his lungs. He couldn't scream or move. It filled his body until there was no more Manfred, just sand— above and below. *This isn't too bad*, he thought. Sand didn't have to worry about the realms. It didn't have to fear death. It just was. Soft and warm.

He felt a small hand tug on his arm from the abyss. It was his sister, eight years old and laughing. His other sister stood just behind her. "I told her not to cover your head," she said, giggling all along.

Manfred stood up and brushed himself off. He was a child, flamingo bespeckled swim trunks under a sunburnt torso. His sisters ran from him, their hair absorbing the golden light of the sun. He chased them and couldn't help but laugh.

"Manny-Freddy," they yelled.

His father stood at the ocean's edge and cast from a long fishing pole. His mother sat next to him and read aloud. The two girls huddled around their father. He was the safe zone. The protector. Manfred plopped down next to his mom and looked up at her. She wore large round glasses and a sun hat. Her nose and cheeks just burnt.

"What're you reading?"

"A book about a captain and a whale," she said and ran her fingers through his hair.

"Can we stay here forever?" Manfred asked. He was surprised by his childlike voice.

She looked up from her book at her husband and asked, "Can't we quit our jobs? Stay out here forever?"

Manfred's father laughed.

The ocean was black and grew darker by the minute. His father cast out farther and farther, hoping to get his hook all the way to the middle of the sea. Manfred watched his father closely, the old man's growing beard and yellowing eyes looking out over the blackness.

"Look, Mr. Fred," he said. "That's Orion's belt. And just there, that's the Big Dipper. And there, if you look closely, that's the North Star."

When did it become night? thought Manfred, feeling suddenly cold again. He blinked once and his father disappeared. He felt his stomach tense and he began to cry. His mother asked what was wrong, but Manfred knew what was next. He blinked again and she was gone. His two sisters reached out toward him.

"Manny-Freddy," they yelled. "Where are you?" Their voices were older this time.

He stepped toward them, but they faded into the ocean— blue and bluer, then nothing.

Manfred fell to his knees, no longer the child on the beach— elsewhere, terrified and alone. He wanted to walk into the crashing waves, but soon even they disappeared and the world returned to darkness.

He felt around for a while, only certain of the sand below him. But even that came with questions. Was it the sand of his childhood beach, or the sand that he had watched devour Bealzut? Or was he in the desert again, where he had first set eyes on Liadra and her crew? He punched and cursed until his knuckles were marked with tiny cuts.

A small dot and a sound like moving icebergs appeared in the distance. With nowhere else to go, he crawled toward it. The sand was cold then hot then cold again. The noise grew louder but the dot stayed the same size, never changing, always just far out of reach. He recognized the sound from somewhere, but like the dot, its memory remained beyond his grasp, just at the periphery of his memories.

"How're you holding up?" said a voice.

Manfred knew the voice but dared not call out. He just kept crawling.

"They sent you to the Realm Unknown? What's it like? I heard it's strange and dangerous. Strange and dangerous. But I suppose it's all strange and dangerous to you." There was a laugh. "Don't worry though, newfriend. Just do like I do. Breathe."

"Os," Manfred whispered. "Is that you?"

"It is."

"You're in the realm unknown?"

"No, Manny. The Kin and I are in deep practice. Preparing. In practice."

"For what?"

There was a long silence.

"Don't worry. It'll all be over soon. As clear as day."

Manfred lay on the ground. His neck was warm and wet.

"But it hurts," said Manfred.

"Breathe through it, newfriend. Into the gut. Into the realms. The gut. The Saint transfers a great power to you."

Manfred's eyes closed and opened to see Ernie standing over him, covered in blood. The Ulis in the distance. Bealzut lay unmoving.

"Old man," yelled Ernie. "You best be right, old man. Old man."

A blueness emanated from the Ulis. He was awake and made signs as quick as his hands could move. Colored shapes filled the room and flickered the yellowed walls with shadows.

Manfred tried to sit up, but Ernie held him down. "I'm sorry, my boy. The old man," Ernie looked back at the Ulis, "The old man said it was the only way."

"Bealzut," Manfred said, trying to reach for his friend.

"Had to put him down. Fast. Doesn't listen though." Ernie tugged on the Ulis' arm. "Old man, we need to leave. To the Den."

The shapes the Ulis had been making started to join together. Squares fit against triangles and rested on rectangles until they formed a large circle behind him. Manfred scanned the room the best he could. Yarley sat in a corner. Manfred didn't see him before—he looked so old, so frail. His knees were pulled up to his chest and he rocked back and forth.

"Yarley?" Manfred pointed.

Ernie looked at him quickly. "He's doing his best. Poor old man. Poor old body. Took the brunt of the Young God. We were so unprepared. Can't worry about him, now, he does his best. Now we connect the realms and make a path," Ernie said impatiently. "Come on. Hurry. Hurry."

"Sit down," barked the Ulis. "Be quiet."

"But… I," as Ernie tried to respond, the blueness around the Ulis pulsed.

Ernie sat down next to Manfred.

"Over soon," he whispered and held Manfred's hand. "The end of war."

Manfred recognized the circle behind the Ulis, it was a portal. The Ulis scrunched his face like he was lifting something heavy and Bealzut's body lifted off the ground. Manfred tried to sit up again but Ernie held him down and whispered, "Do not worry, my boy."

Bealzut's body entered the portal and disappeared in a flash of light. Ernie stood up and threw Manfred over his shoulder. "It's almost over, Mr. Bugsbee."

With each step, Ernie took toward the portal Manfred felt a jolt of pain. His head ached and his eyelids were heavy. Ernie's body was frail beneath him. His shoulders were boney and there was so little muscle around the frame. Manfred wondered where all the power came from, the lithe stepping and grace. The body that carried him was old and tired. His feet barely lifted, long shuffles echoed in the room. Soon Manfred passed out from the blood loss.

When Manfred opened his eyes, he was back, alone in the garden. When he touched his neck there was no blood. He was weak and hungry but felt no pain. It was night and a cool breeze came down from above the walls. Ernie and the Keeper entered and Manfred sat up.

"Ole boy. Ole crow," Ernie said and tried to run to Manfred.

The Keeper grabbed his shoulder. "Slow down, my love. He's just coming to."

Ernie hiccuped.

Manfred raised his hands in front of his face.

"You're safe now," said the Keeper. "Nothing to fear."

Ernie nodded, his nose and cheeks red.

"Take your time. We have much to talk about," said the Keeper.

"Bealzut?" Manfred asked.

"Ole boy. He's a fighter that Beal … B … Zuts," Ernie laughed and hiccuped.

"He's safe," said the Keeper. "Resting. The Realm Unknown can be hard on a man."

"The Ulis?" Manfred continued.

Ernie and the Keeper looked at one another.

"Not safe, ole boy," Ernie said and sat down next to Manfred. "But what is a Ulis if not a dangerous place?"

Manfred looked to the Keeper.

"The Ulis and what's left of Yarley protect us. The Oarygus has nested in Yarley's body. The Ulis is with him now, trying to slow the cursed inevitable. The two will hold it off. Hold it in the White Room. Not forever. The incarnation will free itself. All in due time, Mindiidus. Now you must rest."

"My boy," said Ernie as he patted Manfred's back. "My Freddy. My Manny. You've done all right. What a time to do all right, ole boy. What a time."

The Keeper pulled Ernie back to his feet.

"Where exactly di'yuh put muh drink, woman?" Ernie said.

The Keeper glared at him then looked down at Manfred. "Come on now. You'll rest. Then we'll sort things out."

"What about Looma?"

Ernie touched his chest and stood a little taller. "The girl returns. That woman. Small warrior. The wolf and her three," he laughed. "Proud father. She stands above the Village."

"War is coming to the Old Guard, Mindiidus," said the Keeper. "Looma is its protector now."

TUNNELS OF HEYON

The next morning Manfred, Ernie, Bealzut, and the Keeper sat together in the banquet hall. It was much quieter than when Manfred had been pulled through by Ernie all that time ago. Together they ate sweet bread and eggs. Bealzut was quiet and pale. Ernie slapped his back.

"Felt the same my first time through. The egg of the Lori will help. Eat up," Ernie said and pointed a fork of food at him.

Bealzut nodded and took slow bites.

"Your work will not be forgotten, Hols'Beal," said the Keeper as she nudged Ernie.

"Yes, yes. You have done good, boy. We'll keep you around. Keep you close."

Bealzut sat up straight. "An honor."

Ernie grunted then looked at Manfred. "How you feel, ole Fred?"

"Fine, I guess. Tired."

"We're all tired. How's the neck?"

Manfred rubbed it. "Stiff."

"Thought I killed you."

"Guess I'm harder to kill than you thought," Manfred said.

Ernie laughed and took a bite of food. "We will be seeing."

"Erneel," said the Keeper. "You've joked so much about death. It's at the door now. Fenk says the Cloud's army is not three days from the village. Tansrit has evacuated the farmers. There is a fear, my Ernie."

Ernie bowed his head. "What can we do with death, dear? Not much but laugh."

"What happened to my neck, anyway?" asked Manfred.

"Ah," began Ernie. "The Ulis, he's old. Older than I thought he'd make. Mind is all bones and prophecies anymore. Another trick."

"You still doubt him? After all of this?" asked the Keeper.

"I don't doubt. I never said doubt. But the Ulis, dear, even he's unsure."

"Of what?" asked Manfred.

The Keeper and Ernie both looked at him. The Keeper spoke first, "We know that the Oarygus is weak. Lost, maybe. Out of its depth. Lured by Liadra and the fanatics, the Harvestors. But a weak Oarygus only grows stronger. When Yarley's body dies, there will be nothing left to hold it."

"My neck?" Manfred urged.

"We killed Mr. Bugsbee," said Ernie.

Manfred smiled. "I don't feel dead."

"You're not. Manfred Bugsbee though, he's gone. You've been cut free. Combined with a Relic. Becoming a Relic."

Manfred sat back and massaged his temples. "What now?"

Ernie took a bite of food. "I was sure it would kill you. I mean dead-dead. Not half-dead. Full gone. Dead as the Drilding desert. The Ulis wanted to do it on day one. Figured we'd try a different route to deal with the Harvestors. And it worked. You were powerful. You were courageous. But now we deal with entities whose full force could eat an earth. Could tear a hole in all of existence. We don't need powerful. We don't need courageous. We need sacrifice, my boy."

Manfred took a large bite of the sweet bread. "I don't feel any different though."

"Feel, feel, feel," said Ernie. "Worry less about how you feel. When the time comes, you'll put up a fight or you won't."

"Erneel!" the Keeper said quite agitated, then looked toward Manfred. "Much of these rituals are ancient. Untested for generations, if at all. Much of the evil we now face has never been seen before. Not like this. I apologize, Mindiidus, but we are learning just as you are. We know that the Oarygus will wish to take your body—started with Liadra, she was easy, weak. Yarley was next, frail, but none more powerful than he," she said as she looked into the distance. "Poor Yarley is combined with the thing. Fighting it from the inside. When Yarley dies," she covered her face for a moment. "When he dies the thing will be released and search out a new place to nest. With the Relic embedded in you, your power will be protected for a time. The Oarygus needs a body. Needs to be solid. It will seek you out."

Manfred shrugged his shoulders. "What then?"

"The Cloud and their armies have seen the commotion above the village," said Erneel.

Manfred cocked his head. "Above?"

"I saw it," said Bealzut. "Some small star being born."

The Keeper nodded. "The White Room is held above. If not for the Oarygus power we would pitch it into the sun. Kaseen and the Keepers of the Sign will hold it as long as they can. As long as Yarley and the Ulis can control it."

"So, what do we do?" Manfred asked impatiently.

"We go back to the Village. Looma and Tansrit will fight the armies of the Cloud. That is what they're sworn to do. What they're prepared to do. We will lure the Oarygus out, put you up against it, and hope to pull it from Yarley's body. If the Ulis is still alive and we're not killed by the Cloud in the desert, we'll try our best to kill the thing. To send it back." Erneel gave a nervous chuckle.

"Across the desert?" asked Bealzut.

"It's the fastest way."

"Not quite," Bealzut replied.

Bealzut led them up the beach and bent down here and there to pick up handfuls of sand. It was still cold as they walked and the ocean was a green foam. They could still see the Keeper's Den when Bealzut raised his hand for them to stop.

"Right over here," he said.

"It can't be," Erneel replied in disbelief.

"The Holst are everywhere," Bealzut continued.

He leaned down next to a large rock between two lone trees. The roots of the trees grew over the rock and spread out into the sand and dirt on either side. It was just at the edge of the tide and right below a high finger of land that reached into the ocean.

Bealzut put both hands on top of the rock and gave it two good tugs while Manfred and Ernie stood by.

The rock moved. The roots of the trees lifted and stretched aside and gave the rock a path to follow. It all unfolded in a mechanical sort of way, the roots moving like the levers and cogs of an old clock. Ernie was astounded as the opening revealed itself just large enough for a person.

"So close to the Den," said Erneel as he ran his hand through his beard.

"The Rivers Dald and the Tunnels of Heyon. Holst are at every turn, under every village."

"I'd seen them below the Northern territories, used them during the Great Fires." Erneel shook his head as he spoke, "But so close to the Den?"

"The Guard aren't the only secret holders, Saint. Now, follow me."

The tunnel was pitch black and went nearly straight down. They slid on their butts to keep from toppling into the abyss. The tunnel seemed to end throughout and Bealzut would feel around for the next opening. All the while Manfred felt so claustrophobic that he could hardly breathe.

"How can you see in here?" Manfred asked.

"What's to see?" replied Bealzut. "We're almost there."

Almost there felt like miles. The slope of the tunnel began to even out and soon the men were crawling head first, one hand always brushing aside roots and hanging clods of dirt. When they stopped again Bealzut adjusted himself and pushed on a smooth stone with both feet. The stone rolled forward and light came through. The three men stepped into the opening and emerged in a massive cavern. A serene body of water stretched out in front of them.

Crystalline forms grew up from all sides and met each other in luminescent shapes, somehow lit from within. There were no true walls, only open spaces which disappeared into the stalactite teeth of the ancient crystals. Minerally stone pillars crisscrossed above them and curved down into the clear water. The water was so still it was hard to tell where it started and the rocks ended, occasionally catching some light or some shadow to reveal its depth. It was impossible to see how large the system of rivers was as it dipped out of sight and beyond the monolith formations.

"Sit," Bealzut said and motioned to a flat spot. He stripped off his robe and stretched his arms above his head. His whole body was covered with deep burn scars. Ridges of flesh twisted together up his torso and down his ribs. Dark rivets and knots traversed his hips and legs.

Bealzut took a few deep breaths and dove into the water. Manfred moved to stand but Ernie held him down.

"What is this place?" Manfred asked.

"One of the Holst's many secrets, I suppose. I knew about their tunnels. It's even said they know of a few folds in reality itself. Something so simple, though, so near the Den. Were we not already faced with such extreme and unbelievable circumstances, I'd say I was dreaming, ole boy," Ernie said as he rubbed his beard contemplatively.

In the time it took the two men to relax onto the flat rock Bealzut emerged from the water and pulled behind him a weathered rope.

"Pull," he said.

They worked themselves hand over hand until a raft appeared in the distance. It was so rotted and crooked, a miracle that it could even float. But it did, and it was all they had.

"This is the Holst's great secret," Manfred joked.

"The way. One of many," replied Bealzut as he swung his arms about to dry a bit, before tying his robe around his waist.

"This'll take us to the Village, then?" asked Ernie.

"Close to. Much faster than by land. Straight. A few bends," Bealzut boarded the small raft and waved for the others to join.

"And if the Holst find out?" asked Ernie.

Bealzut smiled. "Pray they don't."

Bealzut used a long stick attached to the back of the raft to push it forward. Where the water wasn't shallow enough for the stick to touch the bottom, its flat end was used as a paddle. Manfred and Ernie sat up front as Bealzut steered. The water was full of living algae and sandy spires in its depths. Undercurrents pulled them along and Bealzut's expert use of the pole kept the raft from capsizing. The water forked and bent in every conceivable direction, Bealzut somehow knew where each one led. To Manfred, it felt like a never-ending shell game, a guess of left or right. Only once did Bealzut hesitate, but with an "ah yes," he pushed against a boulder that had closed in on them. He paddled from one current to the next until one took hold and rushed them toward an opening.

Manfred laid down the best he could and let his hand drag in the cool water. He was relaxed, even as he thought back on the many misadventures that had led him here. Running from Ernie in the woods. The awful desert. The unimpressed glare of Looma. Manfred looked up at Ernie. The old man was sitting cross-legged in deep thought. Certainly calculating every possible next move, contemplating the many ways that he and his party may die. He used to be afraid of Ernie, afraid of everything, but now Manfred felt confidence or at least something like it. He even thought for a moment that he no longer feared death, that it was right around the corner and he'd gladly lay down his life for Ernie. The end of his journey was coming.

As he got comfortable, he kept his eyes open and imagined they were in the belly of some beast. The stone shapes of the roof were its teeth and tongue—rotten, in need of dental work. The cavernous spaces above and beyond them were its hollows, its stomach, the negatives of its ribcage. Bulbous roots grew into one another like cancers of the lungs and heart. Its breath was a salty, sometimes sour smell that wasn't altogether unpleasant. It reminded him of the fairgrounds by his house growing up. The mass of people and their sweat. The farm animals and cotton candy. And the beasts' eyes were many.

Manfred sat up. "Eyes?"

In the darkness above them, there was movement. Silty, furred creatures moved from spire to spire, their radiant eyes catching the light. Manfred whispered and pointed. Bealzut spoke without looking up from his task. "Boagly Fai. They know my scent."

Manfred looked at Ernie who only shrugged his shoulders and he was suddenly quite afraid of death again.

Once he noticed one of the animals, they were all he could see. They moved in and out of the caverns, over and under one another. Some human qualities, some subterranean. Their bodies were arched little things covered in hair. The light of the caverns was rarely good enough to make them out completely, but in places, the reflection and power emitted from the water cast the creatures in perfect relief. Most of them were covered in matted, ragged fur from toe to ear—mangy devilish things. Bald spots here and there revealed red wrinkled flesh. Claw-like hands and feet gripped around the different hangings of the tunnels.

The creatures seemed harmless and even uninterested in the boat below them, but there was something about their movements that unsettled Manfred. They didn't move like monkeys or squirrels, rather, it was reptilian, slithering for position. Their little square-shaped heads turned independent of their bodies.

"They rarely eat humans," said Bealzut matter-of-factly. "Although, on my first transport mission, we'd been hired to bring a young man home to the Ingay Coast. The Boagly caught me off guard and snatched him up. Was a wicked sight. Were not acquainted with me then—my scent."

Ernie reached for his sword.

"As I said, *rarely*," said Bealzut.

Ernie kept his hand on his sword. "When Looma was young, Delute would tell her stories, give the poor girl nightmares, that dirty crow. In one of Kaseen's books, in one of her libraries, was his favorite. Explorers set out to conquer every piece of the world. River and ocean. Mountain and skyline. They followed each bath and bog to its conclusion. There were rumors of underground cities older than time. Explorers raced to discover these unmarked catacombs." Ernie followed the path of the critters as he spoke. "Each time they found a new entrance, a new body would float up in some port. Gutted, bones gnawed on. And the settlers who made a home below the Harper

Mountains. In the span of six days, they all went missing. Weren't found, but arms and legs."

Bealzut nodded.

They continued through two more dark tunnels which dipped ever-deeper into the earth. The creatures came and went, never stopping for more than a second to observe the small craft. Eventually they emerged into a well-lit pool and Bealzut guided them to some flat rocks where they docked the boat.

Beazlut returned the raft to the waterway, hiding its anchor deep below the surface. He led the way toward an opening in the wall where they were met by three of the creatures, much larger than the others—manes of thin, criscrossing, filthy hair.

The creatures stood upright, slightly hunched over, the knuckles of their fore claws loosely touching the ground. One approached Bealzut. Its face was a mess of burrs with eyes just above center. It opened its mouth as if to speak and Manfred felt the itch of battle in his stomach. All around the creature's now revealed mouth were clods of dirt and tangled pieces of some poor small mammal's meat. The creature's breath was rotten and pungent. The Boagly, as Bealzut called it, chomped its oddly human teeth together in a quick rhythm and extended its hand toward Bealzut's face. Ernie moved to present his sword, but Bealzut shook his head in protest.

"Should not be here, I know," Bealzut said to the creature who used its long fingers to examine his face—clicking its tongue as it did. The other two creatures seemed uninterested and sat down.

Bealzut motioned for Ernie and Manfred to move closer so the Boagly could examine them as well. It touched Manfred's face with its massive hand. The Boagly's fingers, mostly covered in fur, were bony things protected by a calloused flesh. Remnants of entrails and earlier feasts remained in the crags of their fingernails. Manfred felt his bravery wavering as the Boagly moved on to Ernie. The creature revealed its teeth a final time in something like a wide smile then turned and kicked the others out of the way.

"Knows your scents as well," Bealzut said.

THE VILLAGE FALLS

Their path out of the cave system went nearly straight up. Manfred was in the back, constantly being struck with small rocks broken loose by his partners.

"Where are we?" Erneel asked impatiently.

"Close," Bealzut replied. "Just under your village, now."

Erneel shook his head. "The Holst are clever, but not even they could get this close."

Bealzut laughed and the party pushed on.

The dirt turned into stone and the grade lessened. Soon they were switchbacking in relative darkness. Manfred had to listen closely for the footsteps to find his way. The path turned into stairs. And then there was light—a splinter, the arc of a crescent moon.

"Do the honors?" Bealzut said to Erneel.

Ernie reached out toward the light and his hands were met with cool slats of wood.

"Push," said Bealzut.

As he did the slats moved in a spiral pattern and revealed more and more light until a passageway opened up. Ernie was the first to go through.

"How?" he said. "How could they?"

Bealzut and Manfred came through next.

"This is Greikor's Pub. I know that seal." He gestured to a lighted corner of the room. An emblem of a bird in a triangle was painted on the ceiling.

"Greikor's father was Holst," said Bealzut.

"Traitor," Erneel snapped.

The three of them stood in the cellar of the pub. A place that Erneel had been going for years and years—a place he had shared many a story of conquest and defeat. The room was lined with barrels of wine and fermented fruits. The passage they had come through had already closed—the fake top of a cask of wine, spring loaded.

Erneel was still shaking his head in disbelief as the chaos above them began to settle in. The Village was being torn apart by war. It was easy for them to forget as they made their way through the tunnels and were preoccupied with the Boagly Fai below them. Dust shook from the rafters and the whole building echoed from the battle above.

"The villagers could use your tunnels to get to safety," said Erneel.

Bealzut shook his head. "The Boagly Fai, Saint. Your villagers wouldn't survive. They're safer taking cover here. And if the Holst catches them, they'd be sold to the slavers."

Ernie shook his head. "After this is through these passages will be filled. I'll kill every Boagly Fai and Holst that gets in my way." He stepped toward Bealzut.

"I'm no longer Holst. I took you two through the tunnels. I'm unmarked. You know that. Your fight is not with me, Saint."

Manfred moved to comfort Ernie.

There was a commotion ahead of them and three members of the Cloud crashed through the basement door. One of them dragged a young woman by the hair.

"Saint Ernie," she cried out in surprise and desperation.

"Herki?" Ernie replied. It was Greikor's daughter, no older than thirteen.

One of the members of the Cloud ran back out on seeing Ernie and Manfred chased after him.

"Close your eyes, dear," Ernie said to the young woman and moved through the remaining men in two quick slices—they fell to the ground in unison, dismembered and still shaking. Ernie grabbed the girl and held her close.

"I'm so sorry. Where is your father?"

She looked at him and burst into tears.

"My dear. I'm so sorry. You'll be safe here. When we leave, barricade yourself. We'll get you when it's all over." Ernie's face was covered in blood and the young girl looked up at him in horror. "I'm sorry."

Bealzut and Ernie dragged the bodies out of the room and closed the door. They could still hear Herki crying on the other side.

Manfred had caught up to the other in the hallway.

When Bealzut and Ernie made it to his side, Manfred had already disarmed the man and held the man's crude knife to his neck.

Bealzut looked at Manfred, surprised, and nodded his head in approval.

Ernie knelt next to the man and asked, "my village?"

Manfred dug the knife into his neck.

"Made past the gates in four nights. The rocks," the man's eyes glazed over in a terrible memory, "they killed so many. But we pushed through, our Abominations have breached the walls. It's over."

Ernie touched Manfred's shoulder and forced eye contact.

Manfred only hesitated for a moment and pulled the knife across the man's throat. A splash of blood and the man went limp.

The three of them exited the pub just as a bridge collapsed above them. Fires had broken out in the older districts and terrified villagers were trying to escape into the streets but were quickly pushed back by the fighting. There was chaos in every direction and Manfred had no idea who was a friend or foe. Tansrit's men flooded the bloodied streets and grappled with the Cloud. Flames and smoke billowed from every side alley and crawl space. The fog of war upset all sense of direction and Manfred could do nothing but stay low and follow Ernie. No one seemed to acknowledge them, everyone was caught up in a struggle to kill or be killed.

Ernie led the way toward the Citadel. They had to get to the Oarygus. The village could only survive if the Young God was destroyed.

A white sphere floated above the Citadel. Shimmers of heat hovered around it in swirling patterns. Smoke billowed all around as the fires of the village continued to build. The Ulis and Yarley were inside doing their best to slow the chaos of the Oarygus finding a new body.

"Kaseen will release the room as soon as she senses us," Erneel said as they moved forward. "And we cannot hesitate. Attack with everything you have." They rested under a stone awning. "How do you feel, Manfred?"

Manfred nodded his head. "Will it be over soon?"

Ernie smiled. "I hope so, dear boy. It seems that it has to be."

Most of the time Manfred had been on this earth he felt sick. He had watched friends die. He had killed. He had spoken telepathically to strange beasts. He was calm now as if his purpose was coming. He looked from Bealzut to Ernie and couldn't help but smile. Two of the realm's greatest warriors had his back. And Manfred knew that Looma was standing above them at the gates and charged with protecting the village. No one could do it better.

Tansrit's men had done well to push the Cloud into the side streets. Their numbers didn't matter as much in the smaller spaces. The villagers were under strict orders to stay indoors, but some of them took to the streets and used pots and kitchen knives to fight where they could.

At first, the help of the villagers was a burden, even a danger, Tansrit and his men had to protect them while trying to protect themselves, but as the battle waged on the extra hands became a necessity. Tansrit and his men were better trained but outnumbered and the use of the Kin's Abominations was more than the gates could take.

There were four Kin in total and they came in two waves. One and then three. The first was taught a lesson for the whole of the Cloud army. In the early morning, it charged the front gate. Most of its gangly body was covered in large rings of chain-mail. Archers tried to slow it down. They used the cover of the farmhouses and silos, but it was of no use. It was large and knob-headed and nearly came eye to eye with Looma above the gate.

Days before, while Manfred and Erneel waited to meet with Liadra in the White Room, Looma had been preparing. The Keeper's Three are a weapon as old as the realms, seldom used, and only as a last resort. Three rocks, each no bigger than the palm of one's hand, had been imbued with an ancient power. A similar energy to that used by the Oarygus in their building of worlds—an artifact of their creation. The Keeper and those that came before her protected and studied the stones—learned how to manipulate them. When ultimate force was needed to be used to protect the secrets of the Old Guard the Three were unleashed. Small at first, like skipping stones, smooth earthen things, but with the proper guide, Looma held the mantle, the Stones could grow to the size of houses. Once the stones take on their final shape, they become an extension of their guide. Looma and her mother before her, and so on, can move them through the world as if they were their own appendages. A task of superhuman strength and constitution that would exhaust even the greatest of warriors. Kaseen and other Keepers of the Sign became conduits of energy to sustain Looma, two standing at her side and the rest in the Hall of Signs, all meditating on her, all surrounding her with their protection.

As the Cloud prepared their final attack drawing all their forces to the valley, Looma performed rites and scattered the Three in the farmland below the village. Each stone once placed on the battlefield rattled with primordial energy—powers created before the dawn of time, built in them and as it did, they grew. Once Looma took her post above the village the stones had become monolithic versions of themselves. Each one was twice the size of the quiet huts that scattered the terrain. As the first Abomination approached, she was as calm as she had ever been. Washed over with the power of the Three, she took a deep breath and raised two of the stones, unsettling the Abomination as it awkwardly slid through. It fell to three limbs and slowly found its footing. The trap was set and Looma was energized. She pulled the stones forward and knocked the beast off balance again. It tried to grapple with one of them, but it was no use. She was fortified and the Stones were unmovable except at her command. She made the stones fall to the ground and the ensuing quake took the legs out from under the beast. With the flick of her wrist, the stones moved over its torso. The beast cried out in anguish as blue-black blood sprouted from its armor. Legend has it the whole Cloud army froze in fear.

And they did.

After killing the first abomination, Looma pressed the Stones out as far as she could and used them to congest the Cloud's approach. It worked for a while, but once they passed into the open fields, she wasn't able to track back. Tanrsit elected to keep most of his men inside the village walls. It was only a matter of time before the Cloud closed in on the gate.

The remaining Kin, as thick as redwoods, made it through the valley unscathed and slammed themselves into the gate. Their bodies were adorned with armor and heavy chainmail that clanked against them and sent waves of sound echoing out.

Arrows came down from the towers that protected the main gates but made little impact—like flies against a lion. Fire was out of the question. If the Abominations caught fire and made their way through the gates, they'd set the whole place alight in a matter of minutes. It took no time for them to create a crack in the ancient walls.

Looma continued to use the Stones in the field. Large swaths of the Cloud were smashed into bits as the Three rolled over them. It was carnage like nothing she could have ever imagined. The power flowed through her. To kill her enemies from a distance like this didn't feel right—the disconnection sickened her. With each person she tore through her resolve lessened, but she was resigned to the mess of war and these were her tools.

It was a remarkable sight. In no time the stones were caked in gore. They didn't roll, instead, they dragged through the marshes and fields, upturning everything in their wake. Slow impending objects that made mush of anyone who dared test them. At first small units of the Cloud tried to fight the stones directly, but they couldn't create enough force to disrupt Looma's connection. As the battle unfolded the Cloud learned to avoid them at all costs, counting on Looma's hesitation to destroy the farmhouses of the people she was sworn to protect, but in the end, she bowled over everything. It was an all-out war—complete and total destruction.

Men and women of the Guard jumped down from the towers and grappled with the Abominations, looking for any break in their defense. Tansrit's men wore harnesses tethered to the wall and carried swords and axes. The Abominations were hyper-focused by their nature and continued to hurl themselves against the walls, even as small humans slashed at their bodies and crawled on them like ants. Members of the Cloud threw spears and launched rocks at them and would pull them down and slice their harness whenever they could. The fight localized to the ground below the village gates. The Abominations kept up their bludgeoning and Tansrit's men did their best to slow it.

Soon arrows became useless—there were too many on both sides in the folds of battle. Any long-range attacks risked injuring one's own forces. A few archers were left to protect Looma and the Keepers. The rest replaced their bows with swords.

When the gate did fall it had been beaten so badly that it opened with almost no sound. An eerie sight for the men and women on either side. Weapons at the ready, the Abominations burst through and slid into the large courtyard. Having finished their initial task, they were left in a moment of undirected rage and they smashed everything in sight, tripping and falling over one another.

Waves of the Cloud entered the village. Mostly men with long twisted spears, their bodies covered in thin sheets of steel and their faces covered in their enemies' blood and gray mud. Followed closely behind them were horsemen with longswords, the tips dragging on the ground in sparks.

A horseman of the Cloud carrying a large warhammer dismounted his horse. With a guttural howl and a wave of his hand, the Abominations fell back in line and huddled in front of the amassing forces. The man had a large square head with tufts of unkempt hair covering much of his face—Pencaut Elo, the Bone King's successor. He had scars over both eyes and a sickly jaundiced complexion. His arms were nearly as thick as his torso, the odd body of a lifelong soldier.

"Give up now and you have my word—we won't execute the civilians," Pencaut yelled out toward the readied Guard. He pointed his sword at the floating room above the village. "The battle is lost, Tansrit. No one else needs to die."

Tansrit moved forward from the line of armored warriors who blocked the main path into the city. He lifted his visor as if to speak, but instead pointed his sword to the right then left of where the Cloud had mostly gathered. Explosions erupted from where he signaled and centuries-old masonry crumbled down onto the Cloud.

Two of the Abominations avoided the falling buildings and charged at the Guard's line. Many of the members of the Cloud were either caught in the wake of the falling stone or on the wrong side of it. The surviving members climbed over the wreckage, many of their horses now hobbled and worthless.

A troop of the Guard confronted the abominations and tried to lead them down a sideroad. Many of them carried arched spears and razor-sharp pikes. They wore light armor and moved in unison, attacking and retreating in lockstep. Their long weapons clanked and sparked against the armor of the Kin. Smaller members of the troop carried rusted iron chains, three for each, and tried to trip up the beast. It worked to frustrate and slow them down, but the Abominations were too strong and the chains broke free under the strain and scattered the chain-bearers, stretching the focus of the troop. It quickly devolved into a game of containment. The Kin wreaked havoc down the deserted side streets of the Village. They tore down bridges and hurled ancient timbers dislodged from the framework at anything that moved. Structures twisted and crumpled to the flat stone and dirt of the roads.

The third of the Kin freed itself from the rubble near the gate. It limped into formation with the surviving members. Horns of war erupted from both camps and stoked the fervor of battle. Having made it through the gate and rubble, the Cloud wasted no time and charged into the foreign streets, colliding head-on with Tansrit and his men. It became a vision of pure hell as blood and sparks flew from blade to bone. The Kin, although injured from the explosions, got low and swung its long arms across the ground, uprooting whoever wasn't quick enough to move, its appendages becoming a gnarled mess, swords and arrows sticking out in all directions.

The other two Abominations still ran amuck. Slowed only slightly from the blades and arrows that had made it through, nothing but destruction in their wake. They had separated, the rounder of the two barreling forth and pulling down balconies and tossing them at the approaching soldiers. The other zig-zagged through side streets and alleyways as it made its way toward the Citadel with a singular focus. It slipped out of the iron chains the Guard was throwing with ease, its movements so powerful and unpredictable.

The wide cobblestone roads shook under the heavy trample. Halfway between the Abomination and the slope to the Citadel, a line of heavily armored horsemen leaned forward on their animals and whispered to one another. They all knew they were facing death. Foot soldiers had been tasked with collecting used cooking oil from the villagers. They poured it out as the

Abomination was nearing. When the beast stepped in the first puddle it lost its footing and slipped toward the horseman—who pushed on full force. Some dove off of their horses and grappled with the appendages of the creature, others made passes and sliced off what they could.

The Kin stopped moving after it killed a few men and broke the necks of a few horses. As the last hiss of breath came out from within the furnace of its stomach, the beast exploded. Plumes of fire billowed into the sky from the explosion and left a large shadowed crater of its body—a stain of death. The buildings on either side of the road caught fire.

Looma had only dared to look back into the Village once as she prepared for the second and third waves of the Cloud. She wished to be on the ground with Tansrit, to have Delute's back one more time as the village burnt. As the second wave made it past the Stones, Erneel, Manfred, and Bealzut made their way to the Citadel.

OARYGUS

The White Room floated above the Citadel. Erneel and the other two had no time to assess the wreckage of the village as they moved forward. There was carnage down every alley and over every hill.

They reached the flat of the Citadel just under where the White Room hung like a strange egg. For the millionth time, Manfred thought to himself, *I've never seen anything like this*. It didn't matter though. As the village burned and the shrieks of war echoed against every wall he knew where his battle was. Above him was some sort of destiny.

Ernie wasted no time. He did not bother to ask Manfred and Bealzut if they were ready. He drew his sword and cast a shape above his head, a green circle with two black exes in its center, and pushed it toward the White Room. In an almost soft way, as if the earth coaxed the room into its embrace, the White Room crashed to the ground—violence in its last moments. Splintering into kaleidoscopic sections, leaving jagged membranes of itself scattered about.

The body of Yarley emerged from the wreckage, the pieces of the room surrounding him and seemed to jostle in his gravity as he stretched to his full height. He walked in long strides and dragged some formless object behind him. With every step, fractured light rose from his feet and spilled out of his head. The light moved around and through him, flickering in the absences of his eyes. Sounds of dying animals welled up from the caverns of his chest. When he finally stopped walking the light lost its intensity and settled into a dense fog on the stones beneath him.

When Ernie realized what Yarley was dragging, he cried out, "No". It was the body of the Ulis. Yarley lifted and threw the body, which landed just in front of them. Less than a carcass, only skin and his ornamental robe were left. Manfred looked down in horror.

"What is this place?" said a voice from within Yarley. "You have kept me trapped." He pointed at the Ulis' body. "A powerful body. An old earth."

"You are lost," Ernie yelled out. "That is all."

Yarley stretched his neck and looked down toward the village. "There is war?"

"Not yours," Ernie replied.

"And these bodies?" Yarley stretched his arms out and the shell of the Ulis moved slightly.

"What do you mean?" asked Ernie.

"They are not my kin, but they are quite strong. Not gods. But what?"

"Protectors," Ernie replied.

"Of?"

Ernie looked around himself. "Of our earth."

Yarley's body rose until he was high enough to see much of the world below him. Beyond the village, the valley was almost completely engulfed in flames. Fire poured off the still standing farmhouses and moved in dark twists and turns. The sludge of viscera amassed throughout the clearings. Death was all around.

Inside the walls of the village, rubble and dust spun up. The old structures leaned and fell into one another. The last of the Abominations limped down a side road and whipped its hand into groups of the Cloud and the Guard. It no longer cared who it killed, it only wished to assert its power while it still lived. Piles of weapons and limbs formed and soldiers fought on in pure desperation.

Ernie, Manfred, and Bealzut watched as Yarley floated back down. He was close enough now that the men could make out his features. Yarley's body was dead. His eye sockets empty and his mouth agape, his charred tongue stretched over his chin. The voice of the Oarygus came from within.

"Nothing to protect. This place is dead."

"It's only dying," said Erneel. "And there's nothing wrong with that."

Yarley turned and walked toward the Citadel. He stood under its high marble walls and the pillars that framed it against the mountain. Ernie, Manfred and Bealzut inched forward.

"Did you build this?" Yarley asked in contemplation. "A wonder in a sick world?" He motioned down the steps where Tansrit's men had dug in to stop the Cloud. "My others built it all, each drop of rain constructed in our image, each turn of the wind."

The three tried to encircle Yarley as he spoke.

"Where is the one who called on me and brought me to this place?"

"You killed her. She is dead." Ernie said.

"Ah. Children of death. Bounded only by life."

Manfred and Bealzut looked at one another. Bealzut had both weapons drawn, the smaller of his swords held low. Manfred's hands both glowed in preparation but nothing manifested. He could feel the burn of the relic pulse through him and pull him toward Yarley.

Yarley turned toward Manfred.

"I recognize you. I tried to burrow in your body. Too strong. Not a god. Not like me. Some shifting, changing shape."

Manfred looked toward Ernie for help. Ernie charged and Rocinallia flashed brilliantly but could not touch the Oarygus. Yarley's body slid just out of reach. Bealzut attacked from the other side. Both weapons moved in lightning-fast precision, but he was met with the same strange distance as if their movements alone repelled the entity. The dance went on for only a few moments. Yarley's arms raised and the two men were pushed away. Ernie slammed into a stone pillar and Bealzut against a half-wall above the steps.

Yarley's body moved just outside of time. The world around him was slow and secondary. His movements had a rigidity to them, something like a new foal finding balance. Yet it seemed to operate just beyond the corporeal world. Bealzut and Ernie were back on their feet but their attacks were worthless. Manfred tried to help, but whatever power the relic had inside of him only made him feel heavy and warm. His hands glowed but only produced occasional pops and hisses of light—no weapon.

"Come closer," the Oarygus said and Manfred floated toward him. Bealzut and Ernie kept up their attempts, circling, throwing themselves at Yarley though they couldn't gain an inch on the being.

Manfred's body hummed with pain and the world around him faltered in and out of his periphery. Soon he could only see Yarley's face in a gyrating mist. His eyes formed two tunnels that reached into the depths of hell. His beard and the hair on his head moved as his face twitched.

Manfred felt his thoughts pull out of his head as the Oarygus reached into him and scraped at his memories. There was his first kiss—a girl named Laura. They were thirteen, behind a convenience store. She was wearing peach-flavored lip gloss. Yarley's eyes became hers, wide and hopeful. There was the night he found out his parents had died. The whole world was icy and black. Ran off the road by a drunk driver. Both dead in a flash. He cried as he remembered feeling relieved that neither of them suffered. He remembered seeing his sisters for the first time after, the complete and utter emptiness. The way nothing was the same with them after.

Manfred could do nothing but form dry sounds of anguish. Bealzut and Ernie lay against the rubble, both of their heads bloodied. Bealzut held his weapons in both hands and tried to sit upright but his body failed over and over again. Manfred could see the skin of the Ulis as his own body was being drained. The memories became tangible. Objects pulled up from his guts, through his pores, and into the air.

Below them, Tansrit and his men held their line against the Cloud as the Abomination made its way toward them. It was only a matter of time before they'd be crushed. Manfred could see and feel it all from somewhere outside his body. He felt Tansrit tense as he parried an oncoming strike then he felt his blade dig into a member of the Cloud—a tall blonde man with scattered freckles and young eyes. The young man was full of rage and fear as blood filled his throat.

Tansrit yelled for his men to hold fast, but their resolve had weakened. Some of them scattered as the great beast barreled toward them. Members of both sides cowered, one eye on their enemy and one eye searching for a place to hide. Tansrit could not stop. He grabbed his men by their armor and pushed them forward. He told them to fight. And with that, he continued to hack through any member of the Cloud within range. Blood slicked the steps of the Citadel when the Abomination finally reached them. The beast was stuck through with arrows and howled with each step. It carried a mangled, armored body and used it as a bludgeon and smashed its way through both Guard and Cloud, kicking and swinging its full might against them. With Tansrit's last breath he stabbed his sword through the demon's face. The blade stayed in place as Tansrit's neck and back broke in a single blow.

Manfred could feel the blade in the beast's face. It went in just under the eye and barely missed the space where its brain should have been. Instead, there was a glowing mass that spread out from its head and into its limbs. Manfred could feel the light vibrate through the thing. The glow originated in the beast's stomach and worked its way around the dark sinews that made up its innards. There were no organs, just denser areas of illumination. Its blood was a byproduct of the light as it poured through the concentrations and created pools of weighted heat in the caverns of its body.

With each step the Abomination took something rose to meet it. From deep beneath the stones that made up the village and the dead dirt below another energy built.

"Hold him a little longer. Longer," said a voice from below, and for a moment Manfred could see Os'halla's face.

Manfred returned to his own body to see Yarley hanging in the air. The old man was contorted in an angular way, unmoving except for waves of black light that pulled from his face. Manfred was connected with the monster that controlled Yarley—their bodies and intentions bound through an intense energy that coursed through the both of them.

The Abomination was still moving toward them.

Ernie and Bealzut were back on their feet. Both men were exhausted and nearly defeated, but the power of Manfred gave them hope.

"Hold him, hold him," Erneel cried out.

The light between Manfred and Yarley formed mirages of their bodies, crashing into one another and folding over until it clustered into a sphere. Manfred could hear the Oarygus crying out, the sounds of a dying machine—unoiled, screeching halt.

The Abomination reached the top of the stairs, its whole body covered in a thick crystalizing sap, its life force pouring out its many wounds, Tansrit's sword still stuck out of its face like some grotesque appendage. Ernie and Bealzut turned to face it, both slumped over but ready, prepared to give their last breath. The beast arched its back and howled. With its arms above its head, the demon may well have been a thousand feet tall. Before it could bring its hands down, a yellow flower sprouted from its head. Then a silver one. Another yellow. A few blue and light red. Its face was soon covered. It tried in vain to pull them out, but with each tear, another two would appear. The beast panicked and its howl became a distinct cry. Ernie and Bealzut attacked. With each slash of their weapons a burst of leaves spired out of the beast. The tears and cuts of its wooden flesh were born out with new life.

The beast tried to fend them off, but the pain of this transformation was too much and soon it stood frozen. A tree once again, bent and spiraled against the darkening sky.

Manfred and Yarley remained locked. The form of light between them shifting shapes, casting horror shadows across every inch of earth, turning in on itself and folding against the world around it. Flashes of lightning cracked in the distance.

The bodies of Tansrit's men and the warriors of the Cloud began to deteriorate. Branches of green and brown boughs sprouted from their lifeless eyes and ears. The more mangled their bodies, the more blood, the more brilliant green they became. The blood in the streets became a rising moisture that formed clouds around the rubble. Sheets of rains sprouted downward from their hollows and fed the new plants. The whole city was being cleansed and muddied all at once. The warriors of both sides stood dumbfounded, uncertain. Some cried, some fought on.

Looma remained above what was left of the village gates and looked out over the valley. Skirmishes still erupted in the far corners but most of the battle had made its way into the village. Her ears and eyes were bleeding, a symptom of the Keeper's

Three. Her mind and body depleted—her soul overwrought with anguish.

In her life, Looma had fought countless battles, killed countless foes but this was different. The Stones could crush ten men in the time it took her to point. As she weakened, she used the Stones to guide the Cloud toward death, pushing them into gullies and ditches, back toward mountain passes. Those who dared stand their ground were quickly turned to mulch. Those who made it past the gates would never want to return to the valley.

She could feel the village change behind her but dared not turn around. The three archers that protected her took turns looking over their shoulders. It was almost over, they said. There was nothing left to do. Looma laid down and the Stones rested in the ash of the valley. The archers did not leave her side. It didn't matter anyway, no one would enter the village as it changed. The Keepers knelt next to her and cried.

The rubble of the place was soon overgrown with trees that grew up from the mangled bodies beneath. Where there had been stone for thousands of years new roots burrowed down. Living vines traced the architecture and went over doors and through open windows. Villagers peered out from their homes, only to retreat for fear they'd become transformed next.

The Oarygus was now formed in front of Manfred, no longer bonded to Yarley, whose body fluttered empty in the wind. Held up by a friction in the air, an electricity that bound the two, Manfred looked out over the village. In his mind, there was no separation between himself and the world below. He couldn't see where his body ended and the newly sprouted flora began, his pores becoming conduits of some new energy. The whole earth shook in and around him. It was all so terrifying. He felt the hooks of fear digging into him, coursing through his whole universe. But beyond that he felt something else, he was compelled to continue, to not let the Oarygus regain control.

The only distinction in Manfred's reality was between himself and the Oarygus. It had become a being of pure light, contrasted against every shadow visible or imagined. The two of them hovered in space, their bodies a simulacrum. Manfred could feel the Sacred Kin pouring life into the world. It swelled through him and into the void that he and the Oarygus had entered.

"Was called on. Invited in to eat. To nourish," the Oarygus cried out.

"You must leave. Or I will kill you," replied Manfred.

Their words were only echoes.

"Kill? Cannot die. Only wish to rest. Sleep in the womb of this place."

Manfred felt a violent tug somewhere inside his body.

"What is this inside of you to make you strong? Will not let me enter—not let me sleep." the Oarygus asked.

The pain intensified.

"Some old bones. Some ancient power." It continued and scraped through Manfred's organs searching for the Relic.

"Leave," Manfred begged.

"You are a precious life form. A magnificent little creature. But I grow weary. Grow bored."

Manfred was below the Citadel again, the smell of the world green and wet and his body ached. Erneel and Bealzut were at his side, trying to lift him to his feet. His legs hurt and his brain felt like mush.

"Is it gone?" asked Erneel.

Manfred tried to speak but was overcome with exhaustion.

"The Kin?" Erneel said looking out over the village. "Os set a trap—used the power of that demon—sapped its energy—turned our village into a breathing forest."

"It... isn't," Manfred spoke between long breaths, "it isn't gone. Ernie. It hasn't..."

Manfred jerked to his feet and felt the atoms and very makeup of his existence rattle. He heard a sound like rushing water as the Relic pulled out of his body. When Erneel had stabbed it into him it was solid and could fit in the palm of his hand, but it broke down inside of him and spread through his veins—into his brain, his kidneys, his lungs, into the hollows of his bones. It pulled out in barely visible, bloodied, white bits. Manfred did not scream. The pain was complete. It took every ounce of fortitude he had just to exist, to stand there as his body was eradicated from the inside out.

As the pieces floated out of him the mist of the place began to lift. The new plants were magnetized to the forming relic. The Abomination looked to be alive again, but it was only an illusion of the swaying leaves and branches. Bealzut and Ernie stood back and watched.

Once the relic was completely out of Manfred's body it formed the crude shape of a man, strung together by the bits and pieces of its former self, all within a cloudy substance that fluctuated from light to dark, infinite to nothingness. It lit up like the neural pathways of some foreign intelligence. The blades of grass and trees that had been pulling toward the creature began to wither. Just as soon as they appeared, they were dying.

With each dead plant, the new form of the Oarygus grew, the mists surrounding it nearly reaching the top of the Citadel and the body within stretched out and collapsed over and over again. Manfred, Ernie, and Bealzut were trapped in its folds. Their bodies warmed from the inside as the world around them dried up. The Abomination was the first to catch on fire. A plume of smoke erupted from the foliage of its face and the bodies it had torn through were soon engulfed as well.

Manfred laid on the ground and watched as Bealzut caught fire. It did not seem painful, he was there, then he was ash. Ernie raised his sword against the coming death and laid over Manfred as the flames of the place passed over them. It was hot and it was coming to an end.

Once the Oarygus had stopped growing it moved away, down the steps and into the city. Everything crumbled at its touch, absorbed in smoke and heat. The foundations of the buildings cracked and bent until they gave way and toppled down on the floating form. Villagers were tossed from their homes in heaps. They never touched the ground. Their bodies charred then evaporated in gusts of wind.

Manfred was dead. At least as dead as he could have ever imagined. His breath and his thoughts were slow and barely there and what seemed like all of his blood had formed a pool below him. Ernie pulled him to his feet, one arm wrapped around Manfred while the other held the sword in protection. The heat and light of the Oarygus moved through the village and grew in intensity. Rocinallia made a barrier against the flames. Ernie dragged Manfred under a stone awning that had yet to come down.

"It's over, my boy," Ernie could barely speak. "I'm sorry."

Manfred let out a few feeble coughs.

"Had I known, I'm so sorry, I'd have never brought you here, my boy," Ernie had begun to cry. "You'll die, but not here, on your own earth. I'm so sorry. The least I can do is let you die at home. The Ulis," Ernie stifled a sob, "gave me the key—the final signs of his power."

Ernie cast a sign above Rociniallia then cut a tear in the realms. He was so exhausted that he dropped his sword and fell to one knee. Manfred could see street lamps on the other side, billowing in and out of his view as the tear wavered.

Manfred knelt and hugged him and kissed his cheek. "I could've done more," Manfred was able to whisper.

"All you could, dear boy. All you could." Ernie said, completely exhausted.

"What happens next?" Manfred asked.

"We die. And your earth is next." Ernie tried to stand but couldn't. "It has been an honor, Mindiidus."

Manfred hugged Ernie one more time and they both cried. Then in one swift movement, Manfred pushed Ernie through the tear. As the tear closed Manfred thought he heard the Saint laughing.

Manfred sat down; the endorphins of death poured through him as his body prepared for the inevitable. He closed his eyes.

The archers at Looma's side turned toward the village and launched arrows at the Oarygus. But in vain. The arrows burned up long before they reached the demon god. It continued its slow crawl through the village. There were no more living plants and the buildings had all begun to char. Death stacked on top of death.

Looma rose to the warmth at her back, compelled to face the oncoming dread. The archers laid down their weapons and held her up at each side. She called on the Three. The stones had changed. Moss and fungal bits grew out of their chips and crags, reinforced by the Kin's magic. They grew behind her until each one's shadow nearly reached the village walls. The Keepers moved in unison with her, shouting out their ancient spells.

Looma whimpered and her knees nearly gave way as the stones floated above her head, each one covered in blood and new fauna, red droplets falling from the sky. She pushed the archers back and stretched herself up the best she could. Starting at her chest she made a half circle with both hands and the stones followed suit. The archers cowered but stayed by her side as the three crept across the sky. They hovered like small planets as they closed in on the Oarygus. All of Looma's energy was used to keep them steady. If not for the Keepers at her side she could not have gone on. She rocked back and forth with her palms pressed forward.

The Oarygus waved for the rocks to move, but they remained steady. They moved in a flat line and tore through some of the still-standing buildings. Looma could not help but cry as she watched her village crumble in front of her, and at her own hand. She had to slow down the beast—she had to try.

She could feel her mother and Kaseen help guide the Stones. When she had left the Keep, she knew she wasn't ready. They had trained so little and wasted so much time letting her go on adventures with her father and Delute. With each movement of the Stones, she became more connected with them. A molten feeling poured through her and connected her across space. The power of the Kin now hummed through her as well—a verdant, primordial glow sustaining her.

The Three pressed against the Oarygus and held it as a small vine broke through the earth below. One, then two, then hundreds. At first, they caught fire in quick sparks as they tried to reach the Oarygus. They never came anywhere close to the beast. But the vines persisted, some as thin as a blade of grass, some as thick as a mighty oak. They darted out of the earth with lightning speed. The ones that didn't burn up began to move around the ever-changing shape of the Oarygus, searching for its essence. Once they found the Oarygus they wrapped around and penetrated to its core. A thick bark began to form around the Young God. The Three pressed harder into the Oarygus as each new vine entwined it. The Oarygus was able to peel back some of the vines, but each one that broke loose produced another one elsewhere. The vines grew thicker and thicker and constricted around the floating beast.

All the while, Manfred felt his own body being surrounded. Grass grew up next to him where he lay. Each new blade sent a crack through the marble staircase under him until he was completely supported by this new, moving organism. He took a deep breath in and felt warm and light as the grass pushed through his nostrils and into his brain—his ears and eyes, his stomach, filled up with it. He felt his body sink into the crumbling mess below as he was filled to the brim with new rising nature.

The archers and the Keepers next to Looma were dead. They, too, were overcome by the Kin's magic. Their bodies were frozen trees and their screams were its wind. Looma didn't notice that the valley behind her had become a forest or that ancient rivers had sprouted from the depths. She could only feel the stones growing and pressing against the power of the Young God.

DEATH

Manfred rose and moved toward the center of the village. Something was different. Reality was being upended. The buildings of his own earth towered over him and flicked in and out of existence. The bricks and cement shook with dust and the iron insides rusted in a flash. Fires of Ernie's village overlapped everything, their heat creating mirages against every shadow. Trees and human carnage hummed on his periphery. With every step, new images would emerge and deteriorate— children playing in the destruction, Boagly Fai crawling out of the earth with their long pink tongues scouring the freshly dead, Harvestors chanting and banging their chests, Fu Kai Va floating and comingling with the clouds—now here, now gone. He could see Ernie in the distance, his golden sword raised above his head and pointed toward the Young God, the Oarygus encased in a vibrating cocoon of bark. Except that it wasn't. It was free and trapped at once—arms and legs and heads—a thousand pieces of moving light.

Looma floated above him, her arms outstretched and weapons at the ready. She charged the beast, disappearing into its folds and reappearing in the distance, her hair matted in viscera and dirt. Each movement she made covered the world in more blood. Manfred yelled out her name.

The Keeper's Three were no longer rocks. They had become swirling, insubstantial masses of kaleidoscopic color. They moved toward each other at lightning speed, rising above the village until they were no longer visible, then crashing down. Manfred could feel their growth in his bones and hear Looma's commands.

"Hold fast. Hold the enemy. Hold on."

A single tree was manifesting around every object and closed in on Manfred's world, creating fibers from whatever he could see. It zeroed in on the Oarygus until nothing was left of the Young God except this new organism, a tree that stood in the middle of the village and stretched its leaves into space. The sky only existed as fragments in its infinite canopy with Manfred beneath it.

Ernie stood on one of the branches and swung his sword, the same arc in repetition, swinging at nothing. Looma stood on another, the Keeper's Three swirling around her head, moving with the motions of her arms, the same movements over and over again. They were all stuck in a loop.

Manfred touched the tree and felt the whole of the universe. Visions of vast oceans and worlds he could never imagine filled his mind. Beasts as large as planets breathed into one another, their breath thick and full of electricity. Within their massive bodies were other worlds. Planets and stars swirled around one another in the great beasts' hearts. Luminescent, unformed beings inhabited their stomachs and brains and crawled over and through one another. They built realities that Manfred couldn't understand, no matter how long he stayed with them. With each exhale Manfred felt his body dissolve into the many, divergent sensations around him. He was transcending space and time and witnessing the structures and building blocks of reality. Some he recognized, some appeared in fractals and wavering dimensions. He was overcome with horror and elation.

"Breathe. Slowly. Breathe," Os'halla's voice came from the belly of one of the creatures.

Manfred sat down and focused on his breathing. The small creatures floated through his veins like the tunnels he had been in with Bealzut and Ernie. He began to cry when he thought of Bealzut, the poor warrior. He had done so much for them. Brought them back to the village, all to die in the same way he was born—in flames. He felt the tears pour out of his face and the small creatures rode them to the ground and splashed against the earth, spreading out in the thousands. The tree moved in front of him and he touched it again.

"Why do you contain me?" the Oarygus asked. "I only wish to rest. Will you not let me sleep?"

Manfred tried to respond.

"Was brought here to sleep. Was brought to eat. But cannot, this mouth will not work. Will not chew."

"Where are we?" Manfred finally asked.

"*We?*" replied the Oarygus. "Occupy creation. Trapped me for no reason. Undone, my nature. To eat. To sleep. In the crown of origin. Where your history is not visible. Does not exist. I am bound. Bound by what? What binds me?" The Oarygus' voice echoed and the tree shook and grew and grew. "Was called upon to eat. Called out of time to swallow up the stones and roots and rocks."

The Oarygus continued to beg Manfred for release, but a closer voice had his attention. Os'halla was right in his ear.

"We've got it right where we want it. I've never seen anything like this. You're outside of it all. Outside."

"What do you mean, Os? Where are you?"

"I'm in the grove. We are all together working to protect, to fix the realm."

"But where are you, where are we?"

"Our minds are the grass and trees. When Looma slowed the Oarygus down we were able to trap him. Hoped to sap him of energy. Return him to dust. Return. We moved to protect you, pull you into the cover of grass, but you disappeared. Changed. Yet you're still close. A part of the realm and not. I speak out to you from our garden, but where do you speak from, Man of Regular Earth?"

"From nowhere, Os. I'm just speaking. What do I do now?"

"Rid yourself of the beast or it will consume you."

Manfred looked down at his body. He had been pressing his hand against the tree and the bark of it was starting to work its way up his arm, the inner workings of it growing into his veins, first through his fingernails then through the lines of his fingers. The bones of his hand began to solidify, each joint connected by fibers of wood and earth. He tried to pull away, but it moved up to his wrist.

"If you will not free me—we will be one," cried the Oarygus.

The fibers worked toward Manfred's heart. He could feel bits of it, like sawdust in his lungs and the gaps of his brain. With each new space filled, memories flooded him.

He was on the ship watching Delute fall, tangled up in the rigging of the sails.

The first time he laid eyes on Looma. Her beauty. The fear he felt.

The Saint in his apartment.

His left arm was completely absorbed by the tree. He felt his skin extending into the tree, the marrow of his bones flowing through it, seeking out its roots. The scars and cuts on his arms melted and tugged more flesh to the tree's center. He'd soon become another vessel of the Oarygus.

In his other hand rested Rocinallia. The Saint's great weapon. It was weighted so perfectly he could feel it in his core and even though he floated through space, the weapon was somehow rooted him. The fibers of the tree struck another nerve in his brain and Manfred could see Erneel leaning against a building in Manfred's homeworld. The streets around him were mostly deserted. Small scavenger animals picked over mounds of garbage. Erneel looked up as if he knew he was being observed then looked away.

Manfred saw Looma next. She was digging through the rubble of the village and pulling up those still alive. Her face was smeared with tears and ash.

The bark of the tree worked its way up the side of his neck. Pinpricks of pain vibrated through him as its splinters wove their way toward his bones.

"A powerful home you'll make," said the Oarygus from somewhere inside of him.

"What now?" Manfred asked Os'halla.

"Breathe, I guess," Os'halla responded.

Manfred began to laugh. The bark worked its way down his ribs and up the side of his face. He took a deep breath and brought Rocinallia above his head. Its steal was so bright it was all he could see. He brought it down as hard as he could against his shoulder. A thin layer of bark chipped away and hurtled through space. He swung again and more bark lifted away and with it a ringing in his ears. Again. This time he hit his own flesh. The ringing in his ears became a piercing agony, tied itself to his physicality, and sent shockwaves through every cavern of his body. He clenched his teeth together as he yanked the blade out of his skin, blood and wood arching together into the nothingness. Another swing and he hit bone. Barbs of the tree had worked their way into his heart— his lungs and stomach were solidifying. He rocked the blade back and forth and it broke loose. The fibers of the tree and Oarygus that had been working their way into him began to come undone.

"Will you not give me a body?" the Oarygus asked.

Two more swings and his arm was severed. The bark on his ribs and neck could no longer hold and fell beside him. Moments before the tree took up the whole universe, but as the bark fell from his body the tree shrunk. Smaller and smaller until what was left fit in the palm of his hand. He and the Oarygus floated through the blackest, farthest reaches of space. Manfred let go of Rocinalla and watched it disappear into the distance, the mighty sword hovering for a moment at his side. The battered thing caught some light, in an almost human way and reminded Manfred somehow of Ernie's wry, mischievous smile when he first met him at the bar, then it tumbled into the infinite nothingness.

With his remaining hand, Manfred grabbed the tree and held it close to his face. The roots of it fluttered as he exhaled, the bark golden brown and shimmering with lines of purple and silver. The leaves wilted and dropped one by one as Manfred breathed in its dust. The smell reminded him of the Aushwary coast—clean and brisk with a slight fetid note—decay or something like it. The Oarygus was still trying to free itself and cried out from the depths of the plant. Manfred held it to his ear, but the sounds from within were unintelligible—an alien birdsong, a supernova, an unknowable melody. He reached back and threw it into the darkness.

The light was so vibrant as it fell that he was sure it could never be lost, farther and farther away, carried on some unseen wind. He thought of the Keeper's eyes—how they had swallowed him up when they first met, how they had momentarily stilled his mind after Ernie dragged him through the forest. Manfred cried and clutched his stomach until all he knew was breath. In and out. As slow as he could until the breath too was gone, the tree and the whole universe turning black then milky white. Then nothing. Pure and simple.

Os'halla stood over him when he opened his eyes again. The Kin were in the distance and breathed in unison and chanted in their guts. Manfred laid on thick blades of grass so dense that his body didn't touch the dirt below. Large heart-shaped leaves covered most of the sky above him.

He tried to sit up, but Os'halla shook his head.

"Not yet. Still incomplete. Incomplete"

Manfred looked at the arm he hadn't chopped off, bruised and weak. He brought his hand to his face. The veins pulsated and it was more weathered than he remembered, dry and cut and gnarled. He looked toward his other arm. It wasn't there. He let out a sigh of agony and tried to bring its phantom to his face. He tried to recreate it with his mind. Nothing.

"It'll be okay. It's almost over."

Os'halla reached down and touched Manfred's head, his hand cool.

"You've banished the Young God. Cast it out. Banished."

"Dead?"

"Can't die. They take on forms. Took Yarley. Tried to burrow in the earth, in you. But we trapped it. Held it. Don't die." Os'halla looked toward the rest of the Kin all stretched out in their form of meditation.

Manfred tried to sit up again.

"Not yet. You're still in pieces."

Manfred looked back toward his shoulder. Small gray wooden fibers sprouted from the sight of his severed arm, much like the roots that grew out of Os'halla's head.

"You'll be different," smiled Os'halla. "But you'll be whole."

"Then can we go home?" Manfred asked.

"You may. Quite divinely. The realms are yours."

"What about you?"

Os'halla shook his head. "We're no longer of the earth. Not like before. Death, in a way. Separation. Cocooned." He laughed. "Like the elders. It hurts and it echoes. But the Kin is gone. Returned. Gone."

Manfred sat up and leaned on his good arm. The other was still forming. The roots spiraled around one another, almost to where his elbow would've been.

"What do you mean?" he asked.

"It's just the one body. The one body dies. The arm dies." Os'halla pointed at Manfred's growing arm. "When we first met, we all knew what the price would be. The storm that would come through. Cleansing. Scorching. Cleansing. Now the bodies of the earth, of the Kin, are dedicated to rebuilding. The forests of Harth'a. The brooks and rivers of the ancient Mesc. It will take us all. Take us generations."

"I didn't want you to die," Manfred said.

"You don't understand death. That is all."

Manfred's arm was nearly complete. The gray roots turned yellow then green. They wrapped around one another and reinforced his movements. Small sinews sprouted out and began to make up the delicate joints of his hands. They stretched and repeated themselves in geometric patterns.

"You wielded Rocinallia, with great honor," Os'halla said.

Manfred squinted his eyes at him.

"The last great weapon of our realm. You held it. Had you not severed your arm with it there would be nothing to repair. Nothing."

"It was beautiful," Manfred said.

Manfred held both hands in front of his face. The new one was still moving, settling into itself. It had taken on an ash color over the wooden fibers. He felt it with his other hand. They were both rough. The old one had new scars, uneven pits of skin rolled into themselves—reminders of his recent misadventures. The palm was dry and the knuckles hardened. The new hand and arm were strong and pliable. A young sapling rooted in his heart.

"Now what?" Manfred asked.

"I can't be sure, Old friend," said Os'halla and reached out for Manfred's hand.

NEW GIFTS AND
NEW JOURNEYS

The Kin were gone and Manfred felt his body being crushed. He looked down to see his torso and legs covered in rubble. He was back in the village—reality reset. A man in the armor of the Guard pulled on his hand and another tried to clear the rocks and mounds of earth that covered him.

"This one's alive," the man yelled over his shoulder. "Barely. He's only part tree. Not like the rest. Give me a hand."

The rubble shifted and Manfred's body broke loose. He tried to stand.

"No, no. We'll get you out of here, old boy."

Manfred's heart lifted, but it wasn't the Saint. Some other warrior, some broken face.

"Just lie there. We'll get you some water," he looked over his shoulder. "Get this man some water. What's your name, son?"

"Bugs… Bugsbee. Manfred."

"By the light," the man exclaimed. "It's Mindiidus. It's him." He waved in excitement for more to come and help.

Manfred drank some water. "What happened?"

"Don't worry about that. We thought you were dead. It all came crashing down."

Manfred drank water and felt sick as he got his bearings. He was somewhere in the heart of the village. It was in complete and utter ruin. The pillars that made up the buildings were laid out in all directions. New trees and ash covered every inch of the place. Bloodied people limped around trying to resuscitate the dead, trying to find life. All around him members of the Guard were yelling out for help as they dug through the wreckage.

The man who helped him had already moved on. Manfred was now able to stand. He could feel the bones of his legs press against the skin. Everything throbbed with a dull pain. He walked in a shuffle and tried to help where he could. But his new arm was useless, heavy, and immobile, so he held it to his chest.

Then someone called out his name.

Looma. She walked toward him then ran. She looked much older. Dressed in clean white, her eyes were darker, held back in shadows. Even now she moved with such grace. Her beauty in this place of death was too much and Manfred had to sit down. He sat against the remnants of a building as she called out his name. They embraced and Manfred felt a hollow pain in his chest.

"I thought… we thought you were dead," she said.

He didn't know how to respond.

"I see you've lost my father again," she said and smiled through her watery eyes.

Manfred shook his head. "He tried to send me away. He tried…"

"I know," she said. She put her arm around him and they held each other.

"You did right, Bubsbee. You did what you had to do. Wherever he is… he can handle himself."

"I'm sorry."

She shook her head then spread her hands out in front of her. "If not for you, even this rubble would be gone. It was pure devastation Manny, but because of you, all is not lost. The old man is somewhere. He has always been hard to keep track of," she smiled. "We'll find him. At least there are some still alive, some to look for him. Some to rebuild."

She grabbed his now wooden arm and looked it over. "Some trick of Os'?" she asked.

Manfred nodded

"The Kin are gone?" she asked.

"I think so," he said. "Somewhere doing their work."

The two of them were so exhausted that they fell fast asleep in each other's embrace right there in the street. The ruined world around them went on. All through the day and night bodies were pulled from the ground. Those that had been absorbed into trees and grass weren't as hideous as the crushed ones although there was something truly grotesque about the human shapes that peeked out from branches and bark. Human eyes and fingertips, teeth and exposed bones lurched out of many of the newly formed trees.

Two soldiers woke them—a tall man and a taller woman. They wore the colors of Fenk's army and were followed by Kaseen. She was covered in the dust and the dirt of the place but finding Looma and Manfred brought a light to her face.

"My children," she said. "The protectors," she leaned down and kissed Looma on the forehead. "The lighted body," she grabbed Manfred's hand and pulled him to his feet. "Come with me."

Kaseen and Looma stood with their heads pressed together and held hands.

"I've never been so tired," said Looma. "Did the Hall survive?"

Kaseen let go of Looma's hands and turned away from them. "There are pieces of the map still intact below. Where our dear Ulis had," she paused for a moment, "lived and done his work. I will show you."

Looma and Kaseen held hands as they walked. Kaseen asked about Manfred's arm without looking at it.

"I lost it," he said.

"You didn't lose it; you gave it up—gave it up for the realms. And that new thing?"

The new arm was loosening up as they walked and he no longer had to hold it to his chest. "I'm not sure," he said and examined the wood fibers of his hand. "The Kin. Os'halla."

"Does it hurt?"

"Everything hurts," Manfred said.

Looma half-laughed, half-sighed.

Kaseen stopped and stood in front of the two of them. "You are great warriors. Both of you. And the great battle has been fought. But it's not over. Not exactly."

"My mother?" Looma asked.

"Safe."

Looma looked at Manfred and back to Kaseen. "And my father?"

Kaseen smiled and turned away. "We're almost there."

All around them, the carnage was incredible. Every step they took, every turn, was met with more death and blood. A black tree arched over them, in its trunk, two bodies could be seen. They looked to have been holding each other in their final moments.

"The Kin have always been ultimate in their help," Kaseen said. "I cannot say I'm glad they came to our aide. So many lost. They only know destruction before rebirth, fire before cleansing. They are like the Cloud in that way."

They approached what was left of the Hall of Signs. The dome was mostly caved in. Massive vines sprung out of the new cracks. Looma couldn't help but gasp when she saw it.

"I remember when you were no higher than my knee, dear girl, running around outside the hall. Such trouble. The Keepers tried to watch over you," Kaseen laughed and touched Looma's face. "We'll rebuild, Looma, your mother, and I."

Tears welled up in Looma's eyes.

"Come, come." Kaseen led the way into the Hall. They had to duck and step over rubble to get to the wax statue that once protected the Ulis. Candles still burned all around, somehow untouched by war. Kaseen made her sign above the statue. It was intricate but somehow different than Manfred remembered. Before when he watched signs being thrown above his friend's heads, they seemed almost random. Blocks of light and shapes moving about. Now, he could see the patterns, like keys being lined up with locks. First, a square was made, its sides multiplied into a cube and then the lines shifted and collapsed and formed a spinning pentacle. Next, a dozen smaller shapes nestled against each corner of the moving star—it slowly filled with light and then settled toward the statue, each pattern and line divined from Kaseen's fluid, brilliant movements. It all somehow made sense to Manfred. As clear as day, as simple as turning the knob of a door.

He watched Looma's face too. She followed each movement, the colors reflecting on her cheeks, first red then dark blue. She moved her head side to side and her lips moved like she was trying to make the sign with her tongue.

The wax statue fell away and they made their way into the belly of the Hall. Manfred thought back to when he first visited this place, having just been woken up by Looma in one of her hurried, impatient states. It felt like a different world then. The darkness then was foreboding, the countenance of both women different. Looma had hated and didn't trust him and Kaseen had looked at him like a curiosity. Now it was somber and quiet. The darkness was thick with tradition. Mostly there was intense sadness. They walked toward an old friend's house who would not be there. He'd never be there again.

As they walked Manfred smiled as he remembered Ernie chasing him through his city. Then, Manfred had been afraid of everything, terrified of a little old man. How little he had known. That that old man would become a true friend.

Manfred watched Looma ahead of him. A battle-hardened warrior whose side he had fought at, whose home he had protected—at least he had tried. His old life felt like a dream, punching in and out each day. He chuckled to himself as he thought of the throw-pillows, the only meaning in his life back then. Kaseen and Looma looked back at him quizzically and smiled, his new friends, a strange little family.

Kaseen opened the door to where the Ulis kept his map.

The three of them sat down and for a moment and took the place in. The ceiling was still filled with cobwebs that hid the bulk of the work of the Ulis.

"Shall we take a look?" Kaseen asked. "I'll need you close, Looma. Usually, it would take your mother or father's physical presence to get the light or our dear Ulis. But you have proven yourself to be just as powerful, if not more. I'd never imagined the Three to be so magnificent. And used so masterfully. We owe much to the powers of Mindiidus, but the stories of you moving through the Cloud, of you holding the Oarygus at bay, those will be told, sung for all time."

Manfred looked at Looma and smiled. He had never seen her blush before.

"I don't know what to do," said Looma.

"I just need you close. Put your head on my shoulder, child."

Kaseen pulled her long hair into a bun and stretched her hands in front of herself.

"Innate to the Ulis was this power, but to see and to track through the countless maps of existence, he learned that from the Keepers." Kaseen held her hands in prayer and mumbled words under her breath. Dim lights pulsated above them, some brighter than others, but nothing like the magnificence of when the Ulis worked it. Kaseen took long deep breaths and her words became louder—more light. Flickers of color traversed the cobwebs. They started brilliantly then burned out in a flash.

Manfred's wooden arm felt heavy again and he had to rest it on his legs. Each time a new light would appear his joints felt a little tighter. Kaseen then threw both of her hands up and a map appeared. A few corners of it and small sections in the middle remained cloudy and hard to make out, but Manfred immediately knew which light was Erneel. At this point his arm was so stiff he felt it would break if he tried to move it. It was one dense and solid piece from shoulder to fingertip.

Gold dust fell from the ceiling and the map moved toward them. Soon they were completely immersed. The lines gyrated and sparked like pathways of the mind. Somehow all of reality was contained around them, broken up into ever-changing spiral shapes that became clearer the harder you focused. The different worlds were sectioned off by large unmoving black swaths.

Kaseen shook her head. "He's in here somewhere—saw him this morning. Not so good with the map."

Manfred pointed his wooden arm. "There."

In an outer region surrounded by flickers of intense light, like the static of a television, there was a small sign. A spiral cut in half with three dots above it that moved and rotated toward its center. As Manfred pointed the whole map became that region.

"Yes," said Kaseen, unable to contain her excitement. "You've found him, Mindiidus. You've found him."

Manfred's arm was still outstretched and he touched the space that represented Erneel. He felt a shock run through his body and for a moment was looking down at Ernie. The Saint was bloodied and hiding behind a large rock. He looked frail and tired as he drank from some hollowed vessel and laughed to himself. The world he was in was mostly dark. Tall rocks in all directions created shadows that danced about and frightened Manfred. But Ernie seemed okay. Just as Manfred felt himself returning to the ladies and the map, he got a glimpse of what Erneel was hiding from.

A long-legged leathery creature lumbered just around the corner. Large blood-cracked knuckles pressed into the earth. Its face looked like the flat of a palm, with small cracked lines, but no eyes or mouth. It was guided by other smaller creatures who pointed and yelled.

Ernie moved from rock to rock, drinking where he could all the while.

Kaseen had pulled two books down from the Ulis' shelves and skimmed them while muttering to herself.

"The dumb ole crow," she said. "How did he end up so far away?"

She flipped through the pages of one of the books with aggravation and threw it on the floor. She opened the next book. "Hillismire," she said. "Good light, the old man is in Hillismire. Of all the crusty broken worlds of all the realms. Why? How?"

"I thought they couldn't travel that far," Looma said.

Kaseen looked at her and then back to another book. "Can't and shouldn't aren't always the same." Kaseen touched her face and sighed in desperation. "The Oarygus must have crossed up the realms, the pathways, while Ernie tried to save you," she pointed to Manfred. "Be glad he didn't. Hillismire is a dark corner of the realms. An awful place."

"Couldn't be worse than the Oarygus," Looma said hopefully.

Kaseen shook her head. "We've spent generations preparing for the Young Gods to return. At least we had studied them and knew what they were capable of. Your father, always your father, always finding trouble, has ended up in a realm we know very little about."

"Then we'll go get him," Looma said and looked at Manfred who nodded.

"No Ulis, No Saint. No portals, no bridges. I'm afraid it is not so easy," Kaseen replied.

"We can't just leave him. My mother must surely have a way."

Kaseen squinted her eyes and touched her face in thought. "The Northern…"

"The Guides? Of the Scorched Regions? Aren't they all dead?"

Kaseen was still touching her face. "There are rumors they have emerged in the Wailing Hills. Rumors. But I wouldn't be surprised. With Mindiidus, with the Young Gods, our realm is full of change and reawakenings."

"Wailing?" Manfred said quietly.

"Fine, the Northern Guides then. Come on," Looma stood up and grabbed Manfred's shoulder.

Kaseen couldn't help but laugh. "The two of you will need help, Looma. The two of you are strong, yes. Stronger than much of the realm has seen. But you'll never succeed alone."

Manfred had already half stood up.

"Who?" said Looma on the verge of tears. "Delute is dead. Bealzut dead. Os'halla has become what he always wanted to be—a weed. We're all that's left."

Kaseen held out her hands and Looma took them. "There are others, Looma. And how do you know Mindiidus doesn't wish to return home to rebuild his own earth?"

Looma looked at Manfred in disbelief, as if he had already abandoned her.

He shook his head. "I just want to take a nap."

The map above them began to fade away and Manfred felt a dull exhaustion sweep through his body.

Kaseen nodded. "Yes, yes. The two of you need rest."

"I *have* rested," said Looma half-heartedly.

"I know, dear girl," said Kaseen. "You two have done so much already. Mindiidus is right. You'll need rest. You'll need plenty of it. There is no certainty going forward."

"Has there ever been?" Looma asked.

Kaseen smiled. "I suppose there hasn't." She looked at Manfred and reached out to touch his wooden hand. "We'll have the Keeper take a look at this before we let you do too much. The Kin, for all their help, are still mostly a mystery to us. I'm sure you're happy to be whole again, but something like that always comes at a price."

Manfred looked at her and nodded along with her words.

"We'll find somewhere nearby for you two to recuperate."

Looma shook her head. "Take as long as you need, Bugsbee. But I won't be resting. Not while our villagers lay in the rubble." She stood up. "When you're ready, come find me."

Manfred never stopped nodding. He was so tired that he was afraid he'd fall asleep in his chair.

"There are a few rooms in the Citadel that weren't demolished in the wake of the Young God. We'll put you up, Mindiidus. We'll take care of you."

Manfred smiled.

When Manfred laid down that night his dreams were so vivid that he may well have been awake. At first, he dreamt of his family back home. The last time he visited his youngest sister was nearly five years ago. She still looked young when he saw her, but more and more like their mother. She even had the same laugh. Manfred dreamed of sitting in her studio apartment and telling her about everything he had seen. She told him that she was proud of him and wished he would have stayed home, that while he was gone the whole world had come apart. After the sun began to burn out, wars had cropped up all over the world, from tribal ones on the coasts to large-scale nuclear conflicts. Everyone was scared. He wept throughout the nightmare.

She told him she loved him before turning to ash.

Next, he dreamt of Erneel. Lost and alone, the old man wandered through some metallic desert with beasts and critters in all directions. He had somehow been reunited with Rocinallia and held it at his side, unafraid. From where he had come there was a mass of carnage. The limbs of animals of all kinds were stacked up, some still twitching.

"Ernie," Manfred called out. "We're coming for you."

Erneel stopped in the dream and looked around to see where Manfred's voice came from and kept moving when he couldn't discover it.

Manfred knew Erneel was moving toward something, but the beasts closed in as the dream ended.

He could see the tree floating through space somewhere at the edges of reality. The Oarygus was still alive inside, pulsing and fuming—plotting its escape.

Manfred sat up in bed. He was so comfortable. The pillows were fluffy and the linens so clean. Even though he was in a root cellar below a city governed by magic and overrun by death, he felt at home for the first time. He stretched his arms above his head, one still feeling foreign to him. He took a deep breath and laid back down. This time he fell into such a deep sleep that no dream could disturb him.

The End

AUTHOR BIO

Michael Farfel's work joyfully unpacks the emergent realities we so often take for granted—be it the strange rituals of domestic life or the potential unreality of home appliance repair. He's even been known to write speculative fiction about reluctant, out-of-shape, interdimensional warriors. When he and his wife aren't arguing about run-on sentences, they can be found playing Scrabble, avoiding strangers and walking their dog, Heidecker. His work has appeared in publications such as *Hobart, X-R-A-Y Lit, Juked* and *Maudlin House.* Those pieces and more can be found on his website, MichaelFarfel.com.

Made in United States
North Haven, CT
09 June 2022

20061235R00221